Praise for
The Death Wizard Chronicles

"Adult Harry Potter and Eragon fans can get their next fix with Jim Melvin's six-book epic *The Death Wizard Chronicles* . . . Melvin's imagination and writing equal that of J.K. Rowling, author of the fantastically popular *Harry Potter* series, and Christopher Paolini, author of *Eragon* and *Eldest*. Some of his descriptions—and creatures—even surpass theirs."
—*The Tampa Tribune*

"Jim Melvin's *Death Wizard Chronicles* crackle with non-stop action and serious literary ambition. He has succeeded in creating an entire universe of interlocking characters—and creatures—that will undoubtedly captivate fans of the fantasy genre. It's a hell of a story . . . a hell of a series . . ."
—*Bob Andelman, author of* Will Eisner: A Spirited Life

"Jim Melvin is a fresh voice in fantasy writing with a bold, inventive vision and seasoned literary style that vaults him immediately into the top tier of his genre. *The Death Wizard Chronicles* . . . is scary, action-packed and imaginative—a mythic world vividly entwining heroes, villains and sex that leaves the reader with the impression that this breakthrough author has truly arrived."
—*Dave Scheiber, co-author of* Covert: My Years Infiltrating the Mob *and* Surviving the Shadows: A Journey of Hope into Post-Traumatic Stress

"Action-packed and yet profound, *The DW Chronicles* will take your breath away. This is epic fantasy at its best."
—*Chris Stevenson, author of* Planet Janitor: Custodian of the Stars *and* The Wolfen Strain

"Triken truly comes alive for the reader and is filled with mysteries and places that even the most powerful characters in the book are unaware of. That gives the reader the opportunity to discover and learn with the characters . . . Melvin has added to the texture of the world by integrating Eastern philosophies, giving the magic not only consistency but depth. He has worked out the details of his magical system so readers can understand where it comes from and how it works."
—*Jaime McDougall, the bookstacks.com*

Forged in Death

The Death Wizard Chronicles
Book One

by

Jim Melvin

Bell Bridge Books

Dear reader:
I hope you
enjoy the
magical world
of Triken! Jim

Bell Bridge Books
PO BOX 300921
Memphis, TN 38130
Print ISBN: 978-1-61194-168-5

Bell Bridge Books is an Imprint of BelleBooks, Inc.

Copyright © 2012 by Jim Melvin
Chained by Fear (excerpt) © 2012 by Jim Melvin

This book was originally published as *The Pit* by Rain Publishing in 2007

Printed and bound in the United States of America.

We at BelleBooks enjoy hearing from readers.
Visit our websites – www.BelleBooks.com and www.BellBridgeBooks.com.

10 9 8 7 6 5 4 3 2 1

Cover design: Debra Dixon
Interior design: Hank Smith
Photo credits:
Figure (manipulated) © Andrei Vishnyakov | Dreamstime.com
Background (manipulated) © Unholyvault | Dreamstime.com

:Lifd:01:

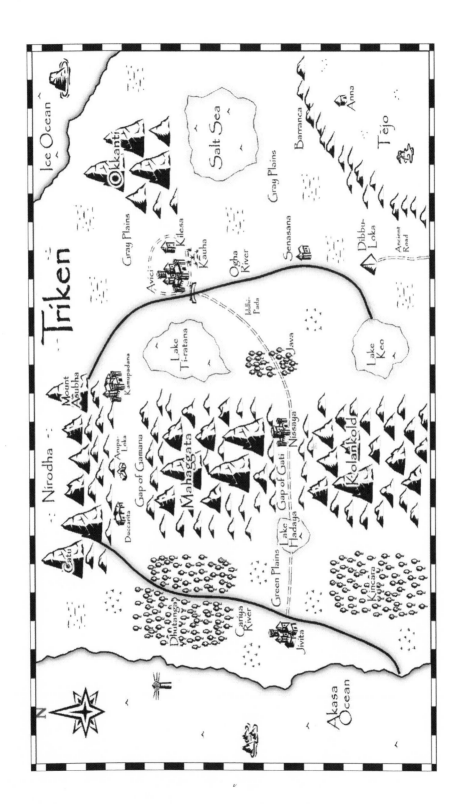

Acknowledgments

Any and all descriptions of meditation in this volume were based on the Buddha's teachings in the *Mahasatipatthana Sutta*.

Dennis Chastain enriched the beauty of the land, by answering endless questions.

Jackson Parris put weapons in my hands.

Stefan Locklair and Rick Loveday lent credence to the fights.

And Margo McLoughlin was the true master of the ancient tongue. Any inconsistencies in the translations are my fault, not hers.

Dedicated to Jeanne,
my wife in every sense
of the word.

Table of Contents

Prologue   3

The Noble Ones   5

Warrior's Sacrifice   31

Escape from the Pit   84

Peak of Despair   107

Beneath the Mountain   124

The Trappers   151

The Other Death-Knower   183

Slaughter and Solitude   214

Glossary   231

"Death is unacceptable,
for one so great as I."

—The Lord Bhayatupa,
most ancient and powerful of dragons

Jim Melvin

Prologue

Such darkness he had never known. In all the centuries of his long life, the wizard had never felt anything as loathsome. Torturous days and weeks lay behind, endless horror ahead. He was helpless in the grip of an eternal doom.

For a millennium he had freely roamed the planet Triken, using his prodigious powers to unite the forces of good. But now a sorcerer held him captive in a pit bored into the solid rock of a frozen mountain. Beyond the walls of his prison, a war would soon take place that would dwarf all others. An evil had arisen that threatened not just Triken but the fabric that held together the universe. Only the wizard could stop it. But first he had to survive.

The pit was two hundred cubits deep but only three cubits in diameter. The prisoner lay curled at its bottom like a snake in a well. Fetid dankness swirled about him, creeping in and out of his nostrils as he breathed. A chill like no other clung to his body, freezing his heart.

All he had left were his memories, which provided his only relief from the relentless blackness. He immersed himself in them, focusing on the past rather than the present. Doing this went against all that he held true. But now it kept him sane.

For a fraction of a moment. And another. And another . . .

The Noble Ones

1

In his mind the Death-Knower wizard replayed what had led to this hideous imprisonment. He fled to a land of fresh air and sunlight where courage and hope still existed. In this place he was known as Torg—king of the Tugars—and he led his desert warriors against Invictus, a sorcerer who threatened to ensnare the world in a prison as terrible as the pit.

Seventy-two days ago, Torg and twenty Asēkhas—the Tugars of highest rank—had set out from their encampment on the western edge of the Great Desert. As dawn approached, the desert warriors had walked across a dry ravine strewn with crumbled rock, their long strides barely disturbing the loose ground. Few living things noticed their presence. Even a tiny elf owl, hopping from stone to stone in search of beetles, never saw them pass, though its yellow eyes were clever and keen.

Many believed that Tugars were magicians capable of invisibility. Others considered them gods who were immortal in battle. Tugars knew invisibility was a state of mind: silence the mind, and the body became difficult to see. As for their perceived invincibility, Tugars trained under the guidance of Vasi masters for fifty years before attaining the rank of warrior. No greater fighters had ever existed. But they were not immortal.

In the fiery heat of late summer, the small band had traveled westward for three days, marching twenty-five leagues across the rocky wasteland of Barranca, which partially encircled the Tējo desert. At dusk of the third day, Torg and the Asēkhas finally passed through the wastes and into lowland choked with scrub. They scrambled over creosote bushes that stank like skunks and strode past giant sagebrush that stood thirty spans tall. If the task before them had not been so crucial, Torg would have had them stop and collect parts of both plants, which the Tugars used for medicines and dyes, and to weave hats and bags.

They camped that night in a remote hollow that was a three-day march from their destination: the city called Dibbu-Loka, the realm of the noble ones. All was quiet, and the Asēkhas slept, except for Torg and one other. The pair stood together on a nearby hillock—two imposing figures dressed in black. Curved swords hung at their hips.

"Lord, is your mind set?" Chieftain Asēkha-Kusala asked. He was the most powerful Tugar in the world besides Torg. "Must you remain with us on this mission? Your people need you more than does our small company."

Torg stood with his back to Kusala, staring at the golden orb in the night sky. For the past several months the full moon had called to his heart in a confounding manner. He ached when he looked at it, a sensation that was sweet and sour. He didn't understand why he'd begun to feel this way. It was unlike him. But he recognized this puzzling development as far too powerful and persistent to dismiss as mere imagination.

"My mind *is* set," he said. "I am a Death-Knower. I have lived for a millennium, yet I have died a thousand times. The paradox makes me wise. Do you doubt it?" He turned to glare at Kusala, who was a shorter but slightly thicker man. "You have been at my side for centuries, chieftain. Do you doubt me?"

"Forgive me, lord," Kusala said, his expression momentarily downcast and obedient. Even he, revered among the Tugars and throughout Triken, knew better than to oppose his king. "I meant no disrespect." But then his countenance quickly changed, as was his custom. He lifted his gaze and his eyes glowed, bathed in the moon's reflected light. "My love for you inspires my speech, and I fear for you."

Torg smiled. He knew Kusala too well. The chieftain was preparing to give his king a spirited lecture.

"The rise of Invictus threatens Triken and its free people, but we have been slow to respond," Kusala said, his voice rising. "Even the Tugars have stood like statues in this storm. If not for you, we already would have closed the doors of Tējo and vanished from the world, away from the young sorcerer's grasp. But you have taught us that sloth would merely postpone our demise. Invictus grows strong beyond his merit, and those who would see goodness prevail depend on you more than ever. Who else but a Death-Knower can stand against a Sun God? Who else but you? And yet his soldiers prepare a trap. An *obvious* one. And you enter it . . . willingly."

Torg allowed him to finish. Then he calmly said, "There has never been such a dangerous threat in our lifetime. And it comes from someone who—compared to you and me—is relatively young. But this has not stopped Invictus from surpassing us."

Torg closed his eyes and breathed in the hot night air. He leaned against his walking staff, which was carved from the ivory of an immense desert elephant found dead of old age at the base of a dry lakebed. He had named the staff Obhasa, which in the ancient tongue meant *container of light*. An impressive weapon, Obhasa crackled with Torg's own magic.

"Invictus' armies, though powerful, are not yet invincible," Torg continued. "But what of the sorcerer himself? Against him, I have not been tested. Still, as his might spreads throughout the land, my confidence diminishes."

"All the more reason for you *not* to go to Dibbu-Loka," Kusala said. "Let the Asēkhas rescue the noble ones. Return to the desert and await us there."

"You are a brilliant chieftain," Torg said. "But your vision can be short-sighted. You are underestimating the scope of Invictus' malevolence. The noble ones of Dibbu-Loka believe there is only one way to defeat such malice. They say, 'Hatred is never appeased by hatred. Hatred is appeased by love.'"

"They are a gentle and beautiful people," Kusala said. "But they are helpless against such evil."

"Helpless? Is a tree helpless against the wind? The wind blows and fades. The tree bends and remains. Kusala, there are those among the keepers of Dibbu-Loka who are far older than you or me. And they do not waste their long lives on meanderings. Instead they wisely use their time to learn the true nature of love and hate, good and evil, pleasure and suffering. What you mistake for helplessness is actually a deep understanding of what is and isn't real."

"You are right, lord. My vision *is* short-sighted. Their 'deep understanding' is beyond my comprehension."

Torg chuckled. "Ah, Kusala, now it is my turn to say that I meant no disrespect. I do not intend to demean your courage or loyalty. It's just that I have spent much time among the noble ones and have grown to cherish them. I could not bear to see such an intense and sincere people perish from the world. I would rather fail in an attempt to save them than not make the attempt at all. A trap? Of course. Do I enter it willingly? Yes. But you must trust that I am not without a plan."

Again Torg looked at the moon. When he sighed, a bluish vapor flowed from his mouth, floating seductively in the thick air. Kusala flared his nostrils and inhaled, then visibly relaxed. Torg's essence imbued a calming strength not unlike drunkenness, yet it wrought clarity instead of intoxication.

"You are my king," Kusala said. "I would cast myself off Mount Asubha, if you but said the word."

"Do not speak of Asubha," Torg said. "The prison on the mountaintop is Invictus' most terrible creation. I will beg the snow giants to cast it down, if we are able to defeat the sorcerer."

Without further speech, Torg and Kusala strode back to the hollow where the others slept. This close to the Great Desert, they had little to fear.

Nevertheless, Torg knew that danger lay ahead, and it was greater than anyone else had yet begun to realize.

Three days later, Torg stood again with Kusala, this time on the precipice of an escarpment overlooking the temples of Dibbu-Loka. Although it was midday and the air was clear, they were far enough away to be undetectable to anyone within the holy city, enabling them to remain in the open and take their time studying the surroundings. Thousands of golden flashes burst from the three-cornered conurbation, resembling a wind-ruffled lake sparkling beneath a setting sun.

Two scouts made their way up the side of the cliff. Kusala was so eager to hear their report, he could hardly stand still. But Torg already knew much of what they would say. The flashes were reflections coming off the armor of the golden soldiers of Invictus. Invaders occupied the holy city.

Asēkhas Rati and Sōbhana, wearing black silk jackets tucked into their breeches, reached the roof of the escarpment and strode forward. Both were excellent scouts. Sōbhana, especially, was held in high regard. She stood a finger-length shy of four cubits, which was considered small for a Tugarian woman, but she was strong, limber, and could run almost as fast as a wolf.

Despite her well-documented prowess, Sōbhana, like many Tugars, was visibly intimidated by Torg's presence. The Tugarian nation considered him to be not just a king, but a king of kings. Sōbhana had once told him she'd take out her dagger and slit her wrists, if he but commanded.

Torg, of course, would never demand such a heinous act. He loved Sōbhana like a little sister. Her nervousness amused him, and in less troubling times he would have teased her until she grew comfortable. But there was no time for that now.

Sōbhana looked at Torg, and her face began to flush. She lowered her gaze.

"Speak," Kusala demanded, with his typical impatience.

Rati stepped forward instead. "Dibbu-Loka is overrun. At least two thousand golden soldiers control the temples and surrounding walls. The monks and nuns offer no resistance. Daggers are held to every throat. Even a surprise attack by a thousand Tugars would save just a few of the prisoners. The soldiers would be easily defeated, but not before most of the noble ones were slaughtered."

Kusala looked at Torg somberly, as if hoping to see some form of resignation that might indicate he would give up the mission.

But Torg paid the chieftain no heed, instead focusing on Sōbhana. "What say you?"

Sōbhana looked up, her cheeks still splashed with red. Though she opened her mouth and seemed about to speak, nothing recognizable came out.

"Sōbhana, are you a warrior or a child?" Kusala said. "Report to me, if not to your king."

When Sōbhana turned toward the chieftain, her clumsiness vanished. Her cheeks remained flushed, but this time with anger. "It is worse than Rati reports," she said. "One of their captains stands boldly on the upper steps of the main temple and calls over and over for *The Torgon* to come forth. He says they'll sacrifice three monks and three nuns for every hour that passes, beginning at sundown of this day, unless our king enters the city and surrenders himself."

"The captain claims our king is a traitor to the free people of Triken," Rati added, "and that he must stand trial for his crimes before the seat of Invictus. He promises a *just* trial. The noble ones roll their eyes. Despite their predicament, they keep their sense of humor. They seem to have no fear. They are warriors, as well, it seems."

"We could have killed the fool, we were so close," Sōbhana said, "but it would have done little good. Rati and I suspected our approach was long witnessed, yet we were permitted to enter the city without resistance. It was too easy. Too many heads were turned in the wrong direction. They are poor soldiers, by our standards, but they are well-armed and all too capable of killing."

Torg could sense that Sōbhana was holding something back—and so he continued to fix his gaze only on her. There was a period of silence finally broken by Kusala, who cleared his throat and touched Torg lightly on the shoulder. "What *is* it, lord?"

Torg twisted around and glowered. The chieftain hastily removed his hand from his shoulder. Torg grunted impatiently, then returned his gaze to Sōbhana. "You fear more than just a fool of a captain or his pathetic soldiers. I can sense it in your bearing. What do you keep from us?"

Sōbhana took a step back, then sighed. Her full lips trembled, ever so slightly. "I saw something else. Or I think I did."

Kusala's eyes almost bulged from their sockets. "*Sōbhana.*" He spoke so sharply that all the Asēkhas whipped their heads in his direction. "Tell us everything . . . *now.*"

Seemingly ignoring the chieftain, Sōbhana moved slowly toward Torg and then stood on her toes so that her mouth was just a span below his. Her features softened, and at that moment Torg saw her as startlingly beautiful, even by Tugarian standards.

Kusala was clearly amazed, perhaps perceiving her approach as a burst of arrogance, and he seemed prepared to discipline her.

But Torg waved him off. "Sōbhana . . . speak," he said gently.

"Lord," she said, "I saw something . . . someone . . . in the doorway at the top of the temple stairs. There was a deep shadow near the opening, and the sun's glare prevented a clearer view. But I saw glints . . . or glows . . . that did not resemble the reflections off armor. Two figures loomed within, and one of them was huge—much larger than any of the soldiers, or monks and nuns. I believe, my lord, that it was the great monster we name Mala. And with him, a Warlish witch."

Though he was born deep within the recesses of the desert Tējo, Torg had resided at Dibbu-Loka many times during his long lifetime, and he knew its history as intimately as anyone. Even as he made his way toward the city, he replayed what he had learned in his thoughts.

A greedy king had built the holy city ten thousand years ago to serve as his final resting place. King Lobha was to be buried in the center of the city in the bowels of a great pyramid. Lobha had originally named the city Piti-Loka, which meant *Rapture World* in the ancient tongue. The king had been a connoisseur of sexual gratification, especially when he forced it upon helpless victims.

The temples of Piti-Loka were adorned with a myriad of statues, carvings, and jewels. The exterior walls were sheathed in contrasting marbles, shimmering in an ever-changing variety of colors, depending on the time of day. The interior walls were slathered with erotic paintings of naked men, women, and children.

Because of his frequent atrocities, Lobha had acquired many enemies, and an army of Lobha's vicious soldiers inhabited the inner grounds of the temple. But in truth, the king feared nothing except the demise of his own body, which had somehow retained its sexual prowess despite the feebleness of old age. His hands ruined many lives.

One fateful day, the king made the mistake of molesting and murdering a woman who had been captured during a slave-hunting expedition on the border of the Great Desert. She was a member of a mysterious tribe which dwelled within Tējo. Even as Lobha lay in the throes of ecstasy, and his chained victim breathed her last, the desert dwellers invaded the city. Though outnumbered ten to one, they routed Lobha's army with ease and slew the king.

After that, Piti-Loka was renamed Dibbu-Loka, the ancient word for *Deathless World*. A remnant of the desert dwellers remained in the city for several years, allowing only peaceful people intent on goodness and charity to enter its walls. Their leader, a wizard of great renown, saw to it that Dibbu-Loka became a holy place. Thirty-three generations later, the trail of that wizard's seed had led deep into the desert. A boy emerged that day during a birth so violent it killed his mother.

His father, an Asēkha Chieftain named Jhana, was devastated, as would be expected. But Jhana loved his newborn son, nonetheless, and he named the boy Torg, which meant *Blessed Warrior*. His proper name for ceremonial events was *The Torgon*.

In the current day, Dibbu-Loka remained an enchanted place. However, it was the monks and nuns who now resided there that made it special, not its desolate location. Dibbu-Loka rested atop a hill that rose out of dusty land pockmarked with canyons and ravines on ground almost as inhospitable as the desert that lay to the east.

The central shrine of Dibbu-Loka dominated the interior of the city. Bakheng, originally designed as King Lobha's tomb, had been grandly built to match his excessive tastes. The pyramid contained three entryways leading to three main chambers. The top chamber was intended to house Lobha's head, the middle his arms and torso, and the bottom his legs.

Now, other more wholesome uses had been found for these chambers.

Three smaller temples surrounded Bakheng, and hundreds of single-story buildings formed a triangular frame around these three. Originally built to house Lobha's army, the chambers now were the residences of the five hundred monks and nuns who occupied the holy city.

All the other interior buildings of Dibbu-Loka were set amid courtyards linked by a maze-like pattern of paved causeways. The main causeway led from the grand entrance to the central shrine. Smaller roads scattered in unusual directions, often ending abruptly in empty pavilions, without doors or windows. Newcomers to Dibbu-Loka frequently became lost if they strayed off the main streets. The noble ones, of course, gently set them back on course. Torg, too, knew all the ways.

As the sun began to fall, he strode purposefully with the Asēkhas through the grand entrance, his pace solemn and hypnotic. Torg was dressed entirely in black, wearing a silk jacket belted tightly at the waist and tucked inside his narrow breeches. Cloth gaiters covered his calves. His hair, which hung to his shoulders, matched the color of his clothing. His tanned skin and blue eyes provided a startling contrast to his monochromatic outfit.

The Asēkhas looked almost identical to Torg. Tugars who had not crossbred with other races always had black hair and blue eyes, and most were between four and four and a half cubits tall, considerably taller than almost all of Triken's humans. Sōbhana was shorter than most purebred desert warriors, but that made her no less dangerous in Torg's mind.

When Asēkhas were adorned in black, they were in a killing mood. The desert warriors who had defeated King Lobha's army had worn black, but while those warriors had been outnumbered ten to one, Torg and his Asēkhas now were outnumbered one hundred to one. Still, he wasn't overly concerned.

Their first sighting of noble ones was not a pleasant experience. Golden soldiers had forced more than a dozen monks and nuns to stand along the roadside with daggers held to their throats. The soldiers grinned maliciously behind their plated helms, which glowed crimson in the fading light.

Some of the noble ones had trickles of blood on their white robes, but the monks and nuns did not appear to be afraid. Torg knew they did not fear death. In their perception it was as natural as breathing. Even so, they prized life above all things because it provided them with the opportunity to overcome suffering and achieve enlightenment, either in this existence or in one of the countless that followed.

Kusala walked on Torg's right, one pace behind. Torg looked back and saw the chieftain's eyes ablaze and tears streaking his dusty cheeks. If not for Torg's steady presence, Kusala already might have lost control and succumbed to what the Asēkhas called *frenzy*, butchering any soldier within reach. Torg sensed the other Asēkhas also struggling to contain their fury. It was not inconceivable that the small band of twenty could kill all two thousand of their enemy, if they were given the time and enough room to maneuver.

"Remember your vows of obeisance," Torg said in a loud voice, bending them to his will. The fate of the prisoners depended on it. "My order was clear. You must not act unless I command it."

Several dozen enemy soldiers laughed, moving their daggers even closer to the throats of their prisoners.

"Yes, do not act unless the *King of Death* grants his permission," a soldier said, his voice echoing in the otherwise silent streets. "He, at least, is wise enough to know that if you attacked, you would be cut down like helpless women."

A dagger suddenly buried itself in a wooden pillar next to the soldier's head. The blade hummed and quivered.

Torg shot Sōbhana a fiery look.

"I missed on purpose," she said, shrugging her shoulders.

Several of the Asēkhas chuckled nervously.

Even Torg could not resist a wry smile. Then he raised his right hand and cried, *"Kantaara Yodha tam!* (A Desert Warrior calls!)" The dagger sprang from the pillar and spun through the air, its handle landing crisply in his palm. Torg noticed a tiny scratch near the tip of the blade before tossing it back to Sōbhana and then continuing onward.

The others followed, probably relieved that he had chosen to ignore her insubordination. They marched into the city's depths, but as they neared Bakheng, Torg heard the captain's dreaded mantra, which erased his brief mirth.

"Come, *Torgon*, or the killing will begin. Sundown approaches."

Again.

"Come, *Torgon*, or the killing will begin. Sundown approaches."

13

Torg ignored the chanting and continued to lead his Asēkhas up the main causeway toward Bakheng. He was relieved that the incident with the dagger had not caused a skirmish. He'd have to discipline Sōbhana, but it would have to wait for later. In truth, he probably wouldn't follow through. He treasured her spirit and hoped she would someday bear children, continuing her precious bloodline. Though that too he doubted. More and more, his Tugars failed to proliferate. When needed most, their numbers dwindled. It had become especially troublesome the past one hundred years, coinciding with the birth of Invictus, whose evil had had a deadening effect that reached all the way to Anna, the Tugars' Tent City in the heart of the desert.

More golden soldiers appeared along the road. Monks and nuns, each with a dagger less than a finger-length from their jugulars, were held on display. Without exception, the noble ones' faces remained calm. During their many years of meditation they had studied all things—without prejudice. Death was an empty threat. They did not demand or expect rescue, but Torg refused to accept the sacrilege of such a slaughter. The noble ones were an invaluable counterbalance to Invictus, an antivenin to his toxic existence. Without their gentleness, the balance of power would irreversibly favor the sorcerer.

Torg struggled to contain his anger. He could hear the grinding of his own teeth. However, he had a plan that he would follow through success or failure.

Bakheng finally came into view. A thick formation of golden soldiers was arranged at the base of the huge pyramid. Several hundred more stood on the steep steps that led to the upper entrance, their swords drawn and their shields pressed to their chests. Archers lined the highest landing.

Torg and the Asēkhas marched to the bottom of the stairs. They looked upward—and beheld an abomination. An elaborate wooden bench had been placed on the balcony at the top of the shrine. Cruelly strapped to it was the High Nun of Dibbu-Loka.

Sister Tathagata, the *Perfect One*, was more than three thousand years old. But her eyes—ah, her eyes—were as clear as a child's. Torg had spent many years with her in conversation and meditation. She liked to call him "young man" before throwing her head back and guffawing. Her laughter was like a waterfall, pleasing more than just the ears. Torg felt insignificant in her presence. For Invictus' minions to threaten her in this way was an insult against anything sane.

Someone had shoved a pewter funnel into Tathagata's mouth, attaching it to her jaw with a leather strap. A bronze cauldron hung two cubits above her head. It contained a bubbling liquid. Even from where he stood, Torg could hear her gagging.

Torg sensed the cauldron's contents. Molten gold—superheated by magic.

He was enraged. Swirling specks of bluish flame crept along his fingertips. Tiny sparks spun about his ears and nostrils. His hair floated and danced, as if electrified. He was a volcano about to erupt, but he knew that if Tathagata and the other noble ones were to survive, he would have to somehow remain calm until he enacted his plan.

The obnoxious captain stood next to Tathagata. He smiled wickedly. Torg smiled back.

At that moment, however, there were greater evils than the captain. The Warlish witch, her face full of filth and fire, loomed over Tathagata. But she was not the worst. Not even close. Inside the dark entrance to the shrine stood the witch's true master, an unholy being whose very presence in that sacred place was blasphemy—and it was on that creature that Torg now focused his formidable gaze.

The captain with the loud voice, seemingly unaware of his peril, walked to the edge of the balcony and leered down at Torg. Surrounded by archers and armor-clad soldiers, the annoying little man must have felt brave and powerful, believing that he was the one in control. But Torg saw him as nothing more than a mouthpiece.

"So, you have finally arrived," the captain said. The timbre of his voice was the most impressive thing about him. "Thank you very much for taking your time, *Desert Peasant*. Did you walk here so slowly because your boots were full of sand? Or was it simply because your legs would not stop shaking?"

What happened next came as no surprise to Torg, for he had designed it to astound his enemies. But even the Warlish witch, who stood guard over Tathagata, seemed caught unaware. Suddenly Asēkha-Podhana was halfway up the stairs, standing amid a tight group of golden soldiers. The warrior let out a scream that rose in pitch to an impossible intensity, causing dozens of soldiers to tear off their helms and clench their ears. While the attention was focused on Podhana, there was a shuffling sound higher up, away from the diversion. The obnoxious captain cried out, and then his head sprang from his shoulders and tumbled all the way down the stairs—thump, thump, thump, thump, *thump.*

Podhana screamed again. All eyes returned to him. Meanwhile, something dark streaked down the stairs, quick as a fox.

Kusala stood next to Torg, flicking blood off the blade of his *uttara.*

Afterward there was much shouting and confusion. A slew of arrows rained down on the Asēkhas, but none were capable of penetrating Tugarian flesh.

Torg reached down and grabbed the captain's head by its long yellow hair. He lifted it high in the air, its face still wearing an expression of disbelief.

"Mala, we could not abide this one," Torg said. "His death was not negotiable. I'm sure you understand."

For a moment everyone appeared unable to move. Evoking the name of Mala had stunned the gathering into silence. But in place of the monster, the Warlish witch stepped into view, and a noise far more unpleasant and painful than any scream Podhana could have conjured disrupted the eerie quiet.

In Torg's perception it began as a low growl, like that of a large feline sighting prey, though it was interspersed with tiny cackles and high-pitched profanities. The bizarre mixture of sounds was designed to breed despair, as if confirming the worst fears of all living beings: Hell was the only true reality and eternal suffering the fate of all. The effect on the gathering was widespread. Several of the noble ones, temporarily freed from the grasp of their captors, bent over and vomited. Sōbhana and the other Asēkhas spat and reflexively drew their curved swords. Kusala bared his teeth and growled in return, one dangerous beast squaring off with another. But Torg held up his hand, as if to stay them all.

When he spoke, the spell was broken—at least enough to relax the Asēkhas. "I did not come all this way 'with sand in my boots' to deal with the likes of you," Torg said to the witch. "Let your master show himself. He is the only one here worthy of my regard."

Despite Torg's bold words, the witch did not appear dismayed. Mucus squirted from her nostrils and fell to the stone at her feet, smoking and sizzling. She stomped to the edge of the balcony and kicked the captain's headless body off the platform. It flew sideways and tumbled halfway down the stairs before crumpling in a bloody heap. Those nearby backed away in disgust.

"Youuuu," she purred, pointing a finger at Torg. "I come for youuuu."

To Torg, the words themselves were harmless, even comical. But there was a madness in the way she uttered them that seemed to cause nervousness and trembling among most in attendance. The witch's eye sockets were empty, but they blazed with rancid light. Her scraggly hair was gray, and it danced on her head like a tangle of snakes. Worst of all she stank, as if long decayed. Torg could smell her even from where he stood. The soldiers could not abide her, and they fled the balcony and scrunched together on the lower stairs. Only the witch remained—with Sister Tathagata lying beneath her on the wooden bench.

The hideous thing put a gnarled hand on one of the nun's small breasts and squeezed. Tathagata made no sound. If she was afraid she did not show it.

"Are you rrrready?" the witch said to Torg. "Are you rrrready for me? It's time for some fun."

Though Torg did not move or blink, the witch began to laugh. Sōbhana lifted her hand, as if to throw her dagger again. But the witch was too quick. When she raised her skinny arms there was a flash, followed by a violent boom and a cloud of black smoke. The air cleared slowly. Where a monster had once stood, there now was a woman of incalculable beauty. She still wore a ragged dress, but on her it looked, even to Torg, like a priceless gown. Intoxicating green eyes filled the once-empty sockets, and waist-length auburn hair replaced the tangled gray. A perfume as sweet as spring spread outward in waves, enriching the air and making the fear and hopelessness of a few moments ago feel like a foolish misunderstanding. The soldiers, now entranced, raced back to the balcony and bowed low.

Chal-Abhinno, queen of whores, stood before the gathering. Like all her kind, Chal had two forms: one hideous, the other excruciatingly beautiful. The far-more pleasant version now stared down at Torg. When Chal smiled, hearts raced, and men began to sweat. Her allure appeared to weaken even the Asēkhas. Sōbhana covered her face. Torg wondered if she felt ugly in comparison. Kusala seemed puzzled and looked at Torg as if seeking guidance.

Torg clenched his left hand in a fist. His right held his walking staff in a death grip. Obhasa's white ivory glowed, causing the air to crackle.

The next move belonged to Torg. All others waited and wondered.

Torg turned to Kusala and then to the rest of the Asēkhas. "I have forgiven Sōbhana, for now," he said softly enough so that his words were barely audible to anyone not standing nearby. "If you wish to mistake that for weakness, so be it. But starting now, I will forgive nothing. Any of you who disobey me will suffer at *my* hands. The stakes are high. Do you doubt it?"

Only Sōbhana answered. "It is I who faltered, lord. We . . . I . . . will not fail you again. We . . . I . . . do not doubt you."

"That remains to be seen," Torg said. "But I say this only once more. Stay where you are until it becomes clear that I need you. You may defend yourselves, if you are attacked. And if I'm destroyed, you may kill any and all that you choose. Otherwise, do not act, other than to shield innocents from harm."

Not even Kusala protested. Torg's tone had achieved its desired effect. He'd tried to lead with respect, rather than intimidation. This was different—and not open for debate.

Torg turned back to the stairs. "May I come up?" he said to the witch.

Chal smiled, exposing teeth white as milk. She spread her arms wide. With the coming of dusk an enchanting breeze had arisen, causing her now-lovely hair to swirl enticingly about her slim shoulders.

"Of courssssse, *Torgon.* You and I need to get to know each other. Let the others bide their time while we discuss matters that are beyond them. If you are reasonable, all of thissss (she waved a hand at Tathagata) will become unnecessary."

"Very well," Torg said.

He bounded up the steps five at a time, and soon stood face to face with Chal. His quickness stunned several guards, who rumbled forward to contest him, but the witch ordered them off.

"Back!" Chal said, and her voice temporarily took on its former hideousness. Then she regained her composure and became sweetly seductive. "*The Torgon* is our guesssst. Give him room to stand."

Torg still held Obhasa. The staff vibrated wildly, as if struggling to contain a bolt of lightning within its dense fibers. Torg leaned down so that his nose was just a finger-length from hers. Her physical beauty was the greater, Torg knew, but it was artificial.

"I find it tedious to repeat myself," Torg said, slowly enunciating each word. "But if I must, I must. I did not come here to bandy words with a witless whore. Invite your master to show himself."

The smile on Chal's face was replaced by a snarl of such vehemence, even *her* beauty was scarred. Black smoke oozed from the pores of her skin. Her green eyes faded to gray and then white. Her transformation from hideousness to beauty had come with fire and smoke, but this transformation—from beauty back to hideousness—was slow and cruel.

Her skin bubbled and popped. Strand after strand of auburn hair curled and turned gray. The lithe muscles of her tanned arms became lumpy and gruesome. The perfume grew sour, bitter and rotten. The golden soldiers fled her presence.

Torg did not flee.

Chal growled and swept a clawed hand at his face. The force of the blow could have shattered a pillar, but he easily caught her wrist and twisted her arm downward.

The witch yelped and dropped to her knees. Acidic tears fell from her eyes, hissing on the stone.

While continuing to grip her arm, Torg knelt and whispered in her ear. "You are not my match, but at the moment you are also not my concern. Despite what you have done to Sister Tathagata, I will give you one chance. Submit now and live. You and I will cross paths again, I believe."

"Bastard," she said. "Basssstard!"

Torg pressed Obhasa's rounded head against the small of her back. Where it touched her, blue flames arose.

"Submit. Or I will end your life. Not even your master will be able to save you."

"I . . . will . . . not."

Torg stood and lifted her by her arm. Then he flung her in the air. Chal spun off the balcony and appeared headed to her death, but Torg knew it would not be that easy. The witch landed with the deftness of a cat about fifteen steps below the upper platform. There she crouched on all fours—a vile beast full of hate—and glowered at him. Crimson beams sprang from her empty eye sockets, scorching the stone at his feet. Red flames spat from her mouth and swirled about the wooden bench that held Tathagata. Before the flames could take hold, Torg touched the bench with his staff. Blue liquid spilled over the wood, extinguishing the fire.

"I will kill youuuu . . ." Chal screamed. And then she scrambled down the rest of the steps with the speed of a hunted animal, rushing past the Asēkhas in a torrent of smoke.

Kusala or Sōbhana could have struck her with their swords, but Torg knew they dared not move, more fearful of his wrath than hers. Chal was a formidable creature, the greatest of all the Warlish witches. But as Torg had said, she was not his match. Chal would have to bide her time.

The golden soldiers and the Asēkhas remained still as stones. The brief struggle between Torg and Chal seemed to have engrossed all who watched—even the noble ones, who had not tried to escape though their captors were temporarily preoccupied. Torg reached down and with one bulky hand broke the leather straps that pinned Tathagata to the bench. He gently removed the funnel from her mouth. With a mere fraction of effort he lifted the tiny woman—who was barely a third his weight—up and away from the precariously balanced cauldron, then set her carefully on her feet. The High Nun staggered briefly before regaining her balance.

Tathagata smiled and started to speak, but then her tongue froze in her mouth, and her eyes grew wide. Torg had never seen her react so strongly to anything. He turned around ever so slowly and faced the dark entrance of the shrine's upper chamber. The figure that had long lurked there, watching the proceedings from the shadows, slowly emerged.

Finally, Mala deigned to make an appearance.

2

On the rooftop of Bakheng, twilight changed to darkness in just a few breaths. Torches, already lit, were joined by the glowing moon and stars, and the balcony on which Torg and Tathagata stood shone brightly, as if on fire.

Mala emerged from the dark opening of the upper shrine, squeezing through the entryway and unfolding his enormous body. Though he was more than twice Torg's height and weighed more than seventy stones, he was limber and quick. Few but Torg matched his strength.

Before Invictus had ruined him with sorcery, Mala had been a peaceful snow giant, one of the most wondrous creatures on all of Triken. Torg even knew his previous name: Yama-Deva. The only beauty Mala had retained from his previous existence was his silky white mane, which ran down his spine to his waist. Everything else was hideous to behold. His eyes were now red and swollen; vile liquid oozed from their sockets. Two blood-stained fangs hung over his lower lip; venom dripped from their pointed tips. His tongue was long and black; it probed and fluttered like a snake's.

Yet Torg believed few who dared look directly at Mala would notice much about his face. What would captivate their attention was something even more sinister. The Chain Man lived up to his name. A single chain wrapped around his shoulders, crisscrossed at his waist and lower back, rode down his hips and looped around his bulky thighs. The chain had six-inch-thick links of gold blended with magical alloys, making it supernaturally strong. It glowed incessantly with a golden fire that appeared as hot as magma, burning Mala's thick hide and causing a stink that was reminiscent of rotten meat cooked over an open fire. Was his pain constant and hideous? Torg could not believe otherwise. But Mala's madness seemed to ignore the pain. It just made him angrier and more dangerous.

The monster loomed over Torg like a fully grown man staring down at a ten-year-old boy. Tathagata covered her face and staggered backward. She gagged and collapsed to her knees.

"I'm sorry, *Torgon*," she managed to say. "I've spent so many years harping on your spiritual weaknesses, yet I see now that I am far weaker than you. I could abide the witch, but in this creature's presence I am pathetic."

Urine slid down her thighs.

Torg placed himself between the sister and the monster.

"Dear one," he said, still staring at Mala but speaking to Tathagata, "do not mistake disgust for weakness. This one is an affront beyond all others, save Invictus himself. I have fought many battles and seen many gruesome things and am more used to such horror, that is all. I would never presume to question your courage."

"My lord, you embolden me. I shall stand and face my doom with dignity."

Mala watched this exchange with a smirk on his hideous face. The Chain Man did not appear to doubt his superiority.

"The one who called you 'Desert Peasant' now lacks his head," the monster said. Then he laughed. It felt like poison to Torg's ears. "Yet I dare to call you something worse. *The Torgon* is a fool and a coward, worth less than the filth on the soles of my feet. Tell me, little one, will one of your Asēkha rats come up and try to take *my* head?"

Mala laughed again. With each spasm of his gigantic midsection, gobs of liquid fire blurted from the chain, smiting the stone stairs. Flames engulfed several golden soldiers, who vaulted off the pyramid, howling as they died. The noble ones dropped to their knees and covered their faces. But the Asēkhas easily stepped out of the way of the scorching liquid that reached the bottom steps—and there they held their ground, continuing to watch their leader's every move.

"Call me what you like," Torg said. "But I name you Yama-Deva, for you were once a snow giant, and it is still possible for you to return to your former glory. I can help you, if you will take me into your heart. Yama-Deva can live again."

Mala clenched his teeth and bit his lower lip, spewing blood. The chain seemed to glow even hotter, black smoke rising from its links. "Fool . . . *fool!*" The booming power of his voice carried far into the deepening night. "Braggart. *Idiot!* You are nothing compared to me. *Nothing!* And you dare . . . you *dare* . . . to offer your aid to me? I am Mala, you little worm."

"Nonetheless, I do offer my aid. Your anger and hatred are an illusion burned into your mind by your master. But I can see the real you, trapped behind the ruin of your eyes."

The Chain Man seemed beside himself with rage. He sucked in a huge gulp of air and spit a gob of rancid liquid onto Torg's face. Few could have survived this assault. Blindness would follow disfigurement. But the foul acid did not harm Torg, sizzling and then evaporating soon after it touched his skin. However, a few droplets slipped past Torg and fell onto Tathagata's cheeks. Torg spun around, faster than the eye could follow. Then he willed precise beams of blue light to spurt from the head of his staff and incinerate the poison before it could do any damage.

The High Nun smiled.

Torg turned back to Mala. "I am not one of the noble ones. I have neither their patience nor their dignity. I am who I am. But for now, that is enough."

Torg took a step toward Mala, pointed Obhasa at the Chain Man's chest and then swung full circle, smashing the ancient ivory against the chain that wrapped around the giant's torso. A conflagration of flame—Torg's blue and Mala's golden—exploded at the point of impact, and for a moment the two dueling colors blended into a brilliant green. Despite the enormity of the collision, Torg's power proved greater, and blue prevailed. The Chain Man staggered backward, flailing his arms before falling flat on his back and smiting the balcony with the force of a fallen pillar. The entire pyramid seemed to quiver.

Torg shouted words from the ancient tongue. "*Kaalakaala! (Deep darkness!)* . . . *Santharaahi! (Spread!)* . . . *Bandha! (Bind!)* . . ." Thick blue fumes swirled from his staff and rose into the night sky. "*Mano! (Mind!)* . . . *Paccosakkaahi! (Retreat!)* . . . *Niddaayahi! Niddaayahi! Niddaayahi! (Sleep! Sleep! Sleep!)*"

Smoke spun like a tornado, expanding and encompassing first the balcony, then the temple, and finally what appeared to be all of Dibbu-Loka. It grew as large as a thunderhead. The Chain Man rose up on his haunches, staring at the broiling sky. The golden soldiers raised their swords and prepared to charge, but then froze in place as the blue smoke fell upon them, seeking their mouths and nostrils. Even if some of the more alert soldiers tried to hold their breaths, it would not matter. The fumes would find their way into their lungs. In a show of trust, Tathagata breathed deeply. One by one the captors and captives began to sag. A sudden and irresistible exhaustion overcame them. Within a few moments all but Torg, the Asēkhas and Mala were sleeping like children who had been kept up long past their bedtimes.

A frisky breeze whisked away the smoke. Soon after, Torg sank to his knees. He had never performed this feat on such a grand scale, and he was weary from the extravagant expenditure of energy. The Asēkhas charged up the steep steps and encircled him, *uttaras* drawn.

Torg's chin rested on his chest, his breath coming in short gasps. But his eyes remained alert.

Mala took a long time to stand. His chain glowed less brightly, but his anger now seemed more calculated. "Aaaaah, *Torgon* . . . I have underestimated you. You were outnumbered and overpowered, but you have managed to even the odds somewhat with this cute little trick."

Kusala spoke on Torg's behalf. "Mala, I warn you to stay where you are."

Mala paid no heed to Kusala, glaring at Torg instead. "Do you think these annoying mice can defeat me? And look at you . . . so weak you cannot stand. As frail as a boy. As feeble as an old man. You believe you have won, but you are wrong. Do you think I cannot crush you?"

With a great effort Torg raised his head. "Before . . . before you could *crush* me, you would have to deal with the Asēkhas. You might defeat them, but it would not come without cost. By the time you finished, you would be weaker than I am now."

Mala growled and pounded his boulder-sized fists together. The Asēkhas surrounded the monster, their *uttaras* sparking in response to his chain. Each sword had taken more than a year to craft, and each curved blade was a thousand times sharper than the thickness of a human hair. Mala's hide was far denser than ordinary flesh, but it was not impenetrable. The monster seemed to recognize at least some of the truth in Torg's words, and he dropped his massive arms to his sides.

"What do you suggest, Death-Knower? It is obvious you have thought this through."

Torg coughed and almost fell on his face, but Sōbhana sprang to his side and caught him. Torg smiled weakly at her, then returned his attention to the Chain Man.

"I *have* thought this through. My reason for coming here has always been the same." More coughing. "I do not want the noble ones harmed. I came here to barter—to give you my freedom in exchange for theirs."

Kusala's eyes widened. "No, lord, this cannot be. We can crush this creature. Leave him to us. When he is vanquished we will save the noble ones and be on our way."

Torg continued to focus on Mala. "I offer myself to you without further resistance. You and I will leave this place. While your soldiers sleep, the Asēkhas will remove the noble ones and take them to a safe place. I give you my word that your soldiers will not be harmed. We both win."

Perhaps wary of a trap, Mala did not immediately respond. But then he shrugged, as if unconcerned by anything that might threaten him. "Very well, *Torgon*. But order your rats not to follow."

Torg rose unsteadily to his feet. He turned to Kusala, Sōbhana, and the other Asēkhas and gazed from face to face. Mala loomed noisily behind him like a tower of malice.

The disbelief on the faces of his warriors was easily recognizable, and Torg understood why. They could not see inside his mind and know his thoughts. How could they possibly understand what drove him now?

He knew more about Invictus than he'd let on to anyone. He could sense the extent of the sorcerer's power like a wildfire obscured by the crest of a hill. All others could see only smoke, but Torg could feel the fire's heat.

Despite his relative youth and inexperience, Invictus had become the greatest threat the land had ever known. Ordinary means could not defeat him. Torg believed that in order to combat Invictus he would need to perform an act of virtue that would help to even the scales between good and evil. A selfless act on a stage of such magnitude would set larger forces into motion. To save the noble ones Torg was willing to sacrifice his own freedom. He did so, however, with an even grander vision. This war would be fought not just on the physical battlefield, but in an arena invisible to all but the wise.

"The soldiers will sleep for at least a day," Torg said to the Asēkhas. "While they are helpless, transport the noble ones to our place of safe keeping. I will depart with Mala and permit him to bear me to Invictus."

"Lord, this is impossible," Kusala said. "If you—"

Blue light fired from Torg's staff, pounding Kusala in the chest and knocking him off his feet. The other Asēkhas gasped.

"Do not *interrupt*," Torg said, slamming Obhasa down hard enough to crack the marble at his feet. "Listen carefully, all of you. I will leave with Mala. You must not follow, not a single one of you. Carry the noble ones to safety and return to the defense of Anna. Do not harm any of Mala's soldiers. If you are ambushed after I am gone, then you are free to kill any and all—and come after me, if you still can. Otherwise stay away from me, and alert all other Tugars to do the same. If and when this situation changes, I will make it known."

"Listen to your master, little cockroaches," Mala teased. "He, at least, has a shred of wisdom. And don't worry. I will take *good* care of him."

Kusala struggled to breathe but managed to regain his feet. "As you command, my king. It will be as you say."

"Yes, it *will* be as I say. If Mala honors his side of the bargain and allows you to remove the noble ones without interference, then you must not give chase. Any who follow will die at *my* hands. This, I foretell." Then he swung slowly back toward the monster. "As for you, Mala, if your minions attempt some treachery in Dibbu-Loka after you and I have departed, you will regret it."

"Your threats are empty," the Chain Man said. "But they are also needless. Once you and I are gone, nothing will happen to these pathetic *breath-watchers* unless you break your vow and try to escape. I care less for them than I do for your rats. You, I care for least of all. But Invictus wishes to speak to you face to face. I do not comprehend it, but I *always* follow orders from my king. So I'll deliver you to him as promised."

3

The arid land that lay just beyond the northern walls of the holy city fell steeply and was riddled with spiny rocks and hidden clefts. Mala chose this path for himself and Torg. After the ordeal on the balcony of Bakheng, Torg was still exhausted, and his legs felt as if they'd been drained of blood. Nonetheless, Mala drove him mercilessly forward. Torg's discomfort was the least of the Chain Man's concerns.

"Keep moving, you little pig . . . keep *moving!*" Mala commanded, shoving Torg from behind and sending him tumbling partway down the hill. "Do as you're told, or I'll have to carry you. And neither of us will like that."

Torg's anger surged, but he remained weak. Also, he no longer wielded Obhasa, having left the staff with Kusala, who had cringed when he had taken it in his hands. Torg's heart withered when he recalled the chieftain's pained expression.

I'm sorry, Kusala. I hope one day to regain your trust. But for now the stakes are too high. I had to make sure that none of the Asēkhas interfered with my plan.

Mala thrust his foot into Torg's ribs, knocking him farther down the hill.

"Hurry, you pathetic flea. I want to put several leagues between us and this rat hole of a city before I even think of resting."

Torg had never been kicked so hard. Gasping for breath, he forced himself upright and stumbled forward. Knowing that he would have to draw on his warrior's training to survive this ordeal, he cleared thought from his mind and began to move with the instincts of a wild animal, choosing the path of least resistance through the jumbled boulders. Soon Mala was struggling to keep up.

"Wait, wait . . . you weasel. I warned you what would happen to your precious *robe-wearers* if you tried to escape."

"I'm not trying to escape. I'm doing as I'm told. Slow? Fast? Let me know when you make up your mind."

Mala chomped on his lower lip. Blood squirted onto his chin. He reached down, picked up a fair-sized boulder and heaved it at Torg. It missed by a wide margin. Curses and profanities followed. The Chain Man stomped around like a spoiled child.

Meanwhile, Torg felt his strength returning far more quickly than he'd expected. He believed he already was capable of running off and leaving Mala behind. After all, the chain borne by the ruined snow giant was a heavy burden. But Torg had given his word and would remain true as long as the Chain Man left the noble ones in peace.

"Mala, it doesn't have to be this way. All this kicking and shoving won't speed up either of us."

The monster snarled. But somehow Torg's words had a calming effect. For the rest of the night Mala allowed him to choose the path and set the pace. They walked until nearly dawn but managed just three leagues, as the owl flies, being forced to clamber over jumbled rock and crawl through thorny brush. Several leagues to the east or west, the land was far easier to traverse, but the Chain Man demanded they head due north toward the city of Senasana, about thirty leagues from Dibbu-Loka.

"That is where the real fun will begin," Mala said. The monster smiled, and the links of his chain grew red-hot.

As the sun emerged, their pace slowed. Torg found a trickling spring and knelt to sniff the water and then take a drink. Mala snorted and disdained it.

Torg found some edible berries and offered a few to the Chain Man, whose face contorted in disgust.

"I would eat *your* greasy flesh before I would eat *that.* Meat, blood, and bones make the best breakfast—not fruit. You're disgusting."

"Yama-Deva did not eat meat. He loved all animals. He was a shepherd."

"Say that name again, and you will regret it. You live now only because Invictus desires it."

Torg shrugged and then led Mala to a natural stone shelter, where they rested beneath its craggy ceiling for much of the day. The rising sun brought with it a languorous heat. Soon Mala's eyes grew heavy, and finally he slept. Torg lay nearby pretending to doze, but he watched the Chain Man through the slits of his eyelids.

Mala's long white mane was unchanged, but little else remained of his former glory. Torg pitied the monster. He had not known Yama-Deva before Invictus captured him, but he had visited with several of his kin high in the peaks of the Okkanti Mountains, including a snow giant named Yama-Utu, who was Yama-Deva's brother.

"I have heard of you, *Torgon*," Yama-Utu had said to him seven centuries ago. "Yama-Deva is the only one among us who dares to leave the peaks, and he has brought back word of the desert king who can cheat death. Please, young master, tell us more."

Torg had spoken long with the snow giant, his mate and three of his friends, who seemed to magically appear from behind boulders. Their company and conversation had been delightful. Many times they'd bragged of Yama-Deva, the snow giant who dared to wander.

More than seven hundred years later, Torg felt the sting of tears as he studied the ruins of Yama-Deva. He remembered what the noble ones said about the impotence of hatred, but he felt hatred for Invictus growing inside him, nonetheless. Torg hoped beyond hope that there was some way he could help Mala revert to his former self. Nevertheless, he feared only the death of Invictus could undo this terrible wrong.

Eventually even Torg slept, his dreams drenched in sorrow.

Anyone watching from a distance might have mistaken them for friends—rather large friends—traveling together in the wilds. Torg woke and could have escaped, most of his strength returned. But he believed in the power of karma; if he broke his word, more harm than good would result. His vow at Bakheng would not be fully honored until he was presented to Invictus.

Torg had once asked his Vasi master, "What is the meaning of karma?"

The master had answered, "Karma means you get away with nothing."

Torg reflected on those words as he listened to Mala's thunderous snores. When the Chain Man finally woke, the monster sat up so fast he banged his thick head on the ceiling of the shelter, the rock suffering more damage than his skull.

"It's a good thing you didn't run off," Mala said, rubbing the sore spot. "I would have returned to Dibbu-Loka and killed every one of the *bald bastards* myself."

"The noble ones *shave* their heads," Torg said. "Even the women. They are not bald."

"Whatever."

Torg sighed. "I have told you before . . . and I mean it. I will go with you, without resistance, and allow you to imprison me. After that, we shall see what we shall see. As for going back and killing the noble ones, that is no longer possible. The Asēkhas have long since removed them from harm. Now, my word is all that binds me to you."

"So full of pride you are. And so bold. It would bring me great pleasure to strip the flesh from your bones. But my master forbids it, and *his* threats are the only ones I fear. You will fear them too. If you are lucky, he will convince you—as he convinced me—to join him in his quest to rid the land of vermin. Otherwise, you will suffer as he sees fit. And die *when* he sees fit."

Before they set off, Mala allowed Torg to drink from the spring and eat more berries. Quick as a snake, the Chain Man snatched a large iguana off the side of a boulder and devoured it raw, bones and all. Although Torg often had eaten salted iguana flesh, he found this sight less than appetizing. However, the fresh meat seemed to improve Mala's mood, and he again permitted Torg to lead.

The unusual pair walked into the evening and all through the night, rarely resting. In the meantime the rocky land surrounding Dibbu-Loka succumbed to rolling plains. Eventually the remnants of a road appeared before them, and by morning's first light they had traveled more than ten leagues and were almost halfway to Senasana. During all that time they had seen only lizards, snakes, birds and insects. Ravenous flies swarmed around them, but their bites had no effect on Torg's flesh—and undoubtedly none on Mala's as well. The Chain Man, in fact, seemed to enjoy eating them.

Once they reached the road, they made much better progress. On the fourth morning after leaving Dibbu-Loka, they approached within a league of Senasana, where one of Mala's scouts met them. The Chain Man barked out orders, and the scout raced into the darkness. As Mala and Torg drew nearer the city, several dozen golden soldiers marched toward them. A captain came forth and stood at the foot of the monster, trembling as he saluted.

"Did you bring it?" Mala said. "*Tell* me you brought it."

"Yes, lord," the captain stammered. "It is with us . . . as you commanded."

"It was wise of you not to fail. I have not yet eaten breakfast."

The captain swayed on his feet, as if about to swoon. Torg almost felt sorry for the man.

Warrior's Sacrifice

1

Sōbhana watched Mala and Torg scramble down the pyramid's stairs and jog along a causeway that led to the northern wall of Dibbu-Loka. The Chain Man was shouting orders and shoving Torg from behind. It was unbearable to watch.

Sōbhana was a warrior. Pain and sacrifice were second nature to her, but this was something else. Her lord's commands did not make sense. The golden soldiers were subdued. Mala stood alone. He was a formidable monster but not invincible.

"Chieftain, this is madness," she said to Kusala. "We must not permit it."

Kusala held Obhasa in his right hand, but his face remained downcast. "He will slay any who follow. I do not doubt it. I have never seen him like this. Madness or no, we must not pursue."

Kusala turned from Sōbhana and swept his arm in a half circle. "All heard the commands of our king. We must take the noble ones to the haven we have prepared. Find carts and oxen. I want them all far from the city by dawn. Do not harm the soldiers, unless we are attacked from without. However, there is one thing not mentioned by our king that I will encourage: If you feel the need to relieve yourselves, aim for a sleeping face. It will match their gaudy armor."

There was grim laughter and a few guarantees—even from several of the women—that not a drop would be wasted. Then the Asēkhas sprang into action. Thirty ox carts were found, but only enough oxen to haul ten of them. It didn't matter. The Asēkhas were strong enough to tow the carts by hand. The noble ones, still deeply asleep, were laid side by side on beds of hay. The evacuation had begun.

Tugars were not just warriors. They also were hard workers. It was said that twenty Asēkhas could outperform a hundred ordinary men and women. Nineteen Asēkhas could do almost as well.

Nineteen would have to do.

Sleek as a cat, Sōbhana slipped over the northeastern wall. She had not asked Kusala's permission, nor had he demanded it. Regardless, she was on her own.

Now she watched with rage as Mala shoved and kicked her king. It took every shred of her will to resist pouncing on the wicked monster. But she held herself back. If she attacked now, she knew Torg would kill her. Her own death did not concern her, but she would be no good to her lord if she were eliminated. She had to be patient and carefully choose the time and place to reveal her presence.

Plus, she knew Torg's senses were extraordinary. She hoped Torg's focus on Mala would dilute the wizard's alertness. If she stayed cleverly hidden, she might be able to follow undetected for a considerable distance.

She had no plan, other than to be certain Torg did not travel this path with Mala alone. She loved him, after all, but not only as she would love a king. She desired to become Torg's wife.

Sōbhana had begun her warrior training at age sixteen, achieving the rank of warrior at sixty-six and Asēkha at seventy-eight. Both were unprecedented. Torg had not become a warrior until he was sixty-eight and an Asēkha until eighty. But he had become a Death-Knower just two years later. Sōbhana knew in her heart that she could not follow in those footsteps. She would never be a wizard; it was not in her. She could, however, love one.

She was brave. She was loyal. She often was told she was beautiful. Why *not* her?

Kusala would have called it infatuation, but she knew better. Sōbhana *loved* Torg, as a woman does a man. She was puzzled that he had never taken a wife, but at the same time it pleased her. It gave her a chance to realize her dream. And if she had ever seen Torg with another woman, she might have committed murder.

Marriage was relatively rare among Tugars. Most of their men and women preferred sexual freedom—and among their own kind, the warriors were promiscuous. Unlike the others, Torg was not. He *always* slept alone. Sōbhana once asked Kusala about it, and the chieftain had fidgeted, uncharacteristically.

"There are rumors, among the elders, that something terrible happened to him when he was young," Kusala whispered. "He will not speak of it. I asked him once, and the look he gave me shriveled my tongue. I will not ask again."

As Sōbhana replayed the chieftain's words, she burrowed beneath a mound of crumbled stone until only her eyes and the crown of her head were exposed. She watched Mala and Torg as they slept beneath the slanted roof of a rock shelter. She saw her beloved open his eyes every now and then and look at the Chain Man. Tears coursed down his cheeks. She cried too. If Torg attempted to escape, she would rush to his aid, heedless of her own survival.

She followed them for days, all the way to the outskirts of Senasana. There she noted the approach of the scouts, and then the soldiers. As the morning sun climbed in the sky, Torg was led toward the main gates. People gathered along the wide road that ran through the center of the city. Sōbhana stayed far back, away from prying eyes.

Senasana was an active marketplace. Traders came from as far west as the Kolankold Mountains and as far east as the Barranca wastes. More than fifty thousand lived there permanently, and transients doubled its population.

On this day, what Sōbhana saw stunned her. A well-equipped army of more than five-hundred-score golden soldiers occupied the city. In addition to this infantry there were dangerous monsters: several druids from Dhutanga and a Kojin from the Dark Forest. Until now, Invictus had not sent this caliber of force this far south, as far as she knew. But the sorcerer's boldness had grown.

The citizens of Senasana were not warriors. They could not forestall an army. Accumulating wealth was their main talent. Under these circumstances they were frightened—and cowardly. Accommodating their new guardians would be their safest course.

Sōbhana knew most Senasanans admired Torg, who'd been a frequent guest. But this time the wizard was a helpless prisoner. It'd be one thing to join forces with an army of Tugars come to rescue their lord. But without the desert warriors to lead the way, it would be suicide to aid him.

As Torg and his captors marched past her hiding place, someone hurled a tomato from the side of the road. Its aim was true, striking her king in the face. Mala guffawed, along with the crowd.

It sickened Sōbhana—and angered her.

Still laughing, the tomato thrower suddenly bent over and coughed up a ball of blood that resembled the splattered fruit. Needless to say, *he* never laughed again. It wasn't wise to offend an Asēkha.

Sōbhana crept closer to the crowd. A large ox cart, piled high with women's clothing, had been left on the side of the road. The merchant had wandered a few paces away to watch the excitement. Sōbhana stole a loose-fitting kirtle, a pair of low-cut leather shoes, a cloth purse and a hat with a linen band that wrapped under the chin. Kneeling behind the cart, she quickly changed, tucking her *uttara* and dagger into scabbards beneath the dress and stuffing her black Tugarian outfit into the purse. The hat concealed the cut and color of her hair, which would have looked suspicious to those with clever eyes. When she emerged, she looked like a typical Senasanan woman.

Sōbhana wandered through the mob, which was growing raucous. Noon approached. Soon there would be feasting, during which the Chain Man and his soldiers would probably be treated like heroes. This was how merchants dealt with enemies. But if most of Mala's army followed him back to Avici afterward, Sōbhana believed that few in the merchant city would complain.

The teeming market in the heart of Senasana surrounded an enormous temple that was larger and more ornate than the pyramid-shaped shrine in Dibbu-Loka. The temple, called Vinipata, was a bulbous dome made of white marble that towered three hundred cubits above the floor of the square. Four smaller and less impressive domes served as Vinipata's guardians, and exquisite minarets framed the outer corners. Visitors entered through a red sandstone gate, decorated with a multitude of ancient inscriptions. The courtyard inside the gate could accommodate many thousands. Sōbhana had been to this place several times before this latest visit, though the other occasions had been far more pleasurable.

Mala escorted Torg into the square. The mob followed. The temple grounds soon swarmed with soldiers and onlookers. Sōbhana, in her new dress and hat, blended into the throng. She positioned herself as best she could to get a clear view.

Though most areas of the courtyard were packed, an open space remained around Mala and Torg. The Chain Man towered above everyone, and few dared approach the monster and his prisoner. Several golden soldiers stationed themselves a dozen paces away, but would go no nearer. The five druids and the Kojin, however, pressed in as close as they could. Mala's presence seemed to fill them with bliss.

The druids of Dhutanga stood almost seven cubits tall. They were thin and angular but deceptively strong. Their outer flesh looked more like bark than skin, and they had fiery eyes and large mouths, with black holes where there should have been ears and noses.

The Kojin was an enormous ogress with a bloated head and six muscled arms. Only a few of her kind still existed in the world, and those rarely had ventured outside of Java—until the emergence of Invictus. Sōbhana recalled her lone confrontation with a Kojin, which had occurred while traveling with two Asēkhas through Java. A vicious fight ensued—three against one. Despite their most concentrated efforts, the warriors could not seriously injure the beast, and they struggled to avoid its wicked counterattacks. Finally they were forced to flee. Sōbhana had never overcome the humiliation. She hadn't thought it possible for a trio of Asēkhas to fare so poorly against a single foe.

The Kojin who stood near Torg was even larger than the one she'd encountered. It was only a span shorter than Mala, dwarfing the druids in height and, especially, in breadth.

Next to these giants, even Torg looked pitifully small.

"How could anyone stand against monsters so terrible?" Sōbhana heard a woman in the crowd whisper to a man next to her.

He shrugged, looking nervous. "I know I couldn't, is all."

"Where are the Tugars?" another man said. "Where are the Asēkhas? Do they tremble?"

"We all tremble," the first man said.

Mala let out a roar that echoed throughout the courtyard. Flames sprang from his massive chain, flinging gouts of black smoke into the air.

All went silent.

The monster's booming voice was as concussive as thunder. "Citizens of Senasana . . . as you know, *The Torgon* stands accused of treason. He has conspired against King Invictus and his loyal followers. But fear not. As you can see, he has been captured and will be brought before the throne of the king in the Golden City—there to be fairly judged."

Mala's speech was greeted by scattered applause and cheers, but also by a fair share of grumbling.

Hidden near the gates, Sōbhana shouted, "Liar!"

Soldiers raced over, but by then she was settled in a different place.

"Liar?" Mala said. His chain glowed like hot coals. "There is only one liar here, and he kneels before me." Mala looked down at Torg, who indeed knelt, head bowed.

There was a brief silence, broken by a piercing call from a different area of the courtyard. Sōbhana simply could not bear it. "Let him speak!"

Several others, apparently braver than the rest, echoed this request. "Let him speak!"

Ebony fumes puffed from Mala's mouth and nose. Rancid liquids oozed from his ears. The Kojin, infected by the Chain Man's rage, pounded her fists against her hairy bosom. The druids swayed like reeds in a windstorm, humming in unison.

The event was not proceeding as Mala had apparently envisioned. The monster struggled to control his rage. His instinct must have been to wade into the crowd and bust heads, but even he was not that crude yet, was he? His king had not waged war, and a slaughter of civilians might do more harm than good.

"You wish him to speak?" Mala bellowed. "I will honor your requests. Speak, *Torgon*." He lowered his voice and said something to the wizard that Sōbhana could not hear.

The Death-Knower lifted his head. Silence again blanketed the courtyard. Even the druids grew quiet. Torg's beauty stunned Sōbhana. In comparison, Mala and the other monsters were repulsive.

"I will go to Invictus," Torg said, "and be 'fairly judged.'"

The silence broke like shattered glass. Clapping, cheering and cries of woe intermingled in the courtyard.

Sōbhana shouted, "No!" But this time her voice was whelmed.

"*The Torgon* speaks wisely," Mala said. "He trusts the wisdom and mercy of King Invictus. Perhaps there is hope he can be rehabilitated. The journey to Avici is long, however, and I will take no chances with such a dangerous prisoner. Bind him."

Several soldiers came forward alongside a four-wheeled wagon hauled by six oxen. Others bore a restraining device that had been wickedly conceived.

Mala smiled.

The soldiers laid Torg upon a full-length jacket of thick fabric and guided his arms through holes in the jacket before tying them against his chest with cruel leather straps. Then they threaded the jacket from his feet to his chin. After the Death-Knower was secured, Mala wrapped golden ropes, probably steeped in the sorcerer's magic, around the wizard's prone body. Torg was bound like a caterpillar in a cocoon.

The Kojin stomped forward and lifted the wizard high into the air. Making full use of her six arms, the ogress strapped Torg to a wide board that was attached at an angle to the bed of the wagon.

The Death-Knower was helpless. And on display.

Sōbhana had never felt so impotent. All she could do was watch, wait and follow.

And so began the lumbering one-hundred-league journey from Senasana to Avici, the home of Invictus. Mala and his army escorted the Death-Knower along the rolling banks of the Ogha River for thirty-eight days, by Sōbhana's count. During the absurdly slow and dreary march Torg remained bound, apparently unable to move anything but his head. Yet Sōbhana did not once see him squirm or otherwise resist. Instead he lay as still as a corpse, eyes closed, accepting occasional sips of water and spoonfuls of gruel without enthusiasm.

Whenever the procession approached a village, the fishermen and farmers who resided near the river bowed their heads. They were not capable of resisting such a well-equipped militia. Where was Anna? Nissaya? Jivita? Sōbhana heard them say more than once that Torg had been forsaken.

All the way from Senasana to Avici, Sōbhana avoided being seen by any of Mala's soldiers. Twice she encountered Tugarian scouting parties who were unaware of their king's orders not to follow, having left the Tent City before Torg's capture. She told them what she had seen and then sent some of them southeast to Anna and some west to Nissaya and Jivita. Kusala would have advance notice to ready the Tugars, and the armies of Nissaya and Jivita would at least be warned to prepare for battle. If Invictus were willing to send forces as far south as Senasana and Dibbu-Loka, then it was clear the young sorcerer was no longer concerned with reprisal.

Much of Invictus' lack of fear was probably based on the fact his stronghold—Avici and its sister city, Kilesa—was virtually impregnable. An oblong wall that stood thirty cubits tall and nearly two hundred leagues in length protected both cities. Sōbhana had heard it had taken twenty thousand slaves twenty years to construct the grand bulwark. Invictus even had the gall to order large portions of the stone to be slathered with liquid gold.

The Golden Wall, as it was aptly named, encircled Avici, Kilesa and more than twenty-five-thousand hectares of surrounding territory. As the Ogha River flowed south on its winding way to Lake Keo, it roared through Avici, cleaving the massive city in half. A pair of majestic bridges—one north and one south—spanned the river where it sluiced through gaps in the Golden Wall. Immense iron gates swung beneath the catwalks, protecting Avici from attack at these two otherwise vulnerable locations.

From where she hid, Sōbhana could now see the southern bridge, which rose steeply from the main wall, towering above the churning currents. As Mala approached the bridge, the main strength of Invictus' army greeted his brigade of ten thousand. Sōbhana guessed that more than two hundred thousand lined Ogha's steep banks, some of whom stood ten-deep on the bridge and wall. Having a warrior's ability to discern the extent of an enemy's forces, Sōbhana quickly recognized that the majority of the army was made up of golden soldiers. But at least a fifth of it appeared to have been recruited from other places. The druids of Dhutanga, who had spent centuries rebuilding their numbers after their failed war with Jivita, probably numbered ten thousand. The wild men of the Kolankold Mountains had provided another five thousand, and at least five thousand Pabbajja, the Homeless People who lived on the fringes of Java, were there. Added to the horde were five thousand Mogols, who dwelled in the Mahaggata Mountains. Many wicked creatures from Mahaggata's interior also had answered Invictus' call, including dracools, Stone-Eaters and wolves. There were dark places beneath the mountains, as well, and from there Invictus had lured cave trolls and mud ogres, and apparently given them potions to enable them to tolerate sunlight. There were smaller numbers of other zealots: demons, ghouls, and vampires from Arupa-Loka; murderers, rapists, and thieves from Duccarita; Warlish witches and their servant hags from Kamupadana. Also included in the hideous menagerie was a slew of misshapen monsters that Sōbhana had never before seen: a pair of three-headed giants who dwarfed even Mala; creatures who were part human and part animal or insect; and beasts with mouths full of sharp teeth that hungered for human flesh.

The sheer numbers staggered Sōbhana.

But her dismay was minuscule compared to what next appeared before her. Apparently the Chain Man wasn't Invictus' only favorite pet. As if the sorcerer needed any more weapons in his vast arsenal, another mighty ally had joined his army. A great dragon perched on the highest framework of the bridge. Even so far away, she could see the beast was fully two hundred cubits long from head to tail and probably weighed several thousand stones.

Though she had never actually seen one, Sōbhana had heard tales of the great dragons. The eldest among them was named Bhayatupa, who was said to be as powerful as he was ancient. As the legends foretold, Bhayatupa had ruled sprawling kingdoms, fought countless battles and slaughtered many brave warriors during his millennia-long existence.

Could this be that dragon? How could it not? It was huge beyond comprehension.

With the vast gathering watching Mala's every move, the Chain Man strode toward the bridge. The army cheered. Invictus was its king, but Mala was its general. It was obvious that this army had been bequeathed to him. When it came time to unleash its power, the ruined snow giant would be at its helm, and Sōbhana and the Tugars would face their sternest test.

Since departing Dibbu-Loka, Sōbhana had been barely able to tolerate watching Torg endure such ruthless torment. But seeing the dragon pained her even more. Mala was frightening, but not invincible. Invictus, whom she had yet to face, still felt more like legend than reality. The golden soldiers, despite their daunting numbers, were not nearly as well-trained as the Tugars. The other monsters presented certain difficulties, but they could be defeated. The dragon, however, was far more perilous.

From her hiding place in a thick copse several hundred paces from the bridge, Sōbhana saw the behemoth as the coming of doom. As she gazed at the dragon, she felt true fear for the first time in her life. This creature was beyond her in all ways.

Finally she understood Torg's mind. Her king had recognized before any of the rest of them that the Tugars could not prevail against Invictus by force. The legions of good had enjoyed many years of peace and superiority on Triken, but the Sun God, in a mere century of life, had changed all that. Sōbhana recognized that the world now approached a dangerous crossroads, and higher forces—karma, truth, love—would play the determining roles in the outcome. She now understood that Torg had surrendered to Mala in order to set those forces in motion.

What happened next caused her to tremble yet again. When the dragon spied Torg, it spread its colossal wings and sprang off the high bridge, landing on the ground in front of the wizard, who still was confined on the wagon by the magical restraining device. Its crimson head alone was twice as long as Torg's entire body, and each of its fearsome eyes was more than two cubits in diameter. The beast bent its long neck, tilted its right eye toward Torg and glided within a finger-length of the Death-Knower's face.

All went quiet. Even Mala dropped his arms and froze. There was magic in the air—born in a time long past.

Sōbhana was close enough to make out the details of Torg's face, and she saw that he did not flinch. His courage smote her heart.

When the dragon spoke, some fell to their knees. Its voice assaulted the senses. It reminded Sōbhana of the dust in a hoary crypt. "*Te tam maranavidum aacikkhanti.* (They call thee a Death-Knower)," said the dragon, speaking in the ancient tongue.

"*Te tam rakkhasam aacikkhanti.* (They call thee a Monster)," Torg responded.

The dragon snorted. Blood-colored flames spewed from its nostrils, bathing Torg's face but doing little visible damage. When the dragon next spoke, it was in the common tongue that most understood. "I would learn more."

"Tell me why," Torg said.

"*Abhisambodhi.* (Enlightenment)," the dragon said.

"You fear death, as do most," the wizard said. "But what you desire to achieve is beyond you—or anyone ignorant enough to take up with this rabble."

The dragon was startled, and it rose to its full height, towering high above all in attendance. But Mala appeared to have heard enough. He boldly stepped in front of the dragon and slapped Torg across the face. "Shut up, little fool. Do not speak again unless my king demands it."

Then he shook his bulky fist at the dragon's titanic presence. "Until we stand before *our* king, all interrogations of the prisoner will be carried out by me. Do you understand?"

The dragon's head and neck made loud swishing sounds as they swayed through the air. Sōbhana thought the beast might bend down and devour Mala whole. Instead the dragon said, "I understand . . . *Adho Satta.* (Low one.)" But before returning to his perch on the bridge, he said one more thing to Torg: "*Bhayatupa amarattam tanhiiyati.* (Bhayatupa craves eternal existence)."

So it *was* Bhayatupa.

Sōbhana was so amazed, she failed to hear if Torg said anything more.

2

In order to enter the southern gates of Avici, Sōbhana was forced to kill again. When a lone soldier wandered too near her hiding place in the copse, she sprang out and drove her Tugarian dagger beneath the back of his helm into the gristle at the base of his neck. He collapsed without making a sound. With so much excitement surrounding Torg, no one seemed to notice this silent death.

Sōbhana dragged the soldier into the thick shrubs and took a long time stripping off his golden suit of armor, which was nearly perfect for her height but overlarge for her girth. She retained the arming cap but tossed aside the interior doublet and hose, parts of which had become soaked with his blood. Then she meticulously put on the armor, which was difficult but not impossible to perform without assistance. First she slid on the steel-hinged shoes, followed by the greaves, knee-cops, and cuisses. The breast, shoulder and back plates were cleverly blended into one piece that she was able to drop over her head, and she attached the brassards and elbow-cops to the shoulder plates with hinge pins. Finally she donned the single-visor helm, which had narrow eye slits with two dozen breath holes.

The soldier had carried a long sword with a straight blade. Her curved *uttara* would not fit properly into his scabbard, which created a new problem. Up to this moment, she had been able to conceal her sword and dagger beneath the loose-fitting kirtle she had stolen in Senasana. She would not part with her sword, no matter the circumstances, but she could not hide her *uttara* inside armor and also could not use her own scabbard because of its mismatched appearance. The sword had been awarded to her on the day she had become an Asēkha, and she would rather be exposed as an intruder than discard it. Despite all this, Sōbhana wasn't overly concerned. Her weapon was similar enough in appearance to avoid detection, as long as she held it next to the soldier's scabbard and covered most of the ornamented handle with her gauntleted hand.

Even without the padded undergarments, the metallic armor felt more comfortable than Sōbhana had expected, as if it were designed to meld with flesh. She knew little about how it was made, but whoever constructed it must have used magic to enhance its effectiveness. It felt stronger than iron, yet surprisingly pliable and light, the entire suit weighing less than two stones. Nothing worn by the Jivitan riders or Nissayan knights could match its quality; theirs was either much heavier or less protective. This added to her growing sense of hopelessness. Invictus seemed able to do no wrong.

She joined the tail end of the brigade as it entered the gates. Amid the cheering and commotion, Sōbhana's sudden appearance went unnoticed, even by the officers. Soon she was inside.

Avici turned out to be everything Anna was not.

The Golden City swarmed with hundreds of thousands of people. The Tent City in the heart of the Great Desert housed fewer than twenty thousand Tugars and about five thousand others.

Avici appeared before Sōbhana as a maze of ponderous stone buildings and temples, interconnected by wide roadways. Its sheer mass astounded her, especially considering it had been little more than a village less than a hundred years before. Anna was a nomadic kingdom, able to pick up and relocate across the sands of Tējo. It was far older than Avici, but it contained no structures too large to transport by hand.

The citizens of Avici were servants of Invictus, subject to his orders and whims. Despite this, some of the community appeared to enjoy great wealth.

The inhabitants of Anna were free to come and go as they pleased. They worked hard and lived simply—depending on hidden oases for sustenance.

True to her warrior instincts, Sōbhana memorized each twist and turn of Avici's main causeway. Nevertheless her efforts lacked conviction. Of what use was resistance? Invictus was too great. With Bhayatupa as its ally, Avici was a power beyond compare. The forces of good were destined for slaughter.

Even so, on that sunny morning she continued to follow the ox-driven wagon and the hordes, always staying within sight of her king. Sōbhana's spirit was fading, but her love for Torg was not. She would stand by him until doom took them all—even if the mountainous dragon himself tried to stop her.

Mala paraded Torg along a paved roadway lined by two-story cement buildings with elaborate marble facades. Men, women and children wearing white robes leered from the balconies that protruded over the street, the adults shouting obscenities, the children hurling chunks of garbage. Sōbhana was incensed, but helpless. She couldn't kill thousands and thousands.

She knew through her studies that the eastern portion of Avici was built upon the remnants of a volcano that had raged and fumed before the Ogha River was born. The volcano now was lifeless, and its sides had long since crumbled and smoothed. A tangle of buildings—jammed side by side on the hill—blocked Sōbhana's view of what lay beyond. When she finally came to the crest, she was able to see more clearly. At that moment she beheld Uccheda for the first time.

The great tower of Invictus dominated the valley that lay on the northeast side of the city. It filled Sōbhana with the same dismay she'd felt when she'd seen the dragon. The evil sorcerer's dwelling place was by far the largest edifice she had ever beheld, dwarfing the temples in Senasana and Dibbu-Loka. Even the central keep of the fortress of Nissaya did not match this level of grandeur.

Uccheda was spherical in shape, tapering slightly as it grew—and it was so tall, clouds sometimes gathered about its roof. But the tower's height was not its most amazing attribute. What stunned Sōbhana more than anything else was the scope of its decadence. Much of its outer surface was coated with gold. Of all the known bullion in the world, it had been rumored that more than a third had been used in the construction of the tower, which blazed beneath the rising sun like a beacon of despair, blinding anyone who attempted to look at it directly.

The main roadway led downward into the valley. Torg was drawn toward the tower. Hundreds of thousands followed. Mala marched ahead of the wagon. Bhayatupa glided in lazy circles above Uccheda's roof. No one paid Sōbhana any attention. She walked freely in her new disguise.

There were no visible apertures at the tower's base, but fifty cubits above the ground, hundreds of doors and windows opened onto a circular balcony. The largest portal, adorned with jewels and inscriptions, faced the roadway.

Slowly the portal swung slowly open.

The crowd grew silent—and bowed.

Bhayatupa landed on the rooftop of Uccheda. Even at such a great height, she could see him clearly on a day as cloudless as this one.

Then her eyes were drawn back to the portal. Ten standard-bearers, adorned in golden armor studded with diamonds and rubies, led the way onto the balcony, their banners bearing yellow suns outlined in red on backgrounds of white.

Next, a woman of unparalleled beauty appeared, wearing a crimson gown and a bejeweled chaplet. Sōbhana curled her upper lip, recognizing Chal-Abhinno, the Warlish witch who'd obviously chosen to return to Avici after her humiliation at Dibbu-Loka. A pair of dracools, winged beasts that looked like small dragons but waddled on two legs, escorted her. Behind the dracools strode an impressive soldier wearing decorated armor. He carried his helm in the crook of his arm, and his golden locks danced in the breeze.

A stately woman with luxurious blond hair hanging past her waist joined the soldier. She was tall and magnificent in her long white gown. Despite her dignified entrance, she immediately bowed her head, as if uncomfortable.

As soon as the blond woman appeared, Sōbhana jealously observed Torg resist the restraints for the first time since being strapped to the wagon by the Kojin. Her king looked up at the woman, who appeared to return his gaze. Suddenly, pale beams of light leapt from both their eyes and collided in midair. No one but Sōbhana seemed to notice, except for Bhayatupa, who snorted in amusement, and the golden-haired soldier, who looked at the woman—and then Torg—with what appeared to be a mixture of surprise and anger.

A thunderous roar from the crowd shattered the blond woman's reverie. She seemed startled and stumbled sideways. The soldier caught her and held her up.

Then Invictus came through the door, and Sōbhana's jealousy was swept away. The young sorcerer commanded her full attention, and his presence rendered all her emotions impotent. She watched him walk to the edge of the balcony and raise his arms toward the sun.

Morning ended. Noon took its place. Invictus bathed in the glory of light.

Physically, the young sorcerer was not as impressive as she'd expected. He was smaller and less muscular than a Tugar, and less graceful in his manner. His yellow hair was shoulder-length, his face boyishly handsome despite being a century old, and he wore long golden robes that glimmered in the sunlight. In Sōbhana's opinion, he was not as beautiful as Torg—or most any Tugar male.

Nonetheless she sagged to her knees. There was no hope. Invictus' might was irrefutable. From where she stood, she could barely tolerate the power that emanated from the Sun God's body. It felt as if she stood too close to the open door of an immense furnace. Torg, whom she'd long believed to be the most powerful being on Triken, was puny in comparison. This alarming apparition dwarfed even Bhayatupa.

Sōbhana turned to Torg for guidance. His face was far away, but she still could interpret his expression. His eyes were closed, but he grimaced, apparently feeling the same despair as she. Her king was outmatched. And if *The Torgon* was outmatched, so was everyone, and everything, else.

"I will speak to you now," Invictus said to the throng. "Say yes, if you hear my words."

"*YES!*"

Of everyone in attendance, only a few, including Torg, did not respond. Mala leaned over the rail of the wagon and slapped the Death-Knower's face even harder than he'd done earlier. "Did you not hear our king? Are you deaf, little worm?"

From above, Invictus spoke again. A hidden magic amplified his voice, so that it was clearly audible throughout the entire valley. "General Mala, please be more polite. *The Torgon* is our guest. He does not know our customs."

Mala's chain glowed, spitting globules of acidic liquid. Then the Chain Man stepped aside. "As you command, my king."

"Yes," Invictus said. "As I command."

"*YES!*" the crowd chanted.

"Now, where was I? Oh . . . as I was saying, I have some things to tell you all. Can you hear me?"

"*YES!*"

This time Sōbhana unexpectedly shouted along with the obedient crowd. It felt as if the word had been torn from her throat, bringing tears to her eyes. Torg remained silent. Mala continued to glare at the wizard but did not strike him again.

"As you can see, *The Torgon* is our prisoner."

"*YES!*"

Sōbhana resisted the sorcerer's will, but it took all of her strength.

"He has been brought before me to stand trial."

"*YES!*"

"I will interrogate him now."

"*YES! YES!*"

"*Torgon*, you have conspired with others to corrupt the free peoples of Triken. I accuse you of treason. What is your plea?"

When Torg responded, Sōbhana was surprised that his voice also could be heard throughout the valley. "May I tell *you* some things?"

"*YES!*" the crowd shouted.

Mala lunged at Torg with murder in his eyes. But the sorcerer waved his hand—just slightly—and the Chain Man froze.

The Death-Knower's belligerence, rather than anger Invictus, appeared to amuse him. "Of course, *Torgon*. As my subjects will readily attest, I am fair and just. Feel free to say whatever is on your mind."

"*YES!*"

Torg spoke slowly. "I gave my word to Mala that I would allow him to bring me here to you. As of now, I have honored my vow. And I can sense in my heart that the noble ones are safe, which means that Mala has honored his."

"Go on," Invictus said. "This is fascinating."

"Henceforth, I consider myself free of any bonds. I will now make every effort to escape. And there's more. I tell you and all present that I despise you and your servants. This means, I suppose, that I plead guilty to your charges."

Bhayatupa, still poised on the roof of Uccheda, lifted his head and chortled. It was an eerie sound, deep and rumbling. Mala shook with rage, and the Kojin leapt up and down, pounding her numerous fists. The druids also reacted by re-creating their peculiar rhythmic humming, while in the background the crowd chanted, "*YES! YES! YES!*"

Regardless, the young sorcerer seemed unperturbed. He stepped off the balcony, descended slowly to the ground—his golden robes spread like wings—and landed as gently as a fallen leaf. With a quick little hop, he pounced onto the wagon bed and stared into Torg's eyes. The massive gathering was shocked into silence.

Sōbhana slithered within striking distance, but she was terrified. If Invictus attacked Torg, would she have the courage to defend him?

"Ah, such entertainment," the sorcerer said. "You enthrall me, Death-Knower. You are so . . . *interesting*. And nowadays, I find so few things interesting. Being a god can be so *boring*. There aren't enough challenges. Everyone does exactly what I say. Do you understand my predicament?"

"I understand you are a spoiled child," Torg said. "A wicked child, as well, blind to your failings. I can redeem you, if you will allow me into your heart. You will not regret it. But you must somehow find the wisdom to listen."

Somewhere in the clouds Bhayatupa laughed again. The crowd seemed to stir.

Invictus' composure began to diminish. "Do not test me too severely. I find you amusing, but not so amusing that you are beyond punishment. I can see that you do not fear for yourself, but what of your precious others? Do you truly believe that the noble ones are safe? Perhaps I could destroy them all with only a thought. Or even worse, I could infect them with an evil that would force them to perform my bidding."

"Not even you are that powerful," Torg said. But Sōbhana detected doubt in his voice.

Mala stood next to the wagon. Though the monster's feet were on the ground, his eyes were level with the wizard and sorcerer's. "*Pleaaaaase*, my king, I beseech you," he said, his fangs spewing poison. "Allow me to rip him to pieces."

"Nay, I have prepared a place for him of *my* choosing," Invictus said. "There he will endure pain far greater than what you are suggesting. After a time he will *beg* to join us . . . if he manages to survive."

Then Invictus raised his arms, and his voice again boomed throughout the valley. "You have heard for yourselves."

"*YES!*"

"*The Torgon* admits his guilt."

"*YES!*"

"I will now pronounce his sentence."

"*YES!*"

"*The Torgon* will be taken to Asubha where he will be imprisoned until he repents."

"*YES! YES! YES!*"

"No," Sōbhana begged. "Please . . . no."

Invictus abandoned Torg in the wagon at the base of Uccheda for three days, giving him nothing to drink or eat. Apparently Invictus intended to weaken the wizard even further. Twice the skies darkened and rained lightly. Sōbhana watched her king catch water on his tongue. The brief sprinkles appeared to entrance him despite his dismal situation, as if the scattered drops were things of beauty. He even managed to smile.

Sōbhana could not approach too closely. After Invictus disappeared within the tower, the massive surge of onlookers wandered off, and the soldiers returned to their duties, leaving her with fewer places to hide, despite her disguise. Even after the others departed, at least fifty golden soldiers continued to guard the wagon. They were regimented and seemed to know each other well. If she had attempted to infiltrate them, she quickly would have been exposed as an intruder.

Mala, the Kojin and the druids also checked on the prisoner often. Sōbhana doubted Invictus felt threatened so near the great tower, but obviously the king of the Tugars was important to him. You can put a prized jewel in an impregnable chamber and still feel compelled to stand outside and watch the door.

Sōbhana would have sacrificed her own flesh just to speak with her king for a few moments. But even if she had been able to find a way, she remained wary of Torg's vow to kill any Tugar who followed him. She had heard him say to Invictus that his pledge was fulfilled. Did that free her as well? Could she help him now? She wasn't certain.

During the long journey from Dibbu-Loka, Sōbhana had not suffered as much as Torg, but it had been hard on her too. She was hungry, thirsty and weaker than usual. She crouched in a damp culvert and shivered in the autumn cold. The golden armor lay discarded at her side. She could bear it against her skin no longer. Some time during the third morning, her exhaustion overcame her, and she slept.

A while later Sōbhana jerked awake. Now it was almost noon, and the day had grown unseasonably warm for Avici's northern clime. The sky was cloudless, the air crisp and clear. She crawled to the edge of the culvert and gasped. Torg and the wagon were gone, but swarms of citizens and soldiers were pouring back into the valley. Though it disgusted her, she hurriedly put the golden armor back on and blended into the thickening crowd.

Sōbhana searched in all directions, but Torg was nowhere in sight. Tears welled in her eyes, but she fought them back. She was through with self-pity. Whoever had taken him while she slept would pay. She didn't care about her own life. She'd failed her king and deserved to die. How could she have slept so deeply? It was as if her proximity to the sorcerer had drugged her.

The throng began to chant. "Sampati . . . Sampati . . . Sampati . . ."

Sōbhana gazed upward. Bhayatupa circled high above the rooftop of Uccheda, a splotch of crimson in the blue sky. But it was not the dragon that occupied the crowd's attention this time. Instead, it was a shimmering black speck that appeared in the northern sky, growing larger as it approached. Though it was no match for Bhayatupa in sheer size, it was huge, nonetheless. A Sampati, which meant *crossbreed* in the ancient tongue, flew toward Uccheda, its tremendous wings pumping the air. Apparently, Torg's transportation to the prison on Mount Asubha was about to arrive.

From where she stood, Sōbhana couldn't see who or what waited on the pinnacle of Uccheda. Although there were no clouds to block her view, the angle was too severe. Still, she could sense Torg on the rooftop. And if he were there, Mala and Invictus would also be present.

Overcome by madness, Sōbhana frantically removed the armor and stood alone in her black outfit among the thousands who wore either gold or white. She held her *uttara* in her right hand and her dagger in her left, and entered into *frenzy*. She attacked soldiers and citizens alike, first just a few and then by the dozens. Wherever she went, there was shouting and confusion. Blood splattered. Heads fell. She murdered any and all within reach. As the Sampati landed on Uccheda's rooftop, Sōbhana wreaked havoc below—killing, killing, killing. Not even the magnificent armor worn by the golden soldiers could withstand her.

Sōbhana cut off a soldier's leg, slicing through his cuisse as if it were paper. She spun in a full circle, simultaneously severing the head of a civilian woman with her sword and slashing the jugular of a man with her dagger. The woman's head flipped round and round in the air and tumbled into the arms of a boy, who screamed wildly and tossed it aside.

Although most of the crowd still was focused on the approach of the crossbred condor, a few began to take notice of Sōbhana's mayhem. More than a dozen druids rushed toward her, humming in their peculiar fashion. She dove into them, slicing and thrusting. Though they were almost twice her size, they were no match. She had trained for fifty years with a Vasi master and was one of the deadliest of her kind. The druids fell in a torrent of green blood.

Hacked in half. Beheaded. Stabbed through their foul hearts.

She was, after all, Asēkha-Sōbhana.

One of the most dangerous warriors in the world.

She could not kill everyone in the valley.

But she would die, trying.

The flat rooftop of Uccheda had no protective wall or other adornments and was the only sizable portion of the tower's exterior not coated in gold. Invictus did not desire for it to be slippery.

In anticipation of the arrival of the Sampati, the rooftop was abuzz with activity. Ten golden soldiers faced ten others about fifty cubits apart, holding thick ropes between them. When the huge beast finally landed, its sharp claws scratched along the surface, tearing up chunks of mortar. The Sampati slid forward, out of control.

"Now!" Mala commanded.

The soldiers heaved on the ropes, which grew taut just as the Sampati rammed into them. The six-inch-thick strands stretched but did not break. The hybrid bird slammed to a halt. Immediately a pair of soldiers raced over and attached chains to the beast's legs.

A thin but muscular pilot leapt off the condor's neck, strode to Invictus and bowed nimbly before him. "The Sampati and I are at your service, my king."

The condor, crossbred with a dragon to increase its size and strength, was one of eleven of its kind. Only a few remained in captivity. The others had escaped and now flew freely about the peak of Mount Asubha, feeding on prisoners—and sentries.

The Sampati had a black torso with white splotches at the tips of its wings, which measured forty cubits when extended. Most of its body was covered with feathers, but its head, neck and feet were laden with crimson dragon scales. A sturdy platform was attached to its back by thick straps that clung to its torso.

The enormous bird was high-strung, struggling against the chains and flapping its wings. Invictus knew it wasn't wise to keep the creature waiting too long. Its hooked beak could tear and rend. Passengers and supplies—with a combined weight of as much as a ton—were loaded quickly.

"We will need the Sampati, but not you," Mala said to the pilot. "I'll fly the beast to Asubha myself. This one will carry precious cargo." The Chain Man nodded toward Torg, who lay on the rooftop, still restrained and under heavy guard.

"As you command," the pilot said, before stepping aside.

Mala ordered the guards to secure Torg to the platform. Before this was completed, a soldier hustled over and dropped to his knees in front of the Chain Man.

"Pardon my rudeness, Lord Mala," the soldier said. "But something is happening in the valley below that might be of interest to you and King Invictus." Then the soldier turned toward Invictus. "There is an odd commotion, my liege."

Curious, Invictus walked to the edge and looked down. The valley far below was bursting with soldiers and citizens. From the rooftop they looked like a swarm of bugs. Near the base of the tower some of the bugs had encircled a single tiny figure.

Mala joined him at the edge of the precipice. "What *is* going on down there?" he asked, sounding sincerely baffled.

Invictus focused his eyes, which upon command could become supernaturally keen. "There is a woman, dressed in black. She fights anyone who comes near. Her swordplay is impressive."

"An Asēkha!" Mala said, turning to Torg. "You have broken your promise, you filthy flea."

"It doesn't matter," Invictus said. "What can she do? Defeat us by herself? If she kills a few, who cares? But look at her, Mala. See how she fights. How *interesting . . .*"

Mala's hideous face reddened even further. He started toward the wizard. But Invictus froze him in place with another wave of his hand. "Do not cause the Death-Knower further discomfort," Invictus said. "When he arrives at Asubha, I want him to have a little strength left. There will be no fun in any of this if he perishes too soon."

"Arrrggghh . . ." was all Mala could manage in response. He climbed onto the Sampati's back at the base of its neck. Soldiers lifted Torg and strapped him onto the platform. Then they released the chains from the creature's legs.

With one great sweep of its wings, the Sampati was airborne. Mala tugged at its bridle and forced it northward, toward Asubha.

"Fly, you miserable beast . . . *fly!*"

Invictus laughed. And waved goodbye. He was so proud of his pets. So very proud.

Like any god, he was in love with his own creations.

Several times in his long life, Torg had ridden high over mountaintops on the backs of giant eagles. Each time he'd adored it. Once, while grappling with a pack of dracools, he had been lifted more than a hundred cubits into the air and then dropped. He hadn't liked that much. Riding on the back of the Sampati, trussed in golden ropes and strapped to a wooden platform, resembled the latter. It was miserable.

He'd been trapped within Invictus' magical restraining device for more than forty days now. Even so, he'd managed to remain sanitary.

Each time he urinated or defecated, he had disintegrated his wastes with blue flames.

Up until he had greeted Invictus, Torg had honored his word and not resisted his restraints. But once his vow had been fulfilled, he'd fought with all his might to break free. To his despair, he'd failed. Although the leather and fabric binding him were inconsequential, the golden ropes encasing him from neck to feet were irresistibly strong. Every time Torg twisted or heaved, the ropes grew yellow-hot, squeezing with increased vehemence as if they were living beings directed by a devious mind. The more he struggled, the more helpless he became.

Eventually he stopped fighting. When he did, the ropes loosened their grip only enough to allow him to breathe. Escape was impossible. It was all too clear that Invictus' power was greater than his own.

Afterward he had lain in the wagon, desperate and depressed. To make matters worse, he could not stop obsessing over his brief encounter with the woman on the balcony. His attraction to her had been intense. Somehow he knew her—and yet did not. Would he ever see her again? He doubted it, and it smote his heart.

Then there was the matter of the female warrior that Mala and Invictus had witnessed fighting so fiercely at the base of the tower. Torg guessed it was Sōbhana. Only she would have dared such a thing against his direct order. And now she was probably dead.

The Sampati soared at extraordinary heights, higher even than a mountain eagle could fly. Only Bhayatupa could have managed greater altitudes. The cold, thin air seared Torg's lungs; he felt as if he were suffocating. Mala, on the other hand, appeared to be ecstatic; he chortled, sang and waved his arms. The hybrid condor struggled against the cumbersome weight on its neck, swaying this way and that in response to the Chain Man's relentless squirming.

"What say you, little sparrow?" Mala said to Torg. "Do you like the view? Are you comfortable? Is there anything I can get you?" Then he burst into ribald laughter, continuing to bounce on the Sampati's neck.

The beast squawked in protest, especially when the chain touched its scales.

"Yes . . . there *is* something you can get me," Torg said. "Some wax to plug my ears."

Mala found this hysterical. His long white mane fluttered in the wind. Huge gobs of spittle flew from his mouth. Torg could feel tiny droplets of it showering his face.

"Aaaaah, *Torgon*! You have a sense of humor, after all. And you'll need every bit of it. You're going to love the little hideaway Invictus has prepared. It's so . . . so . . . *cozy*. And it cleans up after itself, so you don't have to worry about any messes left behind by previous occupants."

Mala laughed even harder, and then he succumbed to a spasm of coughing. Grotesque balls of sputum spiraled from his mouth. Torg already had grown to hate the monster, but now he despised him more than ever.

"Mala, when you finish your babbling, there is something I wish to tell you," Torg said, through gritted teeth.

"Yes, dear?"

"I no longer have any desire to rescue you from your torment. I'm going to see to it that you die in a ball of fire."

Mala laughed so hard, he almost fell off his perch.

Torg was, first and foremost, a creature of the desert. Heat was his natural clime. In temperatures exceeding one hundred and thirty degrees he could walk barefoot on burning sands without discomfort. However, he also was capable of enduring cold. He had journeyed to Triken's northernmost reaches and lived to tell the tale. But the chill he felt as the Sampati approached the peak of Asubha was like no other. Though winter still was several weeks away, the temperature at this great height was well below freezing, and the severe winds intensified the effect.

As Torg and Mala neared the prison on top of the mountain, another hybrid condor flew into view. Several ordinary condors also approached, flocking around Mala's mount and sweeping in and snapping at the bridled Sampati. Mala found the intruders annoying, waving his massive hands as if shooing mosquitoes.

"Get back, you filthy buzzards. If you come any nearer, I'll pluck the feathers out of you, one by one, and eat you raw."

As Mount Asubha came into view, the attackers dispersed. From then on, the Sampati's flight was undisturbed. The prison appeared beneath them, its courtyard several times longer and wider than the rooftop of Uccheda, giving the Sampati more room to land. But Mala was not as good of a pilot as he probably imagined himself to be, and he forced the beast in too sharply, causing it to smack onto the icy stone, sliding precariously before crashing into a lumpy wall. The Chain Man was thrown head over heels. Then he leaped up, cursing and complaining.

"Where is the warden? The little weasel!"

One guard who appeared braver than the rest ran up to face Mala, though even he kept his distance. "The warden is not here, Lord Mala," the guard shouted into the wind. "He disappeared several days ago. He said that he needed to feed, that he wanted to be strong when the prisoner arrived."

"Well, he *has* arrived, as you can see," Mala said. "Never mind, never mind. The important matters are always left to me. Come . . . and bring others with you. I want the wizard removed from the beast before it tries to fly away."

But the Sampati would never fly again. It had broken its massive neck in the crash. Torg sensed the creature's final heartbeat and wished it well in its next existence.

"Remove the wizard from the platform. Bring him to the pit. Hurry . . . HURRY!"

The guards started forward, but Torg's final attempt at freedom caused them to halt. *Death Energy* sprang from every pore, his body glowing like a small blue sun fallen from the sky. The leather and fabric that encased him disintegrated, along with what remained of his black jacket and trousers. Even the golden ropes began to stretch, and for a moment it appeared they might burst asunder.

Mala leapt at Torg and grasped the ropes in his powerful hands, reinforcing their strength. If it had been only Mala's magic against Torg's, then Torg might have prevailed, even in his weakened state. But the sorcery that coursed through the golden strands was born of Invictus.

Mala squeezed Torg's breath from his lungs. He felt like a rodent in the murderous grip of a constrictor.

He was lost.

All was lost.

When Mala finally removed the magical restraints and lowered him by ordinary ropes to the bottom of the pit, Torg lay as limp as a dead man, barely aware.

His nightmare in the pit had begun.

Sōbhana's body was slick with sweat. Her breath tore from her lungs in desperate heaves, and her heart seemed about to burst. More than one hundred of the enemy lay dead, including a dozen druids, several wolves, a huge cave troll, and a disgusting creature that looked like a spider with a human head. In the great battle Sōbhana had lost the dagger Torg had returned to her at Dibbu-Loka, but she still held her *uttara* along with a dented shield she had plucked from the lifeless arm of a golden soldier. Now, tens of thousands surrounded her. She had no chance. She would continue to fight until she was slain. What else was there to do?

As the enemy closed about her, a tremendous shadow descended from the sky. Suddenly Sōbhana was plucked from the ground and lifted high into the air. The force of the blow knocked her sword and the shield from her grasp. Her beloved *uttara* was lost to her, too, but she was too shocked to feel grief.

Bhayatupa grasped her in the talons of one of his front feet, carrying her into the clouds as easily as a crow might lift a cricket.

"Quickly, do as I say!" the great dragon growled. "Remove your clothing and drape it on this."

In his other front foot Bhayatupa held the naked corpse of a young woman, similar in size and appearance to her.

Sōbhana was terrified, but her warrior instincts took over. She managed, as best she could, to tear off her outfit and wrap it haphazardly around the dead woman.

"That's good enough," said the dragon, before deftly slipping Sōbhana's now naked body beneath a massive scale on his crimson breast. All the while, his back was to Uccheda.

From his vantage point on top of the tower, Invictus watched Bhayatupa swoop down and grab the Asēkha. The dragon flew up into the clouds and momentarily disappeared. When he reemerged, he tossed a black bundle into the air and with one snap of his jaws swallowed it whole.

"Such a shame," the sorcerer said to the pilot who had surrendered his Sampati to Mala. "She was so brave. And so *interesting*. Maybe she'll find what she was looking for inside the dragon's belly."

With eyes that had been open to the ways of the world for eighty thousand years, Bhayatupa watched Invictus enter a doorway at the top of the tower and disappear. Despite being more than half a mile away, Bhayatupa had seen everything in great detail and had heard every word. The sorcerer had fallen for his trick. And why not? Bhayatupa had not yet done anything to elicit distrust.

Invictus did not seem to understand that a great dragon's arrogance would not permit obeisance to anyone. Still, Bhayatupa was no fool. He sensed the sorcerer's rising power more clearly than most. Bhayatupa did not yet fear Invictus, but he knew enough to be careful. Destroying the sorcerer would do him no good, if he then had to face a retaliatory army.

Bhayatupa had lived for eighty millennia, the specter of his own demise haunting almost his every waking moment. By mortal standards, he still would live an extraordinary span of time—another twenty millennia, at least. But to Bhayatupa, the concept of dying was unacceptable. The fear of it consumed him. And though he wielded formidable magic, death remained an enemy beyond him.

This was the true reason he tolerated Invictus: The sorcerer provided him with the most direct access to the Death-Knower.

And not just any Death-Knower. Hundreds had existed during Bhayatupa's tenure, but none like this one. *The Torgon* was different than all the rest. Perhaps ... just perhaps ... the wizard could teach the dragon how to achieve immortality.

Bhayatupa craved the Death-Knower's knowledge, but first he needed to get the wizard away from prying ears and eyes. And if Torg did not then talk voluntarily, Bhayatupa would force him—brutally.

Twelve years before he rescued Sōbhana at the base of Uccheda, Bhayatupa had been deep in the throes of dragon-sleep in one of his many hiding places in the remote heights of Mahaggata. Somehow Invictus had found him in the misty cave. The sorcerer had crouched by his pointed ear and spoke to him, though it had taken several days for Bhayatupa to awaken fully. But even before he achieved the lucidity to open his eyes, he had been aware enough to listen—and he was stunned by the extent of Invictus' knowledge. It was as if the sorcerer could read Bhayatupa's mind and regurgitate his thoughts.

Eventually Invictus explained that he was born of demon blood and knew many things only demons knew. When the sorcerer told Bhayatupa that Vedana, mother of all demons, was his grandmother, the puzzle began to take shape.

Invictus left the cave on Bhayatupa's back, bragging endlessly about the might of his growing kingdom. The pair flew over Avici and Kilesa, and the dragon saw the sorcerer's great army. They visited the prison on Mount Asubha, and Invictus stood proudly by the pit as Bhayatupa squeezed his titanic body into the courtyard and managed to bend down his long neck and peer into the hole, which was barely wider than one of his eyes. The dragon jerked upward, in pain and disgust.

Invictus laughed. "Be thankful you're too large to fit inside," the sorcerer said. "Not even the demons know of the dark magic I used to summon the beings that inhabit the walls of the pit. They are from a place beyond all awareness—save mine."

And now, the Death-Knower would be imprisoned in the pit, and the greatest chance at immortality Bhayatupa had ever encountered was in dreadful peril. Unbeknown to Invictus, Bhayatupa had briefly flown alongside Mala and the Sampati just out of eyesight. He had considered killing the foul-mouthed *Adho Satta* that clung to the Sampati's neck, and then taking Torg to some distant place. He knew, though, that kidnapping the Death-Knower would enrage Invictus and invite open warfare. The dragon was not prepared for that. There had been ages in Triken's long history when Bhayatupa had commanded magnificent armies. But now he was alone except for a few Mogol slaves. For this reason he had to move carefully and choose the perfect moment. So he'd returned to Avici just in time to rescue the female Asēkha.

Perhaps the warrior could free *The Torgon*. It was worth a try. Besides, it now appeared to be his best chance.

Such limited options annoyed Bhayatupa. And he did not like being annoyed. If he achieved immortality he would take revenge on all living beings, including Invictus.

And if immortality were unachievable? Then he would at least force the Death-Knower to teach him how to overcome *Tanhiiyati*, the insatiable craving for eternal existence.

If he were not cured of it soon, he would go mad, if he hadn't already.

Sōbhana felt drowsy. One of Bhayatupa's thick crimson scales held her against the interior flesh of his breast. The pounding of his massive heart—which she guessed was larger than her entire body—lulled her toward sleep. The skin beneath the scale was covered with a sweet silky fleece as warm and dry as a luxurious blanket.

Her warrior curiosity finally overcame her weariness, and she managed to squirm and wriggle until her head poked out from beneath the scale. Thick clouds obscured her vision. Everywhere she looked, the air was white.

Bhayatupa was far larger and more powerful than a Sampati. His enormous wings swept through the air with long, steady strokes. His legs were tucked against his body, and his neck, which Sōbhana guessed was more than fifty cubits long, stretched straight forward, while his tail, which was even longer, extended straight behind his sleek torso. Despite weighing more than several desert elephants, the great dragon flew faster than a diving hawk.

Sōbhana realized she was no longer terrified. Ironically, the closer she got to the dragon, the less she feared him. Perhaps it was because she no longer cared if she lived or died. Perhaps her hopelessness had eliminated fear from what remained of her tattered range of emotions. Perhaps it was the spicy smell of his skin.

There was an occasional break in the clouds. For brief moments she could see land far below. To the southeast she recognized Ti-ratana, the largest lake in the known world. To the west was the Gap of Gamana, where Arupa-Loka and its demon inhabitants lay hidden. She had flown more than once on the backs of eagles, so seeing the land from so high above was not unique to her experience.

The dragon's intentions puzzled Sōbhana. Obviously he had ingested the corpse that wore her black outfit in an attempt to fool those who watched from below. But why? And now he flew northwestward toward the mountains. Was he taking her to a secret place to devour her at his leisure?

"I hear your thoughts," Bhayatupa said, in his indomitable baritone voice. "Your mind is more closed than most, but I do comprehend some of what you say. You wonder why you are not already dead. Is that not so?"

"I often wonder that," she shouted into the rushing wind.

Bhayatupa laughed. The sound was disconcerting, but no longer as eerie as it had first seemed. "You Asēkhas consider yourselves great. But compared to me, you are *Adho Satta*. Do you doubt it?"

His words offended her, replacing her original fear with rising irritation. "What you consider low is not what I consider low. Compared to you, we are physically puny, that is true. But Asēkhas are loyal and honorable, attributes that are beyond your arrogance."

Bhayatupa sneered. Smoke puffed from his nostrils. Traces of it blew against her face, causing her to sneeze. "Loyalty . . . honor . . . only words. Time is the true master. All else pales before it, but you pale far more than I. Your lifespan is but a single breath compared to mine."

"I have confessed my puniness. What more do you want, O Exalted One? Does it please you to denigrate your victims before you eat them? Tell me where you are taking me . . . and why."

"Such insolence! Your bravery is impressive for one so tiny."

"Tiny? Yes. But not helpless. Even when unarmed, an Asēkha does not lack weapons. I am strong enough to drive my fist through the flesh of your breast and punch a hole in your heart. Do *you* doubt it?"

In reaction to Sōbhana's sudden threat the dragon panicked, realizing that he had unknowingly left himself vulnerable. He stopped in midair, rearing like a horse, his great wings beating frenetically as he reached for her with massive talons, hoping to pluck her from his breast before she could attack.

"Whoa," she said. "Relax! Relax!" And then *she* began to laugh. "If I had wanted to destroy you, I would have done so without warning." And then she sighed. "There is only one desire left to me, Dragon. I wish, somehow, to rescue my king."

Bhayatupa warily resumed his flight, but Sōbhana sensed a change in his demeanor. Now there was at least a smidgeon of respect. "I have underestimated you," he finally admitted. "Mogols, witches and ghouls have not your . . . substance. That is a good thing. I am pleased . . . because . . . I have a task for you that will benefit both of us if you are successful."

Bhayatupa landed at the opening of a cave near the peak of a bony mountain. He removed her from beneath his scale and set her down on the stone. A nasty wind blew, causing Sōbhana to shiver in her nakedness.

"Tell me, then, what is this task?" she said, staring up at the humongous creature.

"Your desire is my desire. I want to help you rescue the Death-Knower." Then without saying more, he sprang into the air and flew eastward, faster than the wind.

Sōbhana watched the dragon diminish to a crimson speck. She was exhausted and vulnerable. She had no choice but to enter the cave, which obviously had been Bhayatupa's intent.

The mouth of the cave was five times her height and at least that wide. Just a few strides within its opening, the temperature warmed considerably—to above freezing, anyway. She followed a long passageway that descended into the bowels of the mountain. Cold water dripped from the ceiling onto her bare back and buttocks. It was unpleasant, to say the least. The stone beneath her feet was smooth and slippery. She pressed her hand against the wall of the tunnel, which was oily and wet as if slick with sweat.

The passageway narrowed slightly, growing so dark she began to stumble. But as she walked farther, the darkness lost its intensity. Eventually she saw a glowing light in the distance.

The tunnel emptied into a cavern large enough to swallow the entire temple of Bakheng. The hollow was lighted with hundreds of torches. Sōbhana gasped and pressed her arms against her bosom. Piles of treasure—magnificent to behold—were neatly arranged on the expansive stone floor. Near where she stood was a miniature mountain of gold and silver coins. Another pile contained daggers, swords, and scabbards adorned with jewels. Farther back were belts, buckles and sandals, all exquisitely designed. Still farther were rings, necklaces and bracelets. There were five tall trees constructed entirely of black pearls, and ten silver coffins encrusted with fist-sized diamonds. There were suits of armor made of solid gold, along with axes and clubs, helmets and shields, hauberks and gauntlets. There were plates and goblets, silks and tapestries, crowns and thrones.

A vast sea of treasure shimmered in the torchlight. And it was well maintained. Polished and dusted. By someone. Or something.

Walkways wound between the arrangements, and Sōbhana wandered along them, still naked, her jaw slack. She was a warrior, not a princess obsessed with baubles, but even she was allured. The entire room sparkled.

She found clothing in the back of the cavern. Amid a stack of finery, she chose a pair of tight-fitting silk pants and a matching long-sleeved shirt. Both were black, which was to her liking. She picked up a pair of boots made of black leather with wool insoles, and, finally, a coat of dark fur. The coat was too extravagant for her tastes, but she took it for warmth.

Off to the side, something caught her eye. A gold crown laden with diamonds, rubies and pearls seemed to beckon to her. She placed it on her head. It fit perfectly.

She chuckled. If the dragon took her to rescue Torg, she'd look good in doing so.

There was a sudden movement at the edge of her peripheral vision. She spun, crouched defensively, and then somersaulted forward, grasping a sword from a pile of weapons. Its straight, double-edged blade was longer and heavier than she preferred, but it would do. The crown somehow stayed on her head.

Standing at the entrance to the cavern were a dozen large men, their faces colorfully painted. They held long wooden spears and wore deerskin ponchos and furry moccasins. Despite the cold, their hairy arms and legs were bare.

Sōbhana recognized them as Mogols, the brutal enemies of Nissaya who roamed the Mahaggata Mountains. Tugars despised them, hunting them down whenever they could. They were formidable warriors, but no match for an Asēkha. Sōbhana was already planning her mode of attack. Weapons lay all about her, and she knew how to use each one.

But the Mogols did not strike. Instead they lowered their spears and knelt before her. A lone woman hurried forward, bearing a tray of dried meat, roasted nuts and blue grapes. The woman laid it at Sōbhana's feet, then respectfully backed away.

The Mogols spoke a language unlike any Sōbhana could recognize. She tended to avoid such learning—and her Vasi master often had chastised her for this. Torg could have spoken fluently with them. But her King could do many things others could not.

In the corners of her mouth, Sōbhana suddenly felt something warm and wet. She realized it was her own saliva. She had eaten little for several days, and the fare placed before her was enticingly arranged. She bent down, eyes trained on the Mogols, and grabbed a chunk of meat, swallowing it whole. She stuffed a handful of nuts and grapes into her mouth, chewed once or twice, and devoured them too. She wasn't concerned about being poisoned. Tugars were immune to such things. In a rush, she ate everything on the tray.

The Mogols remained bowed—except for the woman. She approached Sōbhana and removed the now-empty serving dish.

Sōbhana still held the sword. She rose to her full height and glared at the gathering. "Do any of you speak the common tongue?"

There was a long, silent pause.

Finally a sinister voice echoed from far back in the tunnel.

"I do."

The speaker came forward.

It was no Mogol.

A female demon entered the torchlight. "How beautiful you are," she said to Sōbhana. "Bhayatupa has chosen a worthy bride. I wouldn't mind a taste of you, myself."

"What?" was all Sōbhana managed to say.

The demon sashayed forward and stopped just a few strides away. She had chosen to appear as a mature woman who was not particularly well-preserved.

The demon laughed at Sōbhana's bewilderment. "I speak in jest," she said, continuing to cackle. "Lord Bhayatupa asked me to keep you safe until he returned. I told the Mogols you were their god's bride-to-be. Your choice of that crown completed the effect. His last wife wore the same one, more than ten thousand years ago."

"Wife?" Sōbhana said.

"Child, surely you know that dragons prefer human wives," the demon said. "It's all symbolic, of course. They don't actually have *sex* with them. *That* would be a little difficult." She cackled again. Small puffs of gray smoke sprang from her ears, as if her insides were burning.

"Come no closer," Sōbhana said, but her arms trembled, and she could barely retain her grip on the heavy sword. "I will slay you. I swear it."

The demon laughed so hard, she almost fell.

"Why do you torment me?" Sōbhana said.

"You are so . . . innocent. So . . . precious. My dear, how can you slay someone who does not live? Do you not know me?" For a moment, Vedana's eyes went pure white. Then their color returned to a semblance of normalcy. "Ahhh . . . I see that you do not. At least, not fully. Allow me, then, to introduce myself. I am Vedana, mother of all demons, and I am ancient beyond all others. Even Bhayatupa is young compared to me. Your master—the *Desert Peasant*—knows me well. But, alas, he is not here."

At that, Sōbhana's countenance changed. She lowered the sword until its tip pricked the stone at her feet. "Does . . . he . . . live?" she whispered.

Vedana seemed to consider this for a moment, then she smiled wickedly. "You're in love with him."

"We all love him," Sōbhana responded, too quickly.

"Not I, though he will be of use to me. But that is not what I meant. You *love* him. Ha! Don't you know, child, what would happen to you if he fucked you?"

"Shut your disgusting mouth," Sōbhana said, suddenly enraged. She hoisted the sword above her head. "I will smite you where you stand."

Through all this, the Mogols remained bowed. But their chins were raised, and they watched attentively. Vedana took one step back and waved her arms overhead. There was an explosion. A gout of smoke followed. When Sōbhana was able to see clearly, the demon had disappeared.

Sōbhana scrambled into the passageway, past the Mogols. None attempted to thwart her. She left the cave and entered the bitter cold that encased the mountaintop. Now that she was fully clothed, it did not affect her so drastically. Vedana was nowhere to be seen. The demon, for reasons of her own, had vanished.

Sōbhana calmed herself by investigating her surroundings. There was a wide stone balcony outside the cave's mouth that provided plenty of room to move about. But beyond the platform the mountain fell steeply in all directions, its sheer stone walls coated with an ultra-slippery glaze of ice. It would be near-suicide to attempt a descent. The cave was a prison as secure as Asubha. The dragon must have transported even the Mogols here.

She turned back toward the cave. The Mogols were there, still bowing. The servant woman gestured to her, enticing her to come out of the icy wind. Sōbhana lowered her head and sighed. She was at Bhayatupa's mercy.

She walked to the edge of the precipice and shouted into the abyss. Her voice echoed for leagues. "Damn you, dragon! Why did you strand me here? Time is precious. He might already be dead."

The wind rose in response. Within its roar she heard the demon's laughter. Vedana was out there, somewhere. But now she would not show herself. Was the demon's bravado overstated? She didn't seem to fear Sōbhana, but did Vedana fear the sword Sōbhana now wielded?

Sōbhana looked more closely at the weapon, which was plain but heavy. Its double-edged blade gleamed like freshly polished silver, and its hilt was wrapped with a material that resembled blackened leather secured with metal cords. The warrior in her recognized it as a special weapon, despite its simplicity, and she decided to test it. She let out a piercing cry and drove a cutting edge onto the side of a granite boulder, expecting the sword to snap. Instead it buried itself more than a finger's width into the frozen stone, and then slid back out with the ease of a dagger in flesh. This was a special sword, all right. Such a blow would have broken even a *uttara*.

Despite her sudden movement, the Mogols did not flinch. Sōbhana found herself admiring their discipline. Though they lacked proper training, Mogols were respectable fighters. The best of them could hold their own against a Jivitan rider or a Nissayan knight. Of course, they were no match for a Tugar, but who was?

She returned to the cavern and began to make a bed out of a pile of clothing. The servant woman approached her, shook her head and took Sōbhana's hand, guiding her even deeper into the cave. They arrived at a room about the size of an ordinary bedchamber. It was lit by a single torch. A plump mattress on the floor, two low wooden tables and a simple chair filled the rest of the room. Food, wine, wooden utensils and a ewer of cool water were arranged on one table. On the other lay a basin of steaming water, a cake of soap probably made from oils and tree bark, a comb carved from balsa and several wool towels. Before leaving the chamber, the servant drew a heavy curtain across the opening.

Sōbhana was blissfully alone.

When had she last bathed? Other than an occasional dip in the icy waters of the Ogha River, it had been almost two months. Her hair was greasy and knotted, and she shuddered to think what her underarms and private parts must smell like. She laid the sword on the mattress, removed her clothes, and took a long time cleaning herself. Then she laboriously combed the knots out of her black hair, which had grown a finger-length past her shoulders.

Afterward she spread some nutty-tasting butter onto a slice of crusty bread and ate it along with dried meats and grapes. She drank wine, which was potent and flavorful. This made her wonder how the Mogols had managed to get fresh provisions up to the mountaintop, but drowsiness muddled her thoughts. Her life had become filled with too many questions and too few answers. She lay down on the mattress with the sword at her side. Before she slept, she tried to make sense of Vedana's foul words.

Don't you know, child, what would happen . . .

Sōbhana thought she knew: It would be paradise. What did the demon understand that Sōbhana did not? She remembered asking Chieftain Kusala—it seemed like several lifetimes ago—why their king never shared a tent with a woman. Kusala had made it clear that Torg was dangerously sensitive about the subject.

Vedana had hinted at something. What could it be?

Sōbhana didn't believe it was simply a demon's trick.

Finally her mind emptied of thought. Exhaustion overcame her, and she slept deeply, the sword beside her like a cold lover.

Sōbhana spent more than a week in the cave, rarely leaving the small chamber that had become her bedroom. She ate, slept and waited.

Several times a day the Mogols served her food and wine, and they also provided her with clean water and towels whenever needed.

On the ninth night of her captivity she had a wonderful dream. Torg was kissing her on the mouth. How delicately he caressed her lips. How deliciously he entwined his sweet tongue with hers.

In her dream she was naked, and he was upon her, breathing on her neck, licking her breasts, nibbling her belly. And then his beautiful face pressed against her pubic hair, and his tongue went between her legs.

It was glorious.

And all too real.

When she opened her eyes, she recoiled. She was indeed naked, but Vedana was the one between her legs, not Torg. The demon's tongue was as long as a snake and as black as coal. It swirled frenetically.

Sōbhana kicked in disgust.

Vedana tumbled to the floor. Unscathed, the demon bounced up and laughed wickedly. "Why did you stop me? You were enjoying it so much."

Sōbhana reached for her sword, but it was gone. The demon must have put some kind of spell on her. Otherwise the weapon could not have been removed from her side.

"You want to fight, my beauty?" Vedana growled. "I want that too. It makes it so much sweeter."

The demon glowed, her flesh translucent. Sōbhana could see Vedana's bones and bulbous heart, and it made her feel faint. Vedana was too strong, wielding magic that stole the fire from her limbs. The demon rushed toward Sōbhana, intending to defile her.

When all seemed lost, Bhayatupa came to her rescue. A torrential fire blew through the cave, consuming the curtain of her small chamber. The demon seemed to fear the dragon flame, and she withdrew, snarling in frustration.

"Your future has been foreseen," she said to Sōbhana. "You would have much preferred *me* to the suffering that awaits you."

Bhayatupa's deep voice boomed down the passageway. "Vedana! If you have harmed her . . ."

The demon stepped back. This time instead of a smoky explosion, a circular black hole opened in the wall, and Vedana leapt into it. As quickly as it had appeared, the hole vanished.

Sōbhana stood naked in the chamber, wiping tears from her eyes. She fell to her knees. Then darkness claimed her, taking her to the stronghold of nothingness.

Sōbhana inhaled deeply. A curious aroma entered her nostrils, a wondrous combination of honey, spices and sweet smoke. Visions flowed into her mind, wave upon wave, endless in number. Civilizations rose and fell. Brave warriors lived and died. There was glory and shame. Courage and fear. Beginnings, middles, and endings.

When she opened her eyes she lay at the mouth of the cave. Bhayatupa's head was a finger-length away, and a tendril of smoke oozed from his nostrils to hers. She sat up so fast her face bumped against the dragon's enormous snout.

Bhayatupa withdrew and chuckled. "I see you have returned to the living," he said. "Are you pleased?"

The memory of the demon's perverted act flooded Sōbhana's awareness. She spat, and then stood up, leaning shakily against the stone wall. "I . . . don't . . . understand."

"That does not surprise me. You are *Adho Satta*. There are forces at work beyond your comprehension. But *The Torgon* knows and understands. I brought you back for his sake, not for yours."

"What would Vedana have done to me?"

"Who knows? The demon's machinations are often beyond my comprehension. But now that I have rescued you, it has become unimportant. As I said before, you and I have a common goal. This makes us allies, at least temporarily."

"Why were you away so long? Torg might already be dead."

Bhayatupa's face—which seemed capable of very human-like expressions—appeared distressed. "I returned to Avici and flew in the skies," the dragon said in his sonorous voice. "I did not wish for the sorcerer to become overly suspicious. But he called for me. And questioned me. I was severely tested." Bhayatupa's huge round eyes glazed over. At that moment he looked like a wizened king, troubled by the state of his realm. When he spoke again his voice almost trembled. "Let us say that our situation has grown more urgent. I have underestimated Invictus. For the first time, I felt . . . *fear*."

Sōbhana saw an opportunity and seized it. "Then why not join our cause? Perhaps you and *The Torgon* can defeat Invictus together."

Quicker than an Asēkha, Bhayatupa grasped her in his front talons and rose on his hind legs to his full height. At that point Sōbhana was higher than the pinnacle of the mountain.

Bhayatupa's eyes reverted from glazed to fiery and dangerous. "Join your cause? And what *cause* might that be, *Adho Satta*? The cause of insects and worms? You do not comprehend to whom you speak. I am

Bhayatupa, the *Mahaasupanna*, mightiest of all dragons, and I am beyond you. You live only because I am in need of your master's wisdom. But my patience has limits. Do not insult me like that again."

He cast her down onto the balcony, and she thudded on the stone. Cowed by the dragon's outburst, the Mogols threw themselves onto their stomachs and pressed their faces against the cave floor. Sōbhana lay stunned, temporarily unable to move.

"Bring her the sword, and dress her," the dragon said to the servant woman. "Her nakedness disturbs me. Be quick!"

Bhayatupa turned back to Sōbhana. His anger seemed to fade as quickly as it had arisen, and his voice returned to relative normalcy. "If you are sincere in your desire to save your king, then I am your only hope. Time grows short. You and I must fly to Asubha now."

3

Bhayatupa flew at heights above the mountaintops. The air was so thin Sōbhana found it difficult to breathe. At least she wasn't cold. The fragrant flesh beneath the dragon's crimson scale kept her comfortable.

She held the sword in a scabbard at her waist and pondered the extent of its power. Did it possess the strength to destroy what she considered one of the world's great evils? Even if it did, she was helpless to act. If she killed the dragon, Torg would be doomed.

"I hear your thoughts, warrior," Bhayatupa said, his voice superseding all other sound. "Save your strength. You will need it for the ordeal that awaits you."

"Tell me all that you know of Asubha," Sōbhana shouted into the wind. "I need to know what I am up against, if I am to succeed."

"An excellent *suggestion*. Indeed, it is time for me to tell you my plan. Your lord's life hangs in the balance."

"Speak, then. I grow weary of you, and I no longer fear you. If *The Torgon* were here now, he would order me to forsake this quest and drive the sword into your heart."

"You have grown, *Adho Satta*. You remain *Adho Satta*, but at least you now are high among the low."

"Thank you *so* much, O Exalted One. May you die soon, for all our sakes."

"How quaint . . . and I was under the impression that you enjoyed being my wife."

"That's not funny."

"I find it so. But enough prattle. You must listen carefully. I have time to say these words only once. Asubha is not far."

"Once is enough."

"It had better be. Now hush, and allow me to finish. This is what you will face. The prison is not heavily guarded—at least, you would not consider it so—because it is inaccessible to almost anyone who cannot fly. For this reason, Invictus does not fear attack. There are just enough sentries to manage the prisoners, fewer than five score, all told. You killed that many at Uccheda."

"This sounds too easy," Sōbhana said.

"If only that was true. Nevertheless, there is more. I believe Mala remains at the prison. That alone makes your task far more difficult. And the warden also presents problems. He is a Stone-Eater named Gulah. Are you familiar with these creatures?"

"Of course. I'm not a complete fool."

"Then you know of their powers. Gulah is not as great as Mala, but he would be a severe test for you, nonetheless. Invictus also keeps several trolls on hand to do the heavy lifting. And I have described only that which lies *within* the prison walls. There are dangers in the skies, as well. Four wild Sampatis hunt from above, and there are hundreds of ordinary condors. To me, they are annoying pests. But any one of them could be deadly to you. Even if you manage to avoid them, they can cause enough commotion to betray your position. Stealth and secrecy are your greatest allies."

"I have trained my entire life for this moment. There are few more prepared than I."

"As you say. I do not doubt that you are somewhat worthy."

"Why, Bhayatupa . . . that is the nicest thing you have ever said to me. There is hope for you yet."

"My hope lies trapped in the pit of Asubha," the dragon said. "The last hope, perhaps, of my long life."

The dragon flew silently for a brief time. Then he spoke again. "There is one final danger—and next to Mala it is the worst. An ancient evil dwells near Asubha's peak. Her name is Dukkhatu, and she appears as a great horned spider, terrible to behold. Only Vedana and I have survived the passage of more days than she."

"I have never heard of Dukkhatu," Sōbhana said. "But I admit that my learning is not what it should be. I have always focused too much on fighting."

"It is probable that even your lord has not heard of Dukkhatu. In recent times she has shied from the lower lands. Millennia ago she hunted among the foothills of Mahaggata, feeding on the unwary. Hundreds of brave warriors tried to slay her and failed. Her hide is tougher than iron, and her fangs are full of foul poisons. In her old age, she wearied of battle and retired to the highest peaks. Recently, much to her pleasure, she discovered Asubha. Food is her obsession, and the prison provides her with plenty of fresh meat. She waits and watches. You must avoid her."

Sōbhana shivered. "Is this sword capable of killing her?"

"Child, do you not know? It is capable of destroying *anything*. It was here before Dukkhatu. Before Bhayatupa. Before Vedana. Before memory. The Silver Sword, though mundanely named, is more valuable than any treasure on Triken. In and of itself, the blade contains no special magic. But it will hack or pierce anything it touches. No shield, hide, or demon flesh—not even a dragon's scale—can withstand a direct blow."

"And you left it lying in a pile, as if it were a trinket," Sōbhana said. "Are you saying it could destroy Invictus?"

"The best hiding places are often the least likely," Bhayatupa said. "As for Invictus, he has grown beyond the bounds of my awareness. And those are words I have never before spoken."

"Maybe one day I'll find out. Maybe one day I'll put the sword to the sorcerer's throat."

"Perhaps," the dragon said. "But in my heart, I do not believe so. That fate lies with someone else."

For a while longer they did not speak. Darkness consumed the sky, but there was light all about. The moon was huge and full, and the stars sparkled like white crystals on a black coverlet. Sōbhana felt as if she could touch them.

The icy air on the warrior's face froze her tears.

"What will become of me?" she said.

"I care naught," the dragon said. "I care only for myself. Have I not said so before?"

Without warning to those in the prison below, a condor fell from the sky and smote the floor of the large courtyard that contained the pit. The bloodied bird flopped about and squawked insanely, both its wings brutally broken.

While the diversion occupied the sentries, Bhayatupa circled and approached the prison from below. With the grace of a hummingbird, he hovered at the base of the thick wall that partially enclosed the peak of the frozen mountain. The dragon gently placed Sōbhana on the roughly hewn stone, which contained numerous lumps and cracks, good for gripping. Then he swerved away, quiet as a breeze.

Before they reached the prison, Bhayatupa had told Sōbhana he had to go back to Avici for a brief time to avoid further suspicion. She was on her own until midnight of the following day, when he promised to return under cover of darkness and fly her and Torg to safety.

The outcome of the quest rested in her hands, and her entire being was consumed with a desire to rush to Torg's rescue. But she had to remain patient for a little while longer.

Sōbhana had never been afraid of heights, but there was a first time for everything, as her Vasi master liked to say. Though it now was deep night, the full moon and abundant starlight made it possible to see long distances. Asubha and its sister mountains glowed like luminaries. Sōbhana looked down past her feet and trembled. She could see for several hundred fathoms, but the floor of the abyss was invisible. She needed to find a place to hide. Too much was going on inside the prison for her to attempt anything this night—and daytime would be impossible.

She heard the final shriek of the stricken condor, which Bhayatupa had disabled to distract the sentries on the wall walk, and then the cheering of men inside the prison. The sound of Mala's nauseating voice further disheartened her. Bhayatupa had been right. The Chain Man had remained in Asubha.

"Start a fire, lads. But first serving goes to me. I like my meat *raw*."

Sōbhana rolled her eyes. She wasn't sure which she disliked more about Mala: his evil deeds or his obnoxious personality. She began to climb slowly up the wall. Her luck held, and she found a hollow in the stone just large enough to provide concealment. She pulled her dark coat around her body and felt reflexively for the Silver Sword. Its presence comforted her, and she allowed herself to sleep.

Some time later, Sōbhana stirred, then sat up with a gasp, sensing something beneath her though she saw nothing. Was it the spider? She dared not sleep again. She was weary beyond measure, but she would have to stay awake through the rest of the night. Sliding the sword from its sheath, she held it in front of her, awaiting the succor of daylight.

Meanwhile, the men inside the prison shouted and laughed. The smell of roasting bird flesh wafted in the still air. Sōbhana's mouth watered.

When daylight arrived she allowed herself some scattered moments of sleep. The uneasy feeling of being watched dissipated. Perhaps the spider couldn't tolerate sunlight.

It became clear, bright, and unseasonably warm—all unusual events in autumn on the peak of Asubha, Sōbhana imagined. She ate a light meal from a pack attached to the belt of her scabbard, and she sipped water from a leather flask. She could hear sentries strolling along the top of the wall. They sounded pleased. The previous night's feast and the rare pleasant weather must have put them in good spirits—or as good as spirits could be in a place as dismal as this.

By early afternoon the weather had changed for the worse. A stiff wind came from the north, running in circles around the mountaintop. Dark clouds followed. Another storm, most likely born in Nirodha, where few dared wander, marched toward Asubha. The sentries grumbled.

Though she shivered in her tiny hideaway, Sōbhana was otherwise pleased. If the storm raged into the night, it would provide the camouflage she needed to complete Torg's rescue.

When darkness came, the storm fell upon the mountain like a fiend. Sōbhana had never felt such ferocious winds or seen such virulent lightning. She feared she might not make it to the top of the wall, much less reach the pit. To make matters worse, it was wickedly cold. Ice crystals spun in the air like a million miniature daggers, obscuring the moon and stars. Frequent blasts of lightning provided fleeting moments of visibility, during which she looked about in all directions, studying her surroundings. As she peered from her hiding place, hail pelted her. The walls above her were coated with a glaze of ice. Would she have to wait out the storm before attempting her ascent?

She did not allow herself to be distracted by the specter of the spider. Could the beast hunt in weather like this? She didn't know. But Dukkhatu probably was adapted to the cold, so Sōbhana knew she had to be careful. The spider might try to grab her as soon as she began to climb.

Still Sōbhana could not be daunted. She would rely on her innate ability to sense unseen danger. If she perceived Dukkhatu's presence in time, the sword would do the rest. And if she fell, her role in all this would no longer matter.

When she could bear to wait no longer, she got to her knees, faced the wall, and leaned backward just far enough to see beyond the upper lip of her hideaway. From where she knelt, it was thirty cubits or so to the top of the wall. Under these tumultuous conditions, it might as well have been three hundred.

For a moment despair overcame her. It could take her until midnight just to get over the wall, much less reach the center of the courtyard, free Torg from the pit, and get him to a place where the dragon could rescue them. To accomplish this feat, killing would be necessary—*quiet* killing. She had assumed her ascent of the wall would take very little of the time she had left. Now it was obvious that it would be a much larger challenge than she had anticipated.

Reason told her to wait, that the storm would dissipate. If she went now, she might be blown off the wall before she was able to reach the top.

But Sōbhana was finished with reason. Madness drove her—born of love.

With her right hand she grasped a flake of stone. It was not quite as slippery as she had feared. Her powerful fingers crunched through the ice and pressed against the granular surface of the brick. She raised her left hand higher and inserted her fingers into a thin crack. Now both her hands had firm holds, and she was able to stand.

She flung her right hand several inches higher, grasping a knoblike protrusion. Then her left hand swung above the right and locked into a jagged tear. Her black boots rose off the floor of her hiding place and dangled in the air. Bit by bit, she climbed. Bolts of lightning revealed her position, but she couldn't allow herself to think about that now.

Gusty winds punched at her, threatening to knock her into space. At times, squalls lifted her torso off the wall and nearly yanked her hands and feet free. But she continued upward, not to be denied. At less than an arm's length from the top, her spirits soared. She was going to make it. Once over the wall she would be more in her element, and her instincts as a trained assassin would take over.

Suddenly a jolt of intuitive wrongness surged through her body. The inner voice born of her long training warned her to look down. Just then, a blast of lightning careened off the stone, revealing a hideous shape on the rock face below her. The spider was at least twenty cubits wide—if you included her legs—and her gruesome abdomen was twice as thick as an ancient oak.

Quicker than Sōbhana could think, the sword was in her free hand, sweeping down with fantastic speed. Dukkhatu had defeated many warriors, but apparently she had never fought anyone with the prowess of this Asēkha. The blade of the Silver Sword hacked off the tip of Dukkhatu's upper right leg. Black blood spurted onto the stone.

There was another bolt of lightning.

Sōbhana saw the spider leaping sideways along the wall.

Soon after, Dukkhatu was gone.

Sōbhana's counterattack seemed to anger the storm, and its vehemence increased. She cried out and nearly lost her grip on the sword. If she dropped it, she would be helpless against Mala and the Stone-Eater. She would not allow it.

Sōbhana replaced the sword in its sheath and took a moment to regain her composure. Then she climbed the remaining distance to the top of the wall and flung herself over the parapet, collapsing onto the narrow wall walk.

She lay there, gasping.

If she had been discovered at that moment she might have been easy to capture. But there were no sentries nearby. It appeared none had braved the ferocity of the storm. Instead Sōbhana imagined that they huddled in cold chambers and prayed for death.

The storm retained its intensity. Sōbhana had never felt so cold, but she ignored her physical anguish. She had no other choice.

The roiling darkness was her friend—though also her enemy. It hid her from prying eyes, but it prevented her from studying her surroundings. Asēkhas were brilliant at assessing situations and taking advantage of their opponents' weaknesses. But that was more difficult to do when you couldn't see.

Wind, snow, and fist-sized hail pounded Asubha, but the flashes of lightning occurred less frequently now. Sōbhana could no longer depend on them to provide spurts of visibility. She would have to proceed by feel. At least her foes were in the same predicament.

She worked her way along the wall walk until she came to a spiral stair that corkscrewed steeply downward into blackness. For all she knew, a sentry guarded the lower steps. If so, she would end his miserable life.

Bhayatupa had told her there were several guard rooms scattered around the main courtyard. Within one of those she should be able to find lengths of rope. If she tied a rope to a plank laid across the top of the pit, she could shimmy down. She hoped her king would have the strength to climb out on his own. If not, she would carry him on her back. She was an Asēkha. All things were possible.

Sōbhana proceeded warily down the stairs. She could see clearly for about ten paces. Beyond that, vague shapes and ghostly blurs haunted her vision. She reached the floor of the courtyard without encountering resistance. Several stubborn torches burned weakly on iron poles driven into the stone, but they provided scant illumination. Dropping to her hands and knees, she crawled along the ground, peering to-and-fro, until she came upon a one-room building with a single window. An oil lamp flickered inside. Though the storm continued to roar, she heard voices. She peeked in the window and saw three sentries huddled around a table. They guzzled from large mugs; if they were drunk, all the better.

The door was ajar. She slid inside the lighted room. One of the sentries was having a good laugh. He slapped his knee. The other two laughed along with him.

With three blurring strokes, their heads leapt into the air, performed backward flips, and fell to the floor, striking the stone in a series of squishy thuds. She waited patiently until the blood finished squirting from their necks, then she repositioned their heads on their shoulders and put the mugs back on the table.

A keg of wine sat next to the wall beneath the window. Sōbhana picked it up and took several long swallows. It was potent, but not particularly tasty. Still, it warmed her insides. She drank quite a bit more before setting it down.

The room had one small closet. She rummaged through it and found plenty of thick rope and a plank that was just the right size. How absurdly easy this part of the operation had become. It made her wary.

Suddenly, the door swung open. A fourth sentry strode through the entryway. He wore a heavy cloak over his tunic, but still he grumbled about the cold before heading straight for the keg, too stupid to notice Sōbhana's presence. She stepped behind him and slammed the door. He jerked around. She crossed the room and pressed the sword against his throat. She forced him down, beneath the window, and crouched in front of him so close to his face she could smell his rancid breath.

"I will let you live, if you answer all my questions—without pause," she whispered. "Do you understand?"

He nodded fiercely.

"Does the wizard still live?"

"The wizard?"

Her forehead flew forward and butted him between his eyes. Steaming blood oozed from the bridge of his nose. He muttered something that made no sense. "And then I . . . I . . . kissed her . . ."

Sōbhana slapped him. His eyes sprang open, and he started to shout, but she roughly pressed the palm of her hand against his lips. "Shhhhhh . . . shhhhh . . . if you ever want to kiss her again, then you must answer all my questions. I am an Asēkha and can silence you whenever I choose. You cannot thwart me. Do you doubt it?"

He shook his head.

"Does the wizard . . . the prisoner in the pit . . . still live?"

"Yes, warrior . . . I heard noises coming from that accursed hole just yesterday. I almost soiled my pants."

Sōbhana's cheeks flushed. Torg was alive! "What kind of noises?"

"Moans. Shrieks."

"Is Mala here?" she said, through gritted teeth.

"Yes. He won't leave, though we all wish he would."

She pondered this, and then spoke again. "Another question. *Where* is the pit?"

He pointed at the door.

"How far?"

"About one hundred paces."

"Is anything between us and the pit that could get in my way?"

"About fifty strides from here, there is a short wall that encircles the hole. Otherwise, there is nothing."

"Is the pit watched?"

The sentry grimaced. "It's supposed to be. We guard it in pairs. But my friend came here for wine. And I got scared and followed. The storm . . . the cold . . . We were sure that Mala wouldn't bother to check on us. My friend—" He pointed to one of the sentries seated at the table. "—is over there. Why does he not move?"

"He didn't answer my questions. Nor did the others. They are no longer."

The sentry shivered. A single tear slid down his rough, red cheek. "I will . . . I will answer your questions. I promise. I truly wish to kiss her again one day."

Sōbhana felt a twinge of sympathy. "Listen to me *very* carefully."

"Yes. But please don't kill me. I'm not ready to die."

"I won't slay you, if you don't force me to. I'm going to tell you a secret, and if you keep it to yourself, I'll let you live. I'm going to free the prisoner. After that, I'll need a place to hide—for a short time—from Mala and the guards. Where might that be?"

"There is no place to hide . . ." The sword pressed against his throat. "Wait . . . wait! I meant no *good* place. But if I wanted to hide, I would go to the roof of the keep. A narrow stair leads to the top. Few ever use it. No one would think to look for you there, especially in this storm."

Sōbhana considered his suggestion. "If you are lying . . ."

"No, warrior, I speak the truth. But may I say one thing?"

"Quickly!"

"Freeing the wizard is impossible. It hurts just to stand *near* the pit, especially if you're not used to it. If you try to enter, you . . . you will not survive. It is deadlier even than you, mistress. Only the warden has the equipment needed to remove the wizard. It's a special contraption with a large clamp, and it is cleverly made. But it is out of reach—behind barred doors."

"I will find a way," she said. "And the keep . . . how far is it from the pit?"

"It is on the northern wall, several hundred paces beyond it. You can reach the stairs, if you veer around to the left and slip between the walls."

"Very good. You are behaving yourself. One more question: Where does Mala sleep?"

"In a large chamber at the base of the keep. He comes out often—even during the night—to check on the prisoner, but usually not during the worst storms."

"You have been helpful," Sōbhana said. "I'm going to tie you up now. If you struggle, the ropes will strangle you. Do you doubt it?"

"No, warrior. I believe every word you say."

"If you somehow betray me, you will die in a most painful manner."

Sōbhana left the guard house a few minutes later with the sentry gagged and bound and tucked inside the closet. Her knots couldn't be undone without help from others. She left the torch lit and the card players in place. If anyone peered through the window, they would see nothing unusual, except for frozen splotches on the floor, as if they had spilled a lot of wine.

The storm had lessened somewhat, but it still blew with considerable force—enough, she hoped, to keep Mala, the Stone-Eater, and the other sentries inside their chambers.

While the storm raged on, Mala lay awake in his room, his enormous body stretched out on the bare stone floor, his thoughts raging as wildly as the weather. He hated the prison and yearned to return to Uccheda, but Invictus had ordered him to stay on Asubha for thirty days. If the wizard still lived after that, Mala was to remove him from the pit and bring him back to Avici.

Mala doubted Torg could survive much longer. It had been ten days, and Mala could sense that the wizard was near death.

On the first day of the Death-Knower's imprisonment, Mala had peered into the pit. Ferocious pain seared his face, and he shouted and jerked back. Now, as he lay in a heap within his chamber, he grudgingly admitted to himself that he'd grown to admire Torg. Anyone—or anything—able to survive in the pit for more than a day was extraordinary. Ten days was beyond possibility. And Invictus thought the wizard might live for a month?

Lightning stroked the air, followed by a concussive blast of thunder. Mala sat upright. Maybe he should go out and have a look around. Wind and hail tearing at his flesh would clear his mind.

Ten days down. Twenty to go. Would this torture ever end? The things he did for his king.

Carrying the rope and plank on her back, Sōbhana slithered over the low wall that encircled the pit. Occasional bursts of lightning threatened to reveal her position, but she moved so slowly and so close to the ground she was all but invisible.

Before she could see the pit, she could sense it and recognize it as pure evil. Poison, decay, sickness, despair . . . the pit contained them all . . . she experienced the same kind of desperation she'd felt when she first saw Invictus. She wanted to flee.

But of course she would not. She had come too far and fought too hard, and she would rescue her beloved—or die trying. Despite the enormity of her fear, no other scenario was possible.

Buoyed by her immense stubbornness, Sōbhana crept closer. She found it difficult to imagine how the sentries were able to guard the pit; either they were partially immune to its wickedness or she was more susceptible. When she had crawled within an arm's length of the opening, her eyes began to water, her ears rang, and her tongue swelled. Surely the sentry had lied. *The Torgon* must be long dead. Not even one as great as he could have survived inside this monstrosity for a single day, much less ten.

Then she heard a shriek, and it almost stopped her heart. Her beloved was down there, enduring horrors beyond her comprehension. But he was alive.

And she was his last hope.

The perfect circle glared at her. It had its own mind, its own voice, and it challenged her to proceed.

Come inside and play with me, little one. You look so sweet and tasty.

Forcing herself to crawl to the lip of the abyss, Sōbhana peered down into the blackness. Instantly her face was ablaze with pain, and the muscles in her cheeks quivered. Mucus gushed from her nostrils, freezing as it fell toward the mouth of the pit, but sizzling and bursting into steam as it entered. What kind of hell was this?

"I'm coming, my love," she whispered. "I will not forsake you."

A low moan rose, as if in reply.

Sōbhana laid the narrow plank across the opening and looped one end of the rope around it, securing it with a sturdy knot. The cord was three finger-lengths thick and well made. She hoped it could survive the pit's virulence long enough for her to climb down and bring Torg up. If she fell, all would be lost.

First though, she drew the Silver Sword and lowered it partway into the pit, expecting it to melt or wither. But the sword was not affected, and its blade remained cool. Perhaps it would protect her. At the least, it might bolster her resolve.

Reluctantly she returned it to its sheath, needing both hands for the descent. She lowered the rope into the darkness while estimating the distance. Five cubits. Ten. Fifty. One hundred. Two hundred. Did it touch bottom? She couldn't quite tell.

For a moment she imagined Torg reaching for the rope and climbing out on his own, relieving her of the burden of entering the pit. But then she realized this was a false hope. She had to go down—and she had to do it now.

Sōbhana sat down on the plank, which bowed slightly but held her weight, and then lowered her feet into the darkness. Even though she wore heavy boots and tight-fitting pants, her feet, ankles and calves instantly burned like frostbitten flesh submerged in steaming water. She left them there for several seconds, testing her ability to tolerate the pain. It hurt terribly, but at least it seemed to level out. She could not have withstood anything worse.

Summoning her strength, she slid the rest of her body into the hole. To stop from crying out she bit her lip. Blood dripped down her chin and smoked like burning oil.

She was submerged into agony, except where the sheath of the sword touched her leg. So she focused her mind along the length of the blade. It did provide comfort. And strength. In some ways the sword was greater than the pit.

Hand by hand she descended. The agony remained without intensifying, but her stomach soured, and she vomited. Now her entire body was sweating profusely, and she believed she might die of dehydration before anything else.

How was Torg still alive?

Sōbhana coughed. One of her teeth spit out of her mouth and impaled itself in the side of the pit, where it caught fire and shattered, casting blazing shards that provided a tiny circle of light—just enough for her to see a portion of the wall. Black things wiggled and squirmed, like the flesh of a devil.

Down she went, farther and farther. The air was so foul she could barely breathe. Blood replaced the mucus that had gushed from her nostrils. Warmth oozed from her ears and eyes. Liquids poured from her vagina and anus. If she did somehow rescue Torg and return to the surface, she wouldn't be a pretty sight. But then, she imagined, neither would he.

She had to be getting close. It felt as if she had been descending for days. Just when she was about to give up hope, her foot touched an object beneath her. She reached down with her free hand and grasped something solid. It was his shoulder—his wonderful, muscular shoulder.

Torg moaned again. Sōbhana felt around as best she could and determined that he was curled naked on his side. The warrior hated to do it, but she had to relieve the pressure on her other arm, so she gently placed her boots onto his thick ribs and crouched down onto his body. If only he would wake up, they could escape together. But he seemed incapable of movement. She would have to lift him, and it wouldn't be easy. He was almost twice her weight—and dead weight, at that.

No, don't use that word.

"I am here, my beloved," she whispered. "I have come. I will save you. Do not fear."

He groaned, but did not move.

Then to her horror, the rope began to jiggle. Something was yanking on it from above. Someone had discovered her, and if he severed the rope, both she and Torg were doomed.

"I'll be back," she said. "I promise you."

Sōbhana climbed with terrific speed, expecting the rope to go slack and dump her into the abyss at any second. Instead it began to sway violently, throwing her against the wall. Her black coat burst into flame and then disintegrated. The skin on her right shoulder bubbled and blistered. Ignoring the pain, she continued to climb.

When she arrived at the top and reached for the plank, something huge and powerful grasped her wrist and lifted her from the pit. Sōbhana dangled in front of Mala, barely a third his height.

"An Asēkha!" he said, his voice puzzled. "How . . . how did you get here? Are you alone?"

With her free hand, Sōbhana drew the sword from its sheath and whipped it at Mala's neck, but he bent his head back just enough to avoid decapitation. The sword dug into a portion of the chain that was burned into his breast, and there was an outburst of golden flame. The Chain Man was cast backward, dropping Sōbhana as he fell. She landed awkwardly on her side next to the mouth of the pit, momentarily stunned.

When she regained her senses, the Chain Man still was dazed. Sōbhana watched his every move. Almost too late she detected a whisper in the air, and she flipped the sword behind her back. Another sword clashed against hers and burst asunder. Sōbhana rose to her feet, spun around, and cut her attacker—this one man-sized—in half with a single swipe.

"What did she do to me?" Mala said, still confused. "What does she wield?"

More sentries arrived, carrying hissing torches. Though Sōbhana had managed to kill the first attacker, she remained dizzy and disoriented, and her shoulder felt as if it had been shredded by poisoned blades. But rage gave her strength. She had been so close. She had *touched* her king. And at the worst possible moment, the monster she'd grown to despise had thwarted her.

Her screams of frustration echoed in the night. The sentries retreated.

Mala became infuriated. "Get her, you cowards! Slice her up."

Sōbhana regained her wits. Killing was what she did best, and when she faced superior numbers, she eliminated the most dangerous first.

With an anger that had fermented over weeks and weeks, she charged at the Chain Man, intent on making him pay for his cruelty.

Her sudden ferocity seemed to awaken Mala. The monster bellowed, and golden liquid, as hot as dragon fire, spurted from his chain. Sōbhana grunted and leapt to the side, barely avoiding the profusion. She fell at the feet of a sentry, rolled to her knees, and swept off both his legs at mid-thigh. Then she stood up, whipping the blade around. Three more fell. The sword cut through anything it touched with ridiculous ease.

The Chain Man picked up a stone statue almost his size and heaved it at her. Sōbhana sidestepped the massive missile and watched it crush a cave troll who'd emerged from the darkness. Another statue, one of a series that lined the outer court, tumbled by, bowling over several approaching sentries.

The storm joined the fight. A blast of lightning, more powerful than Sōbhana had ever witnessed, blew into the mouth of the pit. A blob of electrical energy spewed upward and exploded like fireworks, casting a blanket of dazzling light that illuminated the entire courtyard and revealed the locations of at least one hundred well-armed men.

Despite the threat of the sword, Mala dared to approach her. Sōbhana believed she could kill him with it, but she had to get close enough to strike, and that wouldn't be easy. His powers were formidable, and she had no magic of her own to counter them.

The Chain Man rushed forward, liquid fire spurting from his chain. Even for an Asēkha the scathing flames were difficult to avoid, and she was forced to duck and run while at the same time slaying any sentry that strayed within her vision. Most feared her wrath and stayed back. But Mala continued his pursuit, and now he held the advantage. He could destroy her from a distance, but she needed to get within the length of the sword to harm him. She began to fear she could not prevail.

Gasping and panting, Sōbhana moved reluctantly away from the pit. More sentries fell beneath her blade, but fighting them and avoiding Mala was exhausting. She already had been pushed beyond her limits, and her damaged shoulder felt as if it were dissolving. A fist-sized brick—hurled from her blindside—ricocheted off her cheek, and her mouth filled with blood. A golden soldier could not have thrown with such force. This one must have come from another troll.

Another bolt of lightning struck somewhere in the courtyard. She glanced behind her and realized she was just a span from the edge of a terrible cliff.

Turning back to her attackers, she held the sword in front of her, grinning crookedly. "Come and get me, you bastards. Every one of you will die. I swear it."

Emboldened by Mala, they approached close enough for the torchlight to reveal their grim faces. Sōbhana saw anger, but then fear. Suddenly they stopped. Even Mala.

She didn't see—or sense—what rose behind her until it was too late.

Silk threads from the spider's spinnerets wove around her, pinning her forearms against her torso and encasing her entire body from her shoulders down. As if by magic, the threads tore the sword from her grasp and wrapped it in a separate cocoon. Then she was yanked into space.

"No . . . no!" she wailed. "Please save me . . . my lovvvvvvvvvvve!"

But there was no response as the spider took her—from one hell to another.

Escape from the Pit

1

As he had told Kusala that late-summer night on the outskirts of Barranca, Torg had died a thousand times. Each *Death Visit*, which lasted fewer than thirty long breaths, enriched Torg with magical powers. In that short time Torg fed on supernatural energy, and when he returned to life, he felt paradoxically more alive than most could imagine.

Torg's first *Death Visit* had occurred more than nine centuries ago. Ever since that amazing breakthrough, he had planned the time and place of each "temporary suicide" in precise detail, preferring to wait about a year between visits, though a few times in his life—depending on his needs—he had done so with slightly more frequency.

Now it was mid autumn and well below freezing in the mountain prison on the peak of Asubha. The air was bitter and useless, failing to nourish Torg's lungs. His breaths came in raspy gasps and moans, and he shivered as if in a constant state of illness.

Dehydrated and starving, Torg was no longer able to accurately gauge the passage of time. He spent most of it in various states of unconsciousness, but when he was awake every second felt like a week.

Even Torg could not bear much more. The insidious magic and acidic poisons imbued in the walls of the pit had ravaged his naked flesh. The hair on his body had dissolved, and his teeth had fallen out and been consumed. He could feel his immense strength leaking out of him, like blood draining from a gaping wound.

Torg's lone hope, he knew, was a *Death Visit*. He needed to feed on death's abundant might. But something in the pit prevented him from achieving the required level of concentration.

If I cannot die, I will go insane. I must find a way past the barrier Invictus has erected.

And so, he attempted to meditate, again.

Inhale . . .

Exhale . . .

Even before the completion of the first exhalation, he lost control of his concentration, and his mind wandered aimlessly, still puzzled by the sensual lure of the full moon. His long years of mindfulness training had taught him to recognize these inevitable drifts and gently return to the breath. So he discarded the thought and continued to . . .

Inhale . . .

Exhale . . .

Inhale . . .

Exhale . . .

An itch tormented the tip of his nose. Torg knew that this, too, could be used as an object of concentration. Without judgment or prejudice he watched the itch rise and fall of its own accord, studying its beginning, middle and ending. He observed how it affected the workings of his body and mind. When the prickle abated, he returned to . . .

Inhale . . .

Exhale . . .

Inhale . . .

Exhale . . .

Inhale . . .

Exhale . . .

Torg was making progress, but the mysterious barrier continued to thwart his concentration. The walls of the pit made strange sizzling sounds, occasionally spurting blobs of caustic liquid that burned his bare skin like dragon fire. But the pain alone did not prevent him from emptying his mind or managing his thoughts. There was something else—a madness like no other.

Despite all this, he continued to try.

Inhale . . .

Exhale . . .

Invictus toys with me.

Inhale . . .

Exhale . . .

I will go insane.

Inhale . . .

I must find a way.

Exhale . . .

I will find a way.

Inhale . . .
Exhale . . .
Inhale . . .
Exhale . . .

Watch the breath. Eliminate movement. Watch the breath. Eliminate thought.

Inhale . . .
Exhale . . .
Inhale . . .
Exhale . . .

No movement. No thought. Quiet mind. Peaceful mind. Only the breath.

Inhale . . .
Exhale . . .
Inhale . . .
Exhale . . .

As the torment of the pit further eroded his sanity, Torg struggled one last time to enter the Realm of Death, where he could feed on its power and absorb enough strength to survive a few more days. A successful *Death Visit* was never easy for Torg, even in the best of circumstances, requiring a magnificently intense form of meditation, even greater than that practiced by the noble ones of Dibbu-Loka. Torg's mind had to be emptied of all thought—not just for a few breaths, or a series of breaths, but for hundreds of breaths.

A wise Vasi master had taught Torg the art of meditation when he was a young warrior just beginning his training. Concentration creates a state of extreme relaxation. If performed at a deep enough level, meditation can slow the rise and fall of the breath and the beating of the heart to undetectable levels. But it has nothing in common with sleepiness or daydreaming. The meditator is supremely awake. Every thought, emotion, sensation, and occurrence is monitored with ultimate awareness.

Because of their genetics, Tugars enjoyed a remarkable asset. Their flesh was unusually dense, making it highly resistant to injury. This impregnability continued even after death. An ordinary body began to decay soon after it perished, but Tugar bodies remained relatively unchanged for more than a year, and it took centuries for them to deteriorate into skeletons. Torg was the ultimate Tugar. His physical strength was unrivaled for a creature of his size, but it paled in comparison to his supernatural puissance.

During his lifetime Torg averaged slightly more than one *Death Visit* per year. The act was too dangerous for more frequent attempts. Each episode required that he achieve a state called *Sammaasamaadhi*, the supreme concentration of mind. During *Sammaasamaadhi*, Torg's heart rate progressively slowed until his body ceased to live. At that instant his karmic energy exited his flesh and entered the Realm of Death, where it fed and grew strong. But unlike an ordinary death, Torg was able to return to his body before the process became irreversible. His dense tissues—though temporarily deprived of life-giving oxygen—remained receptive to their host.

Now, imprisoned on the rooftop of Mount Asubha, Torg lay in the pit and continued his final attempt toward *Sammaasamaadhi*. If he had been stronger, he would have sat up in a comfortable position to begin his meditation. But he was too weak to twitch a finger.

Invictus' magical barrier continued to wreak havoc within his mind. Torg searched for its source with single-minded determination. Since his first successful Death Visit more than nine centuries before, he had never experienced such difficulty in achieving *Sammaasamaadhi*.

Torg remembered words spoken to him by the Vasi master who was the first to recognize that he had the rare potential to become a Death-Knower. At the time, Torg was a juvenile approaching the middle years of his warrior training.

"Live in the present moment," Dēsaka said. "Nothing exists but the present. All else is illusion. To live in the present moment, you must become the master of your mind." The teacher tapped his temple with a long finger. *"Thought is the thinker.* To empty the mind of thought, do not think. It is that easy and that difficult. If you empty your mind of thought, you will become its master."

Thought is the thinker . . . that was the key.

For the first time since being lowered into the pit, Torg felt hope, though for a moment his mind drifted back to a distant time before even his first death when he was a forty-year-old youth who had not yet become a warrior. Ever curious, Torg had harassed his Vasi master with endless queries.

"What force could cause the world to fall into ruin?"

"Ignorance," Dēsaka said.

"What is the greatest bliss?"

"Awakening is the greatest bliss."

Dēsaka sat cross-legged in the sand at the base of a great dune. A cotton veil covered his head and face, revealing only his eyes. Torg wandered in circles around the Vasi master, waving his arms.

"Who holds the sharpest sword?" Torg said.

"A person who speaks out of wrath holds the sharpest sword," Dēsaka said.

"My sword is sharpest."

"Your sword is sharp, but your mind is dull. You can see beyond the dunes, but you cannot see what is in front of your eyes. Even worse, you blame your stupidity on others rather than take responsibility for it."

"But you call me your greatest student."

"I say that you could become great. That you should become great. But you are not yet great. You know your strengths, but you are blind to your weaknesses. Until you can see what is in front of your eyes, you will remain an apprentice."

Torg smiled. His master's insults did not have the feel of wrath. "What is the most precious treasure?" he asked.

"Enough! Enough!" Dēsaka said. "Now I have a question for you. Will you answer?"

"Yes, O Exalted One."

"What is the greatest weapon?"

"Wisdom," Torg said, without pause.

"Ah, child . . . you are full of surprises. The only thing that can stop you is yourself. Your father says you are too smart for your own good. He is correct."

Now, as Torg lay shivering in the darkness of the pit, he replayed this tête-à-tête several times before the answer he had long sought arose.

"You can see beyond the dunes, but you cannot see what is in front of your eyes."

Torg finally understood what was in front of his eyes. Invictus had never intended to disrupt his concentration; the sorcerer was too confident to consider it a necessity. But Torg's sensitivity to the insalubrities of Invictus' power had *felt* like a barrier, effectively preventing him from emptying his mind. The magic that created the pit swirled like a filthy tornado. But Torg saw through it, and his sudden clarity gave him a chance . . . which was better than none.

More of his master's words, spoken in a time long past, entered his awareness:

"Breathe in. Know that you breathe in. Breathe out. Know that you breathe out."

Torg felt chaos start to drain from his mind . . .

Inhale . . .

Exhale . . .

The wisdom of silence was his greatest weapon. It also carried a reward: the sweetness of empty mind. Awareness bloomed like a flower in morning's first light.

Each breath has a beginning, middle and end. The inhale has a beginning, middle and end. The pause in between has a beginning, middle and end. The exhale has a beginning, middle and end.

Torg had observed this millions of times, and therefore knew it to be so.

The breath is a microcosm of all existence. Torg knew this also.

Torg used his breath as the focus. But he did not force it out of its natural rhythm. He simply became aware of it.

When his mind wandered he drew it back—gently, but persistently—by releasing his distraction and returning the attention to the breath.

Inhale . . .

Breathe in and become peaceful.

Exhale . . .

Breathe out and become peaceful.

Inhale . . .

Breathe in and concentrate the mind.

Exhale . . .

Breathe out and concentrate the mind.

Inhale . . .

Breathe in and slow the breath.

Exhale . . .

Breathe out and slow the breath.

Inhale . . .

Breathe in and slow the heartbeat.

Exhale . . .

Breathe out and slow the heartbeat.

Inhale . . .

Exhale . . .

Inhale . . .

Exhale . . .

With one final surge of mindful concentration, Torg willed his heart to stop beating. When *Sammaasamaadhi* arrived, his temporary suicide began. What he experienced next occurred to all that ever live—from the simplest bacterium to the most complex animal.

And that is what made Torg so special.
Only a Death-Knower can die.
And live again.
Only a Death-Knower can return from death.
And remember.
Only a Death-Knower can tell us what he has seen.
Not all care to listen.

Torg's lifeless body lay at the bottom of the pit, but his mind—or what some might call his soul—exploded out of the hole like a fiery boulder heaved into the night sky by a volcano. Torg became a swirling sphere of karmic energy, and he leapt great distances across time and space, drawn by a force far greater than gravity.

The silence of meditation was nothing compared to this silence. There was no sound at all—neither was there taste, touch nor smell. There was only sight.

Torg tumbled toward his future. He could not see his own karma; death did not permit reflection. But he could see what surrounded him. Countless other spheres—in a variety of shapes, sizes, and colors—streaked alongside him like an army of comets. Torg could sense that the spheres were looking at him and at each other in mutual fascination.

In the far distance, beyond the planets, beyond the stars, Torg knew from vast experience that a deep-blue ball awaited their arrival. It was larger than a galaxy, and billions of karmic spheres dove into it from all conceivable directions, while just as large a number rocketed outward. The ball was a cosmic headquarters for the natural cycle of life and death, directing and redirecting karma throughout the universe.

In this realm there was no fear or pain. No pleasure or joy. In fact, all emotions were muted. Torg felt only a dry scientific curiosity. It was cold, but he did not shiver. It was bittersweet, but he did not taste. From his experience, the abilities to hear, taste, touch and smell were reserved for life.

Death was a temporary condition. *Life is short,* the Vasi saying went. But death was far shorter.

The lure of the natural order was seductively strong. Torg's karmic sphere yearned to enter the ball and continue on its way to its next existence. His dead body was trillions of miles away on a distant world. His only chance of return was to stop short of the immense ball and hover just beyond its surface. If he entered, there would be no turning back.

Torg had accomplished this feat a thousand times before—but never while so diminished. A large part of him wanted to give in and let the living beings he had left behind fend for themselves. What did it matter, anyway? All of them, except for the demons, would eventually die. All of them would pass through here on their ways to their next existences.

At that moment Torg's thoughts strayed to Sister Tathagata, as they often did during his *Death Visits*. Her wisdom had brought him back from the brink before.

"Use your time wisely, child," the High Nun of Dibbu-Loka had said to him. "Time is precious. What do you gain if you are allotted a million lives but never learn? Do not waste this life hoping that the next will be superior. Halt your suffering now."

Once again, Tathagata saved him. Torg stopped just outside the surface of the ball. Countless other spheres sped past him, seemingly puzzled by his decision. But Torg's mind was made up. He would feed on the boundless energy of death and return to his body in the faraway pit.

Was this a *wise* use of his time? That was yet to be seen.

Like a bird hovering just above the surface of a stormy sea, Torg positioned his essence at the edge of the mottled cloud. All around him, spheres plunged into the broiling blueness, but Torg ignored them. His focus was too intense for distraction.

He inhaled with great effort. Tendrils of the dark ooze crept slowly up, probing his sphere like cautious fingers. He inhaled again. This time, a great draught of the cloud flowed into him.

Torg swallowed hungrily, feasting on death's power. The blue fire engorged his essence with immeasurable pleasure. His sphere bloated to ten times the size of the others, then one hundred. He grew as large as a planet. Fiery blasts of blue light danced around and through him. Incoming and outgoing spheres avoided his presence. If they crashed into him now, they would be obliterated.

"Use your time wisely, child," the mortal from the distant world had said.

In Torg's awareness, the words were quiet and soft, holding little meaning.

But a small part of him tried to listen.

Wanted to listen.

Knew it had to listen.

Opportunities as precious as this should not be wasted.

Aglow with reckless might, Torg reversed his course. He left the cloud behind and roared back to his flesh.

When he returned to life inside the pit on Mount Asubha, his karma tore through his flesh like a bolt of lightning, and he cried out.

The wizard's cry startled a pair of sentries who stood near the opening of the pit, and they yelped and leapt backward.

No sound had come from the pit in more than a week. Everyone at the prison believed the wizard was dead—except for Mala, who claimed to sense the Death-Knower's essence, no matter how diminished. With the Chain Man stomping around, they were all on edge, including the lookouts. When the sentries heard Torg's shout, they nearly dropped dead.

Dawn was approaching, but in these lonely heights the air was as dark as midnight. Enraged winds swept through the gaps between Asubha and its sister mountains. Few places on Triken were as miserable as this peak. Prisoners rarely survived more than a couple of months. Depression and fear grew until they became unbearable. Suicide was common. More often than not, the dead were found frozen at their posts or in their beds—with hopeless looks in their eyes.

"I've got to tell the warden that the wizard still lives," one of the sentries said, managing to regain some composure. "He'll want to go straight to Mala. Might even have to wake him."

The other sentry, his nostrils clogged with frozen mucus, grabbed his partner by the arm.

"You're not leaving me alone," he barked into the wind. "Having to stand guard next to this accursed pit is bad enough, but if that nasty wizard crawls out of it, I'll soil my pants. Let me go tell the warden. *You* stay and watch. I've suffered enough. It was only twelve days ago that the Asēkha almost killed me."

"Don't be a fool. You think you're scared now? Think how it'll be if the Chain Man hears you've messed things up again. It'll make soiling your pants seem like a nice, hot bath."

"Nothing good's going to happen to me up here, I'll grant you that. But I'm not staying alone, no matter what. If you go, I go . . . Chain Man or no."

A dagger appeared. A speckle of starlight that somehow had weaved its way through the swirling clouds reflected off the deadly blade. The cowardly sentry grasped his stomach, his hands feeling warmth for the first time since arriving at Asubha. Steaming blood gushed out and bubbled on the gray ground.

"Thank you," he said. "I'm ready to die now." He staggered, slipped on a patch of ice, and fell backward, tumbling into the pit's hungry maw. At first his corpse clung to the narrow opening, arms and legs draped outside of the perfectly round hole as if making one last effort to avoid termination. Then his lifeless body folded and disappeared into the black cavity.

"Thank me in hell," the other sentry yelled. Before sprinting into the angry darkness, he paused and whispered, "It can't be any worse than this."

Torg's eyes filled the bottom of the pit with blue light, and for the first time in many days, he could see something other than blackness. The walls of his prison were horrid and lumpy, writhing as if alive.

To his surprise Torg felt, more than heard, a commotion above him. Then he sensed that something was falling down the long shaft of the pit straight at him. Just in time, he raised his hands to shield his head. A hard bundle crashed into his side, striking him in the ribs, and the force of the blow rocked Torg. A man-sized body had fallen roughly upon him. Torg closed his eyes and lay still for a dozen long breaths, trying to regain his composure. Though he was sick and exhausted from the accumulation of his ordeals, his inner power now blazed. But he was also stretched dangerously thin.

The body smelled salty and stale. The man was dead; the fall alone would have killed him. But there was more. Torg felt warm blood and acidic goo dripping onto his naked chest, making it probable the man had been stabbed, probably in the stomach. But why? What was happening up there? Torg could not begin to guess.

The man's arms and legs were propped above his torso and pressed against the sides of the pit, which was only three cubits in diameter. The poison that Invictus had magically imbedded into the stone walls began to dissolve the exposed skin on the corpse's wrists and ankles.

Torg gagged from the stench.

He considered his options. Since achieving *Sammaasamaadhi*, he had become dangerous again. He could use his powers to incinerate the body that lay atop him, but he needed to conserve whatever strength he still possessed. Just getting out of the pit could prove impossible, much less accomplishing anything once he was free. If he were somehow able to climb out, dozens of soldiers, and who knew what else, would be waiting for him. Mala still might be up there, and the prison on Asubha was home to other horrors. It was even possible that Invictus would be part of the welcoming committee.

"One thought at a time," Torg said aloud, and the corpse's head flopped down noisily onto its chest.

"I'm glad you agree. You seem like a nice enough fellow. I could use a friend down here."

Torg opened his eyes and willed their bluish glow to illuminate the bottom of the pit again. Then he studied the man's face. His jaw was thick and square, and there was a recently healed wound on his forehead. His dark-brown eyes were wide open, exhibiting an unsettling combination of horror and relief. If you cleaned him up and dressed him in golden robes, he would look like a cousin of Invictus, or a younger brother. He even had the long yellow hair, though a lot of it already was dissolving.

Despite his bizarre predicament, Torg managed to lie still and breathe slowly. In order to plan an escape he needed to find out what was happening on the surface. Though the corpse's weight continued to press uncomfortably against his side, Torg managed to delve into his own memories in search of an answer to his quandary. Whether directed by fate or otherworldly forces, Torg's mind seized on a single memory.

2

Three times in the early years of his long life, Torg had journeyed through the Gap of Gamana and entered Arupa-Loka, which meant Ghost City *in the ancient tongue. The first two times, he had gone with Asēkhas at his side, and the city's stone buildings had appeared to be deserted. The third time, when he was three hundred years old, he went alone, still curious to see if Arupa-Loka was worthy of its notorious reputation as a haven for demons and other monsters. He was not disappointed. The inhabitants of the* Ghost City *opened their doors.*

For a long stretch of time during the deep darkness of a moonless night, Torg had stood transfixed on the center median of a street in the heart of the city. Now he could see wicked faces peering from windows and doorways. A collective hatred beat upon his mind. Torg wondered what might happen if they all attacked him at once. But he was not overly concerned. None in the Ghost City—*save the demon Vedana*—*would dare to stand alone against him. And Torg was certain that Vedana was not present. If she were there, he would have sensed her strength.*

A ghost-child appeared in front of him. If she had been alive, Torg would have guessed her to be about ten years old. She smiled at him, her mouth curling upward at its corners. The beauty of her face stunned Torg. She beckoned him to follow.

In the cold of midwinter, they wandered along many winding roads. Some areas were so dark that Torg could see nothing but the slight sway of the ghost-child's petite dress, which glowed like phosphorous in a black sea. Obhasa also glowed, as if in reaction to her power.

Finally she led him to the outskirts of the city, where they came upon a modest house of gray stone. The ghost-child stepped inside the front door. Torg had to bend over to clear the entryway. Demonic torchlight lit the interior. Sitting in a decrepit chair facing the door was the long-decomposed corpse of what had once been a tall man.

"He has a story to tell you," the girl said, her voice as sweet as innocence.

"I'd prefer to hear your story," Torg said.

"They are the same."

Torg looked at the skeleton's face, then turned back to the girl. "I would listen to his story, but he seems incapable of telling it."

The ghost giggled. She walked over to Torg and waggled her finger. She wanted to whisper something in his ear. He bent down. "The sirens can make him speak," *she said, ever so softly.* "I *know* where they hide. I *know* when *to listen."*

"And what do you hear?" *Torg said.*

"The word . . . the magic word."

"What is the magic word?"

More giggles. The room seemed to wobble. "You have to *hear* it before you can say it."

"I don't understand."

She reached for him. Her tiny hand barely filled his palm, but it burned like ice. "Come with me," *she said.*

The torchlight blinked out, and Torg found himself in utter darkness. For the first time in his long existence, he entered the Realm of the Undead. Never before had he seen such unbroken blackness. The souls of the undead were trapped between life and death, and it was horrid and hopeless. He sagged to his knees.

But the girl was there to guide him. "Do you hear them?"

As Torg knew from Sammaasamaadhi, *the lone sensation of death was the ability to see. But he now discovered that the lone sensation of undeath was the ability to hear.*

Female voices were chanting. "Yakkkkha. Yakkkkha. Yakkkkha."

"I hear them," *Torg said.* "But tell me what it is you need of me. You know something I do not."

Suddenly there was a flash, and they again stood in the dusty room lit by magical torchlight. The girl pointed at the skeleton. "His spirit is gone, but his bones remember. Ask him to speak."

"I don't know how."

"Say the magic word."

In a remote corner of his mind, Torg could still hear the chanting. "Yakkkkha," *he said, though the word sounded like garble in the Realm of Life.*

Torg was surprised to see the skeleton begin to move. Its bones flailed, and its head lolled from side to side.

"I told them we shouldn't attempt the pass."

"Who are you?" *Torg said.*

"Who am I?" *the skeleton said.* "I am no longer. I am gone."

"Who were you?"

"I was her father."

"Ask him what happened," *the little ghost said to Torg.*

The skeleton stood, clicking and clacking, and it tilted its skull toward the girl. "Peta? Is that you?"

"*Yes, father,*" *she said.* "*But please . . . tell this man what happened. I'm afraid she will make him leave before he can help me.*"

"*I won't leave,*" *Torg said.* "*There is nothing here that can make me go anywhere.*" *He walked to the skeleton and looked down at its hollow face.* "*Her name is Peta? And what is yours?*"

"*I do not remember. I am no longer. I am gone.*"

"*Your daughter needs me. To help her, I need you. What can you tell me?*"

"*I told them we should go south,*" *it said.*

"*His bones remember,*" *Peta interrupted.* "*Please ask him to speak.*"

Torg nodded. "*I think I'm beginning to understand.*"

The skeleton's karmic energy was gone, moved on to countless other existences. But its bones remembered *like a painting that had retained the vision of the artist.*

"*What happened in the pass?*" *Torg said to the skeleton.*

"*They came for her.*"

"*Who?*"

"*The demons. They took Peta. And they took me. But they killed her mother and all the rest. It was Peta they wanted. They only took me along to keep her calm.*"

"*Why did they want Peta?*"

The little ghost was jumping up and down.

"*Because she is special,*" *the skeleton said.*

"*Special?*" *Torg said.* "*How so?*"

"*She is blind.*"

Torg was confused, but he sensed he was on the verge of a breakthrough. "*Why did the demons believe her blindness was special?*"

"*Yes! Yes!*" *Peta said, wiggling like a worm.*

"*Because she could* hear," *the skeleton said.*

Torg thought back to his brief visit to the Realm of the Undead. In that dreadful place he had been blind—just like Peta. But at least he had been able to hear. In life, Peta's blindness must have enhanced her senses, including her hearing. Was it enhanced among the undead, as well?

"*Where is Peta's body?*" *Torg said.*

The little girl screamed with delight. "*Yes! Yes! Tell him. Tell him!*" *she said to her dead father.*

But the skeleton's response made no sense. "*Her body is forgotten.*"

"*I don't understand,*" *Torg said.*

"*Neither do I,*" *the skeleton said.*

Torg turned to Peta. Fluorescent tears now lined her cheeks. "*Can you tell me anything? He says your body is forgotten. What does that mean?*"

"*Ask him to speak.*"

"I have asked him to speak. But I have no more questions. Why can't you tell me where your body is? And tell me also why you want me to find it."

"He knows. Ask him."

Torg sighed. He walked to the side of the room, leaned against the wall, and slid down to his rump. The skeleton also attempted to sigh. Dust puffed from where its nostrils used to be. Then it stepped back and flopped down in its chair, bones cracking and snapping.

Peta wailed. "He knows . . . he knows . . ."

"Peta?" the skeleton said. "Is that you?"

"Oh, shut up!" she said.

"Yes," the skeleton said. It sounded sad.

Torg stood up, unsure of what to do next. He leaned against the doorway and looked out at the street. They were not alone. Hundreds of the undead stood nearby, still as stones, staring at him but not daring to approach.

Torg shouted at them. "Where is her body? Tell me."

One by one they fled from his wrath. The street was empty again.

"Her body is forgotten," the skeleton said.

Suddenly Peta's face grew bright. She had thought of something that renewed her hope. "Tell him to walk," she said, her head held proud.

Torg looked at the skeleton. "Stand up."

The skeleton regained its feet, but not without a price. Its left arm fell off at the elbow.

"Now walk to where Peta's body is hidden," Torg said.

"Yes," the skeleton said, and it tottered toward the doorway, bumping hard into the stone frame, crunching several ribs and busting a knee. Seemingly undeterred, it staggered into the street and moved awkwardly along the sidewalk. Torg followed. Peta pranced after them, bursting with merriment.

"Tell him to walk," she said, over and over.

The skeleton made poor progress, banging into anything in its path. Large chunks of bone broke off and clattered on the stone roadways. Torg feared that Peta's father would fall apart before they could reach their destination.

"Are we close?" Torg asked, his breath smoking in the frozen air.

"I do not remember. I am no longer. I am gone." But it continued its slow march.

They came at last to a strange tower that stood alone in a cobbled courtyard. Though the tower was just ten cubits in diameter, it was at least fifty cubits tall. An elaborate bas-relief wound upward from its base, and near its pinnacle was a small window where an eerie light shone from inside.

The skeleton had had enough. It collapsed into pieces and said no more.

"Goodbye, father," Peta said, without apparent sorrow.

There was a single door at the base of the tower. Torg pushed against it, but found that it was barred. He raised his staff and smote the ancient wood, which splintered and gave way. Then he stepped inside.

The interior of the tower was dark. He willed Obhasa to glow, providing enough light for him to view a steep, spiraling stairwell. He started up. Peta did not follow.

"Will you not come?" Torg said.

Peta bowed her head. It was obvious that something disturbed her.

As Torg stared at the ghost-child, he saw movement behind her. The undead had returned. Thousands were in the courtyard, watching but not approaching. This time he disregarded them. Whatever was at the top of the tower now consumed his attention. He strode up the slippery stairs.

At the top was another locked door. It was no more capable of stopping him than the first. He blasted through it and entered the chamber. It was small with a low ceiling, and it glowed with a sepulchral light.

Peta lay on a stone pallet in the center of the room, her body untouched by the passing of time. If it weren't for the stillness of her chest, Torg would have believed she was sleeping. She wore the same dress as her ghostly form, and her face was just as beautiful. If she had been allowed to grow to womanhood, she would have been splendid.

Torg hunched over and approached the pallet, which barely came to his knees. He looked down at her. A tiny gold amulet lay on her chest, and it shimmered and purred. Torg could sense it was a talisman of great power, perhaps created by some long-ago demon or sorcerer to preserve flesh. Peta's body was unmarred, but Torg somehow knew that the little girl had lain in the tower for thousands of years.

He took the amulet in his right hand. Its thin chain snapped off her neck. Instantly Peta sat up and opened her eyes, which were pure white, without iris or pupil. She screamed, and her body flailed. For the briefest of moments, she again was alive.

Then her flesh began to curl, hiss and disintegrate. The little girl writhed in unimaginable agony.

"Kill me," she screamed. "Hurry! Pleeeeaaassseeeee . . ."

Tears filled Torg's eyes. He could not bear to harm her, but neither could he leave her like this. He closed his left hand around her tiny throat and broke her neck with the slightest shift of his thick fingers.

Peta stopped moving. Silently her flesh withered, and her bones turned to dust. Her body was gone. When Torg left the tower, the ghost-child was gone too. He wept.

Afterward he departed Arupa-Loka. The undead followed him to the outer boundary of the city and watched as he slipped into the wilderness. For a month Torg wandered in bitter cold. North of the Gap of Gamana, the Mahaggata Range split into the shape of a Y. Torg headed northwest. In this far realm, the mountains were a jagged jumble of rock and ice. Torg had never felt so lonely.

Though he studied the amulet, he could unravel none of its mysteries. He decided to destroy it, so that it would never again perform such a heinous deed. But the amulet's power was too great. He could not even scratch its smooth surface. Finally he chose to hide it.

On the peak of Catu, the northernmost mountain on all of Triken, Torg discovered a hidden cave. He crawled deep inside on hands and knees and covered the amulet with a shaving of granite. It was a relief to leave it behind.

Soon after he left the cave he witnessed a strange occurrence. A shadow had crept across the sun, consuming it bit by bit until the day became as dark as night. Torg had stood and watched in amazement. Two weeks later, as he'd journeyed back to Anna, the same thing had happened to the full moon.

3

With startling suddenness Torg's thoughts returned to the present moment. He was back on Mount Asubha, trapped at the bottom of the pit, desperate to find a way out, and eager to rid himself of the corpse that had fallen on top of him. He looked the dead sentry in the eyes. He needed to have a little talk.

During Torg's imprisonment in the pit, all of his teeth had fallen out, so it was difficult to enunciate the syllables he had learned from his visit with Peta to the Realm of the Undead.

But it would take more than that to cause him to falter.

"*Yakkkkha*," he said.

The dead man's eyes sprang open. "You're not leaving me alone. I'll soil my pants."

"You're *not* alone," Torg said, his speech slowly improving as he grew more used to talking without teeth. "And I'm sorry to say that you've already soiled your pants. But I need to ask you some questions."

"Who am I?" it said.

"You are who you were . . . but that doesn't matter. I need to ask you what you know."

"I am no longer. I am gone. I will never kiss her."

"Kiss her? Who?"

"I don't remember."

"Never mind," Torg said. "Just listen to me and answer my questions."

"Let *me* go to the warden. *You* stay here and watch."

"Why do you want to go to the warden?"

"That nasty wizard is making noises again. He's crawling out of the pit."

I must have shouted when I returned from death, Torg thought. It was probable that others had already been alerted.

"Was anyone else with you when you heard the 'nasty wizard' make noises?"

"Yes. And the bastard stuck me."

"Where did he go?"

"I didn't see."

"Who else is up there?"

"Up there?"

Torg realized the man must have been dead before he fell into the pit. The memory that remained in his corpse still thought it was on the surface. But at least he was newly deceased. His recollections would be strong.

"Who else is near the pit?"

"No one. There was just the two of us."

"Is Mala somewhere close?"

"The Chain Man? Yes. And he's fearsome, I tell you. I soiled my pants around him more than once."

"And Invictus, the sorcerer? Is he nearby?"

"No. I heard the warden talk about him, but I've never seen him. They say even the Chain Man is afraid of Invictus. But I don't believe it. How could Mala be scared of anything?"

"Is there any way to escape the prison?"

"Escape? Ha! If there were, don't you think I would have done it?"

"What if you *had* to try? Where would you go?"

"There is nowhere to go. All the walls are watched. More than just sentries are on guard. And even though he's small, the warden is almost as dreadful as the Chain Man. It's hopeless. There is nowhere to go."

Torg sighed. The corpse had told him little, other than to warn him that it was likely the pit would be guarded if he were somehow able to climb out. Torg struggled to his knees and, with great difficulty, stood up. In order to fit within the pit's cramped confines, he had to lift the dead body up with him. He now stood almost face to face with the corpse, though Torg was more than a span taller. The claustrophobia was intense, but Torg resisted its contagious effects.

"I ask you again: If you had to *try* to escape, where would you go?"

"The only place would be over the cliff," the corpse said. "There is no wall there. But if you didn't slip and fall into the abyss, then the birds or the spider would get you. I'd rather fall."

"Where is the cliff? Is it near the pit?"

"Yes . . . too near."

Now at least, Torg had something to work with. He released the dead body. As it collapsed to its knees, its head again flopped against its chest.

"Good luck in your next existence," Torg whispered. "May you be healthy, happy and peaceful. After what you've been through, you've earned it."

The corpse began to sizzle. The acids and poisons in the walls of the pit had eaten through the uniform and now were working on the flesh. Within a short time, the body dissolved into bloody slush before finally vaporizing and vanishing. The smell was terrible. Torg might have vomited, but he had not eaten or drunk for almost a month. His stomach was as empty as a dragon's heart.

Torg's tissues were far more durable than the corpse's. Perhaps no living creature could have resisted the pit as long as he. All the same, touching the walls was painful, even to him.

At least the floor of the pit was ordinary rock. A prisoner could lie at its bottom and not immediately perish. Invictus intended to extend the suffering a bit. In Torg's case, it had worked even better than planned.

He ran his hand along his body. His skin, once tanned and flawless, now felt mottled and hairless; and in addition to his teeth, his fingernails and toenails also had fallen out. He could only imagine how hideous he must look. Probably even worse than Mala.

Torg didn't believe he could escape the prison. His return from *Sammaasamaadhi* had recharged his body, but he still was a reduced version of his former self. If Mala were waiting for him on the surface, Torg knew he could not defeat him. If Invictus were there, Torg would be even more helpless. He clung to one slight hope: If he could climb out of the pit and somehow get over the side of the cliff, he might catch them off guard. Torg had visited the snow giants more than once in his long life, and they had taught him how to climb and descend difficult cliffs without ropes or other devices.

The pit was three cubits in diameter. Torg was four and a half cubits tall. He flattened his bare shoulder blades against the spongy wall. Acids flared. Poisons seeped down his spine and buttocks. The toxins chewed on his skin like a million voracious mouths. He cried out. The pain was abominable, but his flesh did not turn to slush; it was too great, even for the might of this malignancy.

Torg pressed one bare foot against the side of the pit. The disturbance caused the noxious surface to splutter. He jammed his other foot against the wall. Golden flames flared angrily. The effort paid off—his quivering body was suspended a cubit above the floor. For the first time in weeks he was not at the deepest depth of hell.

Torg flattened his hands against the sides of the pit. His fingers sank into the wall, which had the same texture as a gooey mass of worms. The large muscles of his back, shoulders, and thighs pulsated, and his biceps and forearms shivered. Where the acids and poisons oozed onto his flesh, golden flames erupted. Torg moaned. He had climbed only one cubit.

The pit was two hundred cubits deep.

He slid his shoulders up another cubit, dragged one foot upward, and then the other. Now he was two cubits above the floor, his knees bent, his buttocks facing downward. The last surviving hair on his body, a single black curl on his left big toe, burst into flame and disappeared in a tiny puff of smoke.

Three cubits. Five. Ten. Frustration caused Torg to shriek. He wriggled like a tortoise flipped onto its back.

Just one hundred and ninety cubits to go.

Torg sighed. It was obvious that his physical strength would not suffice. Instead he needed his magic. Though his body was drained, he still was internally aflame. *Death Energy* roared through his flesh.

The power inside Torg obeyed his will like a loving servant. His ability to wield it had been refined over many centuries. He could spray it like a rainstorm. Or launch it like a bolt of lightning. He could heal with it. Or kill. He could build with it. Or destroy. And now he would use the power within him to save his own life.

Torg enveloped his body in death's broiling might. The golden flames flickered out; the acids and poisons retreated. Blue flames burst from his back, resembling the fiery tail of a comet. He began to rise, slowly at first, but ever quickening.

Ten more cubits.

Fifty.

One hundred.

Far above, Torg saw a trickle of radiance, and he roared in delight. For a moment it didn't matter what happened once he reached the surface. Escaping the pit was his only concern.

Like lava racing upward through a fracture in bedrock, Torg surged toward the surface. When his body catapulted from the hideous hole, all of Asubha seemed to tremble. The pit—as if ashamed of its failure to contain him—exploded.

Then it collapsed upon itself and was no more.

Torg soared into the air, somersaulted, and fell a long, long way as if in slow motion.

He struck hard stone and lay still.

A short time later, he shook his head and struggled to his knees. A storm raged all about him, a combination of wicked winds and snow-choked air. Through a brief gap in the clouds, he caught a glimpse of the moon, which was waning crescent in the midpoint of the sky. As a desert dweller, Torg was well-acquainted with the phases of the moon. Now he truly comprehended the duration of his confinement. He had been in the pit more than three weeks.

Torg shook his head and struggled to his knees. Dawn approached, and with it streaks of jagged light. He scanned his surroundings. He felt as if he were witnessing the end of the world.

Asubha rumbled. Torg's emergence from the pit had awakened the mountain's inner violence. The stone split and shattered, as if crunched by the hand of a god. As the ground beneath him buckled, he was thrown against a low stone wall. He grasped it and managed to stand, looking eastward into the first glow of the rising sun.

Despite the tumult, Torg could make out the silhouettes of several dozen guards teetering at the edge of a cliff. One of them started to fall, but even before he disappeared from Torg's view, a condor swept out of the sky and seized the guard in midair. Then it soared over his head, with the screaming victim in its huge beak.

Torg recalled the words of the dead sentry; *the only place was over the cliff. There is no wall there. But if you didn't slip and fall into the abyss, then the birds or the spider would get you.*

Torg had seen one of the birds. Would he also encounter the "spider" before much longer?

A dreadful voice boomed through the hysteria. Instantly Torg recognized it, for he had spent more than six weeks learning to hate it. Mala stood in the center of the prison, waving his arms and bellowing at anyone within range.

"Stay away from the cliff, you stupid donkeys. Come to me!"

Another massive quake shook the prison. Buildings shuddered and began to crumble. Torg was tossed to-and-fro. He had expended almost all his remaining strength during his escape from the pit, but he wasn't ready to give up. Now, with the mountain threatening to explode around him, he crawled shakily toward the cliff.

It was his last chance.

The Chain Man had not yet seen Torg, but a much smaller creature, less than a third Mala's height, ran toward him, waving its stubby arms.

"Here! Here!" it said. "Don't you see him? The wizard is free. *HERE!*"

Torg watched the creature approach. He recognized it as an ancient enemy. He had defeated its father's army in a great war many centuries before.

"A Stone-Eater." Torg sighed. "And I am already weary."

Peak of Despair

1

"Here! Here!" Gulah said. "The wizard is free. *HERE!*"

Another immense reverberation jolted Asubha, almost knocking the Stone-Eater off his feet. After regaining his balance, he saw Torg squirming toward the edge of the cliff. Somehow the Death-Knower knew where to find the quickest escape route, which puzzled Gulah but also secretly delighted him. The mountain did not blow itself up every day. This opportunity would never come again. Now he just needed to find a way to keep Torg alive long enough to meet the doom he had devised for his ancient enemy.

Asubha continued to rock and sway, yet Mala—the wretched bastard!—was lumbering toward Torg with surprising quickness. None of the pathetic sentries could stop the Death-Knower, even in his weakened state. But the Chain Man was more than capable of ruining Gulah's vengeful plans.

Gulah had to do something fast, while not looking too suspicious, so he stepped in front of Mala and clumsily fell against his stocky legs. Though he was only a third Mala's size, he still was able to knock him sideways. The Chain Man slipped and crashed against the stone floor, cursing wildly. When he tried to stand, Gulah tripped him again.

"You puny fool. You pathetic *ass*," Mala said. "If you can't help, at least get out of my way."

From the raging darkness Gulah watched as a wild Sampati swooped down and attempted to grasp the Chain Man in its talons. In an extraordinary feat of strength, Mala grabbed one of its clawed feet and flipped the beast over his back. It struck the stone floor and blew apart. Feathers, scales, flesh and bone splattered in all directions, and a steaming chunk of gore struck Gulah in the face. When he cleared his eyes, his worst fears were realized. The Chain Man was closing in on the wizard, who was just a stride or two from the edge of the cliff. Would Mala catch him at the last moment?

Perhaps not. A slab of granite tore itself from the mountaintop, rising between Torg and Mala like a tidal wave. The stone screamed, as if in pain. It towered above Mala, teetered momentarily, and then fell. The Chain Man scrambled backward, barely avoiding the shattering collapse. When the debris cleared, Mala remained standing, waving his arms. But Torg was gone.

The Death-Knower had made it over the cliff.

Gulah smiled, regained his footing and worked his way through the tempest to a secret exit, leaving Mala and the doomed prison on the peak of Asubha behind forever. Gulah knew the ways better than any other. Even a cave troll could not have kept up with him.

He beamed.

So much had gone right. If fate allowed, he would encounter the wizard one final time. And when he did, he would rip Torg's heart from his chest and devour it raw to avenge the long-ago murder of Slag, his beloved father.

Whom he missed . . .

. . . so very desperately.

The mountain had become a symbol of impermanence, tearing itself apart like a man ripping off his own head.

Torg crept to the edge and peered over the side. The icy stone was as slippery as a demon's tongue, and he couldn't judge the depth of the abyss. The precipice dove downward into a morass of tornadic winds, fist-sized hail, and jagged lightning. In the last breath of darkness before the arrival of dawn, he could see less than a stone's throw. He believed that if he fell, he would not strike bottom for a long time.

Torg could sense the Stone-Eater behind him, closing fast. He knew the beast well, but it had been many centuries since their last encounter. Besides, Torg had many enemies, and right now it was Mala who was his main concern. If the Chain Man caught him in his current state, Torg would be doomed.

Behind him came a whining roar, and the rooftop of the mountain vomited a titanic slab of granite. Torg was cast over the edge of the cliff and would have fallen to his death had he not thrust out his right hand and caught a tiny lip of stone with his fingers. Precariously he hung there by one hand before finally grasping hold with his other.

The mountain trembled again. Torg searched for footing with his bare toes, but the cliff wall was too smooth and slippery. He had hoped his rock-climbing skills would be sufficient to get him down, but he now feared he could not go much farther without falling, especially in such gusty winds and poor visibility.

The slab of stone above him collapsed, shattering ferociously. A disgusting barrage of screams and curses from Mala soon followed.

With his face pressed against the wall, Torg began to move horizontally along the cliff's edge, hand by hand, hoping to find some sort of foothold. As if his predicament weren't bad enough, a wild Sampati chose that moment to emerge from the broiling darkness and hover behind him, reaching out with its talons. Forced to call on his draining energy, Torg turned and sent a blue flame from his eyes toward the creature, striking its leg. Squawking in pain, it swerved away from the cliff. Half a dozen wild condors—a third of the Sampati's size but still very dangerous—sensed the crossbreed's distress and attacked, tearing at feather and scale.

Above the confusion rose Mala's obnoxious voice.

"Help me find the Death-Knower, you slimy worms. Where is Gulah? If the coward has deserted, I'll squash his little head."

Doing his best to ignore Mala's ranting, Torg continued to creep along the wall. His arms ached, and his bare toes could not find the slightest indentation. If he lost his grip, he would fall a thousand fathoms.

Dawn continued to push against the darkness in an apparent attempt to overthrow the night. But Torg held little hope that visibility would improve with the arrival of daylight. The storm was too intense.

Before hope faded entirely, Torg discovered a tiny fissure just large enough to contain the big toe of his left foot. The farther he moved to his left, the wider the crack became. Soon, both his feet were rooted in the rock, and he was able to hold on with only his right hand while he felt along the wall with his left.

At waist level, he discovered a knob of stone and gripped it with his left hand, which freed his right. Then he thrust out his buttocks and squatted. It was a precarious position, but at least it was a start.

The fissure descended, and he slid his left foot a few inches along the crack, followed by his right. Then he released the knob with his left hand and grasped it with his right. This enabled him to feel along the wall with his left hand, and he finally was able to grab a protruding flake and use it as leverage to traverse several more inches along the face of the cliff. Now his head was five cubits below the edge. But his progress was agonizingly slow. And he was so weak. If the mountain shook again, he probably would fall.

"There you are, you ugly rat!" Mala yelled from above. "Where are you *going?*"

The Chain Man peered over the edge. His eyes glowed red, and not even the surging winds could disperse the stink of his breath.

A bolt of lightning crashed nearby, momentarily illuminating the night.

"Look at you," said Mala, laughing in the manner Torg had grown to despise. "You're as ugly as a toothless monkey. How did you get down there without falling? *Everyone* falls. Unless the spider gets them."

Torg hung on five cubits below the edge of the cliff, but Mala's arms were at least six cubits long. The Chain Man dropped to his chest and reached down, trying to grab Torg by the scruff of his neck. With his free hand Torg swatted Mala's arm, knocking it away. The Chain Man shouted in frustration and lunged for him again.

Torg didn't have much strength left, but he managed to conjure a weak blast of blue fire. It leapt from his eyes and singed Mala's face, but it lacked the potency to do much damage. Still, the Chain Man snarled and drew away.

Suddenly Torg's left foot was yanked from the fissure. Something huge and powerful ensnared his ankle. He looked down and saw a dreadful black shape clinging to the sheer wall beneath him. He scrambled for any kind of hold, but he was torn free of the rock. As he fell he heard Mala's desperate shrieks: "No . . . no . . . *no*! He is not for *you!*"

Whatever grasped Torg's ankle had no problem negotiating the precipice. It descended the wall with an agility that far surpassed the snow giants or any other great climbers. It dragged Torg a long distance in just a few moments, his body slamming against the lumpy stone as they descended.

Torg tried desperately to free his ankle, but the black beast drew him into a hole in the side of the cliff. His head banged against the cold stone.

The rigidity of the stone gave way to spongy silk, softer but more insidious. The silk clung to the surfaces of the tunnel. Torg felt fresh threads fall upon him in gobs, encasing first his arms and then his legs. He was trapped in putrid darkness and could not move.

The huge creature hovered by his feet, but then squeezed past him toward the opening of the hole. Torg felt the disgusting folds of its thorny hide press against his face. His attacker stopped at the breach and paused there, as if guarding a newly won prize.

Torg strained against the silk. The threads were dreadfully strong, and his strength was fading beyond resistance. *Death Energy* kept him alive, but his ordeal in the pit had weakened him too much. All he could do was lie there, miserable and hopeless. *So, this is how it ends. As breakfast for a spider?* It was absurd enough to make him laugh.

At the opening of its lair, the beast shuffled angrily. Something passed close by—probably one of the wild condors—and the spider took a swipe at it. Torg watched with disinterest. He made one final attempt to break free and failed. Now there was nothing more he could do. He was defeated. Unconsciousness crept ever closer, like a hungry predator. But he could not allow darkness to overcome him.

Torg sensed movement even deeper in the hole. Then he heard a moaning sound. The intricate assemblage of silk trembled in response. Torg could not see, but he strained to figure out what lay near.

Someone else was trapped with him—one of Asubha's prisoners or sentries? The poor fool sounded even worse than Torg felt. What hell was this? It was not as bad as the pit. But it was close.

The moaning intensified.

And then the spider returned. Was it ready to eat?

Torg waited. And listened.

2

The spider advanced until its horrific mouth drew within a finger-length of Torg's face and neck, the only parts of his body not encased by silk threads. A pair of curved fangs, each as long as one of his arms, snapped upon his upper torso, easily piercing the silk but failing to puncture his flesh. Torg's body remained impenetrable, even in his crippled state.

The spider hissed and chomped on him again—with the same result. It crept backward several steps, then dove forward and drove the poisoned fangs against him. Even then, the fangs and their toxins were ineffective.

"Begone, foul beast," Torg muttered. "I am not for the likes of you."

But there still was a lisp in his speech, and his words felt impotent.

And then to his horror, something responded—from deeper in the hole. "My king, have you come to rescue me?"

Instantly the spider reacted, bounding over Torg in the direction of the voice. He heard a scream and recognized his fellow prisoner. Sōbhana. But how did she come to be here? Confusion and sorrow made him nauseous.

She screamed again.

Torg could not bear it and fought to escape his silk prison. His panicked anger flooded through him, and his magic became wildly dangerous. Blue flame erupted from every pore in an orgasm of anguish. The silk threads caught fire like dry grass, turning the passageway into a conflagration. The spider exited the hole in a panic.

Torg was free of his bonds, but the flames roared on. With every shred of his remaining strength he willed the blaze to diminish, but it still sizzled in pockets throughout the tunnel. When most of the smoke cleared, enough light remained from the glowing embers to provide visibility.

Sōbhana lay close by, her naked body mutilated. Torg's flames had burned off her hair and scorched her skin, but it was obvious that worse damage already had occurred before his fiery outburst. Large portions of her ears were gone, disintegrated by the spider's persistent attempts to feed, and her right arm and right leg displayed gruesome patches of exposed bone. Her right shoulder was mangled and diseased. The warrior looked like a flesh-and-blood body slowly transforming into a skeleton. How long had she been here? A day? A week? Longer?

Torg cried out. Anger and sorrow grasped his heart and squeezed. Tears gushed from his eyes. He crawled over to her and cradled her in his arms. He had never experienced such bitterness.

Sōbhana looked at him, and her eyes widened. "I feared how I might look to you, if you ever found me. But you have not fared much better, my lord." She managed a tattered giggle.

Torg was mortified. "Sōbhana. Brave one . . . loyal one. How came you here?"

"I could never forsake my king," she said weakly. "You are my life." Then she took a long breath and sighed. "I have never told you—or anyone—but there is no reason to hide my feelings any longer. I love you, *Torgon*. I always have and always will. I would have made you an excellent wife."

Torg's tears drenched her face and dripped into her mouth. Though she was disfigured, he recognized her true beauty for the first time. Then he hugged her so hard she moaned.

Torg heard a noise near the opening of the hole. In his despair he had forgotten the spider. It stood close by, glaring at them, torn between fear and desire.

"Her name is Dukkhatu," Sōbhana said. "She is almost as ancient as Bhayatupa. The dragon told me so."

"Bhayatupa? What do you mean . . ."

Sōbhana coughed. Greasy blood spewed from her mouth. She grimaced, struggling to breathe. An ordinary creature would have been long dead. And yet Sōbhana, with the strength of an Asēkha, had endured this torture for how long? Torg couldn't bear to even think about it.

"My life is over," she said. "My body will soon perish." More coughing. "We both . . . know what must be done."

"No, Sōbhana. You will not perish. I will carry you down the side of the mountain. We will return to Anna together."

"And I will become your wife?" she said. Despite her horrific appearance, her smile was beautiful. In the final moments of her life, Torg fell in love with her. But if they had ever become husband and wife, they would have been forced to live in celibacy, which would have been a greater torment than either could have borne—though she knew this naught.

"Yes, my love. You will become my wife, if you so desire."

She coughed some more, the pain gnawing greedily on the remains of her consciousness. Still she managed to smile again, and the tenderness in her ravaged expression brought fresh tears to his eyes.

"When Mala took you, I followed despite your orders," she said. "You vowed to kill any who pursued. Yet I still believed I would somehow rescue you. Now I see how both will occur. We must perform *Sivathika*. Nothing else remains."

Sivathika had existed among the Tugars from the beginnings of their history, though it remained a secret ritual, unknown to outsiders. When a desert warrior was mortally wounded in battle, another Tugar would approach and—if granted permission—press his or her mouth against the other's. The dying warrior then breathed what remained of his or her *Life Essence* into the survivor's lungs, where it was absorbed into the blood like psychic nourishment. The survivor became physically stronger and even possessed a dual personality for a short time afterward. It was a rare and high honor to give or receive *Sivathika*.

"Kiss me, my love," Sōbhana said. "Do not deny me."

The spider crept closer.

"Do it now, before it's too late," she said, her words barely recognizable. "I will be gone from this body, regardless. It will be my privilege to join your spirit. In that way I will become more than a wife; I will become a part of you."

"No . . . *no* . . . I'm not ready. Your loss will cost too much. I would rather die here alongside you."

"Do not dishonor me with such worthless speech," she rasped, each word growing weaker. "Kiss me, my love . . . and then avenge me. A weapon is near that can destroy Dukkhatu. When I become a part of you, you will know where to find it."

Sōbhana reached up and wrapped her left arm around his neck, pressing her mouth against his lips. For a few moments they kissed like lovers. But Torg felt her body fail. At the last instant before her death, she blew her hot essence into his mouth. He inhaled with equal strength.

The Torgon and Asēkha-Sōbhana became one.

At that moment she learned the truth about Torg's perplexing celibacy. He had spent almost his entire existence learning how to bridle the savage might of *Death Energy*. For the most part he had succeeded, except in one crucial area—sex. When he achieved orgasm he lost control of his power. Nine centuries before, on the night after he had successfully returned from his very first *Death Visit*, Torg had made love to a Tugarian woman. During his climax he had incinerated the woman and the tent in which they lay, turning the sand beneath them to glass.

Torg was devastated, and he hastily arranged an assembly of Vasi masters to confess his crime. But as far as the Tugar elders knew, nothing like this had ever happened to any previous Death-Knower. Because there was no forewarning, Torg was vindicated. But he never forgave himself. Though Torg's people—none of whom were as long-lived as he—had lost most knowledge of the incident, his guilt continued to haunt him.

Torg now shared his guilt with Sōbhana.

And he felt it dissolve.

As a Death-Knower, Torg believed that nothing in life compared to the wonder of death. All other experiences paled. In his mind the fear of death was a waste of energy. Why dread something so magnificent and so inevitable?

But when Sōbhana's psychic force entered his lungs and flowed into his blood, Torg was as tantalized and amazed as he had been during any *Death Visit*. A symphony of thoughts, emotions, and memories set his senses ablaze. The sizzling bundle of karmic energy once known as Sōbhana surged into every cell of his being, sharing residence with his mind and body.

When he opened his eyes, Sōbhana's flesh was dead, but her karma was very much alive. He gently laid her carcass upon the floor of the spider's lair and then sat up to gather his wits. She already was conversing with him internally, disappointed to discover he had thought so little of her—at least in terms of her potential as a mate.

"I'm sorry, my beloved," she said, within his mind. "But even without sex, I would have been a good wife. Just sharing ordinary life with you would have been enough."

"I did not perceive your intentions," he said. "You seemed so young. And I felt so old. But as you now know, I have long admired you for other reasons."

"I know much that I did not know before. Such *wonder*. I can only hope to carry some of this wisdom to my next existence. If so, I will perform miracles."

"That, you have already done. I will see to it that the Tugars rank you among the greats."

"If you survive. There is still the matter of the spider," Sōbhana said. "She is tensed and prepared for another attack. Now that we are joined, you know how to kill her."

The Silver Sword lay a short distance from Torg (and Sōbhana). Apparently, the spider had chosen to hide it, rather than discard it. But Torg's conflagration had revealed its location.

Torg (and Sōbhana) reached for the sword, causing Dukkhatu to hiss and retreat. Torg (and Sōbhana) grasped the Silver Sword in his right hand. Instantly he recognized aspects of it that Sōbhana had not—and now, she saw the sword through his perception and was amazed. It was not made of silver or any metal native to Triken. Instead, it had been forged in some ancient time using otherworldly ores. In and of itself the Silver Sword was lifeless; unlike Torg's ivory staff, it harbored no internal magic. But nothing that it struck could withstand it. Mala had survived Sōbhana's glancing blow only because it had not been a direct hit.

When Torg rose to his knees in the tunnel, his desire for vengeance melded with the Asēkha's. Though still physically drained, Torg was as dangerous at that moment as he had ever been. His sudden burst of strength wouldn't last forever—Sōbhana's essence would fade, and Torg's torture-induced exhaustion would return—but for the time being, he, she and the sword were a lethal combination.

The passageway was tall enough for Torg to stand upright, but it was not wide enough for Dukkhatu to fully extend her legs. Inside the hole, she probably was far less mobile than outside on the cliff wall. Her best chance to kill her prey would come in the vertiginous open.

"You are hideous," Torg said to Dukkhatu. "You have destroyed much that is of value. But your reign of terror has come to an end. Prepare to meet your doom."

The last five words were spoken with the woman's voice and facial expressions, which puzzled the spider. The great beast froze—paralyzed by uncertainty—as the larger man moved toward her. Dukkhatu's compulsion to rend and devour was immense, but her dismay continued to expand. First the prey had unleashed a deadly fire in her lair, and now it wielded the strange weapon. Its eyes held no fear, but they burned with anger. Should she flee? The thought ate at her evil mind like noxious poison.

The man moved faster than she expected. Dukkhatu was forced to turn and run, but not before she felt the tip of the sword cut through several spans of her abdomen above her spinnerets. She leapt through the hole and dropped at least fifty cubits before catching hold of the craggy wall. When she looked upward she saw a blurry shape moving at the opening of her lair. The deadly thing was searching for her. She was enraged—and terrified. Her fangs clattered. Her wound dripped black blood. It was little more than a scratch, but it burned.

Never in her long life had Dukkhatu been so ably thwarted. And now this had happened *twice* in just a short time. The other food had resisted her as well. The meat of the first one was so tough she had had to work days and days just to drink a few drops. And this second one was even more difficult. She could not so much as scratch it.

Dukkhatu desired food, but now revenge had become her greater hunger. The female was dead—as far as Dukkhatu could tell—but the male still lived, and his very presence haunted her. She already felt the vibrations in the stone as he began his descent.

But this wasn't over yet. She knew hundreds of places to hide. She would watch, wait and follow.

If she could attack him unawares, she could wrest away the weapon and have her way with him. Or at just the right moment, she could sneak up and knock him off the side of the cliff and watch with glee as he fell to his death.

Maybe after he splattered on the stone, he would be easier to eat.

3

Torg peered over the edge of the cliff and saw the spider clinging to the wall. A trick of perspective made Dukkhatu look larger from a distance than she had close up. He pounded a fist against the stone. The spider scampered farther downward and disappeared beneath a ledge.

"Dammit. I was not fast enough," he said in a nasal voice. "I should have killed her when I had the chance."

"It's my fault, beloved," he said this time with Sōbhana's voice and mannerisms. "I distracted you with my silly romantic talk. I'm sorry."

"It was both of our faults, then," he thought, attempting an internal laugh. "But now we have to find a way to get down. That would be difficult enough, even if she weren't out there somewhere."

"We'll find a way." She spoke within his mind, but already her voice was fading.

The air was calm but wintry. The storm that had wracked Asubha during Torg's escape had since relinquished its fury. Snow still fell, but softly. Torg was naked, and he shivered in the morning chill. On top of everything else, he would have to make the descent with little hope of finding warmth.

Out of curiosity, Torg rolled onto his back on the icy stone and took a moment to look upward at the peak of the mountain. From this vantage point he could see a fraction of the previous night's destruction. He wondered what it might look like from a dragon's perspective. He supposed it would be blown apart. But from where Torg lay, there was little to observe other than several large scars along the wall that probably had been caused by falling boulders.

He rolled back onto his stomach and searched for signs of Dukkhatu. He could not see her, but he knew she was down there somewhere. What were her intentions? Perhaps he had injured her sufficiently to scare her off for good.

"You don't believe that, and neither do I," he said in Sōbhana's voice. "Dukkhatu will not depart without a fight."

To emphasize this point, Sōbhana replayed her memory of Bhayatupa's description of the spider. Torg became enraged at the dragon for using Sōbhana to get to him, but he didn't blame Sōbhana for not resisting. It was an unusual partnership, but they had needed each other. Torg wondered if he would ever meet Bhayatupa again.

"I believe you will," Sōbhana whispered in his thoughts. "But I now understand that the answers he seeks from you will not succor him."

"His cravings have no merit," Torg spoke in his own voice. "His lore is great and his experiences many, but his wisdom has failed to flourish. His ego is so strong he fails to comprehend that ego doesn't truly exist."

"I know, my lord," Sōbhana said silently. "I'm a part of you now, don't you remember?"

"And I'm treasuring every moment."

"I know that, too."

"Please don't go."

"I won't . . . not yet."

Still on his stomach and now facing the opening of the tunnel, Torg dropped his legs over the ledge. He was forced to hold the sword in his mouth. The frozen blade burned his toothless gums.

"I must be quite the sight," he said, his voice muffled.

"You look terrible, to be honest," she said. "You have no hair, your skin is covered with sores, and you sound like an old man who has misplaced his wooden teeth. Compared to you, Mala is handsome. But I love you, nonetheless."

Torg laughed so hard the sword fell out of his mouth and clattered on the ledge. The sound was a strange mixture of male and female tones.

Then Sōbhana said, "A wild Sampati comes. I'll keep quiet, until we dispose of it."

"How do you know? I don't see it."

"I am fading, beloved. I exist in both worlds and can sense things beyond your awareness. This might prove useful to you—until I am no longer."

Sure enough, the Sampati appeared a moment later from around a bend in the mountain. When it saw Torg, it dove toward him like a hawk attacking a pigeon.

Torg, however, was no pigeon. He hauled himself back onto the ledge, picked up the sword and stood to meet the hybrid monster. As the Sampati made its first pass, Torg hid the sword behind his back, not wanting the beast to sense its power.

The Sampati circled and came for him again, this time intending to strike. Torg waited until the last moment before bounding off the ledge. With the sword again in his mouth, he somersaulted and fell onto the creature. Then he dug his fingers and toes between the feathers and scales, and held tight.

The Sampati veered away from the mountain, twisting and shaking like an angry stallion—but failing to throw him. When Torg drove the sword into the thick of its back, the Sampati shrieked and tumbled out of control, slamming into the mountainside and bursting asunder.

Torg struck the stone and was knocked unconsciousness. His limp body slid down the wall and came to rest on a flattened outcrop.

The sword clattered beside him.

Both lay still.

Torg dreamed sweetly *of a tender woman. Together they stood holding hands beneath the largest and brightest moon he'd ever seen. Torg assumed he was with Sōbhana, but when he turned to look more closely he saw someone else. The woman's hair was the first thing to attract his attention. It was blond and hung past her waist—unlike Sōbhana's, which was black and shoulder-length.*

The pale stranger was taller than Sōbhana, but less muscular and more voluptuous. Her blue-gray eyes contained a sparkling power that Torg found both intimidating and enticing. He had seen her before, but could not remember when or where.

Was she a Warlish witch? Despite the flawlessness of her beauty, he did not think so.

Was she a sorceress? That seemed closer to the truth.

Was she good or evil? To Torg, she felt mysterious but unthreatening.

The woman smiled at him, causing his heart to thump. An erection surged beneath his trousers, and he backed away. Don't you know who I am? Don't you know what I do to women who get too close?

The sorceress did not seem afraid. On the contrary, his presence seemed to please her. And yet she remained silent.

Then Torg heard a faraway voice and spun toward it. In the moonlight, he saw the glowing silhouette of a figure on a distant hill. It was waving, slowly.

"Farewell, my love," Sōbhana called.

Her words caused him so much pain. He dropped to his knees.

"You and I were not meant to be," she said. "A part of me will always love you, but I am no longer. I am gone."

Then she leapt into darkness, but not before shouting an urgent warning: "Wake up now. The spider comes."

Torg opened his eyes. At first his vision was hazy. When he finally was able to focus, he saw Dukkhatu standing nimbly on the wall just a short distance above him. He sat up. The monstrous spider reacted to his sudden movement, rearing on her back legs, fangs snapping.

Torg looked about for the sword and saw it lying two paces to his left, on the flat ledge that had broken his fall. He lunged for it, but in his dazed condition the spider was too fast for him. She swatted the sword off the ledge with the tip of her damaged front leg, and the weapon tumbled off the ledge and spun downward, sparking as it struck the floor of the talus far below.

Dukkhatu retreated and reared again, her front legs stabbing at the air, hypersensitive to Torg's slightest movement. He was surprised she didn't attack right then. Perhaps her predator's instincts were making her cautious; she hoped to stare down her prey until it panicked and fled, then ambush it from behind. But Dukkhatu had more reason to be afraid than she knew. Exhaustion made Torg vulnerable, but some of Sōbhana's strength still surged in his body.

When he stood, the spider retreated a little farther, apparently sensing something in his manner that made her wary. Anger overwhelmed Torg, shoving his spiritual training aside. The High Nun of Dibbu-Loka would have admonished him: *Hate never dispels hate.* Some part of Torg knew his teacher was correct, but he was beyond caring. He missed Sōbhana too much, despising what had been done to her—and to him. He had grown to hate Invictus and Mala and the wicked creature that now trembled uncertainly above him. Revenge was ugly and ignorant, but it offered sweetness that Torg could not resist, especially on this miserable day.

Torg's wrath demanded penance. This time, sword or no sword, he would not fail. He jumped toward the spider.

Dukkhatu attempted to skitter backward, but Torg grabbed a thick segment of her left front leg and held on tight. Her ancient exoskeleton began to crack. She leaned forward and tried to stab her fangs into his eyes, but he caught one massive tooth in his free hand and snapped it in half. Poison spurted from the break, sizzling on Torg's bare chest, but he ignored the pain. The *frenzy* was upon him. He would settle for nothing less than her death.

Dukkhatu must have sensed the extent of his malice, because she drew back, trying to shake him. He defied her, scrambling up her leg and onto her back, pounding his great fists against her thorax. There were cracks and crunches and more black blood.

In a final attempt to escape, she curled into a defensive ball and rolled.

Torg dug his hands into the grotesque hair that sprang from her bloated abdomen.

The spider and the wizard rumbled toward the ledge, struck it hard, and bounced over the side. They fell in airy silence onto a knot of sharp stones. Torg landed on top of her, his fall cushioned just enough to keep him alive. Then he rolled off her shattered bulk and lost consciousness, again.

This time there were no dreams. When he opened his eyes the ruins of Dukkhatu were sprawled before him. The spider lay on her back, pierced in many places by prickly black rocks. Her hideous legs quivered, and a wet, whistling sound came from her mouth.

The same mouth that had tortured Sōbhana's flesh.

The *frenzy* returned. Torg tore a chunk of obsidian from the ground, climbed onto the spider's exposed belly, and stabbed the stone into her hide, perforating her long, tubular heart. Dukkhatu let out a final, ear-shattering scream—and went still. But Torg didn't stop. He drove the stone into her again and again, punching huge holes in her carcass.

Her body shredded and tore apart.

Her entrails splashed in his face.

Hate and despair drove his madness. When he no longer had the strength to move, he collapsed face-first in Dukkhatu's gore.

He didn't remember standing. He wandered naked and shivering through and around the crumbled stone . . . staggering, falling, crawling. Tears rinsed a little of the filth from his face, but his broken body reeked of the spider's stink.

Heaps of razor-sharp obsidian were scattered among the jumble of smoother stones, as if planted there with tiny black seeds. It took all of Torg's remaining will not to grasp another shard and drive it into his own heart, ending his pain.

His life had become nothing but pain. Why breathe any longer? His endurance was gone, his hopes destroyed. Who could blame him for giving up? Not even Sister Tathagata could ask any more of him.

What did it matter anyway? All things were impermanent—he, certainly, as much as anything else. The time of his ending had come. A future lifetime beckoned.

Perhaps he would live it in a better place than this.

Beneath the Mountain

1

The Silver Sword had come to rest amid a tangle of obsidian, the volcanic glass protruding from the ground like black fangs. Yet the great weapon appeared unharmed. Through his tears, Torg saw it glimmering in the bright noon sun.

He crawled toward the sword. He wasn't sure why he wanted to retrieve it; he barely had the strength to pick it up. But on this stark and frozen ridge between Asubha and one of its sister mountains, the sword was his last connection to his former self. Though he had held it for just a little while, it felt like his only remaining friend. And it reminded him of Sōbhana, who also had wielded the weapon.

As he struggled forward, Torg laughed and cried as if deranged. If a young Tugar had seen him—naked, hairless, toothless—the child probably would have fled in terror, mistaking him for a sinister monster that had slithered from a cave.

But Torg was delirious with grief and had no concern for his appearance. Not even he could endure such prolonged torture. He had been placed in the pit while already weak, and had spent many long days trapped within its black horror. Finally he had escaped, only to discover that the person in the world who loved him most had suffered in ways every bit as terrible as his own—and all because she was trying to rescue him. Torg had once thought of Sōbhana as a young sister, but her true connection to him was revealed in her final moments of life. Flashes of her memory and personality still clung to his psyche. Torg mourned her loss as if she were his longtime lover.

Hill-sized heaps of stone, torn from Asubha's crown, stood in Torg's way, but he clambered over them like a drunken chameleon. He approached the obsidian and climbed onto the razor-sharp rocks. He reached for the sword and closed his hand on the hilt.

Suddenly a heavy foot stomped on his fingers.

Torg cried out and looked up. The sun blinded him.

Something kicked him in the face and sent him tumbling into the teeth of the obsidian. When his sight cleared a few moments later, he saw a stout figure looming over him. Flames flared from its flat nostrils, smoke seeped from its pointed ears, and its hide had the texture of an elephant halfway turned to stone. The creature had grabbed the sword from Torg and now held it in one hand while waving a spear of obsidian in the other. The beast brought the black volcanic glass to its mouth and began to chomp on it, as if snacking on an ear of corn.

"You killed my father," it said. "For that, I will enjoy a long-awaited revenge. But first, I have promises to keep."

Several other Stone-Eaters stood nearby.

"Give him a sip of Asava," Gulah said. "We need him alive, but barely. He could still be dangerous. Do not underestimate him, despite his pathetic appearance."

One of the Stone-Eaters lifted Torg's head and poured scorching liquid down his throat. He felt like he was swallowing lava. Though his stomach burned, strength surged through the rest of his body, along with a drugged weariness. Soon afterward, sleep strode forward and claimed him. He could not resist it.

Torg did not know how long or deeply he slept, but he regained partial consciousness several times and was able to look about. Gulah and his fellow Stone-Eaters had strapped him to a crude litter and were dragging him across the rocks. It was a bumpy ride.

More of the Asava was splashed into his mouth. He gagged, but Gulah slapped his hand against Torg's lips and forced him to swallow. Once again, Torg felt the odd combination of strength and weariness. It was the first nourishment of any kind he'd received in almost a month. But more than anything, he craved cold water. If he could take a long drink and pour the rest over his head, he might be able to shake this drowsiness.

Again he slept, but his dreams raged out of control. A particularly wicked thud shook him awake, and he looked up and saw they were approaching the mouth of a large cave in Asubha's sheer side. Several Stone-Eaters stood guard at the maw of the cavity, as well as an enormous troll who shied from the bright sunlight. There also were three women, two extremely beautiful and one extremely ugly. Warlish witches . . . just what he needed.

But the Asava—whatever it contained—had re-energized Torg's spirit. Though he was drugged and barely able to move, he felt his body responding internally to the sizzling sustenance, increasing his desire to resist.

When the Stone-Eaters dragged him into the cave, the ground became smooth and the ride less chaotic. Torg was able to sleep in relative comfort.

He dreamed again.

This time he wandered in absolute darkness, but his hearing was acute, and he could sense objects before bumping into them, which enabled him to move boldly forward, unperturbed by his lack of vision. Torg heard a small figure rise up beside him. It grasped his hand. He could not see it, but he knew who it was.

"Peta, I have missed you so much, my dear little friend. But how came you here?"

The little girl giggled. Torg remembered the sound of her laughter with fondness.

"You rescued me from the tower. For that, I am grateful. When you saved me, I foresaw your future and knew that you would need my help. So I chose to stay and look out for you."

"I don't understand. When you died—when I released you—your karma should have moved on. Only demons are immune to the natural cycle of life and death. You aren't a demon. This should not be."

"I cannot defy my future forever, but a few hundred years is no great matter. In my reckoning, you ended my suffering just a moment ago."

Peta squeezed his massive hand. "But we have already spent far too much time in greeting. I must tell you some important things before she returns."

"She?"

"The demon . . . Vedana."

"Was it the demon who imprisoned you in the tower?"

"Vedana recognized my abilities."

"Your father told me you were blind. But he also said you had powers that the demons found valuable. What did he mean?"

"They—she—found my powers valuable enough to imprison me for ten millennia. The amulet you discovered on my chest kept my physical body intact while Vedana's magic controlled my spirit. She used me . . . for terrible things. And eventually, for the most terrible thing of all. You see, without my clairvoyance, she could not have created Invictus."

"You foresaw his birth?"

"I cannot deny it. Vedana had spent almost her entire existence breeding with mortals. Her offspring were magical and powerful, but none attained the might she desired. When she discovered me, her hopes were renewed. She knew I could guide her, in all the ways that mattered. And—against my will—I did guide her." Peta paused for a moment, as if deep in thought. Then she said, "But you came along and disrupted her plans, removing me from her sway before she was ready. In most ways I had already

shown her enough. Due to my guidance, she was able to mate with a man whose bloodlines were interwoven in just the right order, and from his seed she bore Invictus' father, who in turn bore the greatest bane in all of history.

"However, when Vedana lost my guidance she also lost the knowledge that would have enabled her to control Invictus. And now no one is his master. The Sun God is like wildfire in a forest long plagued by drought. He threatens more than just our land. If he continues to grow unimpeded, he will endanger all things."

"I know not how to impede him," Torg said.

Peta nodded, as if in agreement. "Invictus' rise has not gone unnoticed. There are beings beyond all known laws, natural or otherwise, and they are watching the sorcerer with growing interest—and making plans for his demise."

"How do you know this? Who are you, really?"

Peta giggled again. "I am just a little blind girl who can see too well for her own good. But allow me to finish, before the demon comes to stop me. There is more you must know. Vedana still desires control, but her grandson has become her most lethal enemy. Invictus wields enough power to eliminate the demon and her kind. She and her minions fear that more than all else. For this reason—and others—Vedana schemes to dethrone him. The first step in a long process is for her to become impregnated . . . by you."

"Then her plan will fail. I cannot impregnate anyone. I can only burn and destroy."

"You are wrong. There are three females on Triken who can abide you. Vedana is one. She is great enough to withstand the fury of your orgasm and retain the wonder of your seed."

Such words, coming from a child, made Torg uncomfortable. But then again, was Peta really a child? "If that is so, then how do I thwart her? I am a prisoner and lack the strength to resist."

"I beg you . . . do not thwart her. Do not! She must bear your child."

Torg felt pressure on his arms. The skin on his face began to sting.

"She comes. Farewell!" Peta said.

Thick hands shook him, and Torg was torn from sleep. Someone slapped his face, hard and often. When he finally opened his eyes, it took several moments for his vision to clear.

There stood Vedana, the mother of all demons. And she was not alone.

"Bastards! Asses! Fools!" Vedana shouted. "I told you, 'Do not let him sleep.' She has *spoken* to him."

"Who has spoken to him?" Gulah said. "What are you talking about? No one has been near him."

"You don't understand, you idiot," Vedana said. "Who knows what *she* is capable of? She sees. She *sees!* Are you blind, as well as stupid?"

Gulah drew the Silver Sword and waved the point in Vedana's face. "Be careful with your words, Demon. I have endured enough abuse in recent days from Mala, and my patience is gone. Because we are allies, I will allow you to have your way with him. But be quick. I will not tolerate you much longer."

"Put away the ssssword, Gulah," a voice purred. Chal-Abhinno's beautiful self strode forward. Then she turned to Vedana. "No serious harm has been done, mistress. Who cares what the wizard might have been told. He is our prisoner, and he is far too weak to ressssist us. Your plan cannot fail."

Ignoring the witch, Vedana continued to glare at Gulah, her eyes blood red, her flesh eerily translucent. "You are too much like your father," the demon said, with a fanged snarl. "*My* patience is gone as well."

The tone of Vedana's voice seemed to disconcert the Stone-Eater, but he held his ground.

Chal intervened again. "We are all friends here, Gulah. We wish to ssssee the Death-Knower punished as much as youuuu. But Vedana needs him first . . . for one little . . . *thing*." This last word caused her to giggle. Chal sounded like a virgin shyly attempting to flirt.

Then she turned to Torg and bent over the litter, which had been placed on a flat stone bed. Her gorgeous, sweet-smelling mouth came within a finger-length of his lips.

"Ssssso, *Torgon. We* meet again. And as youuuu predicted at Bakheng, I have been given a second opportunity for revenge. As pathetic as you now look, it hardly ssssseems worth the effort. Still, you should have killed me when you had the chance, my darling. A lady doesn't forget these things."

"Lady?" Torg said. "Where?"

Gulah slammed the sword back into its sheath and burst into laughter. The other Stone-Eaters joined him. Even the cave troll grinned and grunted. Torg wasn't sure if they were laughing at what he said or how oddly his voice sounded. Either way, Chal became enraged and unwillingly began to transform to her hideous self. But then she reined in her anger and somehow managed to maintain her attractive appearance.

The witch stepped back and folded her arms beneath her large, round breasts.

"A *lady* doessssn't forget," she said, her voice as cold as a mountain spring. "I will take great pleasure in your death, *Torgon*."

"Take pleasure where you will. I care naught."

Gulah laughed again. The cave troll slapped its massive knee. This time the witch could not hold back her rage. Her flawless pale skin seemed to catch fire, her long auburn hair wrinkled and turned gray, and her perfect breasts flopped against her suddenly bulbous stomach. Reeking like rotten flesh, Chal reached for Torg with clawed hands.

Gulah stepped in front of the witch and held her back. "As amusing as this is, I have heard enough," he said, shoving Chal out of the way. Though Gulah was shorter than Chal, it was obvious that he was far stronger. "Vedana, I vowed to deliver the Death-Knower to you, and I have kept my promise. Now keep yours. Get on with your business. And then leave him to me."

"On this, we agree. There is no reason to delay any longer," Vedana said. "Too much is at stake. Prepare him for me. Gulah, you can watch, if you like. And Chal, I *know* that you like to watch."

"Missssstress, you honor me," the ugly witch said with a touch of sarcasm in her voice.

"I will watch," Gulah said. "But only to make sure he doesn't escape."

Vedana cackled. "Come then, my *friends*. Come and watch our . . . *business*."

The cave troll thundered over, grabbed the ends of the litter and dragged Torg toward another dark tunnel. Gulah, flanked by several Stone-Eaters, led the way. Vedana and Chal walked on either side of Torg. More Stone-Eaters and witches followed behind. The tunnel, lit sporadically by flickering torches, dropped steeply. The farther they descended, the warmer the air became. Torg felt himself beginning to sweat—an unusual sensation, after so many days of torturous cold.

As they traveled deep into the bowels of Asubha, Torg could sense the immense weight of the stone. All of them were minuscule when compared to the might of the mountain; even in its broken state, it would exist long beyond their short, bitter lives.

They marched for what seemed like half a day. After a while, torches were no longer needed. A blazing light rose beneath them, heating the air like a cauldron. Torg found it difficult to breathe.

The Asava had given Torg vigor, and he tested the straps that bound him to the litter, believing now that he was strong enough to break them. It would take weeks of rest and healing to return to anywhere near the fullness of his former strength, but at least he now could put up a fight. However, Peta's words haunted his consciousness: *You must not thwart her.* Torg trusted the little girl. He would do as she said—even though he felt disgust rising in his throat like bile.

They finally entered a cavern of immense proportions. Stalactites hung perilously from the ceiling, and the floor was littered with stalagmites as tall and thick as trees. In several places the stone growths met, forming thick towers that helped support the high ceiling. There were no torches in the cavern, but it was as bright as the desert under a noon sun—and much hotter.

Torg soon saw why. A circular pool of bubbling magma dominated the center of the cavern floor.

"Welcome, Death-Knower, to the asthenolith," Gulah said, his voice sounding prideful.

The asthenolith was at least twenty paces across, and it radiated an intense, skin-searing heat. Torg believed no ordinary beings could have stood nearer than ten paces, but everyone in the party was extraordinary, in some sense. Gulah strode within a few spans of the pool, but even he could go no closer. The magma was hot enough to liquefy metal.

A pair of enormous granite slabs flanked each side of the pool. They appeared ancient, yet still strong. U-shaped grooves had been chiseled into the top of each slab, and a rounded column of stone—about six cubits in diameter—had been placed on top of the slabs, fitting securely into the grooves. The column spanning the pool of magma reminded Torg of an oversized spit. A massive crank was attached to one side. Only something monstrously strong could turn something that size.

"Give him my potion," Vedana ordered.

With a hand as large as a tortoise shell, the troll grasped Torg's head and held it securely in place. Chal came forward with a steaming stone cup and pinched Torg's nostrils, forcing open his mouth and pouring a nocuous brew down his throat that tasted like a grotesque mixture of honey and blood.

If he had been at full strength, Torg could have incinerated the potion before it entered his bloodstream. But he had neither the strength nor the desire. Instead he heeded Peta's warning: *Do not thwart her.*

As the potion overtook him, a pleasant drunkenness saturated Torg's awareness, causing him to smile. Suddenly this situation didn't seem so bad. In fact he became quite pleased with everything. He hadn't felt this good for as long as he could remember.

"It's working, misssstress," he heard Chal say. "Look at him. He's an assss. And sssso ugly. No teeth. No hair. And he stinks. Why, he makes Gulah look almost attractive."

"You're one to talk," Gulah said. "I've seen you both ways."

Still in her ugly state, Chal snorted.

"Quiet, both of you," Vedana said. "I'll be the one to decide if my potion is working. Watch this . . ." The demon took Torg's penis in her hand and stroked it.

Chal gasped, and then sighed, wantonly. The five other witches in the cavern put their hands to their mouths. Gulah rolled his eyes. The cave troll grunted and looked between his own legs.

"I would have to say that your potion is working, misssstress," Chal said.

Vedana cackled, obviously pleased. "Yes. Be quick now. Strap him to the spit."

Two Stone-Eaters released Torg from the litter and carried his naked body up a set of stone stairs on the opposite side of the crank. Though the column was rounded, it was wide enough to walk on without slipping. The Stone-Eaters hauled him to the middle of the pillar, where four iron cuffs had been pounded into the granite. Then they laid him on his back and locked his wrists and ankles into the cuffs.

The witches and Stone-Eaters encircled the pool, as close to the magma as they could bear. Chal and her sisters began to sing and chant. Gulah and the other Stone-Eaters stood with arms crossed at their chests. The cave troll walked over to the crank. Torg lay helplessly on the column, his erection resembling the stalagmites that rose from the stone floor.

Vedana removed her robes. Like the witches, the demon was a shape-shifter, but she was more versatile, able to appear as almost anyone or anything relatively close to her physical size. When Torg turned his head to look at her, he saw Sōbhana's naked body, tanned and erotically muscled. He quivered with passion.

Vedana, in the form of Sōbhana, glided alluringly up the stairs and across the pillar. The demon stood above him, straddling his prone body with her athletic legs. The witches' strange mantra filled the chamber, increasing in volume, and their bodies changed from beautiful to ugly, ugly to beautiful—over and over. Gray smoke, emanating from their transformations, choked the air.

Slowly Sōbhana lowered herself onto Torg's rigidity. He succumbed to bliss, moaning as he writhed. Sōbhana moaned too, and the witches sang louder. Even Gulah's Stone-Eaters became entranced, and the troll's drooling tongue lolled from its mouth.

Blood-red tendrils from the asthenolith leapt from its surface and licked the sides of the spit. Miniature bursts of lightning crackled between the tendrils, followed by snapping claps of thunder. The cavern was as hot as an oven.

Sōbhana's well-built warrior body rode Torg deliciously. She growled and screamed, digging her nails into the thick muscles of his chest. Torg began to scream as well, his head jerking backward and his eyes clamping shut. At one point he opened them again to look at Sōbhana, and he saw that Vedana had lost control of her illusion and become her true physical incarnation, a translucent being with visible bones and internal organs. To avoid further disgust, Torg turned his head and watched the others.

The witches succumbed to frenzy, flinging their heads wildly and transforming back and forth so quickly that no single appearance held sway. They were beautiful and ugly, at the same moment. The cavern was ablaze with perverted sexual energy.

Torg's approaching orgasm surged out of the depths of his frustration. It had been more than nine hundred years since he had been with a woman, and the abysmal aftermath of that encounter had left a permanent scar on his psyche. His supernaturally vibrant body burned for intimacy, but he had been forced into a centuries-long celibacy that tormented his every waking moment—as well as his dreams.

Now Torg howled uncontrollably, and his back arched ferociously, almost casting Vedana into the pool. But with a demon's agility, she held on tight. The pair climaxed simultaneously.

Cathartic energy erupted from every pore of Torg's body, and the cavern filled with blue fire. Next came a concussive blast of sound, which boomed inside the chamber. Though his mind was lost in the throes of lust, Torg still was able to see fissures forming in the surrounding stone, racing this way and that like cracks in a weakening sheet of ice.

First to die was Gulah. His eyes popped from his skull and ruptured. His stony hide burst into flame and incinerated. His skeleton cracked apart and clattered to the floor. The sword, released from its sheath, bounced on the stone and slipped into the broiling magma.

The other Stone-Eaters suffered similar fates. They were no match for such power. The troll ran toward the tunnel, but his enormous backside caught fire, and he split in half along his spine. Then his body blew apart, splattering fiery chunks of flesh onto the cavern walls. His bare skull tumbled through the air and landed on top of a stalagmite. It stuck there, jaw sprung open as if pleased to find a less-fragile body.

The conflagration also swept away the witches. Even Chal-Abhinno was consumed, screaming in wild-eyed horror as she realized, too late, how she had been betrayed. Her revenge would not be sweet. Nor would Gulah's. Apparently Vedana had wanted no witnesses. Was this a secret she chose not to share? If so, the loss of a few underlings would be a small price to pay.

Torg's orgasmic fury sluiced through Vedana's undead flesh like a torrent, but it did not destroy her. After she was sure of his completion, the demon leapt into the air and somersaulted over the pool. Fast as a spider she fled on all fours, skittering past the carnage into the safety of the passageway. Torg heard her wicked cackles echoing long after she disappeared.

As if in response, the stone column shattered into a thousand shards.

Torg tumbled toward the asthenolith and then sank into its blistering depths.

2

Few beings in Triken's history could have withstood the fury of the asthenolith. All but the mightiest would have been consumed—flesh, bones, and sinew—in just a few dreadful moments. But the aftermath of Torg's orgasmic firestorm still clung to his dense flesh, protecting him from the molten stone. He sank deeper and deeper into the viscous magma, tumbling slowly head over heels.

The pain was unbearable, and he could not breathe. As the blue fire that encompassed his body diminished, the agony intensified.

Yet he continued to live.

The asthenolith's hard walls tapered like a funnel. Torg finally struck bottom and lay on his side in the superheated goo. Although his iron cuffs had already melted, he now pressed against something else metallic—and still cold. It was the sword. Its supernal alloys were impervious.

As if guided by an invisible will, a current of magma lifted and carried him into a passageway that ran through the surrounding wall. Torg was drawn into the tunnel head-first, his broad shoulders barely squeezing through. He could not see, but somehow he managed to grab the sword before he was swept away.

The tunnel ran straight for several paces before bending sharply upward. Torg ascended slowly, lifted by the bubbling surge. At first his body was limp and unresisting, his blue fire nearly gone. The grime and disease in his flesh sizzled away. Soon the pain reached new levels of anguish. Torg began to writhe and scream, praying for some form of mercy.

Then, suddenly, his head was free of the fire. And his hands. And arms. With the final remnants of his strength, he pulled his body and the sword out of the magma and up into a small chamber.

The room was aglow, enabling Torg to see for several paces. He slithered away from the molten rock as far as his strength allowed, finally collapsing on hot stone.

He lay still, fading in and out of consciousness, his body a screaming bundle of misery. Each time he awoke, he sobbed and moaned, then fainted again. This went on for a long while.

When he finally regained full consciousness, Torg lay face-down and listened to the magma as it bubbled near his feet. It had the sound of hunger and desire, as if beckoning him to return to the depths and be devoured. He heard another noise—or imagined one, at least—coming from the other direction. It sounded like trickling water, and it drove him mad. He had gone without water for almost a month.

The enormity of his thirst inspired him to move. Otherwise he might have lain there and succumbed to the lure of death. Bit by bit, he dragged himself away from the magma, away from the dim light and into the darkness of the tunnel. It soon descended, making it easier for Torg to move forward. But the farther he journeyed the darker it became. The fading blue glow that emanated from his flesh provided scant visibility. He clung to the sword, as if it were a comrade.

The trickling grew louder. Torg crept toward it. The walls of the tunnel became smooth and slippery, and he half-crawled, half-slid, endlessly downward, into the bowels of the mountain.

Into places where there was no light and no life.

His grave, he feared, would never be discovered. His corpse would decay slowly, and his bones would lie alone, with the sword at their side, lost and forgotten in the great depths of the mountain.

A droplet of water struck his forehead, and he reached upward with his hands. The roof of the tunnel was moist. Torg screamed out of joy and relief, and an infinite series of echoes raced through the tunnel. He pressed his face against the stone and licked. Then he scrambled forward several more paces and found the main source, a tiny but steady trickle of water issuing from a prick in the ceiling. The water was lukewarm and metallic in flavor, but to Torg it tasted as sweet as nectar. He drank for what seemed like forever, until his stomach was too bloated to hold any more.

After that, he slept fitfully. Peta did not visit his dreams, but Sōbhana was there, naked and alluring. Or was it Vedana?

Torg jerked awake. It was utterly dark. The blue glow of his skin had faded to nothing.

For the first time in weeks, he urinated. It burned his flaccid shaft as it drizzled onto the floor of the tunnel. When he finished he was thirsty again, and he drank his fill of the precious water. Slowly, hydration worked its way into his cells. With it came vitality. His body still needed food, but it had needed water more. With his thirst quenched, his mind opened to the possibility of survival.

"*Eso aham idha* (Here I am)," Torg said out loud.

Eso aham idha . . . Eso aham idha . . . Eso aham idha . . . Eso aham idha . . .

How deep *was* this tunnel? Did it ever end? And would it become too narrow for Torg to navigate? He could barely squeeze through it now.

In a sudden burst of awareness Torg felt the weight of the mountain all around him. Panic crept into his thoughts, threatening to suffocate his sanity. There was nowhere to escape. If he backtracked, the magma would trap him. If he continued forward, he would descend farther into uncharted territory, ensnared in the fatal grip of a trillion tons of bedrock. He began to sweat profusely. His heart thundered in his chest. He could not catch his breath. The air was so stale. His body trembled. He became dizzy and nauseated. He felt an irresistible urge to pound his way free, to smash his fists against the underbelly of the mountain until it collapsed around him.

Torg shrieked in childish terror. It echoed along the never-ending length of his cramped prison, alerting all who might listen to his despair. He scrambled downward in a mad rush, scraping his elbows and knees on the smooth stone, dragging the clattering sword alongside. His panicked shouts outraced him, piercing the darkness. He went on this way for a long time.

Finally, he fell on his face.

Shivering. Moaning. Whimpering.

The passageway echoed his suffering.

All that he had been taught was a lie.

There was no beginning.

No middle.

No end.

There was only fear. Now and forever.

But this time, exhaustion—long his enemy—came to his rescue, and he succumbed to sleep.

Peta remained noticeably absent in his dreams, as if Torg had delved too deeply even for her to follow. Instead nightmares made an unpleasant visit. The tunnel closed around him, attempting to digest him. Worms chewed on his immobile flesh, and he could not escape their hunger. They devoured his nose, ears and tongue. They ate his fingers and toes. His screams sounded like Sōbhana's.

Torg sprang awake, banging his head against the low stone roof. When his brain cleared he found that—for whatever reason—his madness had receded. He had never been particularly claustrophobic before, but his confinement in the pit had given birth to that fear. Now he shut that door with a bang. He probably would die here, but it would not be of fright.

He was *The Torgon*. Or at least, what remained of him.

"*Natthi me maranabhayam* (For me there is no fear of death)," he shouted with as much conviction as he could muster.

Natthi me maranabhayam . . . Natthi me maranabhayam . . . Natthi me maranabhayam . . .

"But I don't want to die," he whispered.

That echoed, too.

Again he crawled forward, bringing the sword along with him, though it made it more difficult. He was able to loop his right pinky finger around the crossguard and drag it along without losing too much dexterity. He was amazed to feel that even the leather grip had survived the heat of the lava. Was it warded by ancient magic? He wasn't sure why he continued to carry the weapon, anyway. It wouldn't do him much good down here in this enclosed space. But out of respect for Sōbhana, he kept it with him.

After blindly feeling his way in the darkness for a long time, Torg came upon a fork where the tunnel split in two directions. He had no idea which opening to choose. Both appeared to continue downward, but the one on the right felt larger and cooler. Torg had no desire to encounter any more magma, so he went that way.

As he descended along the new tunnel, it quickly became very cold, and Torg began to shiver. He hadn't felt this cold since Gulah had captured him, but he soon became re-accustomed to the discomfort. He certainly had experienced enough of it in the pit.

After a while the tunnel split again. Torg felt around with his hands and discovered at least three different openings. This time, the left tunnel was the largest and coolest, so he went that way.

However, this passageway soon tightened, and he was forced to press his shoulders together just to squeeze through. He put the sword in front of him, sliding it forward, afraid that if he continued to drag it and then lost his grip he wouldn't have the will to back up and retrieve it.

Eventually the tunnel split in several more directions. Torg realized he was hopelessly lost, then laughed aloud. Since this journey had begun, when had he not been lost? His laughter bounced off countless walls. He was trapped in a maze of passageways that wove in a thousand directions. Even if the tunnels were lighted, he could not hope to escape a labyrinth of such scope.

From then on, whenever there was an option he chose the middle path. As Sister Tathagata always said, "The middle path leads to enlightenment." Luckily, he found more trickling water—cooler and clearer than before. He drank his fill and slept again. What other pleasures were left to him? Quenching his thirst and sleeping had become the extent of his entertainment. And, of course, the nightmares. In one, Vedana came toward him holding a squalling baby. When she held it up, Torg saw that it had a human head and torso but legs like black worms. Torg recoiled, then reached out with his right hand and broke its neck. The thing turned to dust.

Torg shrieked and bumped his sore head on the ceiling of the passageway yet again. A cacophony of his own echoing screams taunted his awakening.

When silence returned, he lay still and began to watch his breath. It was his first attempt at meditation since his escape from the pit. He had no intention of achieving *Sammaasamaadhi*; his broken body was incapable of surviving another *Death Visit*. But the benefits of meditation were many and varied. At the very least it would calm him. He doubted there was any way he could escape this predicament, but a clear mind was always superior to a clouded one, no matter the precariousness of the situation.

The darkness and quiet aided his concentration. He felt his breath whistling in and out of his nostrils. The skin on the tip of his nose tingled ever so slightly. After several inhalations and exhalations, a thought entered his mind: Where was Vedana now? Was she pregnant with his child? He acknowledged the thought and gently pushed it aside, returning his focus to the skin surrounding his nostrils. Inhale. Exhale. Peaceful mind.

Why had Peta believed it was so important not to resist the demon? Why would a child with Vedana be able to provide him with the weapon to destroy Invictus?

Return to focus. Inhale. Exhale. Inhale. Exhale. Peaceful mind. Quiet mind. Clear mind.

Abruptly, his concentration was interrupted.

He heard something.

Scraping and slurping on the stone.

And it appeared to be headed his way. Fast.

3

Whatever was approaching Torg came at a speed that was impossible to evade. To make matters worse, the darkness was disorienting. Torg couldn't tell from which direction he would be attacked. All he could do was grasp the sword, brace his body and prepare for the inevitable.

Suddenly something bit down on his left foot and swallowed his leg up to the knee. It chomped with terrific force, attempting to devour him, but it could not bite through his flesh. Torg spun the sword around and drove it into the monster, piercing something thick and cartilaginous. With a hiss the tentacle withdrew.

Although Torg's leg burned, he touched the wound and felt no blood. Then he attempted to illuminate the tunnel with his magic, but he was too weak. He would have to wage this fight in total darkness. And the creature he faced must have been born in darkness.

It attacked once more, driving between his legs and snapping at his groin. To protect his genitals, Torg slipped his free hand between his legs. He felt the thing gnaw on his inner thighs, then it reared back momentarily and rushed forward.

This time, the creature shoved him more than twenty body lengths. The passageway narrowed too much to accommodate his girth, and Torg was wedged wickedly into the hole. He managed to retain his grip on the sword, but his arms were locked against his sides.

He couldn't move.

The creature sensed his helplessness and renewed its attack. First it bit his right foot. Any normal being would have been dismembered, but Torg's dense flesh was too great for the toothy mouth to penetrate. Then the creature pulled away and drove forward again, swallowing most of Torg's right leg and crunching on his thigh. Again, it did little damage and was forced to withdraw.

Torg twisted and squirmed, but could not free himself. He could barely wiggle his fingers. With terrific power the tentacle struck again, pounding against his feet, ankles and calves. It bit, hissed and spat.

Over and over it smashed against him. The more it failed, the angrier it seemed to become. Had it ever encountered a prey so defenseless and yet so invulnerable?

One final time, it crushed its colossal strength against Torg's underside. He felt excruciating pressure build along his torso, and his shoulders were pressed forward until they touched. Suddenly, impossibly, his body squirted through the tiny hole into a wider portion of the tunnel.

The tentacle continued to propel him forward at fantastic speed.

Finally Torg exploded from the tunnel into an open expanse—and fell a long way, thudding against the hard floor of a magnificent cavern. The sword clattered beside him.

Torg was dazed.

But there was light.

Splendid and dappled.

He gazed upward. What he saw amazed even him.

Flaming torches were jammed into clefts in the cavern's sheer walls. A treasure trove of multicolored gems protruded from the stone, reflecting the flickering light. The wall from which Torg had emerged was pockmarked with hundreds of round holes, each less than two cubits in diameter. From each hole a black tentacle extended, flipping and flopping.

At least twenty furry creatures were leaping athletically from tentacle to tentacle. They used sharp stone daggers to hack at a limb before pouncing to another—just quick enough to avoid being snapped up by a snarling set of teeth. The daggers could not fully sever the writhing tentacles, but they sliced off small chunks of steaming flesh. The cave monkeys—Torg could think of no other words to describe them—scooped up the raw meat that had fallen to the floor and then moved to a safe place away from the wall.

One of the monkeys paused from its frenetic activity and crept within a few paces of Torg, staring at him with obvious curiosity. Instantly Torg was charmed by the creature's expressive face, which appeared capable of humanlike expressions. Was it smiling at him?

The cave monkey had a pointy nose and a mouth full of flat teeth. A pair of bioluminescent eyes three times larger than a Tugar's dominated its small head. Its face and long bushy tail were black, but the top of its head was white and the rest of its body reddish brown. Torg guessed it weighed less than two stones.

As the creature's eyes glowed, Torg felt a tingling sensation inside his skull. The monkey was using telepathy to probe his mind. Was this how they communicated with each other in the darkness?

The tingling increased slightly, but Torg felt no discomfort. The monkey lacked either the power or desire to force itself into his thoughts. Instead it investigated gently, searching for clues to his intentions. Was he, the large intruder, a friend or foe? Torg sent out a wave of loving kindness, hoping the monkey would recognize his amiability.

It seemed to work. This time, there was no doubt. The creature smiled.

Without warning, a squeal interrupted their pleasant encounter. A tentacle had seized one of the monkeys and yanked it into a hole. A second monkey chased after it, diving into the darkness. Several moments later, the rescuer emerged with the bloodied victim, who was mangled but still alive.

The monkey that stood near Torg scampered off to help, as did the rest. They carried the injured one away from the groping tentacles, which seemed to extend only a short distance from the wall. The monstrous limbs had either come to the end of their reach or were wary of entering too far into the torchlight.

All at once the tentacles withdrew completely, and there was sudden silence in the cavern. The worm monster—again, Torg could think of no better name—had failed to devour even a single one of its prey. Perhaps its frustrating confrontation with Torg had demoralized it.

At least thirty monkeys surrounded him. Each was small but appeared strong, with long flexible fingers and toes. Though Torg was ten times their size, the monkeys were able to work together and lift him off the floor. Slowly they carried him into a dark tunnel.

Torg was too weak to remain conscious. The last thing he remembered was watching one of the monkeys leap along the wall from torch to torch, dousing the flames with quick slaps of its little hands.

Then all went black, as if the lights had been turned off inside his head.

Time passed, but Torg could not gauge it. Eventually he awoke to the most wonderful aroma he'd ever smelled. He took several long whiffs before opening his eyes and looking around. Off to one side, an ancient woman stood over a stone pot heated by a blazing fire. The woman stirred the pot's bubbling contents with a wooden spoon.

Cave monkeys were everywhere. One was perched on each of her shoulders and another on her head. Dozens more scampered about her feet, staring up at her with adoring eyes. She appeared to be their master.

Torg lay on a soft bed of sand in a spacious cave. The Silver Sword leaned against the wall nearby, amazingly undamaged by all that had occurred. He sat up slowly and studied the gray-haired woman. He had no idea whom she was or how she'd gotten here, but he did not sense anything evil about her.

"Where am I, dear lady?" he asked. He was pleased to find that his lisp was almost gone.

She turned to him and smiled. Then she answered—in the ancient tongue: *"Tvam saddhim amhaakam bhavasi.* (You are with us.) *Mayam kataññuu homa.* (We are grateful.) *Dharaama bhojanam tam.* (We bear food for thee)."

One of the monkeys grabbed a clay bowl and held it next to the pot. The old woman filled it with fragrant soup. The monkey carried the bowl over to Torg. Several others followed along excitedly. In the dim firelight Torg noticed the creatures were similar in size and shape, but with wide coloration. Some were reddish-brown, like the monkey who had probed Torg's mind, but with different-shaded faces or tails. Some had gray bodies with black-and-white striped tails. Others were snow-white with black-rimmed eyes and ears.

"We will feed thee," the old lady said, still in the ancient tongue. "We will feed the lovely one."

She waddled over, knelt beside him and took the bowl from the monkey. Using the wooden spoon, she fed him. The soup tasted better than it smelled, containing a rich red broth with delicious chunks of tender meat—sliced from the worm monster, Torg guessed.

Without his teeth Torg could not chew very well, but the meat was cut into small enough bites to swallow whole. Other than the Stone-Eaters' scorching brew, the soup was the first nutritious thing he had eaten in more than a month. When the bowl was empty he begged for another—and another.

"Thou art insatiable. Food will make thee strong. When your strength returns, will thou helpest us?"

After the meal Torg was given several cups of fresh water. He drank deeply and then lay back on the sand bed and took a long nap. But he awoke many times to a strange sensation: The monkeys were cleansing every inch of his skin with their coarse tongues. Then they dressed him in gray robes and a pair of straw sandals.

Upon coming fully awake, he was relieved to discover that some of his former strength had returned. His body was responding to the nourishment, rest and kind treatment. However, his skin itched. He scratched himself all over, finding nubs of hair already starting to grow back. His gums were sore. He skimmed along them with his tongue and discovered the rough edges of teeth, also starting to re-grow. This was not unusual for Tugars. When the desert warriors lost adult teeth—which happened occasionally during battles—they routinely grew back, though it usually took several weeks.

The old woman was by his side, shimmering in the gloom. She stroked his head with her tiny hand. Then she leaned over and licked his nose. Her tongue was coarse. When she smiled, her facial expression was familiar.

Torg knew her. He said, in the ancient tongue: "There is no purpose for this disguise. Discard it. I do not threaten you or your friends."

The old woman sighed. Then she seemed to fold, fade and shrink. In her place sat the little monkey who had first approached him in the torch-lit cavern.

"*Eso tvam avoca yam me upakaaram appekhasi* (You said before that you need my help)," Torg said, sitting upright in the powdery sand. "You have already done so much for me. It would please me—very much—to return the favor."

The monkey wriggled her finger, motioning for Torg to follow. He stood, surprised to find that his legs weren't wobbly. The soup had worked wonders on his battered body.

I must look terrible, he thought, *but I feel better than I have in a long time.* He knew it would take weeks of food, water and rest to return to his former self, if he ever did, but this was an excellent beginning.

Leaving the sword by his bedside, he followed the monkey past the still-bubbling pot of soup into a smaller chamber. There, at least twenty of the creatures huddled in a circle. As Torg came forward they parted, revealing a troublesome sight. The monkey who had been injured by the tentacle lay on the floor. How long had it been since she was bitten? Torg had no idea.

The combined force of their telepathic energy pressed into Torg's mind. A myriad of words swirled within his head. It was confusing, but he understood the general concept.

"Can thou healest her?"

Torg kneeled and placed his ear on her small chest. Her breath arose in staccato bursts. When he touched her, she grunted. Her external wounds had been tended, but Torg could sense there was life-threatening internal damage. He rued the short time he had spent in his own recovery, but he recognized the necessity of it. Had he been any weaker, he would not have been able to aid her.

At least now, he had the strength to try.

Torg yearned for Obhasa. With the aid of his ivory staff, he could have blasted his blue fire in thin beams, making his magic more effective. He had no doubt he could summon enough power to heal the injured monkey, but he didn't know how much control he could muster. It wasn't as simple as bathing the small creature in flame. Torg had to be able to cauterize individual regions of her tiny body, one by one.

Without Obhasa, Torg's fingers would have to serve as the conduit. He placed his right hand on the monkey's chest and focused his concentration on the pads of his fingertips, searching beneath her soft fur for hot spots that would guide him to the wounds. There was a bewildering array of damage beneath the creature's small ribs. Torg struggled to pinpoint a specific injury.

The monkeys perceived his hesitation. As a group they linked their considerable psychic powers to his mind. Their more intimate knowledge of the inner workings of their bodies helped Torg find what he sought.

First, he identified a small tear in her chest that was leaking small drops of blood into surrounding tissue. Torg sent a beam of fire into the wound, closing it with precision.

Next, he discovered a broken rib that had punctured one lung. He disintegrated a portion of the rib and sealed the hole.

Then, he observed poisons surrounding bite wounds on the monkey's chest. He superheated the toxins, turning them into harmless vapors.

Torg's search for injuries continued farther inward. There was a crack in her spine. He closed it and incinerated the leakage. In her right leg he found a splintered bone. He repaired the damage and destroyed the stray splinters. There was mild swelling in her brain, due to a skull fracture above the left ear. He sealed the bone and dissolved excess fluid near the swollen area.

Things were going well.

However, Torg found one injury he could not heal. The trauma had weakened one of the chambers of the monkey's heart. Mending it would require too much precision, even for his abilities. She would have to lie very still for several days and let her body do the rest.

But Torg believed she would survive. As did the cave monkeys. They came to him—now more than seventy in all—and clung to him like bees on a honeycomb.

They appeared to weep with joy. Torg wept, too.

The injured female slept peacefully, her breathing slow and steady.

Torg felt drained. He returned to his bed in the adjoining cavern, ate another large bowlful of soup, relieved himself in the privacy of a back chamber, and then slept for what seemed like an entire night. When he finally stirred again he felt groggy—but otherwise wonderful. He was amazed by how quickly his mind had been able to overcome trauma. In the past few weeks he had endured a lethal combination of physical and mental anguish. But his mind had refused to dwell on it. Instead Torg sat up, stretched and belched.

The sudden noise startled several of the monkeys, and they leaped upward and almost crashed against the stone ceiling. The others chittered, a sound that resembled laughter.

One of the monkeys imitated Torg's belch. Soon they all were laughing, chittering, burping and coughing. In the dim underground chamber they made quite a racket. Torg watched them, smiling all the while.

Several days passed. Torg wandered among the caverns, learning his way, step-by-step. What he saw fascinated him. The monkeys were unendingly clever. They were adept at using fire—always positioning the flames beneath vents in the rock—but they also had other abilities. They cooked, cleaned and bathed themselves. They used knives, spoons and pottery. They even had a kind of school. The youngsters watched the elders perform various skills, including the ultra-dangerous method of collecting their main source of food—the chunks of tentacle meat.

Their artistic abilities were what most astounded Torg. By blending mineral extracts and worm fat, the monkeys created multicolored pigments. Using their fingers as primitive paintbrushes, they adorned the passageways and chambers with images of the other animals that populated their underground world, including many Torg did not recognize. The worm monster played a dominant role in most of the drawings. On a wall in one of the largest caverns, the monster extended from floor to ceiling, its tentacles roaming hungrily through a myriad of winding tunnels. The monkeys portrayed themselves as brave warriors in the illustration, taking on a beast ten thousand times their size.

Torg applauded this depiction—literally. The monkeys clapped along with him.

One day they led him to a well-lit chamber. Its smooth walls were untouched, except for one painting: a life-size image of the wizard—with a huge smile on his face—standing over a pot of soup. For the first time, Torg got to see what he now looked like. At first he was horrified, but then he laughed until tears sprang from his eyes.

Torg stayed with the monkeys more than a week. They led him through dozens of caves and passageways, some brightly lit by torches, others as black as the Realm of the Undead. Occasionally they passed an ominous hole—and the creatures taught him how to duck under or scoot around the opening. Several times a tentacle emerged. The monkeys reacted almost nonchalantly to these sudden appearances.

It took Torg awhile to realize the cave monkeys did not hate or fear the worm monster. For one thing, it single-handedly kept the underground free of vermin. But that was merely a side benefit. In reality the monkeys were utterly dependent on the monster for their survival. If it were destroyed, they also would perish. Without the worm's precious flesh, there wasn't enough food in the lower depths to support their colony. They were ill-equipped to hunt close to the surface and appeared unable to bear the brutality of sunlight. They were—and probably always had been—creatures of the underworld.

On the sixth day of Torg's stay, the monkeys took him on a hunt. He brought the Silver Sword and the monkeys their stone daggers. They returned to the large cavern where Torg originally had met them. The great wall stood before them, full of empty holes.

Before scampering to preassigned positions, the monkeys lit dozens of torches. Then they began to pound the handles of their daggers against the wall, in perfect rhythm. Within a few moments hundreds of tentacles emerged from the holes. The monkeys danced from limb to limb, hacking and slicing and barely avoiding death.

Torg strode forward, holding the sword in both hands. With one lightning-quick stroke he hacked off the ends of five tentacles. Under these conditions, the worm monster was no match for him. It sensed its peril and withdrew.

Torg held his arms aloft like a hero, the severed tentacles wriggling at his feet. But the cave monkeys were not pleased. He had upset their delicate balance and had shamed them in the process. As soon as he understood his mistake, he felt embarrassed and ignorant.

The monkeys eventually forgave him, but they never trusted the sword again. In their minds, it seemed to endanger their symbiotic relationship with the worm, and they wanted nothing to do with it. At one point Torg had considered giving the sword to them as a gift. Now he knew better. So he buried it beneath the sand of his bed and left it hidden there.

On the eighth day, the old woman reappeared and spoke to Torg.

"Lovely one, I must ask . . . how long will thou stayest?"

Torg paused. Then he sighed. "Those far away depend on me. I am one who commands. I am needed above."

"I . . . we . . . understand. Then the old woman sighed, and tears fell from her eyes. "We will prepare, but we will be highly sorrowful."

"Oh, my wonderful friend, so will I . . . so will I."

On the morning of the tenth day, Torg knew it was time to depart. The monkeys gave him a cloth bag containing dried worm meat and raw mushrooms. To find the mushrooms, they probably must have journeyed much closer to the surface than they would have preferred, but providing Torg with food had become an honor. They seemed to love him as much as he loved them.

Torg still wore the gray robes and sandals they had given him. He turned to the leader and asked her where they had gotten the robes and the bag, and also where they had found the wood to make the torches and their eating utensils. There was no way to weave fabrics in a world of stone, and there was no wood so deep beneath the surface.

She answered, telepathically. *We find things down here that shouldn't be here. Something leaves things for us. We don't know who or what. Sometimes, we see a white-haired lady.*

Torg wondered what else they had discovered. Did they have a stash of hidden treasure? He hoped they did—and that it brought them pleasure. But who was the mysterious being or beings that helped his little friends? Perhaps one day he could return and find out.

The reddish-brown monkey who sometimes appeared to him as the old woman came forward and took his hand, leading him toward the middle of the chamber. The colony spread apart, making a path.

Tears flooded Torg's eyes. The monkey who had been injured stood before him, leaning on a small staff. Torg knelt in front of her and bowed, positioning his face just a finger-length above the sand floor. When he lifted his head he recognized gratitude in her expression. She came to him, placed her small hands on his cheeks, leaned forward and licked him on the tip of his nose.

Torg continued to cry. Tears came far too easily these days—especially for one who claimed to be a warrior—but he didn't care. Using his powers to heal a living being, rather than destroy one, pleased him beyond words. He had done far too much killing during his long life. And there would be so much more.

He rose to his full height, towering above the monkeys. The tallest of them did not reach his knees. He started to speak, but what he saw stopped him cold. Every member of the colony had imitated him, bowing with their faces a finger-length from the sand.

Torg was astonished.

Finally he said, *"Sahaayaa me, titthatha. Tumhe ariyaani sattamaani. Tumhe na koci puujetha.* (My friends, please rise. You are the highest quality. You bow to no one.)"

One by one they came to him and clung to him. Some hugged his legs. Others climbed onto his broad back and shoulders. Each one lifted his robes and licked a portion of his skin. Then they left the chamber, wearing expressions of sorrow.

Torg was devastated. The sadness he felt re-awoke his grief over Sōbhana's death. He stood alone in the chamber for a long time.

His friend—their leader—waited patiently in the entryway. Finally Torg composed himself, picked up the cloth bag and the Silver Sword, and followed her along a familiar tunnel. For his benefit she carried a single torch to light their way. As they walked through the winding passageways, Torg caught occasional glimpses of wide, glowing eyes just out of range of the torchlight. Many of the monkeys were following him. They still weren't ready to say their final goodbyes. Torg was grateful for their company.

Torg never could have found his way out on his own. The gallery zigzagged numerous times, opening into countless tunnels and chambers. His guide knew which paths to choose and which to ignore.

The temperatures varied widely. When they came near pockets of magma, the air grew unbearably hot. At other times it was bitterly cold. For much of their journey Torg was able to walk upright, but several times the ceiling lowered and he was forced to hunch over. Sometimes he had to crawl.

All told, they traveled more than three leagues, though they had probably ascended less than a thousand vertical paces. Boulders and stagnant pools of water hindered their progress. Finally they entered an enormous cavern that was well-lit—not by magma or torchlight, but by sunlight creeping down from above. Torg looked at his friend. She already was in pain, her eyes squinting. He understood she could go no farther.

Out loud, Torg said, "I will miss you, precious one. Thank you for saving my life."

She responded, telepathically. *And I will miss you, lovely one. Thank you for saving my sister's life.*

The monkey retreated into the semi-darkness and then waved her thin arm. Torg could sense the sadness in her eyes. He felt the same, and more. She gestured toward a small passageway that exited the cavern. Torg nodded. He walked toward the light.

He couldn't resist turning around one last time. At the edge of the darkness, the old woman had reappeared. As always she was smiling.

Then she vanished.

Torg sat down on a flat stone, disconsolate. To take his mind off his sadness he ate some of the dried meat and raw mushrooms. The upper parts of his teeth had broken through the surface of his gums, and he finally was able to chew, which made the food taste even more delicious. Near his feet was a clear pool of water, and he drank his fill. Part of him wanted to forsake the surface world and return to his primate friends, but he knew he would not be able to find them on his own. Once again he vowed to return one day—if Invictus were defeated and peace returned to Triken—and try to reconnect with the precious colony.

Until that time, if it ever came, he would mourn their absence.

Torg sighed. It was now or never. He stood, picked up his belongings—a simple bag of food and an ancient sword—and ascended the difficult passageway. It was steep and slippery. He soon found himself gasping for breath. But the higher he climbed, the brighter it became, motivating him.

The quality of the air began to change. During his stay underground Torg had grown too used to mustiness. This air was crisp, cold and dry—and engorged with oxygen. The richness of it overwhelmed his lungs, but at the same time it filled them with sweetness and vitality. Torg was a creature of the surface. And it was to there, after his long suffering, that he would now return.

When he stepped from the mouth of the cave, it was near dusk in the southern foothills of Mount Asubha. Though it was still only late autumn, the temperature was well below freezing, and there were scattered patches of snow on the ground. Most of the trees, except a few hemlocks and pines, had dropped their leaves. The darkening sky was clear and deep-blue; almost everything else was white, brown, or gray.

The beauty of it smote Torg's heart.
In response, he held his arms aloft.
Opened his mouth as wide as he could.
And howled.
The sound was deafening.
And frightening.
But he wanted his return to be made known.
To the Tugars. And to all.
Despair had done its best to destroy him.
And it had failed.
Do you understand what that means?
By now, you must.
He was *The Torgon*.
Still.
And he was . . . free.

The Trappers

1

Torg stood at the mouth of a cave, his breath exploding in white puffs. Other than trees, he saw no living beings. It also was well below freezing, and the temperature continued to plunge. At least the sky was clear, and there was no immediate threat of a storm.

The thin gray robes given to him by the cave monkeys provided scant protection. Torg could venture no farther this night. A vast stretch of wilderness stood between him and the nearest city. Until he could find warmer clothing, he would be forced to travel during the day.

Though he had journeyed to many remote areas of Triken, he'd never been this far north on this side of the Mahaggata Mountains. Still, he had studied maps and knew the area well enough. He guessed that Kamupadana, home of the Warlish witches and their hag servants, was about fifteen leagues to the southwest. Avici, the stronghold of Invictus, was about sixty leagues due south. Tējo, the Great Desert, was more than two hundred leagues away.

Torg had some thinking to do, but it was too late to make any decisions tonight. For now what he needed more than anything was a fire. In such a remote location he doubted he had much to fear from prying eyes.

Looking for firewood, he wandered from the cave into the nearby woods. The oaks, birches, and maples were bare. The trees were widely spaced with little foliage beneath, and Torg was amazed to see that portions of the ground were coated with ash from the fallout of the destruction of Asubha. But he found plenty of dead wood and soon had a large-enough pile to burn through the night. Some of the logs were damp, so he used the Silver Sword to strip off the soaked bark. He returned to the cave and chose a flat area to build his fire, using several thick logs to construct a lean-to over a pile of kindling.

During his ordeal with Vedana, Torg had exhausted the majority of his *Death Energy*. With food and rest, a sizable portion might regenerate, though he would not regain full strength until he again achieved *Sammaasamaadhi*. But in order to escape the pit, he had been forced to perform a *Death Visit* just three months after his previous one, which was too soon. He preferred a year between visits—and at the least would have to wait several months before his next attempt. However, he wasn't powerless . . . even now. Effortlessly he mustered a burst of blue flame from the tips of his fingers, and soon the lean-to was ablaze. In the night air the smoke would settle like a fog over the land, and anyone within half a league would be able to smell it. But he didn't care. Even in his weakened condition he was more than capable of defending himself.

The fire sparked, crackled, and grew hot. Torg stood near, enjoying the much-needed warmth. He had leaned the sword against a nearby rock, and out of curiosity, he now picked it up and slid the blade into the hottest flames. Where the sword entered, a pocket of air formed around the supernal metal, as if the fire was unwilling to touch it. When he withdrew the sword, he pressed his fingers against the blade and found that it was as cold as if it had been lying in snow.

Torg stared at the weapon for a long time. The sight of it reminded him of his final moments with Sōbhana. Grief surged over him, and he plopped down on a flat rock, placed the sword at his feet and buried his face in his hands. When he sobbed, his entire body shook.

Afterward he felt a little better, the painful bout of tears purging a portion of his lament. He opened the bag of food given to him by the cave monkeys and investigated its contents. There was enough to last for about three days, if he rationed it. But he wasn't overly concerned. He needed only enough for a meal now and a good breakfast in the morning. After that he would be able to find more food, even in late autumn. There would be plenty of nuts, and the woods were bursting with deer, possums, squirrels and rabbits.

As if sitting down to a feast, Torg ate half of what remained in the bag, pleased that his teeth had already grown in enough to chew. The dried worm meat and mushrooms tasted wonderful. Then he scooped up several handfuls of snow. For now, that was enough to quench his thirst. But in the morning he would need to find water, which also would not be difficult. It was probable that several active streams were within a thousand paces of where he stood.

Tomorrow he would go in search of food and clothing. Although he had the ability to kill game and tan hides, he'd have to stay in one place for a week or more to accomplish it. That was not acceptable. Regardless, he believed he could find warmer clothing. The wilderness was vast but not barren, and it was likely that others wandered these woods. In return for a cloak and boots, he would barter his services. And if he ran into any uncooperative sorts, he would convince them that it was not wise to make a Death-Knower angry.

Soon he would take the first steps on his long journey toward vengeance. But he would have to be patient. There were many leagues to travel, many plans to make. And eventually, many battles to wage. Torg tossed more logs onto the fire. Then he sat cross-legged and meditated for two hundred slow breaths before allowing himself to sleep.

He dreamt of his dead father.

In the fiery heat of midsummer, Torg, who had seen just eighteen summers, and Asēkha-Jhana stood on an escarpment overlooking a dry lake bed. Beyond the mile-wide playa, a series of sand dunes tumbled toward the horizon like frozen waves. Though it was just an hour past dawn, it was more than one hundred and ten degrees in the heart of the Great Desert, and the crusty surface of the lake bed was a good deal hotter. But that didn't stop the Vasi masters from beginning that day's training session with their Tugar novices. Fifty masters wore black jackets and breeches; a thousand novices wore white.

Jhana pressed against his tall, young son. "Today's lesson is called Aarakaa Himsaa,*" he said to Torg. "In the ancient tongue,* Aarakaa Himsaa *means* away from harm, *though the masters prefer to call it 'keeping a safe distance.' The idea is simple: If you stay far enough away from your adversary, he, she or it will not be able to harm you. This does not mean that you should run away. It only means that you should always remain at least a hair's width from your adversary's longest strike."*

Torg watched the novices begin their training with one hundred slow breaths of mindful meditation and follow that with a carefully orchestrated bow in honor of their masters. The bow contained seven separate movements, each performed with meticulous precision to the rhythm of the Bheri, a thunderous drum.

After the ceremony was completed, the students lined up in fifty parallel columns, with a master at the head of each. The first student in every column was given a bo, a wooden stave that was five cubits long. Then the novices were instructed to attack the masters with their bo, thrusting and stroking in a series of sporadic movements. With simplistic ease the masters stayed just out of range, jumping backward, sliding sideways, stepping forward. Torg was fascinated. When the students struck quickly, the masters reacted slowly. When the students slowed their attacks, the masters sped up their defense, constantly changing rhythm but never varying distance.

As far as Torg could tell, not a single instructor was touched.

Jhana laughed. "The masters enjoy Aarakaa Himsaa. *It gives them yet another chance to show off. But it's clearly valuable. During my fifty years of training I spent more than one thousand hours practicing various forms of these movements. As you can imagine, the more you practice the better you get."*

"Fifty years is such a long time, father. I don't know if I have the patience. I want to be a warrior now."

"Think of it as eighteen thousand days, Torg. That way it won't seem so long." Then he laughed heartily. *"All youngsters feel the same. And some do* not *have the patience—and they fail. But a time will come in your training when your resistance will snap. That will be a painful day. But the training becomes easier and far more pleasurable afterward. Besides, if you train hard enough and long enough, a day will come when you can teach your master a lesson. That is a joyful day."*

"You could defeat a Vasi master? I thought they were invincible."

"I am Asēkha—beyond the masters and all others. One day you'll become an Asēkha. For me, that will be a very joyful day. But I'm already proud of you. You have no idea how much talent you possess. If only your mother were here with us. She was an even better fighter than I, you know."

"You have told me that every day of my life," Torg said. *"But I never grow tired of hearing it. I didn't know her, yet I miss her so much."*

"Aaaah, Torg, do not despair. She wouldn't allow either of us to mourn. Dying while giving birth to you was her karma, just as continuing without her was yours and mine. But she lives on . . . in you. Your face looks just like her, my beautiful son."

Then Jhana began to wander backward.

"Father, where are you going?"

A mist swirled about the Asēkha. He floated toward the blazing sky and was swept away by the hot desert breeze.

"Father, wait! Don't go. Not yet."

Torg bolted upright. The first thing he saw was the Silver Sword, pale and lifeless at his side. The sun had risen, but the sky was thick with ugly clouds, and a chill breeze swept across his brow. The fire he'd built the night before still smoldered, but it emitted little warmth.

Torg sighed.

He wasn't eighteen years old.

He was more than a thousand.

And his beloved father was centuries dead, reduced to just a memory that grew dimmer with each day.

It had been a dream, no more.

But the two grizzled men and the white-haired woman who approached from the trees were all too real.

One of the men was huge—tall as Torg and as thick around the belly as an oak—and the hair on his head, face and neck grew together into one grimy tangle. He had small eyes, but his nose was long and oddly shaped. Torg studied him carefully, and soon there was no doubt. This one was a crossbreed—part man, part animal. From the looks of it, the animal portion was a bear.

Throughout the land there were a select few with magic powerful enough to conjure such a creature: Invictus, Vedana, Bhayatupa, the Warlish witches. But whoever had made this one no longer controlled him. He roamed freely, and by the looks of him, was dangerous. In addition to his intimidating height and girth, he carried an axe so heavy few could have lifted it from the ground, much less wielded it.

The second man was dwarfed by the first, even though he was large by ordinary standards. He also had long dark hair and a thick beard, but he was better groomed—and startlingly handsome, his wily blue eyes intelligent and alert. This one was not a crossbreed, but that made him no less dangerous. He held a spear in one hand and had a dagger in his belt.

The woman was the smallest of the three. Her hair was white as snow, accentuating her green eyes, and she wielded a fancy wood bow, probably stolen, that was already nocked and drawn with a flint-tipped arrow aimed at Torg's heart.

"Friend, I says to ya, we wish for no trouble," the smaller man said, his eyes fixed on Torg's every movement. "We miserable wretches are tortured enough, as is. Rest assured, we will leave ya in peace once ya meet our slight demand."

"Let me shoot him dead and be done with him," the woman snarled. "Why waste our time with foolish words?"

The leader glared at the woman. Then he turned back to Torg and smiled. "Don't listen to the Bitch. If it were my choice, I would stay awhiles and make lots of friendly talk. But we have travelled far, and our feet are lamed. We must be moving along."

The crossbreed stomped forward, his breath bursting from his mouth. "The Bitch is right. No more talking is what I wants. Give me the sword, Master Ogre, or I will remove your foul noggin'."

The smaller man shook his head. "Ya heard them," he said, as if resigned to an unwelcome fate. "My friends have not a speck of good humor in their bones. Angry words give me a belly-ache, but what is I to do? I dares not try to control the whims of such frightful peoples."

Torg rose to his feet, the Silver Sword at his side. "You have traveled far, but not as far as I," he said in a voice that sounded almost normal to him, now that his teeth were growing back. "And I'm exhausted and lack my usual grace. In better times I might find the three of you amusing. But today I have no patience. Besides, your demand is unacceptable. The sword is precious to me, and I would not abandon it, even under threat from an army of enemies. But I have demands of my own, and I counsel you to obey them. I am in dire need of warm clothing. Take me to your camp and show me what you possess. Be quick, and I'll reward you. Defy me, and I'll strip the clothes off your backs."

Torg's bold words dumbfounded all three of them. The crossbreed's mouth sprang open. The leader clapped his hand against his forehead and chuckled. But the woman reacted without hesitation, letting the arrow fly.

Despite her quickness, Torg was not caught unaware. He could have knocked the arrow out of the air with his sword, but he wanted to impress them, so he allowed it to strike his chest. The arrow bounced off, as if his flesh were made of stone.

"He is Demon Spawn," the woman said. "Me arrow would've killed a Buffelo."

"None of you wields a weapon capable of harming me," Torg said. "I'm beyond you. Do you doubt it?" Then he willed his eyes to glow with a deep-blue intensity. "I'm no ogre or demon," he continued in a booming voice. "I'm far *greater*! If you test my patience too severely, you'll do so at your peril."

Whether frightened or enraged, the crossbreed could stand no more, and he rushed at Torg with his axe held high, swinging a mighty blow. Torg avoided it easily. One thousand hours of *Aarakaa Himsaa* were more than a match for such a crude attack.

The smaller man flung his dagger. This time Torg didn't allow himself to be struck. He flicked the Silver Sword, knocking the blade out of the air.

Torg believed he was capable of killing all three with ease. But he preferred not to kill unless it was absolutely necessary, and his instincts told him that these odd companions might be of use to him. They were ruthless but not evil. Still, he needed to disable them, at least temporarily, until he could earn their confidence. They were too feisty to be trusted just yet.

The crossbreed dropped his axe and slung his arms around Torg's torso in an attempt to crush him. Torg dropped the sword, placed his palms on the sides of the giant's neck and compressed the main arteries, temporarily cutting off the flow of blood to the brain. During his warrior training, he had practiced this move only a few dozen times, but it was simple to learn and always effective.

The crossbreed's eyes rolled to the back of his head. Then he let go of Torg, took a step back, and said "Huh!" before collapsing into unconsciousness.

"Ya have killed Ugga, ya Bastud!" The smaller man sprinted toward Torg and threw the spear.

Torg ducked as the spear zipped past, clattering against a boulder. The man continued forward at full speed. But in Torg's perception of time, the attacker moved in slow motion.

Torg caught the man by his wrists, rotated on his hips, and flung him face-first into the smoldering remains of the fire. His adversary squealed like a pig and rolled off the embers, brushing himself frenetically.

"Bard, me dears. I comes to save ya!" The white-haired woman leapt at Torg, snarling like a lioness protecting her cubs. But Torg punched her in the solar plexus—lightly, by his standards—and then tossed her aside. She landed awkwardly on the hard stone by the mouth of the cave and lay still.

The one she called Bard stood up warily, bits of charred debris still smoking in his beard. Without the dagger and spear he had no visible weapons, though Torg suspected he had more hidden beneath his cloak.

"Will ya kill us all?" Bard said. "We deserve it, I supposes. But Master Ogre, ya could do me a great favor if ya killed just me and let the others go. I loves them and would hate to witness their endings."

"Put your hands by your side and come to me."

"If I does, ya will skewer me with that blade," said Bard, motioning toward the sword that lay at Torg's feet.

"If you do as I say, I promise not to kill any of you. My word is worth much."

Bard looked down at Ugga, who lay flat on his back, eyes closed, breathing slowly, as if taking a nap. The woman lay still as well, though she was moaning.

"And what of Jord?" Bard said, pointing at the woman. "Will ya defile the Bitch? I could not bear it."

"I'm no rapist," Torg said. "If you could see me as I truly am, you would find my words more believable. Still, you have no choice but to trust me. You cannot defeat me in battle. I say it again, put your hands by your side and come to me."

Bard remained unconvinced. "Ya could not best me again, so easy."

Torg sighed. "If you do not come to me, I will come to you. And we shall see what we shall see."

Bard reached inside his coat and drew out another dagger.

Torg closed the gap between them and grasped the man's hand with his thumb and forefinger. He squeezed wickedly, contorting the wrist.

Bard cried out and dropped the weapon.

Torg drew the man's face close. "*Niddaayahi!*" Blue smoke burst from his mouth and swirled into Bard's nostrils. The trapper instantly fell into a deep sleep, and Torg lowered him gently to the ground.

Next, he walked over to the woman by the mouth of the cave. Scattered patches of ice clung to the stone floor, and he struggled to keep his footing in his flimsy sandals. Jord held her abdomen, groaning and coughing. Torg knew he hadn't struck her hard enough to do serious damage, but he leaned down to get a closer look.

She was craftier than he had given her credit. She kicked at his left ankle, knocking his foot off the ground. His other foot was positioned on some ice, and it slid sideways. Torg fell on his face, amazed. He had never been bested in such a way before.

The woman ran toward the trees. But Torg was up in an instant, kicking off the annoying sandals and chasing after her.

"Wait . . . wait! I will harm you no further."

Even barefoot, Torg was quicker. She must have sensed his approach because she tried to run even faster, which caused her to stumble and fall. She scrambled to her knees just as he caught up.

Torg grabbed one arm, but she spun around and bit him on the wrist. Her teeth were hard and flat but no match for his flesh. Her eyes flew open, as if she had chomped on a piece of wood, and when she felt the strength of his hand, she went limp.

"Do not kill me, Master Ogre! Do not eat my heart or slurp my blood. I will do whatever ya ask. I will be your Concubeen, if I must. But please, don't kill me. I doesn't want to die so young." Then she burst into tears and shivered on the ground at his feet.

Torg wasn't fooled. Her cowardly display was mostly for show, buying her time to think up another way to escape. Grasping a handful of her hair, he yanked her to her feet. She yelped like a dog that had been kicked in the ribs.

Tugars knew more than fifty pressure points on the human body which, when stimulated, were capable of causing debilitating pain. Torg pressed his thick thumb into a spot just below her right elbow. Jord screamed so loudly her voice echoed in the trees.

"I'm beginning to think that all three of you are deaf," Torg said. "I'll try to make my intentions clear, yet again. If you do as I say, I will not harm you. And I have no desire to make you my *Concubeen*, whatever that might be."

Through the long strands of white hair that had fallen over her eyes, Jord looked up at him with renewed anger. "Do ya think me ugly?"

Torg couldn't help it. He threw his head back and laughed. "No, you're not ugly. This has nothing to do with how you look, though you're in more need of a bath than I."

She drew her breath in with a hiss.

"Do not take offense," Torg said. "For now, sex is the least of my concerns. What I need more than anything is warm clothing and a hot meal. I would love some bread. Vegetables. Roasted meat. A mug of beer or a cup of wine. Aaah . . . what I wouldn't do for either."

The woman sat on her haunches and brushed the hair from her eyes. She looked at Bard and Ugga. "Are they dead?"

Torg chuckled again. "The big one—Ugga, you call him?—will have a bit of a headache when he wakes up, and Bard might be groggy. But otherwise they'll be fine. I'm glad you care. You'll be more likely to do as I say, if you fear for their safety."

"I ran like a coward," Jord said. "I'm ashamed. But ya scared me so."

"Make it up to them. Do as I say, and I won't hurt them any more. Do you have a camp nearby?"

"We have a house, less than a league from here. It's *my* house. We were hunting for our breakfast when we smelled your fire. We planned to make off with your sword, which has the look of value."

"It does have value. But it's mine, and I plan to keep it. Do you have any food at the house?"

"I has flour and yeast for bread, and plenty o' hickory butter. There is a barrel with squashes and wild potatoes. And I has spices, too."

"Take me there. We'll prepare a meal. Before this is over, you and I will be friends."

Jord motioned to Ugga and Bard. "Will ya leave them? The cold'll kill them before just a short time passes."

"No, I won't leave them."

"But they are too big to carry."

"Not for me."

2

Torg offered his hand to Jord. The green-eyed woman allowed him to lift her to her feet. He turned away and walked back to the cave, where Ugga and Bard lay unconscious. He reached down, picked up the Silver Sword and slid it into the belt of his robes.

Jord followed him.

Torg imagined she must be tempted to pick up a stone and bash his skull. But she had seen how he fought, and probably didn't dare. First he went to Bard and lifted the smaller man with little effort. Then he laid him alongside the giant crossbreed.

Jord got on her hands and knees and put her ear against Bard's chest—and did the same for Ugga. "Are ya sure they will live, Master Ogre? If they die, it will be the foulest torment to me."

"If they are half as strong as they appear, they will not die. Ugga will wake up first. Bard won't open his eyes until late tonight or early tomorrow, but when he does he'll feel strong and rested."

"Ya have performed these fantastical deeds before? Where did ya learn such trickery? Ya felled Ugga with a slap of your hands. And ya made Bard sleep with smoke belched from your stomach. I would not have believed it possible. Ugga and Bard have never been bested, at least whilst I was watching. Even the blows of wicked savages do not injure them."

"I've received proper training."

"Ya do not fool me. Ya persist in saying ya not be Demon. But I believes ya not be Man. Ya must be a great Conjurer of Magic, arisen from the bowels of the mountains to haunt this world. What is your name, Master Ogre? Can ya tell me that?"

Torg laughed again. "In some ways, you speak the truth. I *did* come from the bowels of the mountains, though not by choice. I'm *not* a man, at least not in the way I take you to mean. And I *am* able to conjure magic, though there have been times in my life when I've been more capable than now. As for my name, I choose not to reveal it. Please do not take offense. I'd make a dangerous ally. Knowing who I am could be perilous."

Jord sighed. "We must call ya something."

"Very well. Call me . . . Hana. That name is as good as any."

Torg retrieved his bag of food and offered Jord a mushroom. To his surprise, she took it without protest. After tasting it, her eyes opened wide with delight.

"Hah-nah, do ya have great quantities of these mushrooms? They are better than any I has ever tasted. I begs to know—from where did they come?"

"As for quantity, I have only what you see," Torg said, opening the bag for her perusal. "As for where, let me just say that the world beneath our feet is not lifeless."

"I hopes to never find out," said Jord, who reached back into the bag, pulled out another mushroom, and chomped hungrily. Torg envied her full set of teeth.

"Wait, Hah-nah! I changes my mind. I wants to go into the cavern and get some more. Will ya show me?"

Torg sighed. He suspected she was exaggerating her pleasure for his benefit. "One day I'll return to the cave, if my karma allows. But for now, my errands are too urgent."

Then he handed the bag to Jord and knelt between the two unconscious men. The woman gasped when Torg threw Ugga over one shoulder and Bard over the other. When he stood, Jord almost swooned.

"Can ya carry Buffelos with your bare hands?"

"I must admit, these two are heavier than I thought," Torg said, trying not to grunt too much. "But I'll manage. Lead the way, Jord. The quicker we get to your camp, the quicker I can put them down. Their stink is worse than their bulk."

Jord found that quite amusing, bending over and slapping her knee. The woman started off through the woods. After a few hundred paces the land sloped downward into a hollow. The footing was treacherous, especially considering Torg was lugging more than forty stones of dead weight. Plus, he was walking barefoot, and his feet were already numb. But his dense flesh was otherwise impervious. Rocks or roots could inflict minor pain, but they could not cause cuts or bruises of any consequence.

They soon came upon a clear-running stream. Torg set down his burden, buried his face in the icy water, and drank deeply despite the cold. Jord joined him, getting down on hands and knees and burying her face in the water, but when he lingered too long by the water, she became annoyed.

"Come. It is yet a far ways."

The white-haired woman traveled much lighter than Torg. All she carried was her bow and arrows, Bard's spear and Torg's small bag of food. She had been forced to leave Ugga's immense axe, though she had hid it under some leaves before they departed.

Jord sprinted as fast as one of his Tugars. Torg wondered suspiciously how he had been able to catch her so easily back at the cave. Gasping for breath and sweating profusely, he was forced to halt several times and drop the men on the ground less gently than he should have.

"Must ya wander along so slowly?" Jord said. "We've gone less than a hectare. Almost a league still lies betwixt here and our neighborhood. Would ya like me to carry the sword? Ya keep trippin' over it."

"If you had any idea what I've been through in the past few weeks, you would be amazed that I could walk on my own, much less carry these brutes. And no, I don't want you to carry the sword. But if your wildness demands it, go on ahead. I'll follow your footprints."

"An excellent idea, Hah-nah. I'll start the fires. Beyond this hollow, ya will find a splendorous wood where the pines rise to vast bigness. Our house lies beyond the great trees."

"Whatever you say. But in the time it takes me to catch up to you, please try to learn a proper language."

"Hmmph! Your speech is the one lacking, Master Ogre."

"You will lack your head, if you're not careful."

She responded with another hmmph! Then she ran off, fast as a filly.

Torg watched Jord sprint along the base of the hollow, scramble up the side of a hill, and disappear into the trees. Despite the presence of Ugga and Bard, who lay at his feet like a pair of logs, Torg felt alone. He fantasized about leaving them and jogging after Jord, ridding himself of his annoying burdens.

But he knew if he ever did something so selfish, his karma would haunt him. Nothing good ever came from such an act of cruelty.

Torg sighed. For better or worse, Ugga and Bard were in his care. He hoisted both men onto his shoulders, slipped a little on the icy ground, uttered some ancient profanities and started forward. His toes were numb. He was in no danger of frostbite, but he was not immune to discomfort.

"Must ya wander along so slowly?" Torg said, mimicking Jord's annoying pattern of speech. "Let's see how fast you could wander with these two Buffelos on your back, ya bitch."

Torg walked clumsily along the floor of the hollow, which was littered with fallen trees and crumbled boulders. Compared to Jord's joyous trot through the bowl-shaped depression, he moved as slowly as a snail. When he reached the hill that she had ascended so easily, Torg looked up with dread. How could he possibly carry these two lugs up there and have the strength to go any farther? He was hungrier than he was thirsty, and he remembered—with renewed annoyance—that he hadn't eaten since the night before. To make matters worse, Jord had taken what little food he had left.

Torg's legs were wobbly. His sojourn with the cave monkeys had strengthened him somewhat, but he was not even close to being fully recovered from his ordeal in the pit. A journey this physically stressful was the last thing he needed. But disabling Ugga and Bard had been his choice, so he subdued his internal whining.

The hill was steep, but not high—no more than fifty paces to its peak. Still, scaling it turned out to be even more difficult than Torg had feared. About halfway up he had to put Bard down, hoist Ugga to the top and return to his smaller companion. By the time all three were out of the hollow, it was almost noon. Torg sprawled on the ground next to the two men, wheezing like a weary old man.

As he lay on his back, he was surprised to hear Ugga moaning. Torg didn't believe it possible that the crossbreed could awaken this quickly. Maybe the bear part of him had better recuperative powers than an ordinary person's. Torg watched Ugga closely, curious to see if he would move.

Suddenly the crossbreed sat up, let out a roar and struggled to his feet. But he didn't stay upright for long. Instead he fell forward onto his face and lay still for a few seconds before rising to his knees. Then he made a strange face—and vomited. The stink was terrible.

Torg stood up and backed away.

"How did I get here?" Ugga said. "Where are ya, Bard? Where are ya, Bitch? My head hurts terrible. And I has lost me axe!"

"Are you able to walk?" Torg said, from behind the crossbreed's back. "I surely hope so. Carrying you has been most unpleasant. You're as heavy as a camel."

Still on his knees, the crossbreed spun around in reaction to the voice. He stood up again, lost his balance and tumbled backward, landing roughly on his rump. Then he sat there with a quizzical expression, staring at Torg with a sort of awe.

"Do ya mean to kill me, Master Ogre? Without me axe, I knows I can't stop ya from ending me days. Have ya murdered Bard and the Bitch? Did ya swallow them while I slept?"

Torg rolled his eyes. "Let me answer your questions one at a time. Do I mean to kill you? Not if you behave yourself and do what you're told. Have I murdered Bard and the Bitch? Bard, as you can see, is sleeping soundly just a few paces away, and 'the Bitch' is already back at your camp, preparing a meal. Or she'd damn well better be. Have I eaten your companions while you slept? I'm not that hungry yet, but if I don't get some normal food soon, I might eat all three of you . . . *raw.*"

Ugga began to cry. It was an unusual sound, coming from someone so large and dangerous. "Please, Master Ogre. Don't kill poor, ugly Ugga . . . or his two nicey friends. Bard and the Bitch have treated me kindly. I *will* behave, I promises." He covered his face with his hands.

"All right," Torg said. "I believe you, Ugga. As I said before, you and the others have nothing to fear from me." Then Torg held out his hand. "Trust me. If I meant to kill you, would I have waited until you woke up? And would I have carried you all the way here on my back? I need food, drink and clothing—not murder and mayhem. And I'd relish some friendly talk by a warm fire after I've filled my stomach."

Ugga's small eyes opened wide, apparently stunned by the strength of Torg's grip. He stood and faced him. They were almost the same height.

"I trusts ya, Master Ogre," Ugga said, bowing his head. "I will do as ya say." Then the crossbreed looked at his smaller companion, who lay on his back on the frozen ground, with a grin on his face. "Will Bard ever wake up?"

"Probably not before next morning. But he won't be sick like you were. Still, we do need to get him to a warm place soon. Is her house—as Jord calls it—comfortable?"

"Her house is small, but it's very nice, I thinks. I takes ya there now, Master Ogre. Would it make ya mad if I carried Bard?"

"Ugga, if you'll carry Bard, I promise to be your friend for as long as we both live. But there's one other thing you must do for me, regardless."

"What's that, Master Ogre?"

"Please . . . *please* . . . call me Hana!"

As they started out, Torg shivered in his thin robes, and his bare feet were now numb past his ankles. Otherwise he felt like he was in paradise. He had forgotten how pleasant it was just to walk on his own, without lugging forty stones of odoriferous weight. Ugga now carried Bard, and the muscular crossbreed appeared to be having an easy time of it.

"I smell smoke," Torg said. "Do you think Jord is cooking something? I can't remember ever being this hungry."

"It's not far, Master Ogre . . . errr . . . Hah-nah," Ugga said, shifting Bard to his other shoulder. "I smells smoke and food, too, I thinks."

"Jord didn't mention anything about fresh game," Torg said, "but I swear I smell venison."

"Knowing the Bitch, she got a deer after she left ya," Ugga said, breathing hard but moving at a steady pace. "There are many in these woods. With her bow, she can slay a Buffelo from a furlong away. With her help, Bard and I kill lots of beasties and tan the hides—and we sell them to the merchants in Kamupadana for gold coins. But the whores tempt us with their pretty bodies. I likes the Brounettos best of all. Bard goes for the Blondies. The Bitch gets angry if we don't bring back more than a smile."

"Does Jord get jealous?" Torg said. "It seems she and Bard are a couple."

Suddenly Ugga dropped Bard to the ground and collapsed, as if he had been struck in the back with an arrow. Torg drew his sword and looked quickly around, searching for signs of an ambush.

Ugga's face reddened, his eyes filled with tears, and he appeared to be in terrible pain. Baffled, Torg started toward the crossbreed to see what he could do. But then he sighed in relief. Ugga wasn't injured. Instead, a titanic fit of laughter had rendered him helpless.

The crossbreed rolled onto his side and held his thick stomach, thrashing his legs and pounding his fists on the ground. Bizarre grunts and squeals came from his mouth. He belched and farted before succumbing to a fit of coughing. A good time later he managed to compose himself, sitting up and wiping his eyes.

"Master Ogre . . . Hah-nah, I means . . . if ya do not intend to kill me, ya won't say such a thing again. In all my life, I has never heard anything so funny. Bard and the Bitch, a Cup-pull?"

Ugga lost control again. As he laughed, gobs of sputum froze on his beard. It went on for so long, Torg finally sat cross-legged on the ground and waited for it to stop.

"Sorry . . . sorry . . . Hah-nah," Ugga said. "After we have eaten, we will tell ya the story of Bard and the Bitch. Then ya will better understand the reasons for my crazy giggling."

"Don't apologize. It's been a long time since I've heard this kind of laughter. To be honest, it warms my heart. And after you tell me about Bard and the Bitch, I'd like to hear the story of Ugga."

"Only if ya tell me about Hah-nah."

"Fair enough."

Ugga lifted Bard and started up the hill, Torg at his side. When they reached the crest, Torg stopped. The land descended toward a narrow creek and then rose again in a series of lumps and ledges before flattening into a high plain. Where the plain began, a row of pines towered like titans over the lesser trees that stood nearby. Each tree was twice as large as any pine Torg had seen—more than two hundred cubits tall with trunks eight cubits thick. There were trees in Dhutanga that were greater in size, but Torg had never witnessed any so majestic on this side of the mountains.

"What makes them grow so mightily?" Torg said.

"Not even the savages can tell us," Ugga said. "Betwixt here and the mountains, there are none so grand. Aren't they handsome, Master Hah-nah? I loves them, I does. I stands and stares at them until the snow freezes my beard. They love Ugga too. They hide Ugga and his friends from their enemies."

"They're magnificent. But I can't imagine why they're here—and only here."

"I does not know. But the Bitch might. When she comes near, the trees sing."

They walked beneath the giant pines. Torg stopped again and counted the wondrous trees. There were exactly thirty side by side, and in a line so straight it resembled a palisade. He touched the trunk of the nearest tree and felt energy gush through his fingers into his arm.

"Ya are brave," the crossbreed whispered. "I dares not touch them. They are too strong for me."

Torg approached another tree until his nose was just a finger-length away. He could sense the life energy surging beneath the furrowed bark, and he took a deep breath. Tendrils of green light squeezed from between the fissures and oozed into his nostrils. The Silver Sword glowed in response.

He stood in silence for a short while, feeling peaceful and safe. Then he gazed upward at row upon row of branches, which grew in circular patterns along the trunks like stacks of plates. The behemoths in the heart of Dhutanga were taller, reaching four hundred cubits tall and thirty thick. But the hearts of those trees were dark and dangerous. These majestic pines exuded wholesomeness, as if tended by a benevolent spirit.

"When the Bitch is here, they sing," Ugga repeated. "They don't seem to mind your sword, but they don't like my axe. I hides it when I'm near." Then Ugga lowered his head. "Will someone steal it while I'm away?"

"Don't worry, your axe is well hidden. Besides, who would have the strength to lift it, much less carry it off?"

Ugga's face brightened. "Ya are right. But I misses it so much. I will go back for it later."

The high plain stretched as far as the eye could see. Beyond the pines, the forest became a traditional mixture of conifers and leafless hardwoods. The smell of smoke and roasting meat intensified. Torg's mouth watered. He had become obsessed with the idea of eating. The cave monkeys had fed him well, but their worm soup—despite its excellent flavor—had grown monotonous. Torg wanted what his Vasi master liked to call a square meal: meat, bread, vegetables, fruit.

"How far, Ugga? Will I die of hunger before we get there?"

"A stream meanders down a ways. Do ya hear its bubblies? Beyond the stream, the timber becomes dense. The Bitch chose that spot, long ago. It is her house, ya know, but she lets us stay with her. I thinks she is clever. But the savages are scared of her. When she's around, they act like she isn't there."

Scared of her? Why that would be? But an increasingly intense aroma drove the puzzlement from Torg's mind. Close to madness, he ran recklessly toward the shadowy area where the house was hidden.

The stream was wide and lively, but Torg leapt over it as if it were a trickle. He charged into the woods, dead leaves crunching beneath his feet. He jumped over fallen logs and tore through tangled branches before reaching a clearing, within which was a small hut. Sweet-smelling smoke poured from a vent in the center of the angled roof, but that was not the main source of the wonderful odor. Jord stood outside, tending a blazing fire, and suspended above it on a sturdy spit was the carcass of a skinned and gutted deer. A metal pot containing a fragrant stew hung over another fire. Jord had been busy. Torg was amazed that she had accomplished so much in such little time, but he was too dazed to ponder it any further.

"The bread is in the oven," Jord said. "Go inside my house and get warm. The Bitch will take care of ya. Ya have earned a bit of rest, me dear."

Torg staggered through the door, and despite his hunger he collapsed onto a bed of leaves and saw no more.

He slept for the rest of the afternoon. Finally loud snoring woke him. When he opened his eyes Bard lay beside him, still overcome by the effects of Torg's spell. But the snoring was a good sign. It meant Bard was sleeping normally and could wake at any time. Apparently his recuperative powers were almost as strong as Ugga's.

A deerskin cloak had served as Torg's blanket, presumably a gift from Jord. He sat up and saw the Silver Sword leaning against the wall near the door. This relaxed him a bit, and he took the time to examine the interior of the hut. A hearth sat in the center of the round dirt floor. Smoke from a well-tended fire leaked out through a vent in the thatched roof. The walls were made of strips of bark woven between vertical posts and plastered with clay and dried leaves. Near the hearth was a crude table with three stumpy chairs. The hut lacked windows, but its door was ajar.

Torg stood and stretched. A pair of boots stuffed with wool socks had been placed near the door. He strapped on the boots and walked outside, unsure of what to expect.

Jord and Ugga were nowhere in sight. Dusk had not yet arrived, but the sky was gloomy, and a breeze blew strong and cold. A storm was in the works, maybe even a blizzard. Torg looked back at the hut with relief. They would need its protection tonight.

The smell of roasting venison drifted in the air. Torg examined the deer carcass with lust in his eyes. Drops of fat sizzled on the fire. Near the spit was an iron pot containing what appeared to be vegetable stew. And nearby on a flat rock were several loaves of dark bread, recently left there to cool. Jord or Ugga had to be somewhere near, or they wouldn't have left the bread unattended. Raccoons, squirrels and other wily creatures were numerous in these parts.

Somewhere beyond the clearing, Torg heard a series of loud crashes sounding like drums or, maybe, the pounding of hooves. He saw flashes of movement, but they were unrecognizable.

"Ya have finished your napping, I sees," said a voice from behind.

Torg fell into a defensive crouch. He was not used to anyone—or anything—being able to sneak up on him. "How did you do that?"

Jord laughed. "Ya deserved a little fright, after all ya have done to me and my friends. The look on your face was a very funny thing—but ya are still an ug-gly booger. Even Ugga is prettier. What manner of beast are ya, anyways, with no hair and such wrinkled skin?"

"I thought you agreed to call me Hana," Torg said grumpily, still disturbed she had been able to come upon him unawares.

"Hah-nah . . . yes," Jord said. "Sorry. Even Ugga calls ya Hah-nah. Master Hah-nah, he says. He's silly, my big Ugga. But he is quite taken by ya. Ugga says ya liked the trees. If that's so, then I likes ya too."

"It's so. Speaking of Ugga, where is he?"

"Where do ya think? He went to get his axe. Couldn't bear to be without it. But he should be back soon. And then we'll eat, before the storm blows in. The night will be nasty, I believes."

"I'm so hungry I could eat a horse."

Jord's eyes blazed. They were the color of pine needles. "We're not Bar-Barians. We don't eat horses."

"Or bears," boomed a voice from the edge of the clearing. Ugga strode into view, his axe slung over his shoulder. "Hello, Master Hah-nah. Ya have a good rest, I hopes?"

"It was grand," Torg said. "Bard's still asleep, but I think he'll be waking up soon."

"Ya think right," came a voice from near the hut. Bard stood just outside the door. "I sees that while I slept, ya all have become a happy family. Is there a story to be told, Ugga? Has the Bitch put a spell on the unfriendly ogre and made him a nicey guy?"

"I'm impressed," Torg said. "Most would have slept through the night. You're strong."

Bard seemed pleased. "Well, whatever ya did, I feels so very good now. I don't feel good enough to eat a horse or a bear, but I could eat most of that deer."

"Let's do it," Ugga bellowed. And he stomped over to the spitted carcass and tore off an upper leg with his bare hand. The shanks already had been removed.

"Ugga!" Jord said. "Where are ya manners?"

"Who cares about manners?" Torg said.

He ripped off another leg. Bard joined them.

"Men," Jord said huffily. "Ya are nothing but a bunch of Bar-Barians." She picked up a clay bowl and delicately ladled a modest serving of vegetable stew.

"Have some wine, Master Hah-nah," Ugga said. He hefted a keg and poured a fragrant red wine into a clay cup.

Torg drank it in three big gulps. "Aaaaaahhhh," was all Torg could manage.

The men proceeded to eat and drink like fiends. Torg felt as if he had been invited to a raucous party. For a brief stretch of time the suffering of the past three months seemed inconsequential. As the evening grew darker, colder and windier, he drank so much wine that even he felt its effects. Ugga and Bard became very drunk, blubbering like fools. But Jord stood quietly off to the side, watching with sober interest. Her eyes sparkled, but otherwise she remained calm. Torg noticed she ate just one bowl of the stew and drank a few sips of wine.

Ugga staggered into the hut and brought out another keg. "Here be more, Master Ogre . . . er . . . Hah-nah."

"Fill my cup," Torg said. "And bring me more bread."

"Bread? Bread?" Bard shouted. "Forget the bread. Cut us some more juicy chops with your axe, Ugga."

Torg lifted the keg over his head. The wine spilled over his face and chest, staining his new cloak. He couldn't remember the last time he had had so much fun. Ugga and Bard could barely stand. Even so, they demanded he hand over the wine while there was still some left.

"Drink up, ya scoundrels," Torg bellowed.

The storm snuck up on them and ruined their merriment. The wind was armed with ice crystals. Nearby trees shrugged and bent. The outside fires were blown out, and it became dark as death. Ugga and Bard crawled toward the hut on hands and knees, disappearing inside. Torg followed, but the vicious winds conspired against him. Then something yanked him backward.

"Come with me!" Jord shouted through the tumult.

She grasped his thick bicep and led him away from the hut. They ran together into the teeth of the blizzard, through the thick trees, over the rushing stream. Jord was supernaturally strong. Where her hand gripped his arm, it burned.

Suddenly they were beneath the giant pines. The power of the storm tantalized the great trees. Torg could hear their singing.

"Allow me do to this," the white-haired woman shouted. "I will heal you. She has left her mark in you. If I do not remove it, her poison will weaken you."

She shoved him roughly onto his back. The snow cushioned his fall. "Allow me."

"What? . . ." Torg muttered. "I don't . . . understand."

Jord tore open his cloak and lifted the thin robes beneath. "Allow me. Do not resist. I must remove the poison."

And then she moved her face between his legs. To Torg, it felt as if liquid fire was consuming him.

"No!" he screamed. "You're in danger. Please . . . *stop!*"

Torg tried to push her away, but she was too strong. He could not extract himself. "Please . . . pleeaaaseeee . . . I don't want to hurt you!"

But Jord continued to caress him. She was not afraid.

"I will . . . destroy you," Torg stammered. "You don't . . . understand."

She lifted her head and gazed into his eyes. "I will not be harmed."

The storm attacked the forest like an invading army. The magical pines danced. Jord returned to her business, her head bobbing up and down, faster and faster. Torg arched, and then howled in ecstasy. The power of his release surpassed the tempest, and his bed of snow melted, bubbled and boiled. Blue light burst from his body, raced up the trunks of the pines, and erupted into the angry sky. In response, green energy blasted downward and permeated his flesh. Just then, he spit up a crimson ball of pestilence, which hovered magically in the air, searching for a way to escape. But the green fire would not allow it. It leapt upon the poison and devoured it.

Jord was not injured. Instead she finished him, lovingly.

Torg lay on his back, still gasping, his body glowing blue-green. The trees towered over him like guardians. He closed his eyes and listened to the storm. Within the strands of howling wind, he heard drums. Or was it the pounding of hooves?

Then the crossbreed was there, somehow sober, and he buttoned Torg's cloak and helped him to his feet. "The Bitch is gone. Ya must come where it is warm."

"Where is Jord? Does she live?"

"She's gone. I doesn't know where." He sounded sad.

Ugga hoisted Torg onto his back and carried him back to the house of Jord.

3

The second time Torg woke inside the hut, he was alone. The door was closed, and the room was dark except for a small fire that bristled in the hearth. At first he had no idea where he was. The memories of his encounter with Jord consumed his awareness, but they seemed unreal. He lay on the bed of leaves for a long time, trying to decide whether it had been just a dream.

But when he sat up, his body felt strong and his mind clear—as if his insides had been cleansed of putridity.

Was it the height of day or the middle of the night? In the dimness of the hut, he couldn't tell. And where were Ugga and Bard . . . and Jord? Was she standing outside the door, waiting for him to emerge? Though he was more than a thousand years old, Torg blushed.

He meditated for three hundred long breaths. When he finally stood up, his concerns vanished as if washed away by a surge of vitality. He felt like a person miraculously recovered from a dreadful illness. Power surged through his flesh and bones. His strength was back, physically and emotionally. The full extent of his magic also had returned. Somehow the green energy of the pines had restored him, and he felt as potent as ever.

The sword still leaned against the wall, its tip buried in the dirt. Apparently his three companions had lost their desire to steal it. Torg swung the door open and stepped outside, entering into a world of infinite alabaster. The ground, the trees, even the sky were white.

More than two cubits of snow had fallen during the storm. As far as Torg could guess, it now was late morning, but he couldn't accurately judge the time of day because he couldn't see the sun. The air was desperately cold, but the previous night's winds had fled. All was quiet.

Abruptly the silence was broken.

"Master Hah-nah. Master Hah-nah." Ugga charged toward Torg and gave him a powerful hug, lifting him off his feet. "Me and Bard were afraid ya'd never wake up. Ya slept so sound, we feared ya might have passed away."

Bard also approached, bearing his spear along with Jord's bow and arrows. "Good morning, Hah-nah. Glad to see ya aren't a corpse, though ya do kind of look like one."

"Thanks," Torg said, "I suppose."

The crossbreed smiled, his small eyes glistening. "The storm blowed away all the food and gear we left outside. Me and Bard couldn't even find the pot we use for stew."

"And what of Jord?" Torg said.

"The Bitch is gone," Bard said. "I looked everywhere. Ugga, too. But there are no signs."

"I misses her," Ugga said. "Where did she go, Master Hah-nah?"

"How would he know, ya dimwit," Bard said. "Hah-nah was sleeping all night, don't ya remember?"

Ugga ignored Bard's insults. "Will ya help us look for the Bitch with your Mah-Gick-Cull powers?" he said to Torg.

Bard stepped between them. "After our party last night, there's not much left in the house to eat. If we want breakfast, we need to hunt."

"I agree," Torg said. "And after we eat, we'll have a long talk and tell each other who we are and why we're here. As for Jord, I believe she will return when she desires and not before."

The crossbreed lowered his head but did not speak.

Bard told Ugga and Torg to stay and build a fire, and then he pounded through the snow into the woods. After his companion disappeared, the crossbreed went about collecting deadwood and kindling. Torg did the same. Neither spoke. Ugga drew a sliver of flint from his cloak and struck it against his axe. The kindling caught fire.

"Are you angry with me over what happened last night?" Torg finally said.

Ugga's great chest heaved. "I is just sad, is all. The Bitch is gone, and I doesn't know why. Will I ever see her again? I loves her, I does."

Torg placed his hand on the crossbreed's shoulder. "Who is she? Who is Jord?"

"Don't ya know? She is me mumma . . . in a way. And Bard's, too."

Torg was amazed. "Your mother?"

As if in response Bard stomped out of the woods, carrying two hares and a plump possum.

Ugga ran to greet him. "Bard, me love! How'd ya get them so quick? Ya've been gone just a blink of an eye."

"I'd like to say I killed them myself," Bard said. "But I did not. A parcel of savages greeted me not a thousand paces from where ya stand.

They rushed to me and handed me these fine critters. Their chief said to me, 'Svakara werricauna.' And then he and the savages ran far away."

"Why are the Svakarans afraid?" Torg said.

"Do ya not know?" Bard said. "They are scared of ya. We're not the only folk who call ya an Ogre. They hope to buy your pardon with hares and this fat che-ra. They fear ya have come to murder the men, rape the women and eat the children."

Torg rolled his eyes. "Why does everyone around here think I'm a monster?"

"Ya looks like a monster," Ugga said. "Ya are as strong as a monster. Are ya not a monster, Master Hah-nah?"

Torg wasn't used to being treated like a bogeyman. He took a moment to examine his body, first rubbing his hand along the top of his head. When he had escaped the pit, his scalp had been bald, but now it was covered with a bristly carpet of hair. He slid his tongue along his teeth. As far as he could tell, they were already about a quarter of the way grown in. The skin on his arms remained scaly and mottled. The asthenolith had burned off most of the disease, but the healing process wasn't pretty.

Torg guessed it would take several more weeks to look relatively normal and half a year to grow his hair back to shoulder length.

"Ugga, I'm not a monster," Torg said. "At least, not in the way you mean. In fact, it's time to tell you who and what I really am. But first, let's skin these 'critters' and put them over the fire."

"Ya and I are alike," Ugga said. "We're hungry all the time."

While the hares and possum roasted, the crossbreed went into the hut and came out with a keg of wine. "This is the last of the spirits. Water is all we'll be drinkin' for a spell, I fears. It's a fair ways to the Whore City. But we got some nice skins put away that we can trade for more wine."

"How long does it take to reach Kamupadana?" Torg said.

"In the summertime we could walk there in two days," Bard said. "But after yesterday's big snow, I thinks it will take three days or more."

Torg took the keg from Ugga and drank several gulps of wine.

"The two of you need to go to Kamupadana for fresh supplies. I need to go there for reasons of my own," Torg said. "Here's what I propose: If Jord doesn't return today, we'll spend tomorrow looking for her. The following day, no matter what, we'll begin our journey. Does that sound fair?"

Bard shook his head. "There's no use searching for the Bitch. She's where she wants to be."

Ugga snarled. "Ya would abandon the Bitch after all she's done?"

"The Bitch is gone 'cause she wants to be. It's not like she hasn't disappeared before. Ya know that as well as I does, ya dimwit."

Ugga lowered his head. "I loves her, Bard. Where does she go? Why does she leave?"

"Ask him," Bard said, pointing to Torg. "He knows her better than us. Ya told me so this morning, ya did."

The small portion of Ugga's cheeks that weren't covered with hair turned bright red. "I told ya to keep it a secret," the crossbreed muttered.

Torg interrupted. "It's obvious we all have much to say. Let's sit in the hut where it's warm, share what's left of the wine, and tell our secrets. I'll go first."

They went into the hut and huddled around the table. Each drank several more swallows of wine before Torg finally broke the silence.

"My name is not Hana, as I'm sure you've guessed. My name is *The Torgon*—and I am a king."

Bard spat a mouthful of wine onto the table. "Ya are a king. And Ugga is a princess."

"Be quiet, ya *katichhei* (rogue)," Ugga said. "Let Master Hah-nah finish his talking. And don't waste any more of the spirits. If ya can't keep it in your mouth, don't drink it."

"I must not look much like a king," Torg said, chuckling. "Master Ogre is a better description. But my recent travails have been hard on my body—and spirit. Others might not have fared as well. But before I continue my story, I must ask you both a question: Do you know of the sorcerer named Invictus?"

"Surely, ya speak in jest," Bard said. "Everyone in these parts has heard of Invictus, even simple wood folk like us."

"Are you for him or against him?" Torg said.

"I'm for Bard and the Bitch," Ugga said. "I cares naught for In-vick-tuss, as long as he leaves us alone."

"We're too small a bunch for his concern," Bard said. "But I thinks we'll have to move on one day. Betwixt the Whore City and Avici, it's no longer safe. More and more, his soldiers wander about, causing trub-bles."

"Good enough," Torg said. "But let this be known: I am Invictus' sworn enemy, which makes me the enemy of any who claim him as friend or ally. I will slay anyone who has joined him as surely as I would slay the sorcerer."

"I believes ya, Master Hah-nah," Ugga said. "Or, should I call ya King Hah-nah?"

"Hana is what I prefer," Torg said. "Besides, it will be safer to use that name while we travel. Even in the wilds, the enemy has eyes and ears. I'm hoping Invictus believes I'm dead, and that's the way I want to keep it for as long as possible."

"We'd better check the meat," Bard interrupted. "It should be cooked by now."

"Let's eat, then," Torg said. "And while we do, I'll tell you why I like the name Hana."

They rushed outside in a fit of hunger, then went back inside with their meal. Torg chomped into the possum's juicy thigh. The white, fatty meat was as tasty as wild boar. Grease dripped down his chin. He wiped it with the sleeve of his cloak before picking up the keg and taking a long swig. Ugga and Bard devoured both the hares and then helped Torg with the remains of the much-larger che-ra.

Afterward, the crossbreed and his handsome friend began to digest more than just roasted game. For most of the morning they listened as Torg recounted the events of the past several months, including the rescue of the noble ones at Dibbu-Loka and his imprisonment in the pit. He told them who and what he was. He even described the death of Sōbhana. But he left out the sexual encounter with Vedana. That was between him and the demon.

Ugga bowed his large head. "I understands why ya want us to call ya Hah-nah. Your Sōb-hah-nah was a great lady. Almost as great as the Bitch."

"In some ways they were much alike—strong, brave and beautiful."

"Ya speak as if Jord is dead, too," Bard said.

"I don't believe she's dead. But I have no idea where she is or why she left. Who and what she is befuddles me, as well. Maybe now, you can tell me your tale and help me to understand. Do you believe what I've told you?"

"I believes ya, Master Hah-nah," Ugga said. "Ya are not a liar."

"I believes ya, too," Bard said. "But does I has to call ya King Hah-nah?"

"Very funny," Torg said. "But now I'm being serious. I've risked a lot just telling the two of you about me. But I trust you . . . as friends."

"Then friends it is," Bard said. "And friends we will be."

"Yes," Ugga said. *"Good* friends!"

The crossbreed smacked a hand the size of a bear paw onto the rough wooden table. Torg placed his hand on top of Ugga's. For a moment Bard hesitated, but then he placed his on Torg's.

"Good friends," Torg said.

"Good friends," Bard said.

"Gooooooooood friends," Ugga agreed.

Bard leaned over the table and stared at Torg. "I'm ready to tell the tale of Ugga, Bard and the Bitch. But first I has to tell Ugga something." He smiled sheepishly at the crossbreed. "I'm sorry, Ugga, but I has uttered a white lie. Ya drink so much of the spirits, I sometimes has to hide some for myself. There is one more keg of wine hidden in the corner where we keep the potatoes."

Ugga smiled broadly. "Some lies are good."

And so, when Bard began his tale, there was plenty of wine to go around.

"What I says now will not be a lie. What I says will be the truth, as I knows it. When I first saw Ugga and the Bitch, I was a boy of just ten winters and . . ."

Bard lived in a small settlement hewed out of the wilds on the northeastern border of the Dhutanga Forest. The wide mouth of the Gap of Gamana was due east. Duccarita, known for its villains and outlaws, was a few leagues north. The Dark Forest lay west and south. And the Mahaggata Mountains, home to Mogols, trolls, and an assortment of bloodthirsty creatures, also loomed nearby. There was danger on all sides.

Many evil beasts dwelled in Dhutanga's interior. The settlers constantly had to watch the trees, never knowing what might emerge. There were fewer than two hundred in the colony, and less than half were adults capable of putting up much of a fight. The elders met often about the perils surrounding their homestead. Though they were close to a large stream and plenty of game, they finally were forced to admit that they had chosen a poor location. Their only hope of long-term survival was to abandon the settlement and move south, nearer the Green Plains.

Less than a week before their planned exodus, a Mogol war party found them. Dawn of a cool spring day had not yet arrived when fifty warriors swept into the hamlet. They wore only breechcloths, but their wild faces and muscular bodies bore grotesque tattoos, and they were armed with clubs, spears, axes, and blowguns. The lookouts never saw them. In a short time all of the adult men and elderly women were dead. The younger women and the children were captured and roped together by their ankles.

"We could make no sense of their gibberish," Bard said, "but they beat us and made us watch their savage behaviors. They builded a vast fire and spitted my daddy and uncle and roasted them like animals. We begged for mercy, but the savages didn't care. Instead they laughed and whipped us."

Bard lowered his head. A single tear fell from each eye, splashing onto the tabletop. Ugga's thick lips quivered.

The Mogols forced their captives to march northward. Because their ankles were bound, the going was extremely slow. The boy staggered along next to his mother and heard her whisper to another woman that they were being herded toward Duccarita to be sold as slaves.

"'I'm so sorry, me boy,' my mumma said. 'If ya have a chance to run, ya take it, do ya hear? Don't look back.'"

The boy cried and told his mother he would never leave her, but then a Mogol warrior came up behind him and kicked him between his legs. The boy bent over and gagged, and the warrior kicked him again.

They stumbled along for two days with little food or rest. The Mogols beat any stragglers and took the weakest from the main group to be clubbed to death. The boy wished he could find a way to die. But he also noticed the knots around his thin ankles coming loose. His mother saw it, too.

"'Ya do what I says,' she whispered. 'If ya get free, I wants ya to bolt. It's better one of us escapes than none at all.'"

The second night after the attack on the settlement, a skirmish broke out among the Mogols. The boy and his mother couldn't tell what was happening, but a rumor passed among the prisoners that a warrior had taken a liking to one of the females and had attempted to carry her off into the woods. The leader of the war party became angry, not wanting to lose any more slaves than necessary. The Duccaritans paid well for young women and children.

"Mumma gave me a look. She said, 'I loves ya boy, but now's the time. I wants ya to run into the woods and hide till we're gone.'"

"'But where will I goes after that, mumma? How will I lives?'" I said to her. "But she had no answer and turned away."

The boy broke free of his bonds and rushed into the trees. It was not until morning that the Mogols noticed he was missing. This enraged the savages. A strong young male was worth even more than a woman. The Mogols sent five warriors to track him, and in less than half a day they found him shivering beside a swollen stream in a tree-choked cove.

The warriors rushed toward him with anger in their eyes. But then a black ball of rage sprang from the trees. The snarling bear leapt upon the nearest warrior and ripped off his head with a single swipe of a huge front paw. But the four remaining warriors surrounded the beast. The darts from their blowguns could not pierce its tough hide, so they attacked with their spears. The clash was violent. The boy was too terrified to move. Soon after, only one warrior remained alive, but the bear was grievously wounded and lacked the strength to continue. The lone survivor closed in for the kill.

"And that is when she arrived," Bard said, taking several gulps of wine as if attempting to drown his pain. "From the woods she appeared, lookin' just like she does now. The savage seemed to know her and was scared. He tried to run, but she caught him from behind and snapped his neck."

The warriors terrified the boy, but there was something about the woman that did not seem threatening. He crawled to the dying bear and petted its coarse fur, which was soaked with blood. When he looked up at the white-haired woman, tears streaked his pale cheeks.

"'I shall give you a gift,' she said to me, 'and one to this fine animal, as well. You both shall stay with me for as long as it takes to heal your wounds—not just the wounds of your bodies, but also the wounds of your spirits.'

"'The bear is dying,' I said to her. 'He is cut here and there.' But she only laughed. And then she said, 'For a beast to be reborn as a man, it must perform an act that lifts it beyond its instinctual behaviors. This bear, I believe, will be reborn as a man. So my gift to the bear is human form—in this lifetime. And my gift to you will be his friendship.'"

While the boy watched, the white-haired woman performed her miracle, lifting her arms and speaking strange incantations that caused a blinding green light to spurt from her fingertips. The boy could not stand the intensity of it and hid behind a tree, but his curiosity forced him to peer around the trunk. A whirlwind of sparkling energy engulfed the bear, lifting its massive body several cubits off the ground, as if it weighed less than a feather. The corpses of the warriors also floated in the air, and they began to spin around the bear—faster and faster—until they blurred.

The woman cried out. A radiant eruption caused the boy to cover his face. When all went quiet, he looked up and saw . . .

"Bard has told me the story many times, but I remembers it not," Ugga said. "Before I met Bard and the Bitch, all I knew was hunting and running, blood and berries, worms and bugs. And then I remembers standing on my hind legs and being amazed by how clear everything was. I saw the boy, crouched on the ground. And when I looked down, my legs were different, long and pale like my fur had fallen off."

After hugging his new friend, the boy begged the white-haired woman to save his mumma. But she refused.

"I remembers 'zactly what she said," Bard recalled. "'I could have saved all of you, but I am not here to rescue the weak or punish the wicked. I am a watcher—little more and little less. Only on rare occasions am I permitted to interfere.'"

The boy lay on the ground and wept, and his new friend knelt and comforted him. But the white-haired woman could not be swayed. She strode off without another word.

"I picked up Bard and carried him," Ugga said. "The Bitch was our only chance. I didn't know any words . . . yet. But I knew enough to want to stay with the lady."

The crossbreed and the boy followed the woman for a long time, passing west of Duccarita, and journeying north almost to Nirodha. They then turned east, traversing steep mountains and remote valleys that were chilly even in early summer. They eventually settled in the foothills of Mount Asubha. Soon after their arrival, the magical pines began to grow.

"She gave us names from the ancient tongue," Bard said. "Bard means *liberated*, Ugga means *mighty*, and she named herself Jord, which meant *guardian*. My old name, before the Bitch saved my life, is lost to my memory. Many winters have passed since those fateful days."

"How many?" Torg said.

"I'm not sure," Bard said, "but I would guess many thousands."

Torg's jaw dropped.

"The pines keep us young," Ugga said. "The Bitch always told us to stay close to them. If Bard and I goes too far away, we start to feel old and lame."

Torg took one last sip of the wine. Bard and Ugga finished the rest. Then they sat in silence for a long time. Bard's tale had taken the entire afternoon, and night's black breath was creeping into the forest. Occasionally one of them threw a fresh log on the fire. Otherwise they barely moved. Outside the hut it was as quiet as death.

Finally Ugga broke the silence. "Do ya know who the Bitch is?" he said to Torg. "Can ya tell us, pretty please?"

Ugga's question prompted Torg to silently recall the ghost-child's dream-like words spoken to him less than two weeks before, when he was the Stone-Eater's prisoner.

There are beings beyond all known laws, natural or otherwise, and they have begun to watch the sorcerer with growing interest—and are making plans for his demise.

Torg gazed at Ugga and Bard. When he finally spoke, he did so with a tremble in his voice. "I believe Jord is who and what she claims to be. She is a . . . *watcher*. But don't those who watch usually report to superiors?"

"Who is the Bitch's soo-peer-eee-er?" Ugga said.

"An excellent question," Torg said. "I don't know the answer—and I'm not sure I want to."

"I has another question," Bard said, whose tone now contained a hint of anger. "Why does the Bitch favor Master Hah-nah?"

Torg again thought back to his conversation with Peta. *There are three females on Triken who can abide you—and you already have met them.* Vedana was one. He now knew Jord was another, though he had never met her before as far as he knew. But who was the third?

"I'm not sure *favor* is the proper word," Torg said. "But I do know this: An evil has arisen that threatens us all. The fate of the land lies in the hands of a few. I am destined—willing or not—to play a role in the outcome. Perhaps the two of you are fated to join me."

Outside the hut, the drums resumed their mysterious beat. Leaning against the far wall, the Silver Sword glowed like a comet.

Torg, Ugga, and Bard paid little heed.

Too much wine.

Too much talk.

The three men—*good* friends, all—succumbed to the lure of drunken sleep.

The Other Death-Knower

1

Upon awakening, the first thing Torg noticed was the pervasive smell of sweat. Bard still sat at the table, but the side of his face was plastered against the splintered wood. Ugga had fallen out of his chair and lay flat on his back on the dirt floor, his massive chest—and even larger stomach—rising and falling. The fire had burned low, but the interior of the hut remained warm. Torg yawned, stretched and sat up. At least, he alone among the three of them had had the sense to crawl over to the bed of leaves, though he had no memory of doing it.

The Silver Sword rested against the wall near the door. Torg walked to it and grasped the black-leather hilt. He noticed for the first time that the asthenolith had damaged it a bit. But for reasons he could not understand, it had not disintegrated entirely. He touched the blade with his left hand, expecting it to be about the same temperature as the room; instead it was freezing cold. Heat had no effect on the supernal alloys. He vaguely remembered grasping the blade while in the agony of the asthenolith; even there it had been cool.

He put down the sword, opened the door and stepped outside. More snow had fallen during the night, and the morning sky had remained gloomy. The fire that had roasted the possum and hares was lifeless.

The downturn in the weather did not surprise him. As winter approached, storms would be frequent, and there would be snow on the ground for at least four months. Most of the people who dwelled this near to the northern mountains would spend the majority of their time indoors, wandering out only to replenish water supplies and to hunt for game.

Speaking of game, lying in a split-cane basket near the hut were the carcasses of two wild turkeys and a che-ra. In a second basket were purple berries, hickory nuts and three bloated skins. A wooden spear at least two cubits longer than Torg was tall had been thrust into the ground between the baskets. White and brown feathers attached to the staff hung lifeless in the dead air.

Torg had the feeling he was being watched, but when he scanned the surrounding landscape, he saw no movement. Whoever was out there knew these woods as well as he knew the Great Desert.

He understood one thing that Bard and Ugga did not. The Svakarans, along with the other native people of the mountains, were not "savages." Some of their actions appeared brutal—especially where the Mogols were concerned—but their ability to live in harmony with their surroundings surpassed most of the "civilized" cultures found on Triken. Only the Tugars, who thrived on the blazing sands of Tējo, were as well-adapted to their environment as the so-called savages of Mahaggata.

Regardless of their reputation, the Svakarans were formidable. If they sensed weakness, they would take advantage. They cared most for their own people and tolerated others only if they feared or respected them.

Torg decided to reinforce the fear aspect.

He removed his heavy cloak and laid it on the surface of the snow. Wearing only his thin gray robes so that his movements would not be restricted, Torg drew the spear from the frozen ground and grasped the center of its well-balanced shaft, admiring its sharp tip made of chiseled obsidian. He hoisted it above his shoulder and drew it back. With a hidden surge of power from the palm of his hand he engulfed the spear in blue-green flame, but just enough to strengthen it without making it too obvious. Then he let out a howl and heaved the spear with the might and precision of a Tugar warrior. It hurtled through the air like a bolt of lightning and struck the trunk of a dead oak more than one hundred cubits away. There was a booming sound, and shards of wood sprayed outward. The spear pierced the trunk, burst out the other side, and buried itself in a living tree several paces farther away.

Ugga and Bard stumbled through the doorway, tripping over each other.

"Here we come, Master Hah-nah," the crossbreed shouted. "Do not fear!"

Ugga brought his axe, and Bard carried Jord's bow and arrows. The pair scrambled next to Torg and stood ready, their haggard breaths coming in large white bursts. They scanned the edge of the clearing, looking this way and that. A long time passed before Bard finally spoke.

"What is it, Hah-nah? We see nothing but the trees. Were ya accosted by savages?"

"Someone or something is out there," Torg said. "They left us a gift and then withdrew."

Bard's cheeks went red. "Are ya trying to end our lives with your wicked shouting? Next time, give Ugga and me some warning before ya go 'round hooting like an animal."

Ugga, ever the opportunist when it came to food and drink, already was investigating the baskets. "We eat well today," he said, with a smile that exposed his sharp teeth. "I likes having ya around, Master Hah-nah. Wherever ya go, food appears like mah-gick."

Then the crossbreed picked up one of the skins and sniffed its contents. "Beer! Beer! *Beeeeeeer!*" He danced about absurdly.

Torg could not help but laugh. "Ugga . . . *my friend*. Ya . . . *you* . . . are a joy."

"Thank ya, Master Hah-nah."

But then the crossbreed's smile faded. "No sign of the Bitch?"

"I cannot sense her presence. Whatever the reason, I believe she is far away—by her own choice or need. Perhaps she has been called by her superiors."

As if in response to Torg's words, there was movement in the woods. Bard strung an arrow to the bow, and Ugga hoisted his axe. Torg scanned the trees with well-practiced precision.

"Someone hunts us, after all," Bard whispered.

Then a raspy voice came from somewhere outside the clearing. "It *is* you, isn't it? If I didn't know you so well, I wouldn't believe it, the way you look now."

"Show yourself," Torg commanded.

"Isn't that just like you," the voice said. "Always showing off and bossing people around. For the sake of Anna, will you never stop?"

Torg finally recognized the voice. "Rathburt? How came you here? Where have you been all these long years?"

A man emerged from behind a tree. Like Torg he had black hair and blue eyes, but he was stooped and appeared frail beneath his bear-skin cloak. He leaned against an oaken staff.

Ugga seemed to distrust him. "Who is the interloper? I doesn't like the way he looks."

Bard agreed, aiming an arrow at the man's chest.

"My, my . . . *Torgon*," the man said in response, slowly approaching the clearing. "Is this how you would treat an old friend?"

With one hand Torg gripped the underside of the arrowhead and pulled it toward the ground. With the other he grasped the handle of Ugga's axe.

"There's no need for your weapons. He is, indeed, my friend, though I haven't seen him in many years. His name is Rathburt—and trust me when I say that he is the only other Death-Knower alive in the world but me."

2

Ugga and Bard appeared unconvinced the "interloper" was a friend, but they lowered their weapons as instructed. Meanwhile, Rathburt strolled over and stared at Torg's face. Because of his poor posture, he was at least a span shorter than Torg and Ugga, while about the same height as Bard.

Up close, Rathburt looked much older than Torg remembered. His face was lined and weathered, which was unusual for an ordinary Tugar, much less a Death-Knower. Conversely Torg must have looked far different to Rathburt. The hunched man was puzzled.

"*Torgon*, what's happened to you? You look . . . terrible."

"Have you not heard? Have you lost touch with our people?"

Rathburt's expression soured. "They're no longer my people, and you know it. Besides, Tugars rarely travel this far north. They prefer to keep their noses buried in the sand, where they belong."

Bard interrupted. "Are ya sure this *occooahawa* (old fool) is your friend? His words are full of the venom of snakes."

Amusement replaced Rathburt's sour expression. "And what would your name be, sir? I would dearly like to know."

"My name is my own biz-nuss. I only gives it to polite peoples."

Rathburt laughed and pounded his staff into the snow. Ugga raised his axe.

"Not even a friend of Master Hah-nah can laugh at Bard that way," the crossbreed said. "Be quiet, rude person, or I will teach ya some manners."

Torg had heard enough. "*Silence!*"

A sudden gale swept through the clearing, causing the snow to swirl at their feet. Bard and Ugga retreated several steps. Rathburt stayed put, but lowered his gaze.

Torg glared at all of them. "As I said, Rathburt is my friend. I did not say he was friend*ly*. In fact, few among our people can tolerate his presence. He's irritating, insulting and sarcastic. But I've always believed there's more to him than meets the eye. And a Death-Knower should *never* be underestimated, regardless of his or her appearance. This man has left his body—and returned to speak of it. More need not be said."

Bard's cheeks went pale. Tears welled in Ugga's eyes. But Rathburt was not so easily cowed. He walked to the crossbreed and wrapped his skinny arm around the giant's massive shoulders. "Don't worry, he's always showing off, demanding this and commanding that. He says our people can't tolerate my presence, but the same goes for him. They act nice to his face but grumble behind his back. He was always the fastest, the strongest, the smartest—and he was the first to let you know. It annoyed everyone. For Anna's sake, *Torgon*, will you never change?"

Torg sighed. "I'm too hungry and irritable for such silliness. Much has occurred since you and I last spoke." He pointed toward the baskets. "In the meantime, I thank you for your gifts."

"These gifts aren't really from me," Rathburt said. "They're from my trusty associate. I'd like to introduce him, if the three of you don't mind. I believe you'll like him. He works hard and is an excellent cook."

"I'm very hungry," Ugga said, his good humor suddenly returning. "If your ah-soh-see-it can make food taste good, then it is all right with me if he joins us."

"Why, *thank you*," Rathburt said. Then he yelled toward the woods: "Elu . . . show yourself!"

A small head peeked out from behind the trunk of a yellow poplar.

"There you are," Rathburt called. "Get over here. It's time you earned your keep." Then he turned and whispered to Ugga. "I speak to him harshly, but he's a worthy companion. He loves me like a papa."

Elu sprang through the woods, entering the clearing at a dead run.

"Come to papa!"

But instead of going to Rathburt, Elu ran to Torg and bowed at his feet. "Elu is at your command," he said to Torg. "Speak, and Elu will obey."

Rathburt looked annoyed. "Show off."

"Rise," Torg said. "That is my command."

Elu was less than half Torg's height, but his face was manly and his body heavily muscled. He dressed in the winter garb of a Svakaran tribesman—a beaver-skin coat threaded with the sinews of a deer. But the Svakaran males were relatively tall. Torg was puzzled.

"Who are your people?" he said to Elu.

Rathburt answered for him, his words sounding rehearsed. "He's a Svakaran. But he was poisoned as a child by a Mogol shaman, and it stunted his growth. His parents were embarrassed and abandoned him, deeming him a blight to their community. But I was kind enough to take him in." Then Rathburt became more animated. "Despite his demure stature, he's not helpless. As I said, he can hunt and cook. And he fights well for someone so small. Why, I daresay he could give even big men like you a tussle. While you're not looking, he'll bite you on the leg."

The crossbreed laughed. "I hopes not to fight ya, little guy. Are ya as good a cook as Master Rad-burt claims?"

"Elu cooks very good," he said in the common tongue. "He will cook for the friendly giant. And for the others." He gestured toward Torg. "Elu will do whatever the *great one* says."

"Well, then, get started, you little booger," Rathburt said. "The 'great one' is hungry. And so is the poor excuse for a man standing next to him. Will you lower yourself to cook for him, too?"

"Elu does what he is told."

"Don't worry, little guy," Ugga said. "I'll help ya."

"I'll help, too," Bard said.

"If the friendly giants will start the fire, Elu will do the rest. Do you have a pot for a nice stew?" He motioned toward the baskets. "The hickories thicken the broth, and the berries add sweetness."

"I found our pot yester-eve," Ugga said. "I'll get it for ya, little guy."

Torg was relieved. "Rathburt and I have much to discuss," he said to the others, and then he grasped the fellow Death-Knower by the arm and guided him toward the hut. "Call us when dinner is ready. And we'll take one of the skins of beer, as well."

Ugga didn't like that idea so much. "Just one, I hopes, Master Hah-nah."

"Why does he call you Hana?" Rathburt said.

"It's a long story. Come inside, and I'll tell you what has happened to me since you and I last crossed paths. And you'll do the same."

"My tale will be less interesting, I'm sure. But then, I've always been less interesting than you."

"Like I said, you haven't changed a bit."

"But you still love me, right?"

Torg held open the door. "I love my people. And I still consider you one of them. Do not convince me otherwise."

"There you go with your threats."

Inside the hut the fire had burned out. Torg threw more logs into the hearth and placed his right hand on top of the thickest piece of timber. Blue-green flame surged into the dry wood.

Rathburt claimed one of the chairs next to the table. "It smells like the insides of an Asēkha's boots in here."

"There are worse smells."

"*You* would think so."

"Listen . . . Rathburt. You commented about my strange appearance just a few moments ago. But now you seem to have lost your curiosity. Don't you want to know what happened to me?"

"I knew you would tell me, without any prompting. You've always enjoyed talking about yourself."

Torg sighed, an all-too-frequent occurrence whenever Rathburt was concerned.

"You seem to blame me for your predicament," Torg said. "But why am I the cause? Your ascension pleased me even more than it did you. I was prepared to welcome you among the greats, and so were the rest of our people."

"I didn't desire to be among the greats," Rathburt said. "My *ascension* was a fluke. I didn't even make it past the first week of warrior training, much less deserve to become a Death-Knower. I'm a freak, *Torgon*, and you know it."

Torg started to protest, but Rathburt waved his bony hands. "I'm five hundred years old. I know that's not as old as *you*, but it's older than any other Tugar, including Kusala. I have been a Death-Knower—if anyone can call me that without laughing—for more than four centuries. And do you know how many times I have achieved *Sammaasamaadhi*?"

"I'm unaware."

"Humor me. Guess."

Torg sighed again. "More than one hundred times."

"More than one hundred? And how about you, *Torgon*? How many times for you?"

"More than one thousand."

Rathburt snickered, but there was no humor in it. "Don't you see, *Torgon*? This proves I'm a fraud. You guessed one hundred? I'd be proud of that number. Try *once*."

Torg wasn't shocked. "Once is one more time than anyone else in the world besides me. Once is one more time than the Vasi masters who terrorized you. Once is one more time than Kusala, who ranks among the greatest men I have ever known. Once is one more time than all but the rarest of Tugars in our long history. Why do you insist on demeaning yourself?"

"Because it was a fluke, as I said. I never even felt the urge of *Dakkhinā*." Rathburt leaned forward and pounded his fist on the table. "I wasn't destined to become a Death-Knower. I was born to be a gardener. Isn't that the funniest thing you've ever heard? A gardener who lives in the desert. But it's all I've ever wanted, really—to tend trees, plants, and flowers . . . to get to know them . . . to treasure them . . . to love them. Which is why I also happened to enjoy meditation. To get close to nature, you have to *think* like nature. Meditation helped me do that—by quieting my mind and raising my awareness. And one night without planning or preparation, my mind cleared, my breath and heartbeat slowed, and my concentration reached a deeper level than ever before. Suddenly there I was, in the *Death Realm*, where you have been so many times. But unlike you, it wasn't talent, strength or courage that brought me back to my flesh. Do you know what it was? I missed my garden. It would have struggled without my care, and I wasn't ready to abandon it. So I returned to my body, coughing and gagging."

Rathburt buried his face in his hands. "I've never made the attempt again. And I never will. I'm a coward, *Torgon*. Our people—*your* people—wanted me to be like you, but I was incapable."

Torg placed his hand on Rathburt's stooped shoulder. "You torment yourself needlessly. You're ashamed of your success as a gardener and your failure as a warrior. But what you don't comprehend is that a gardener is the superior being. Nourishing life ranks among the highest states of wisdom, destroying life among the lowest. I've killed many times—with magic, sword, and bare hands—and each time I've fallen further away from the attainment of enlightenment. Don't you understand? There's *no* justification for violence. But it appears I'm destined to be a warrior, at least in this lifetime. If you're destined to be a gardener, does that make you a freak? Perhaps I'm the freak."

"It's just one more thing I hate about you. You're so *nice*. I deserve to be humiliated for my cowardice, not rewarded. And yet you refuse to discipline me. I abandoned Anna and fled into the wilderness, forsaking our people. Why can't you hate me as much as I hate myself?"

"Because you're the only person I've ever known who has seen what I've seen. It's lonely, being a Death-Knower. Surely you understand that as well as I."

"Yes," Rathburt said, with a sigh of his own. Then he leaned back in his chair and folded his arms over his narrow chest. "Let us trade stories, then. At least for today, we can put our loneliness aside and be joined as friends."

"That's the smartest thing I've ever heard you say. But first, come sit with me by the fire. I wish to meditate together."

After Torg and Rathburt disappeared inside the hut, the others went about their business. Bard and Ugga built a spit for the turkeys and a tripod to hang the iron pot. Elu dressed the turkeys and then went to work on the possum, scraping off its hair, carving out the musk glands, gutting it, and cutting off its head, tail and feet. After that, he carried the carcasses to the nearby stream for a good rinsing. On his way back he searched the woods for herbs and "ground potatoes" to further enrich the flavor of the che-ra stew.

As the turkeys roasted and the stew simmered, the three men sat down and relaxed. Although most of the morning had passed, Torg and Rathburt never once emerged from the hut.

"Do ya have more of this tasty beer, little guy?" Ugga said. "I dearly loves it."

"Elu and Rathburt live in a longhouse half a day's walk from here," the Svakaran said, pointing westward. "We have lots of beer and can get more from my village, which is not far from our house. Elu doesn't know how Rathburt will feel, but as far as he is concerned, you're welcome to stay with us through the worst of the winter."

"If there is lots of beer, I wants to go to your house. Do ya want to go, Bard?"

"I agrees with ya, Ugga. I'd rather go there than walk all the way to the Whore City in winter. It's too shivery."

"It's not safe to wander in the woods, anyway," Elu said. "There are bad men in the forest. More than there used to be. They come from the south with deadly weapons. Some among my people believe it's time for our village to move even deeper into the mountains. But Rathburt doesn't want to go. He has a garden near our house that he refuses to leave behind. When spring comes, he will tend it again. Even if Elu were to go with his people, he thinks Rathburt would stay. But Elu would not abandon Rathburt. Elu owes him his life."

"Why do ya say that, little guy?" Ugga said.

"Elu was not always a 'little guy.' Elu was once a big guy . . . as big as Bard. Rathburt didn't tell the truth about the 'poison.' He made that up to fool you. But Elu trusts Ugga and Bard and would like to tell the real story. Would you like to listen?"

"I would love to hear ya story."

"Me too," Bard said.

"As would I," came a deep voice from behind them. To their surprise Torg stood outside the hut with a weary-looking Rathburt at his side. "May we join you by the fire?"

"Please sit with us, Master Hah-nah," Ugga said. "Elu is going to tell us a very great story about how he got to be so little."

Rathburt didn't look well to Torg. "I've heard this one before, gentlemen. I think I'll go back inside and take a nap."

After the stooped Death-Knower closed the door, Elu leaned forward. "Rathburt doesn't like it when people say nice things about him. He wants everyone to believe he's a coward. That way, they'll leave him alone."

"Truer words have never been spoken," Torg said.

Elu seemed pleased.

"Tell us your story, little guy," Ugga prodded. "I wants to hear it so bad!"

The Svakaran stood and pranced around the fire. Torg, Ugga and Bard sat on a fallen log, but even from that position they were taller than Elu. Torg guessed that the Svakaran was about the same height as a Tugar boy of seven summers. How could he have ever been big?

As it turned out Elu was an accomplished storyteller, changing facial expressions and tones of voice while gesturing with his stubby arms and legs.

The diminutive Svakaran had once been a proud warrior and renowned hunter, wandering far and wide and never returning empty-handed. During one fateful expedition, Elu and three other warriors set out in search of game. It was early spring, and food was plentiful, but the hunting party was in the mood for adventure. The foursome journeyed farther from the village than necessary, traveling along the foothills of the mountains almost to the eastern mouth of the Gap of Gamana.

"The game trails go on for leagues, rising along the sides of mountains before tumbling into hollows and coves," Elu told the three of them. "One night, after we had slain a buck, we set up camp on a flat rock near a stream and built a fire to roast the tenderloins."

"I loves the loins," Ugga said.

Elu nodded at the enormous crossbreed, then continued his story. "While the meat was cooking, we began to hear scary sounds from the upper heights. We all knew what animals howled like that—black mountain wolves. In a panic we doused the fires and hid, hoping they wouldn't find us. But we weren't so lucky."

Elu and his companions left their gear and jogged northward along the trail in the darkness, carrying only their bows, arrows, and knives.

"We believed the wolves would find the gutted deer and go no farther. We could hide in the bushes and get our gear the next morning. But the wolves weren't interested in the deer. They ran right past it and followed us."

The trail rose steeply and then flattened along a narrow ridge. The land dropped down on both sides into thickets of tangled vines with thorns as long and sharp as bear claws.

"It's called mountain laurel," Rathburt said.

Torg looked up in surprise.

"Sorry . . . I couldn't sleep, after all."

"Come and listen to Elu's great story," Ugga said.

"I've heard it before."

"Go on, Elu," Torg said.

In the darkness Elu and the other warriors couldn't see the approaching wolves, but they could hear and smell them. It was impossible to outrun them, but if they stopped and tried to fight, they would be routed.

"Our only chance was to brave the vines," Elu said. "Bears can run through them very fast. There's an open area beneath the laurel about this high off the ground." Elu raised his hand to the level of his own shoulder, about two cubits tall.

"But the black wolves are as big as horses," Rathburt said. "It's difficult for them to hunch down low enough to get through."

"It's hard for men, too," Elu said. "We can't scrunch down like bears."

"Bears can run *very* fast," Ugga said proudly.

"Still, they would have escaped," Rathburt said, apparently unable to resist joining in. "The wolves remained by the edge of the trail, helpless to pursue. But not for the reason Elu and the warriors believed. Something else lived in the laurel, and the wolves could sense it."

Elu lowered his head. "The vines . . . eat you."

Rathburt nodded and then took a deep breath. "Most often, the thickets are harmless, except for the thorns. But there are places in the mountains where another kind of vine grows, hidden among the laurel, and it is anything but harmless. It feeds not on sunlight and rich dirt, but on flesh—usually the flesh of bears and other animals that enter the laurel, but it will consume humans too. At it turns out Elu and his friends escaped the wolves but not the vines."

"I've never heard of these vines," Torg said, "and I've journeyed in the mountains many times."

"Few have heard of them," Rathburt said. "They're rare—though less rare now than before. Lately, they have been spreading. The Mogols call the vines *Badaalataa*, the plant that devours. And that's what it does, gradually and painfully. The animal—or human—doesn't always die immediately. Instead the victim becomes a living part of the plant and sometimes survives for as long as a week."

"When Rathburt found us, it was the morning of the fourth day," Elu said, visibly shaken. "We had gotten no more than twenty paces off the trail when the *Badaalataa* grabbed us. I felt like I was being bitten by an army of fanged snakes. The poison paralyzed my body, but it didn't dull the pain." Suddenly the Svakaran cast himself onto the ground and sobbed.

Ugga knelt down and lifted him in his arms, hugging him against his chest. "Don't cry. I can't stand it," Ugga said, also bursting into tears. "Somebody help Elu . . . *please.*"

"There's little help for such pain of the heart," Torg said. "Not even the passing of time will heal it completely. Let him cry, but don't let him go. Your friendship is what he needs more than anything."

Rathburt also wept. This surprised Torg far more than Elu's outburst. He had never seen Rathburt react to anything with such sincere emotion.

Eventually Elu's sobs reduced to whimpers, but Ugga still held him close. Rathburt's face was buried in his hands. Bard moved beside him and placed his arm around his shoulders.

As if in response to such tenderness, more of Rathburt's words emerged. "I was wandering, as I sometimes do," he said. "I too heard the wolves and hid in the trees, waiting for them to go away. But they didn't leave, howling nonstop for three days. Something a ways down the trail was enraging them, though I couldn't imagine what. Near the end of the third day, they finally gave up and loped back to their dark lairs in the upper heights. A pack of more than fifty passed within a few paces of where I'd cowered for so long."

Rathburt looked at Elu, his stoop even more pronounced. "I wanted to be sure the wolves were gone before I investigated what it was that had befuddled them. I was curious, I must admit, but not enough to overcome my fear. So I slept fitfully through another night and didn't leave my hiding place until early the next morning."

Rathburt began to cry again, as if overwhelmed by grief too large to bear.

Elu squirmed out of Ugga's arms and crawled into Rathburt's lap, calming them both. "I don't know how much better it would have been had I helped them sooner," Rathburt said. "I suppose I'll never know. But it will always haunt me. The Vasi masters say, 'What's done is done.' I'm not so sure. When morning came I finally found the courage to start along the trail, and it didn't take me long to find them—or what remained of them. The *Badaalataa* were enjoying their meal. I could see skin, flesh, hair. Lips. Teeth.

"I remember clearly—as if it just happened—seeing an ear stuck to the end of a pulsing vine. But what I remember most is their eyeballs—eight of them, isolated here and there, but still aware. They stared at me, pleading . . . not to save them, but to end their misery."

"What did ya do, Master Radburt?" Bard said. "How did ya save little Elu from this terrible thing?"

Rathburt looked first at Bard and then at Torg, as if begging for permission to stop. But Torg's expression would not permit it.

Rathburt sighed. "You need to understand . . . for someone like *Torgon*, magic comes easily. But for me it's difficult—and sporadic. I can't just *will* my power to emerge. Sometimes it does, sometimes it doesn't. One day I can heal a dying tree; the next I can't save a blade of grass. I'm not like *him*."

Elu hugged Rathburt even tighter.

"But this time . . . *this* time . . . the magic roared out of me," Rathburt continued. "I strode into the vines, and they parted as if I were their master. Blue fire spurted from my staff and fell upon the *Badaalataa*, withering them. The flow of the magic was addictive. I felt as if I could scorch an entire forest. But as suddenly as the bliss arose, the agony followed. The vines were tamed, but Elu and his friends were still there, ripped into hundreds of pieces."

"And?" Torg said.

"And . . . that's when it . . . came to me." Rathburt then grew silent.

"Tell us," Torg said. But there was no command in his voice, only respect.

"Very well. But only this one time, and never again. Because saying the words makes me relive it, which is more than a coward can bear. What I saw terrified me far worse than the vines. I saw the extent of my power, and knew I could save them. Or, at least, one of them. I could peel the plants off their flesh and mold what remained into a single being. But it would not be pleasant for me—to say the least. The cost to my own body would be immense."

Rathburt placed Elu on the ground and stood up. Then he strode several paces away, his back to the fire, and whirled to face his audience. "It hurt me to exert the power necessary to mend a broken body. It *hurt* me to save them—to save him. Like being burned. Or frozen. Stabbed. Tortured. Dismembered. It hurt like madness."

These last words stunned Torg and the others into silence. The sweet aroma of roasting fowl wafted throughout the clearing, but they did not notice. Rathburt stared at the ground, his tears puncturing the snow.

Finally the Svakaran broke the long silence. "The vines were gone, the pain was gone, and Elu was alive. But Rathburt was lying on the ground, and Elu thought he was dead. His face was white like a ghost's, and he was wrinkled and weak. To Elu, he looked like a giant—ten cubits tall—but Elu didn't know then how small he had become. Rathburt brought Elu back, but only part of him." Then he flexed one of his arms, displaying a bulging muscle. "Elu had the same strength as before, just in a smaller body, and he dragged Rathburt for ten days, giving him food and water when he could. When Elu finally reached his village, his people did not recognize him, and they shunned both of us. Elu tried to tell them who he was. They didn't believe . . . at first. But when Elu told them the things he knew about each and every one, they believed him then, and they gave us the longhouse and asked us to stay away from the village. Once there, Elu tended Rathburt and brought him back to the world of the living. It wasn't as great as what he did for Elu, but at least it was something."

"It was more than just something," Rathburt said. "Thank you, my friend."

Ugga and Bard began to cry again. But Torg did not. He stood and held his muscled arms aloft. "I believe the five of us have been brought together for a purpose," he said in a loud voice, as if speaking to more than just his companions. "The fate of Triken lies in the hands of a few. I stand on the side of good and invite any and all to join me. What say you?"

"We are good friends," Ugga said, as if that were all the answer Torg required.

Then they gathered in a circle.

"Good friends," the crossbreed said again.

"Good friends!" they shouted in unison.

At that moment, an alliance was formed that would change the world.

3

In Torg's perception, it had taken Ugga less than a day to form an adoration for little Elu. And if there were any lingering doubts about Ugga's feelings, the roasted fowl and che-ra stew seemed to erase them forever. The crossbreed devoured the food with the urgency of an animal, and his contagious smile widened farther with every bite. The rest ate with similar passion.

Torg and Rathburt remained silent about whatever it was they had discussed in the hut, but it was evident to Torg that it had taken a toll on Rathburt—and the tale of the *Badaalataa* had made matters worse. The gardener, as Bard had begun to call Rathburt, looked even older and more haggard than when he had first arrived.

It was nearly dark when they finished their meal. A new storm was brewing. The wind increased its vehemence, prompting the pines to whisper urgently.

There still was no sign of Jord. If she were anywhere near, she was well hidden. But Torg believed she was far away.

"It's time to go inside," Torg said. "It's going to be an ugly night. In the morning we'll make our final plans. Rathburt suggests we wait out the worst of the winter at his longhouse, rather than venture to Kamupadana now. I agree. The longer I remain undiscovered, the better for all of us."

Ugga was especially pleased. "Elu says there is lots of beer at the longhouse. I says we stay there all winter—maybe all spring, too."

Rathburt laughed. "Ugga, you're a charmer."

"Thank ya, Master Rad-Burt."

The storm struck not long after they had retired to the hut, sweeping through the forest like a giant broom. But the house of Jord was up to the challenge. Though winds ferocious enough to topple trees surged all around the small hut, its roof and walls held firm while the hearth fire burned merrily, as if unaware of what was transpiring outside. Torg slept side by side with the men, snoring and farting as only men can do, and caring not a whit.

By morning the storm had dissipated, and the sky was as blue as a Tugar's eyes. But it seemed to take all of Ugga's strength to push open the door. More than two cubits of snow had fallen, which would make the march to the longhouse even more difficult. Elu predicted it now would take from morning till dusk to complete the journey. But at least they wouldn't starve. There still was enough roasted turkey left to last through the day, and Elu said there were grapes high in the trees that remained edible.

The stores at the longhouse had been stockpiled to sustain two men, not five. Once there they would have to hunt frequently, and fruits and vegetables would be in short supply, unless they could convince the nearby Svakaran villagers to part with some of theirs.

"That will be your job," Rathburt said to Torg.

Besides their weapons they packed little gear, other than a litter that had been built to haul the impressive stack of skins collected and tanned by Bard, Ugga and Jord during the fall. Torg bore the Silver Sword, Ugga his axe, and Bard his spear and the bow and quiver of arrows abandoned by Jord. Rathburt carried no weapons except for his oaken staff. Elu had a pair of daggers. His spear still was buried in the trunk of the tree, and they left it there. Perhaps anyone who found it would take it as a sign that the hut was not to be disturbed.

"Other than our pretty faces, the skins are the only things we'll have to trade in the markets of the Whore City," Bard said.

"I have no desire to see Kamupadana," Rathburt said, "but if you want to go, I certainly won't try to stop you."

"I likes the Brounettos," Ugga said.

"Aaah . . . I see," Rathburt said. "Beer and Brounettos. What an excellent combination. And what hair color do you favor, *Torgon?*"

Torg reached over and pinched Rathburt on his shoulder near the base of his neck. Rathburt yelped.

"Some jests are beneath even you," Torg said, threateningly.

"Sorry . . . *sorry*," Rathburt said. "Some people have *no* sense of humor."

"I doesn't understand," Bard said. "Does Master Hah-nah not like Brounettos?"

"Drop it!" Torg said, and he grumpily lifted the arms of the litter and strode into the woods. The others shrugged and followed.

Soon they passed into a thick grove. Torg stopped and gazed eastward, the opposite direction of the longhouse. The others watched him, puzzled. Finally Ugga could stand it no more.

"What is it, Master Hah-nah? Do ya see something? I would dearly like to know."

Torg emerged from his reverie. "Do you not hear their song?"

"Whose song?" Rathburt said.

"The giant pines. Jord's pines. They sing to us."

"I hears nothing," Ugga said. "Do ya hear the pines, Bard?"

"I hears nothing but the crunching of our boots. But if the pines call to Master Hah-nah, I would not be surprised. Maybe it's Jord saying goodbye. If so, I hopes it's not forever."

"Me too," Ugga said.

"Elu has seen the pines," the Svakaran said. "His tribesmen believe they're possessed by powerful spirits that protect Bard and Ugga. If not for the pines, our warriors would have raided their hut and stolen their skins."

"We're not helpless to defend ourselves, nor is Jord," Bard said.

"Elu has never seen Jord," the Svakaran said. "Only Bard and Ugga, though Elu didn't know your names until we were introduced. Our warriors call you Man and Bear."

Torg raised an eyebrow.

"If ya know of us, ya would have to know of Jord," Ugga said. "She's with us lots of the time. She likes to pretend she's a helpless woman, just to have fun. But when she's angry, she scares even Ugga and Bard."

Elu shrugged.

"Jord played that pretend game with me," Torg said. "But she has revealed herself. And I will not be so easily fooled again."

"All your strange talking is scaring me," Ugga said. "Without Jord around, this place feels creepy, almost like we're trespassing."

But Rathburt wasn't quite finished. "When we were in the hut, you mentioned these great trees, *Torgon*, but I was too weary to pay much attention. Now you've made me curious. You know how much I adore trees. How far are they from here? Do we have time to see them?"

"We've dallied too long already, thanks to me," Torg said. "We're hardy men and can endure the cold, but I'd prefer to arrive at the longhouse before dark . . . if possible."

"There are more reasons to arrive before dark than just the cold," Elu said. "Beasts roam the wilds that are new to Elu's land, nameless things that can shrivel the stoutest heart. They come from the south in search of prey and take the unwary back with them."

"How do ya know all this, little guy?" Ugga said.

"Elu still has friends in the village. The Svakarans know these mountains and foothills better than anyone. Some stray as far as Lake Ti-ratana. When they return, they speak of the sorcerer's slave hunters."

"In that case, I'll visit the trees another time," Rathburt said. "I have no desire to be captured by the sorcerer, especially if he is as powerful as *Torgon* says he is."

"I don't know *how* powerful he is, but I do know I'm in no position to find out right now. Enough talk. Let us travel in silence for a spell. Elu, you lead the way."

"Yes, *great one*," the Svakaran said. "But Elu must warn you that parts of the trail will be treacherous, especially with this new snow hiding all the roots and fallen leaves."

Then Elu strode through the trees. Because of the pines and hemlocks, the canopy was dense enough to hold back a portion of the previous night's snowfall, and in some areas it was only about knee-deep to Elu, and barely above the ankles of the larger men.

The Svakaran expertly avoided the thicker pockets of snow. By noon they had traveled more than a league, seeing and hearing no humans or animals, not even a rabbit or woodpecker. When they stopped near a tumble of boulders for a rest and some bites of turkey, Elu scampered into the woods to search for grapes.

"The forest has a strange feel—as if a hidden menace is abroad," Rathburt said.

"I sense it too," Torg said. "Also a feeling of being watched. But I don't believe we're in immediate danger. Perhaps what we sense is the evil of Invictus. His grasp expands every day."

"I hope to never meet him, if his strength is so great that he can change the mood of a forest with his will," Rathburt said.

"I agrees with Rad-burt," Ugga said. "I'll leave In-vick-tuss for Master Hah-nah to handle. Or Jord, if she ever returns. Could the Bitch defeat the Sore-sir-err, Master Hah-nah?"

"I'm not sure what she can do," Torg said. "She's beyond my knowledge. But there's one thing I've been meaning to ask you and Bard since we first met. Why do you call her 'the Bitch'?"

Bard laughed. "Ugga and I has heard the whores call her that, when she's not around. They say, 'Ya are grown men. Ya can do what ya want. Don't listen to what the Bitch says. Come in where it's warm and lay beside us.'"

"When we told Jord, she laughed," Ugga said. "She liked it when we called her that."

"Aaaah . . . now I understand. It appears Jord, whatever she is, does have a sense of humor." Torg winked at Rathburt.

Just then, Elu emerged from the trees carrying an armful of frozen grapes.

"There aren't many left. The bears are eating up the last of them. Elu had to climb very high to find these."

"Bears?" Ugga said. "If ya see one, let me know, little guy. I loves bears."

"Elu doesn't like bears. They want to eat Elu. But he will tell Ugga if one comes near."

The crossbreed seemed pleased.

After a cold meal they continued their march. To their right loomed the Mahaggatas, which the company skirted along a bony trail that meandered toward the southwest, rising for hundreds of cubits along gentle slopes and then tumbling into coves. The litter became a severe annoyance, and they cursed it like a hated enemy. But the skins were too valuable to leave behind.

Everyone except Rathburt, who complained of a sore back, took turns hauling the litter. Even Elu managed it for short distances, proving he was far stronger than he looked. Though the temperature was well below freezing, they became sweaty and overheated, and at times two or more of them had to lift the litter over rocks and fallen trees. Other than Rathburt, they were not lacking for physical strength. But the litter was awkward, frustrating, and just plain heavy.

"Are you sure you wouldn't like to give it a try?" Torg said to Rathburt during one of his turns. "A little exercise might do you some good."

Rathburt rubbed his lower back. "It's an old injury that never fully healed. But you, Bard and Ugga are so big and strong. It's as if you were made for this task."

"You've missed your calling," Torg said, his heavy breaths casting balls of white mist into the frozen air. "Instead of a gardener, you should have been a jester. You could make a fortune in the courts of Nissaya."

"Don't forget that Elu is strong too, and he isn't lazy like Rathburt."

"Watch yourself. I'll turn you back into a vine."

The Svakaran didn't find that the least bit funny. He pounded his small fists together and then stomped ahead.

"It appears you are a poor judge of talent," Rathburt said to Torg. "Apparently I'm not much of a jester, after all."

After Elu disappeared around a bend, Torg counted fifty paces before the Svakaran returned.

"This is the worst part of the trail," Elu said. "It will soon become steep and narrow, and there are lots of hidden roots. At the top of the path there is an overlook that is split in two by a stream—and a few paces away is a great waterfall. There is still some trickling, but most is frozen in peculiar shapes. My people believe this is a sacred place, especially in the winter. If you look carefully you will see faces in the ice. But don't look too long. Something evil in the water wants you to fall."

"I've been there several times and never seen any faces," Rathburt sneered. "I've seen carrots, corn and onions, though. And some lovely wildflowers."

"I wants to see no faces in the ice," Ugga said. "Faces are scary."

"They're not as scary as carrots," Rathburt said.

If anything, Elu understated the severity of the path. Under pristine conditions—and not dragging the son-of-an-ass litter—it would have been difficult to ascend. But with the snow, ice and gnarled roots, it was close to impossible. It took all of Torg's strength to haul the litter to the top, and that was with Ugga shoving from behind, braced by Bard. Elu led the way and disappeared again. Rathburt trailed behind, whining endlessly.

"There are easier ways to go," he mumbled, "even if they do add several leagues to our journey. We have to get there *before dark*, after all. Anna forbid we don't get there *after dark*."

When they reached the crest of the path they passed through a wall of trees and came upon the stream that fed the waterfall. From the overlook Torg could see for leagues. An endless vista of hills and valleys extended toward the horizon. The men were transfixed. Even in winter the land was beautiful.

"Elu sees the faces of his brothers," the Svakaran said abruptly, startling Rathburt.

"For Anna's sake, Elu. Give us some warning . . ."

But the Svakaran, who had crept to the edge without any of them noticing, appeared hypnotized. "The vines are eating their bodies, but their faces are still beautiful."

"Are ya all right, little guy?" Ugga said. "Aren't ya too close to the edge? I fears ya will fall. Is Elu going to fall, Master Hah-nah?"

"Elu," Torg said. Then louder: "*Elu!*" The second time he said it, a hot gust rustled the Svakaran's hair, awakening him from the trance. Elu slid far enough backward for Ugga to grab his shoulder and drag him to safety.

"Don't do that again," Rathburt shouted. "You scared us half to death."

"The ice spoke to Elu," he said, his voice distant.

"There *is* magic here," Torg announced, "but I sense neither good nor evil. It came from a far distant place, and it cares naught for our world."

"Then why did the mah-gick make the little guy see faces?" Ugga said. "That sounds evil to me."

"Whatever is here is very old. Older than me. Older than you or Bard. Older than any creature on Triken. Can't you feel it? To this kind of awareness, a millennium is like a single breath. It has been here since our world was born, existing within the rocks beneath our feet. It loves the water that rushes over its back—so soothing and delicious. But in the winter when the stream freezes, it becomes restless. I don't believe the magic *makes* anyone see faces. I don't believe it even recognizes our presence. Rather there is something in this ancient power that awakens our karma. Some of us might see what already has occurred. Others might see what is yet to happen. This is an opportunity we should not take lightly."

"What nonsense, *Torgon*," Rathburt said. "How could you possibly know all this just by standing on these damnable rocks? If I didn't know better, I would guess you've been chewing on poppies."

"What are poppies?" Bard said.

"They're little flowers that grow in the northern mountains near Catu," Torg said. "If you drink their sap, you often have visions. But that's not what's happening here. You ask me how I know this. I am a Death-Knower and comprehend many things others do not. But there's a better reason than that. I've been altered by the pines. Their green magic flows through flesh. And it's similar to what lies hidden in these rocks. It speaks to me, inspiring visions as vivid as any the poppies could provide. But it's your choice to believe or disbelieve."

"I believes ya, Master Hah-nah," Ugga said.

"Me too," Bard said.

Elu nodded vigorously.

"You're always trying to make me feel like the bad guy," Rathburt grumbled.

"Look!" Bard said. "Your sword, Master Hah-nah . . . it has come alive."

Torg slid the sword from the belt at his waist. The blade glowed and was hot to the touch. "The magic of the Silver Sword must be similar to Jord's trees and these rocks," he said. "It comes from an otherworldly place. Triken itself must have once been otherworldly, before it was bound together by the forces that created it."

"Yes, yes, yes," Rathburt said. "Always the philosopher."

Rathburt's behavior seemed to annoy Elu more than usual. "You've told Elu many times that the plants talk to you. Why can't the rocks talk to the *great one?*"

"That's different," Rathburt said, but the expression on his face seemed to lose its certainty, causing Torg to chuckle.

Then Torg said, "Now it's my turn."

"Oh, no, I'm not going *after* you," Rathburt said. "Everyone knows you'll see something grand that will make me feel insignificant."

"I didn't think you even wanted a turn," Torg said. "I'll go next, and then you, if you still desire."

"Always the showoff," Rathburt said. "Always, always, always."

Torg placed the Silver Sword on the ground well away from the drop-off. Then he reached down, picked up a hefty rock and handed it to Ugga.

"I want you to hold my belt," Torg said to the crossbreed, "and if I start to act strangely, take this rock and hit me as hard as you can on the back of my neck—here." Torg pointed to a slightly protruding bone. "It won't injure me. But if you hit me hard enough, it will stun me for a moment, which should give you the time to drag me back."

"I'm afraid I will kills ya," Ugga said.

"No one can kill the great and mighty *Torgon*," Rathburt sneered. "By all means, Ugga, hit him as hard as you can. Give him a really good *smack.*"

Torg smiled. Then he walked to the edge, which was even more slippery than he expected. As he peered down, his inquisitiveness took over. At first he was amazed by the simple beauty of the frozen falls, the ice gnarled and tangled like the exposed roots of an old oak but bursting with color. White and blue were predominant, but crimson and gold danced within the cracks and crevices, sparkling like jewels. Torg gasped. *I could stand here all day and just stare at it.*

But then the bright afternoon sun faded and darkness consumed his awareness. Now the ice glowed like a full moon in a black sky. It squirmed and came to life, forming the sweet face of a beautiful woman.

She smiled at him, the knowing smile of a lover who also is a friend. Torg reached for her, his hands flailing.

The rock crashed down with precision. Ugga and Bard dragged him away. Torg regained his senses soon after sitting on the bank of the stream. But he didn't speak for a long time. When he finally looked up, the others were staring at him.

"Ya tried to jump," Ugga said. "What were ya thinking?"

"I'd like to know, too," Rathburt said angrily. "You frightened us, you moose. What *did* you see?"

Torg rubbed the back of his neck. "I saw . . . my future."

"Huh?" Rathburt said. "Your future? What do you mean?"

"I will say no more."

"No more? *No* more? Isn't that just like you? You get us all so worked up we're about to burst, and then you say, 'I saw my future.' What an absolute ass you are. *Tell* us what you saw, or I'll hit you with the stone even harder than Ugga did."

"I cannot."

"Arrrgggghhh!"

The rest of them sat silently while Rathburt cursed and waved his arms. Finally even he calmed down.

"How about you?" Torg said to his fellow Death-Knower. "Do you still wish to look at the ice?"

"Believe it or not, I do. For once, I'm *guaranteed* to outshine you."

Torg held Rathburt's belt, followed by Ugga, Bard and Elu. Rathburt leaned on his walking staff as he peered over the edge. It didn't take him long to start complaining.

"I don't see anything but a bunch of ice. And a long fall. Were you playing some kind of joke on me? There's nothing here but . . . wait . . . *wait* . . ."

Rathburt grew placid, and the eerie silence returned. The others watched him, ready to pull him away from the edge as soon as they saw signs of trouble.

Without warning Rathburt's face contorted and he cried out, raising his staff and smiting the ice. There was a crackling explosion, followed by hissing bursts of steam, and a massive chunk tore free and tumbled into the abyss, bursting asunder on the rocks below.

They pulled him from the edge and sat him down in the same spot Torg had been before. Rathburt sobbed hysterically. When he regained control, he looked at the others with horror in his eyes.

"What did you see?" Torg said. "Rathburt, what did you *see*?"

"I saw . . . *my* future."

And like Torg before him, he would say no more.

For a long while, Rathburt wouldn't even speak. After his ordeal at the waterfall he appeared frailer to Torg than usual, trudging through the snow like a hunched old man. Nothing cheered him up. Even the ebullient Ugga could not seem to break through Rathburt's self-imposed silence.

Once they left the waterfall, the trail became easier to traverse. But frequent pockets of snow—several spans deeper than Elu was tall—slowed them considerably. At these places Torg was forced to use his magic. The blue-green flames that spouted from his fingertips melted trenches wide enough for the men and the litter. But Torg knew that there were creatures on Triken who could sense such displays of power, and many of them were friendly with Invictus.

"I might as well hand out scrolls announcing I'm here," Torg said. "But I suppose it's better than being buried alive."

"I likes it better, Master Hah-nah," Ugga said. "And I'm sure the little guy does too."

Elu nodded vigorously. Rathburt said nothing, his chin so low it almost touched his chest.

The arduous journey continued. In the quiet calm of late afternoon they heard wolves howling in the distance.

Instantly Elu was on alert. "Those are black wolves," he said in a panic.

"From the sound of them, there are many," Torg said.

For the first time since the incident at the waterfall, Rathburt spoke, though his voice quivered. "We must find a place to hide."

"How far is the longhouse?" Bard said.

"We would not reach it before dark," Elu said. "The wolves can run on snow as fast as on grass. If they're aware of us, they'll catch us long before we reach the house."

"Is there any other place to hide?" Ugga said.

"Elu remembers a small cave less than a league from here that is large enough for the five of us. We could hide there and hope the wolves pass."

Even as the howling grew louder, Torg held up his hand, as if to calm his companions. "You forget who is with you. I am *The Torgon*—and my strength has returned. A hundred wolves are no match for me. If I were alone, I would meet them wherever they chose. But if we're attacked from all sides at once, I fear most for Rathburt and Elu. Rather than hide, we must make a stand."

The Svakaran was offended. "Elu can fight."

"I meant no offense," Torg said. "If it were just one black wolf against you, I've no doubt you would prevail. But if I'm correct, we'll be severely outnumbered. And where there are black wolves, there can be other creatures, some of which are even deadlier. If my attention is diverted, you'd be easy prey. Your familiarity with this land is needed more than your strength."

"Maybe Rathburt and Elu should hide in the cave while you great men do all the fighting," the Svakaran said angrily.

"For Anna's sake, Elu. None of us doubts your courage," Rathburt snapped. "But for once, *Torgon* is right. Rather than complain, help us find a better place to fight than these trees."

Elu stomped his foot and spat. Finally he pointed toward the mountains. "Up there, the land rises sharply. Beyond is a narrow path with great stone walls."

"Good idea, little guy," Ugga said. "Show us the way."

Then the crossbreed swept Elu onto his shoulders. To quicken their pace, Torg melted a long trench in the snow. Bard took control of the litter, and Rathburt, surprisingly, lent a hand, bending over and shoving it from behind.

"If the wolves get too close, we'll have to abandon this," Rathburt said.

"I'll die before I do that," Bard said. "I wouldn't give up the skins to a thousand of them."

"You've been spending too much time around *Torgon*," Rathburt said. "You're picking up his stubbornness."

As the howling intensified, their hopes of escaping undetected diminished, though they could not yet see the wolves. The land rolled and swayed like a stormy sea, restricting their visibility. The wolves could have been just a stone's throw away and still be hidden from view.

"How far, Elu?" Torg said.

"Less than five hundred paces."

"We have to give up the skins," Torg said. "They're slowing us down too much."

Bard started to protest, but Torg cut him off. "It's not what they're after. We'll come back for them when the fight is finished."

They shoved the litter into a dense area of trees and continued their flight. Bard was dismayed—and for a moment it appeared he might stay with the skins rather than follow his companions—but Ugga grabbed his arm and yanked him forward.

"Master Hah-nah is right. What good are they to us if we're dead?"

The terrain became treacherous. Even without snow and ice it would have been difficult to traverse, but in the wintry conditions it was tough on all of them. Rathburt, as it turned out, slowed them down almost as much as the litter, frequently tripping and sliding down the slope ten paces or more each time he fell. Torg and Bard were forced to drag him along.

At the same time the narrow path came into view above, the lead wolves appeared below. At first there were just four, and when they caught sight of the men, they rushed toward them at a full run. They were as large and fast as horses, but far more dangerous. Their fangs and claws were as sharp as the point of a Tugarian dagger.

Bard loosed an arrow that caught the lead wolf between the eyes. It tumbled and lay still.

The second wolf leaped over its fallen brother. Torg shifted to his left and then whipped the Silver Sword in a high arc over his right shoulder. The blade cut through hide, bone and sinew. Blood as black as tar splashed onto Torg's face.

The third went for Ugga, but the crossbreed dealt a death blow with his axe.

The fourth got past the three men and lunged for Rathburt, who tried to smite it with his staff but slipped instead, falling awkwardly onto his rump. The wolf went for his throat, but Elu pounced onto its back and plunged his dagger between the bones of its spine, killing it with one stab. Then the tiny Svakaran pounded his chest.

"The little guy is tougher than he looks," Ugga said.

"Hurry!" Torg said. "The others will soon be upon us. We must reach the narrow way."

They darted upward, dragging Rathburt toward the wall of stone, within which was a crevice just wide enough for the largest of them to enter. It was a perfect place for their defense. Rathburt and Elu squeezed through the opening just as the main strength of the wolves rushed forward, growling and slavering, anxious for the kill. But something held them back. Rather than attack in uncontrolled rage, they approached slowly, side by side, heads down.

"There are too many," Rathburt shouted. "Come with us. We can escape on the other side of the path."

"It would be useless to run," Torg said. "Stay where you are. Elu will protect you."

Torg was flanked by Bard and Ugga, who appeared alert but unafraid.

"The wolves are not alone," Torg said softly. "Something commands them. I can sense its power. Whatever it is, you must leave it to me. It is beyond any of you."

Just then the line of wolves parted, and the woods grew eerily silent. A dip at the base of the slope concealed what approached. But its footsteps boomed.

Suddenly Rathburt screamed, "A Kojin comes!"

The wolves were intimidated and enraged at the same time, the hair on their napes bristling. They tore at the ground with their claws, but it was clear the ogress was their master.

"If I fall, you must flee," Torg said.

The Kojin crawled up the slope like a sister of Dukkhatu, using her six muscled arms to propel herself. When she reached the wolves, she rose on two legs to her full height, twice as tall as Torg or Ugga and almost three times as heavy.

The ogresses were massively strong, yet also agile, and they possessed ancient magic that shielded their flesh. Eons before, when Java was five times its current size, hundreds of Kojins were believed to have roamed the forest, terrorizing any who dared enter. But Java succumbed to the onslaught of a thousand wars and was reduced in scope. Now fewer than a dozen ogresses were thought to survive. But that did not make this one any less dangerous. Torg could see a purplish glow emanating from the beast's scaly hide. An ordinary sword, no matter how skillfully wielded, could not pierce the supernatural buffer.

Kojins were incapable of speech, but they were not stupid. They communicated telepathically, much like the cave monkeys but with not nearly the delicacy. As the ogress strode to meet him, Torg felt the beast's will beat upon his brow like the heat from a furnace. In a posture of challenge the Kojin pounded her fists together, causing the wolves to yip and snarl, maddened by her bravado.

The ogress wielded no weapons other than her club-like arms and the poisoned claws on the tips of her fingers and toes. Torg wielded the Silver Sword. As he confronted the Kojin, the creature seemed to sense his confidence and was puzzled. It was possible that she had never before stood face to face with so bold an opponent.

The wolves sensed the ogress' confusion. As the will that drove them wavered, they rushed forward. But the Kojin let out a high-pitched screech, freezing the beasts in their tracks. Then she seemed to regain her composure and return her focus to the being that approached her.

Wielding the Silver Sword, Torg continued toward the monster, closing within three paces. With long-practiced precision, he grasped the dull portion of the blade near the hilt with his left hand and lowered the sword to his left hip, its point facing behind him, its pommel facing forward. Then he knelt on his left knee.

The Kojin towered above him, seeming to mistake his movement as an act of submission, and she pounded her hairy chest and screeched again. The wolves could barely tolerate the intensity, shaking their heads wildly. Bard, Ugga, Rathburt and Elu made smacking sounds as they clasped their ears. But Torg was unaffected.

What happened next took less time than a single long breath.

Torg grasped the black-leather grip with his right hand, lunged forward on his right foot, and leaped high into the air, whipping the blade left-to-right across the front of his body. The tip gashed the Kojin's throat, and purple light exploded from the wound.

Torg landed at the Kojin's feet and knelt again. From this position, he again swung the blade across the front of his body, this time right-to-left, and cut off the Kojin's left foot above the ankle.

The ogress cried out and collapsed to her knees.

Once Torg had completed the swing, the sword again pointed straight back on his left side. With barely a pause he leapt upward, raised the blade over his head, and drove the edge into the Kojin's skull. A blinding explosion of purple erupted from the gory wound, scattering the wolves and setting nearby trees aflame.

Almost nonchalantly, Torg flicked blood off the blade.

The Kojin collapsed onto its shattered face. It would never again haunt the Dark Forest or any land. It was no longer.

Torg stared down at her ruin. The Silver Sword remained lifeless and cold, as if totally disinterested in its role in the carnage.

Though the ogress was dead, her body still writhed, and the ancient magic erupting from her skull, neck and leg scorched whatever it touched. The wolves went wild, attacking anything that moved, including each other. By the time they calmed enough to turn on their intended prey, fully a third of their own were dead or maimed. But that left more than sixty still capable of wreaking havoc, and these fell upon Bard, Ugga and Torg in a frothy rage. Bard dropped the bow and fought bravely with his spear, skewering two before being driven back against the wall. Ugga killed half a dozen with his axe, but he was forced to retreat to help Bard. Without Torg, they would have been lost. He entered into *frenzy*, butchering two dozen wolves with a variety of cuts, hacks and thrusts refined over a thousand years of practice. The surviving wolves—fewer than thirty in all—finally lost their courage and rushed down the slope with their tails between their legs, yelping as they fled.

But five alpha males remained, still focused on Ugga and Bard. The crossbreed had a deep gash across his forehead that was dumping blood into his eyes. Bard was cut and bruised, and his spear had been sundered. He held just a pair of daggers. But now Elu had joined the fray, and he stood between the men like a boy come of age, waving his own dagger as if daring the wolves to attack.

Still in the *frenzy*, Torg pierced the nearest wolf through its heart. The others turned to face him, but they were no match. A second fell, its legs cut out from under. Ugga swung his axe and beheaded a third. Elu stabbed the largest of the wolves between its ribs before Torg finished it with a thrust to the throat. The final survivor turned and ran, following the others into the forest.

Bard sagged to his knees. Elu and Ugga knelt near their friend. Torg stood motionless, watching his breath until his rage subsided. Finally he motioned for Rathburt to come out of hiding.

"The fight is over, for now. The wolves are routed. Once we regain our strength, we can recover the skins and be on our way."

"Is anyone badly hurt?" Rathburt managed to say.

As a group, they turned to Bard, but he was already on his feet. "Nothing that beer won't cure."

The others laughed—except for Rathburt, whose face was red with shame.

"I'm sorry, *Torgon*. I'm too weak to slay a single wolf, much less a Kojin. Once again I've failed you."

But Torg only smiled. "Sister Tathagata once said something similar to me, and it was foolish coming from her, as well. I inflict death. You do not. Are you inferior? Accept your destiny. And take pride in your accomplishments. They're not as minor as you believe."

Rathburt glared at Torg. "Perhaps there will come a time when I will not fail you."

"You've never failed me."

"Just once . . . hate me. Scream at me. Hit me. I can't stomach your unconditional love. It makes me feel even more worthless."

"I reserve hatred for a select few. And even then, I'm ashamed of it."

"You don't know the meaning of shame," Rathburt said, before stomping off.

"You could not be more wrong," Torg whispered.

But none heard him say it.

Slaughter and Solitude

1

Before leaving the scene of the battle, Torg tended his companions' wounds. The gash on Ugga's forehead was the worst of the injuries. Torg cauterized it with a tendril of blue-green flame from the tip of his right index finger, stopping the bleeding and eliminating the chance of infection. The others stared, wide-eyed and silent.

"What should we do with the carcasses?" Ugga said to Torg. "It will take too long to bury them, and burning could attract evil eyes."

"Let them rot. The forest will consume them at its leisure."

"I likes that idea," Bard said. "We need to go back quick as we can. If the wolves have ruined the skins, I'll come back here and kill them again."

Elu obviously thought that was funny and wrapped his arms around the trapper's leg.

"When you're finished hugging Bard, can we get back to our business?" Rathburt snapped.

"Rathburt is right, we should delay no longer," Torg said. "The wolves have been routed, but there are other enemies in the forest more dangerous in the dark than in the light."

Elu let go of Bard's leg and began to inspect the remains of the Kojin. Sparkles of purple light still spun from the creature's wounds. The beast's chest was thicker than the Svakaran was tall. Elu poked at it with his dagger.

"Be careful, little guy," Ugga said. "It might still be dangerous."

Torg approached. "Stand back, all of you."

None questioned his order, and they retreated down the slope in a rush.

"*Vanadevataayo!* (Gods of the forest!)" Torg said in the ancient tongue. "*Paapam imam visodetha.* (Purify this evil.)"

Torg lifted the Silver Sword high into the air and whipped the blade down upon the back of the Kojin's neck. The bulbous head fell away, and a conflagration of purple light raced along the ground. But the remnants of the ogress' power proved impotent.

Torg rejoined the others. "The Kojin is no longer dangerous. Now even the crows can feast on her flesh without fear."

"Always the showoff," Rathburt mumbled, though he said it this time with little conviction.

After retracing their path, Bard was delighted to find the skins unmolested. Torg had been right. The wolves were interested only in their prey. But after they restarted their trek, the litter regained its status as an enormous nuisance. At this pace they wouldn't reach the longhouse until deep into the evening. Their only consolation was that the sky remained clear.

Now Torg was wary of using his powers to clear paths. The litter slid on top of the snow relatively well, but the men's feet dug deep. The whiny Rathburt wondered aloud if they would arrive at all.

"At least we won't freeze," Ugga said, trying to cheer Rathburt. "We have enough of the skins to keep an army warm."

At dusk they stopped briefly near a running stream, drinking their fill of the frigid water and eating what remained of their food. The quarter moon already had reached midpoint in the darkening sky. Stars winked on, one by one. The air became as icy as a demon's breath. But there was no wind, not even the slightest breeze, and the men—clad in thick cloaks and boots—did not feel the cold.

"How much farther now?" Torg said to Elu, his patience withering along with the rest of them. "It feels like we've been walking for weeks."

"If there were no snow and wolves and skins, Elu could make it to the longhouse in a short time," the Svakaran said. "But as slow as we're going, it will be a while yet. A third of the night will be gone before we arrive. And that's if there is no more trouble."

"I'm surprised we haven't seen someone yet," Rathburt said. "Not that Elu's people make a habit of running around in the middle of the night in the freezing cold, but there usually are scouts about, and I'd have guessed they'd be especially vigilant after receiving the news that the Great Ogre," he nodded toward Torg, "is in the vicinity."

"We should have met someone by now," Elu agreed. "There are more than a thousand in the village."

"What about the wolves?" Bard said. "Maybe the people are afraid to go outside."

"That could be," Torg said. "Regardless, we have only two choices: to continue on or to stop and make camp. But I'm not certain we dare risk a fire. On a night like this, the smoke will cling to the ground like a fog and attract any number of nuisances."

"Nuisances?" Rathburt said. "There are worse than nuisances about. I, for one, vote against a fire. Let's keep walking. Once we reach the longhouse, we can build a nice fire inside and sleep till noon."

For the first time, all agreed with Rathburt. Ugga grabbed the litter while Torg and Bard went ahead and dug a path through the thigh-deep snow. Elu was sent out to look for any signs of a fellow Svakaran, but he reported discovering no other humans out on this night.

Later on, they heard tormented cries. At first they mistook them for snow owls, which make haunting sounds that carry long distances on still nights. But the men became convinced that animals had not made the noises. There were words among the screams.

"Are these woods haunted?" Torg said to Rathburt.

"You believe in ghosts?" the fellow Death-Knower said.

"Of course. I've spoken with them."

"I wants to speak to no ghosties," Ugga said, his small eyes darting about. "Ya talk to them, Master Hah-nah. I will stand behind ya."

"Ghosts are nothing to fear. Unlike demons and ghouls, they lack power over the living. But even if they were dangerous, none would dare approach while I am with you."

"I'm glad ya are here," Bard said. "The ghosties, demons and ghoulies give me the shivers."

"Do you fear nothing, Master Showoff?" Rathburt said.

"I fear desire and aversion. Greed and suffering. But I don't fear ghosts. Does that answer your question, Master Complainer?"

"Do you fear *fear?*" Elu said.

"A wise question," was Torg's response. "I wish Sister Tathagata were here. She could answer better than I."

"Who is that?" Ugga said. "I heard ya say her name before."

"A very wise woman. The wisest of women. Even Jord could learn a thing or two from her."

"Could you learn from her?" Rathburt sneered. "Or are you beyond her teaching?"

Torg did not respond.

The quarter moon had set by the time they arrived at the longhouse. The men covered the litter with several tarps and then went inside, the ghostly cries following them all the way to the door. The weary travelers lit candles and started a fire. They ate jerky and dried apples and then opened the first barrel of beer. But on this rare occasion, they didn't drink very much. Exhaustion overcame their desires, and they cast themselves upon furry blankets and slept like dead men.

In the morning the men woke amid a cacophony of stretches and groans, their legs and backs sore from the previous day's exertions. All except Torg and Rathburt had cuts and bruises that Torg had not had time to heal.

Torg discovered that the longhouse was divided into three rooms: a main area for cooking and sleeping; a storage area for food and supplies; and a stable housing three goats and nine chickens, which had produced several dozen eggs while Elu and Rathburt were away.

The Svakaran built a fire in the hearth, heated slices of salted pork in an iron skillet, and scrambled eggs in the pork fat, tossing in onions and herbs. Then he spread hickory-nut butter onto slices of dark bread. Even Rathburt got into the act, brewing a pot of black tea.

The men sat on the floor around the fire and spooned the eggs out of wooden bowls. The meal was not large enough to satisfy Ugga, but it worked wonders for the rest of them. Afterward they went outside to relieve themselves, and when they returned they drank more tea.

"There's enough food here for two men to survive the winter, but not five, especially the way Ugga eats," Rathburt said. "We'll need to go to the village and barter. Either that or *Torgon* can just scare them into giving us what we need."

"Let's try bartering first," Torg said.

Elu, however, was in no mood for jests. "The village is not far, but it will take until early afternoon to reach it and until dark to return. We should leave as soon as possible."

"What's the hurry?" Bard said. "There's enough food to last awhile. Shouldn't we rest a few days before we go tromping 'round again?"

"Elu is worried," the Svakaran said nervously. "Something is wrong. We should have seen someone. These woods are not usually so empty."

"Your people are hiding from the *great one*," Rathburt said. "Cowering in their huts, afraid to breathe. Maybe they fear he will stomp into their village and burn it down like an angry dragon."

"I feel it too, Elu," Torg said, ignoring Rathburt's sarcasm.

"Did the wolves come this way?" Ugga said.

With that, Elu threw on his deerskin coat and raced out the door. "There are *children*," he screamed.

Without hesitation, the others followed. Each brought their weapons, a bag of jerky, and a single skin over their cloaks to have something to trade if the opportunity arose. They planned on returning to the longhouse by nightfall with more supplies. The weather remained cold and clear, but if a sudden storm arose, they would have to make the best of it.

Without the litter to slow them down, Torg felt as if they were flying. Torg, Ugga, and Bard took turns churning trenches through the deepest drifts of snow. By the time the sun was in the middle of the sky, they were within a league of the village.

That's when they saw the first bodies—or what remained of them. Their small company had stopped to rest, and Rathburt was leaning against a tree when he looked up and screamed. An arm that had been torn off at the shoulder dangled from the crook of a limb. The thumb of its hand was missing, which somehow magnified the gruesomeness.

Elu screamed too, but for a different reason. The dismembered arm seemed to confirm his worst fears.

They found the head a dozen paces away, resting upright on a bank of snow. It stared at them, mouth agape. No tracks surrounded it, and there was little blood, except for a trail of red dots that led to the real carnage. At least three corpses lay beneath the trees, disemboweled and shredded. Elu ran to the tattered bodies.

"Are they *all* dead?" Rathburt said. "Did the wolves slaughter the entire village? There were good people here, *Torgon*."

They rushed on. When they reached the village, what they saw stunned even Torg. They stood on a hillock and observed the carnage from above. There had been no fires—they would have noticed the smoke long before they approached—but many of the huts had been battered to pieces, and misshapen bodies lay strewn about, some of which were as small as babies. Elu charged down the hill, heedless of the others' cries. Torg, Ugga and Bard followed, with Rathburt trailing behind.

Most of the victims had been disemboweled—the work of black wolves. This became even more evident when they found the carcasses of half a dozen wolves, felled by arrows and spears. But the destruction of the huts and other structures made it plain that the Kojin had played a major role in the slaughter. Against such a fiend, even a thousand Svakarans had been helpless.

Elu came to a sudden halt, sat on the ground, and took a corpse in his arms.

Torg knelt beside him. "Who?"

"It's his mother," Rathburt said from behind. "After Elu returned, she never accepted him, claiming he was a devil and banishing him from their home. But he never stopped loving her."

"I'm sorry, little guy," Ugga said. "But we will take care of ya, won't we Bard?"

"That's very right. Ya are our good friend."

Torg slid his hand beneath Elu's cloak, caressing the red-brown skin with glowing fingers. The Svakaran's tensed muscles relaxed, and he gently released his mother's ravaged body.

"All are dead. Should Elu not mourn?" There was no sarcasm in his voice, only desperation.

Torg stared hard into his eyes. "In this lifetime their suffering is no longer. But your pain remains. You must find the strength to overcome it."

"And Sōbhana?" Rathburt said sharply. "Did you not mourn for her?"

"I mourned for myself."

Torg turned back to Elu. "We must do for your mother and the rest of your people what we did for the others. A slaughter of this magnitude must be countered. The insanity of such merciless behavior strains the balance of karma. But it will take far too long to burn their bodies in traditional fashion. For this task I must risk another display of magic. But first let us search for signs of life."

The men moved slowly through the rubble. In every face, Torg saw remnants of terror. None had been spared. Despite Torg's attempts to calm Elu, the Svakaran's agitation intensified. Torg finally told Rathburt to escort Elu to the far side of the hill. He, Ugga and Bard would do the rest.

The trio searched until late afternoon but did not find a single person alive. If any had survived, they had fled far away. However, the assault had left plenty of food and supplies untouched. They even found a four-wheeled cart—probably stolen from villagers who dwelled along the Ogha River—and a pair of robust oxen to haul it. The Kojin and the wolves had been intent on mayhem and murder. Apparently the animals and supplies had not held their interest.

Torg, Ugga and Bard overloaded the cart with carrots, peas and beans; dried apples, pears and figs; venison and pork; cheeses and butter;

salt and herbs; and hay for the oxen. And of course, as many kegs of corn beer and apple wine as they could manage. They were not in the mood for it now, but the winter would be long, and their sadness would fade. *Life is for the living*, Vasi masters liked to say.

"Those who desire to watch should do so from the hilltop," Torg said. "Do not stray too near."

"*Torgon the Showoff* is about to perform another act of derring-do," Rathburt sneered.

"Why don't ya be *quiet*," Ugga said. "Master Hah-nah is only doing what's right for those poor peoples."

"Yes, be quiet," Elu said.

"Hmmph!" Rathburt said.

While the others climbed to the safety of the hilltop, Torg walked to the center of what remained of the village. He stood there silently, counting fifty inhales and fifty exhales without permitting a single other thought. Then he raised his arms toward the sky. Once again, his eyes glowed blue-green, and tendrils of fire danced along his fingertips, earlobes and nostrils. When he opened his mouth, a ball of smoke puffed out.

"*Aggi dahanti, te aamantemi*! (The fire that consumes, I summon thee!)"

There came a low rumble, as if an earthquake were working up the urge to wreak havoc. Torg became engulfed in red fire, but his blue-green power blended with it, turning the flames a tempestuous shade of purple. The fire whirled, slowly at first, but ever faster and more violently, expanding outward and upward, hungry and potent. Bolts of lightning leapt from it, hurtling angrily into the firmament.

The others watched from the hilltop. Torg imagined that even Rathburt would be left speechless. Everything the fire touched was consumed. Buildings, bodies and bones turned to ash. Without warning, a wave of super-heated air blew across the hilltop. A concussive, five times as loud as thunder, followed.

When it was over, the village had been consumed. The flames receded and the smoke dissipated, leaving nothing but white ash that swirled in the air and coated the ground.

Torg stood in the middle of it all—and he remained there, motionless, for a long time. Finally he dusted himself off. His cloak and boots were unharmed, except for the fringes of his sleeves, which were singed. He had protected himself, even his clothing, with a cocoon of magic. The Silver Sword hung from his belt, cold and disinterested. As Torg walked to the top of the hill, flakes of ash still clung to him.

"It's done," he said to the others, all of whom faced him with mouths agape. "I am weary. But we must leave this place."

2

The quarter moon had set by the time Torg and the others made it back to the longhouse. Even with the help of the oxen, the cart had slowed them down, and they barely had enough strength to unpack the supplies and guide the beasts into the stable. The goats and chickens seemed unhappy with their new companions—especially ones that weighed more than one hundred and fifty stones apiece—but Torg knelt and whispered to each of them. After that, the animals got along splendidly.

Rathburt smacked his own forehead with the palm of his hand. "What next, *Torgon?* Will you part the Salt Sea and stroll among the flopping fishes?"

Torg chuckled. "I've considered it."

The exertion at the Svakaran village had taken its toll on him. Before casting himself onto a bed of straw in the main room, he ate a small meal hastily prepared by Bard. Usually Elu was in charge of the food, but the Svakaran had been disconsolate since they had departed what remained of the village, and he went to sleep without eating. While Ugga and Bard built a fire, a storm brewed outside. It had a nasty feel. The weather had been calm for more than three days, which was unusual this far north at this time of year. Now it was time to show the tiny creatures that wandered on Triken's surface what really was in charge.

The storm howled for two full days, piling another three cubits of snow onto an already thick cover. The men drank tea in the mornings, wine in the afternoons and beer at night. They only left the longhouse for quick and shivering sessions of relief. Rathburt finally took it upon himself to heat some water and order each man to bathe.

Torg declined. "When the need arises, I can cleanse myself without the use of water."

"There are merchants in Kamupadana who make their living selling soaps and perfumes," Rathburt said. "I'm sure they're pleased there's only one of you, *Torgon.* Any more, and they would be out of business."

"I am who I am," Torg said, aggravating Rathburt even more.

When the storm finally relented, they went outside for a look around. New drifts of snow—some taller than Torg or Ugga—were haphazardly piled as far as they could see. They were "snowed in," as Bard liked to say, but at least they had plenty of food and drink. Unless they came under attack, there was no need to do anything but pass the time as best they could until winter loosed its grip, which could take as long as three months this far north.

"The cold is dire," Torg said to his friends. "But our enemies will find it unpleasant as well. I think we are safe, for now. If all goes well, we'll be able to renew our journey at winter's end. Eventually I must reach Kamupadana to learn news of the world, but it is well I remain hidden for a while longer."

"And what of your precious Tugars?" Rathburt said. "Don't you want to return to Anna?"

"Avici lies betwixt here and Anna. Besides, I have made Kusala aware that I live, and that is enough. The chieftain is more than capable of preparing the Tent City for whatever dangers might occur. I fear more for Nissaya and Jivita than I do for Anna—and Nissaya, especially. That is where Invictus will strike first. But when? Not before midsummer is my guess. I've seen his army. He has little need for surprise."

"What are your plans after Kamupadana?" Rathburt said.

"My first plan is to remain free. I'll be no good to anyone if I'm recaptured. I must avoid Avici, which means I will need to travel west before going south. The journey to Jivita—if that is where I choose to go—could take more than a month. Any who wish to join me are welcome."

"I'll come with ya," Ugga said. "But I'm afraid what will happen when Bard and I travels too far from the trees. Will we grow old like Master Rad-Burt?"

Rathburt snorted. "You can only hope to look as good as I do at my age."

"Bard and Ugga are not as young as they appear," Torg said. "As for your question, Ugga, I don't know the answer. The trees have played an important role in your longevity. But there's one thing I know for certain: Wherever I go, danger will follow. None of you will be safe, as long as you are with me."

"I'll go wherever ya go, trees or no trees," Bard said. "I doesn't mind a little danger. I gets bored sitting around all day."

"Elu will follow too, if you'll have him," the Svakaran said. "He is weak compared to you great men, but he knows the wild ways and the wild peoples. He might not be the most powerful, but he's the best guide. And he needs to get away from here. This place makes him sad."

"I'd be honored," Torg said. "Your heart is large, my friend. And your strength, as well. Still, we're getting ahead of ourselves. It may be that what I learn in Kamupadana will change everything. And you never know who we'll meet along the way."

The five men went about the task of waiting out the winter. It was tedious, to say the least. When the days were calm, they allowed the oxen to forage for grasses beneath the snow, while the men hunted for game. Squirrels and hares were plentiful, as were possums. Several times they killed deer, and once an elk that was larger than a black wolf. Of course they avoided bears—Ugga would never allow one to be harmed—and they also didn't harm otters. Torg loved them too much to kill them.

"I was an otter in a previous life. If we can't kill bears because of Ugga, then we can't kill otters because of me."

"The Chaunoc are friendly creatures," the Svakaran agreed. "Elu was an otter once, too."

"And Master Radburt was a carrot," Bard said, which sent them all into laughter, including the butt of the joke, who seemed pleased by the jest.

"Better a carrot than a polecat," Rathburt said, slapping his leg.

Ugga found that even funnier.

Next to bouts of heavy drinking, their meals were the highlights of their days. All of them were adept at cooking, but Elu was the master, especially with sauces and gravies. Once after a big meal they walked outside for fresh air and found a Tyger the size of a Buffelo standing a few dozen paces away, sniffing the aromas that drifted from the smoke hole in the roof of the longhouse. Elu and Rathburt ran back inside. Ugga and Bard stayed close to the door. But Torg strode forward, unafraid, until he stood face-to-face with the beast. Vapors seeped from his mouth, and the Tyger became tame, falling on its side in the snow, as if wanting to play.

"Bring what's left of the Che-ra," Torg said to Ugga, but the crossbreed wanted no part of the massive feline. Bard managed to work up the courage, timidly approaching and tossing the roasted remains of the possum a few paces away. The Tyger leapt up and swallowed it whole, then crept to Torg and licked his face with its scratchy tongue.

"Showoff," Rathburt muttered, while peeking from behind the door.

Time continued to pass. Torg and Rathburt meditated several times a day. The others took an interest and joined them. They also passed the time by telling stories. Rathburt enjoyed this as much as any of them, recounting humorous moments involving his failed attempts to become a Tugar warrior. Once, Torg laughed so hard, the inside of the longhouse started to superheat, and they had to rush him outside to cool him off and avoid burning their shelter to the ground.

Elu told many tales of the Svakarans and also of the hated Mogols. Bard and Ugga talked at length about Jord, and how much they missed her. They also bragged of their sexual exploits—paid for with "da skins"—in Kamupadana.

"I likes ya guys," Ugga said one evening, after his tenth mug of beer. "But I *loves* the Brounettos. Will winter never end?"

"I second that," Rathburt said.

3

Oh so gradually, the days lengthened. Oh so gradually, the banks of snow receded. Like a tired old man losing the will to live, winter released its grip. There was rain instead of sleet, followed by delicious wisps of midday warmth.

Even as patches of snow lingered on the ground, a weeping willow growing near a stream about three hundred paces from the longhouse was the first of the deciduous trees to go green. The stream roared again, chunks of ice tumbling down its long throat.

"When do we leave, Master Hah-nah?" Ugga said to Torg one morning, while the men stood together beneath a crystal sky in the late morning. "Now that the snow is melting, Elu says we can reach the Whore City in three days. Our food's low, and we're almost out of beer."

"I'm waiting for a sign," Torg said.

"Don't listen to his nonsense," Rathburt said. "He's always saying things like that. *I'm waiting for a sign.* Ooooooo. He won't be satisfied until the sun and moon perform a waltz for his benefit."

Torg was unperturbed. "Something strange is in the air. Do you not feel it?"

"The only thing strange is you," Rathburt said.

But the Svakaran agreed with Torg. "Elu feels it, too. The birds have stopped singing, and the chipmunks no longer chitter. Something frightens them."

"The little guy is right," Bard said. "Where *have* the birds gone, anyways? And there is no breeze."

Torg raised his head, shielded his eyes with his hand, and gazed toward the sun. The others did the same.

"We are about to find out," he proclaimed. "Behold!"

"What are you babbling about?" Rathburt said.

"Be patient. And shield your eyes. Even a Tugar can be blinded if he stares too long at the sun."

"I sees something," Ugga said excitedly. "Look, a sliver of darkness."

"I sees it too," Bard said.

"You've gone mad," Rathburt said. But then, even he couldn't deny it. "Wait . . . I do see something. *Torgon,* how did you know?"

"I am a Death-Knower. I know many things others do not. Besides, I've witnessed this event before, and I remember how everything felt just before it began. All of us who live long lives will see the moon become enshrouded in shadow many times. But when it happens to the sun, it is a far rarer and more powerful occurrence. The noble ones say that the sun and the moon circle the skies like birds, and sometimes the moon passes in front of the sun and blocks its light."

"The Svakaran legends say the sun and moon take turns eating each other," Elu said. "And afterward, they're so full they rest for a long time before their next meal."

"Come to think of it, I've seen this too," Rathburt said. "But it was so long ago."

They stood silently and watched the eclipse develop. At first a shadow appeared on the western edge of the sun. Then over the course of two hundred slow breaths it widened until the sun was half covered. The sky remained clear, but the blue was less vivid, and the light at ground level was noticeably dimmer.

From there, things happened quickly. The western sky darkened, as if a great storm was creeping over the horizon, and the rest of the sky changed from blue to violet. Now the sun resembled a crescent moon, no longer bright.

"Behold the rising shadow," Torg said, gesturing toward the west.

The shadow rose and widened, resembling the arrival of a winter storm from Nirodha. But there was no snow, lightning, or thunder. Only darkness. The sun shrank to just a sliver. And then, as if in surrender, the delicate crescent sparkled and winked out, becoming a black disk surrounded by an irregular circle of quivering light. Stars were visible in the twilight. The far edge of the horizon glowed like the final moments of sunset. Gusts of cool air stroked their faces. A cluster of bats, believing night had arrived, burst from a nearby cave.

The sun remained dark for twenty-five slow breaths before finally emerging from the shadow. Soon after, it was blazing as before. The bats returned to their hideout. The brightness of day resumed.

"I have my sign," Torg announced. "We leave for Kamupadana tomorrow morning. Beginning now, my name is Hana—to *all* of you. One slip of the tongue could expose our conspiracy. Thus far, our encounter with the wolves was our only misstep. But wolves cannot talk, so their masters will remain confused over who or what defeated them. We must all be like Ugga and Bard: common wood folk looking to trade skins for food, drink, coins and luxuries."

"Brounettos!" Ugga shouted.

Rathburt rolled his eyes, but the others laughed. Afterward Elu took Torg's hand.

"Will we be away for a long time, *great one?*"

"If you join me, it will be many months before you return . . . *if* you return. But as I've often said, I will force none of you to accompany me. The road I travel will be wrought with peril."

"Ah . . . I might as well come, anyway," Rathburt said. "Without Elu around, who will do all the chores? And besides, I've stayed in one place for too long. The soil of my garden needs a rest. A little adventure might suit me. Think of all the plants, flowers and trees we'll see as we wander."

"Tonight we should have a celebration," the Svakaran said. "Elu will prepare roasted goat with mushroom gravy and chicken soup with carrots, onions and wild potatoes. Even Ugga will have a full stomach."

"What a great idea, little guy," Ugga said. "There's just enough beer and wine to have one last party. Let's get started."

After their feast they went to bed late and got up early, feeling queasy and hung over—except for Torg, who never experienced ill effects from drinking. This time they had the cart and oxen to haul the skins and their supplies. The going would be easier, but still tedious. Though the terrain between the longhouse and the Whore City was traversable on foot, some areas would be difficult. But with Elu, Ugga, and Bard to guide them, it could be done.

As they prepared to leave, the oxen became especially docile, as if pleased to have survived the previous night's feast. Torg carried the Silver Sword, but now it was strapped onto his back beneath his cloak. The others laid their weapons in the cart next to the skins. Elu packed cooking gear, bowls, cups and spoons along with what remained of their herbs and spices. By midmorning they were ready to depart.

"This was a good home," the Svakaran said, tears in his eyes. "Elu will miss it."

"So will I," Rathburt said. "There are worse places to live."

"There may come a time when you will return," Torg said.

"I won't return," Rathburt said.

Torg raised an eyebrow. Then he turned, grabbed one of the oxen by its yoke, and pulled. The ox responded, and the cart lurched forward.

The others followed on foot, with Elu the last to leave the longhouse behind.

By nightfall they had managed only four leagues. The oxen moved slowly, and the cart was crudely built. Several times they were forced to circle out of their way to avoid deep streams or dense stands of forest. Still, they were pleased. Anything was preferable to hauling the litter.

The first night was chilly. There was just the slightest sliver of moon, and the skies remained clear. They camped inside a cave several times larger than the longhouse, its ceiling towering twenty cubits above a floor covered with crumbled stone.

Ugga became obsessed with bear droppings he discovered deep in its interior, crawling around on his hands and knees and sniffing like an animal. Torg was more interested in drawings he found on the walls, some of which were brightly colored with amazing detail, while others were barely visible. In one scene a hunting party of long-haired men battled a wooly mammoth. The red and yellow ocher used by the artist had faded over the millennia, but large portions of the painting remained intact.

"Mammoths still live in the heart of Nirodha," Torg said. "The great dragons have eaten most of them, but the decline of the dragons has enabled a few mammoths to survive. They are mighty beasts, twice as large as desert elephants—though not nearly as intelligent. Their hide is covered with shaggy hair, and the males have humps on their backs like camels."

"And I suppose you've seen them and ridden them, and even taught them the ancient tongue," Rathburt said.

"I wasn't able to teach them the ancient tongue."

Elu snorted.

They risked a fire, enjoying a hot meal and some of Rathburt's excellent black tea. Soon after dark, they curled up and went to sleep. Torg saw no need to post a guard. His senses were such that it was nearly impossible to approach him undetected, even while he slept—although Jord had managed it in broad daylight, which still galled him.

"Where are you now, Jord?" Torg whispered to himself. "Are you watching over us, a bird perched high in the trees? Or a bear crouching in the bushes? Ugga would like that. Wherever and whoever you are, I thank you for removing Vedana's poison. And I thank you for filling me with the magic of the great pines. I'll need my strength in the coming months. I hope we'll meet again, one day."

Torg meditated for two hundred long breaths before closing his eyes and going to sleep. He dreamt that he straddled the crest of a fossil dune, somewhere deep in the heart of his beloved Tējo. On his right stood his father, Asēkha-Jhana. On his left was a beautiful woman with golden hair and flawless skin. It was midnight, and a full moon glowed as bright as the sun.

Jhana bent over and scooped up a handful of sand. "I have a lesson for you, my son."

"Tell me, father."

"The Great Desert extends more than a hundred leagues from where we stand. The grains of sand I hold in my hand represent what you've learned thus far in your life. What you still must learn lies beyond."

Torg pondered the enormity of such words, and a slew of questions leapt to mind. But before he could ask any of them, Jhana transformed from flesh to black stone. This frightened Torg, and he turned to the woman for support.

"What happened to my father?" he asked her.

She did not speak, but her smile burned sweet holes in his heart. For a moment Torg's fears receded, and he lost himself in the glory of her blue-gray eyes, which sparkled in the moonlight.

But the pleasant reverie was interrupted when—somewhere in the depths of the darkness—a baby began to wail.

Torg was horrified. Who could abandon an infant in such a dangerous place? Surely, only the worst kind of monster would be capable of such cruelty.

He clambered down the side of the dune and charged across the desert, running to and fro in a panic. But the infant was as invisible as a ghost, and try as he might he could not find her anywhere.

As suddenly as it had begun, the wailing stopped.

And was replaced by cackling laughter.

Torg stood still—lost and alone in a vast sea of sand.

So much to learn, he thought.

And so little time.

So . . . little . . . time.

Glossary

Author's note: Many character and place names are English derivatives of Pali, a Middle Indo-Aryan dialect closely related to Sanskrit but now extinct as a spoken language. Today, Pali is studied mainly to gain access to Theravada Buddhist scriptures and is frequently chanted in religious rituals.

Abhisambodhi (ab-HEE-sahm-BOH-dee): Highest enlightenment.

Adho Satta (AH-dho SAH tah): Anything or anyone who is neither a dragon nor a powerful supernatural being. Means *low one* in ancient tongue.

Akanittha (AHK-ah-NEE-tah): A being that is able to feed off the light of the sun. Means *Highest Power* in the ancient tongue.

Akasa Ocean (ah-KAH-sah): Largest ocean on Triken. Lies west of Dhutanga, Jivita, and Kincara.

Ancient tongue: Ancient language now spoken by only Triken's most learned beings, as well as most Tugars

Anna: Tent City of Tējo. Home to the Tugars.

Arupa-Loka (ah-ROO-pah-LOH-kah): Home of ghosts, demons, and ghouls. Lies near northern border of the Gap of Gamana. Also called Ghost City.

Asava (ah-SAH-vah): Potent drink brewed by Stone-Eaters.

Asēkha (ah-SEEK-ah): Tugars of highest rank. There always are twenty, not including Death-Knowers. Also known as *Viisati* (The Twenty).

Asthenolith (ah-STHEN-no-lith): Pool of magma in a large cavern beneath Mount Asubha.

Avici (ah-VEE-chee): Largest city on Triken. Home to Invictus.

Badaalataa (BAD-ah-LAH-tuh): Carnivorous vines from the demon world.

Bakheng (bah-KENG): Central shrine of Dibbu-Loka.

Bard: Partner of Ugga and Jord, trappers who lived in the forest near the foothills of Mount Asubha.

Barranca (bah-RAHN-chuh): Rocky wasteland that partially encircles the Great Desert.

Bell: Measurement of time approximating three hours.

Bhasura (bah-SOOR-ah): One of the large tribes of the Mahaggata Mountains.

Bhayatupa (by-yah-TOO-pah): Most ancient and powerful of dragons. His scales are the color of deep crimson.

Black mountain wolves: Largest and most dangerous of all wolves. Allies of demons, witches, and Mogols.

Catu (chah-TOO): Northernmost mountain on Triken.

Cave monkeys: Small, nameless primates that live in the underworld beneath Asubha.

Chain Man: Another name for Mala.

Chal-Abhinno (Chahl-ahb-HIH-no): Queen of the Warlish witches.

Che-ra (CHEE-ruh): Svakaran name for a fat possum.

Ciraya (ser-AYE-yah): Green cactus that, when chewed, provides large amounts of liquid and nourishment.

Cubit: Length of the arm from elbow to fingertip, which measures approximately eighteen inches, though among Tugars a cubit is considered to be twenty-one inches.

Dakkhina (dah-KEE-nay): Sensation that brings on the urge to attempt *Sammaasamaadhi*. Means *holy gift* in the ancient tongue.

Death-Knower: Any Tugar—almost always an Asēkha—who has successfully achieved *Sammaasamaadhi*. In the ancient tongue, a Death-Knower is called *Maranavidu*.

Deathless people: Monks and nuns who inhabit Dibbu-Loka. Called deathless people because some of them live for more than one thousand years. More commonly known as noble ones.

Death Visit: Tugar description of the temporary suicide of a Death-Knower wizard.

Dēsaka (day-SAH-kuh): Famous Vasi master who trained *The Torgon*.

Dhutanga (doo-TAHNG-uh): Largest forest on Triken. Lies west of the Mahaggata Mountains. Also known as the Great Forest.

Dibbu-Loka (DEE-boo-LOW-kah): Realm of the noble ones. Means *Deathless World* in the ancient tongue. Originally called Piti-Loka.

Dracools (drah-KOOLS): Winged beasts that walk on hind legs but look like miniature dragons. Taller than a man but shorter than a druid.

Druids (DREW-ids): Seven-cubit-tall beings that dwell in Dhutanga. Ancient enemies of Jivita.

Dukkhatu (doo-KAH-too): Great and ancient spider that spent the last years of her life near the peak of Asubha.

Elu (EE-loo): Miniature Svakaran who is an associate of Rathburt.

Fathom: Approximately eleven cubits.

Gap of Gamana: Northernmost gap of the Mahaggata Mountains.

Gap of Gati: Southern gap that separates the Mahaggata Range from the Kolankold Range.

Golden soldiers: Soldiers of Invictus, mass-bred in his image.

Golden Wall: Oblong wall coated with a special golden metal that surrounds Avici and Kilesa.

Gulah (GOO-lah): Stone-Eater who became warden of Asubha. Son of Slag.

Invictus (in-VICK-tuss): Evil sorcerer who threatens all of Triken and beyond. Also known as *Suriya* (the Sun God).

Jhana (JAH-nah): Father of Torg.

Jivita (jih-VEE-tuh): Wondrous city that is home to the white horsemen. Located west of the Gap of Gati in the Green Plains. Also called the

White City. Known as *Jutimantataa* (City of Splendor) in the ancient tongue.

Jord: Mysterious partner of Ugga and Bard, trappers who lived in the forest near the foothills of Mount Asubha.

Kamupadana (kuh-MOO-puh-DUH-nah): Home of Warlish witches and their lesser female servants. Also called the Whore City.

Kilesa (kee-LAY-suh): Sister City of Anna.

King Lobha (LOW-bah): Sadistic king who built Piti-Loka.

Kojin (KOH-jin): Enormous ogress with six arms and a bloated female head. Almost as large as a snow giant.

Kolankold Mountains (KO-luhn-kold): Bottom stem of the Mahaggata Mountains, located south of the Gap of Gati.

Kusala (KOO-suh-luh): Second most powerful Tugar in the world next to Torg. Also known as Asēkha-Kusala and Chieftain Kusala.

Lake Hadaya (huh-DUH-yuh): Large freshwater lake that lies west of the Gap of Gati.

Lake Keo (KAY-oh): Large freshwater lake that lies between the Kolankold Mountains and Dibbu-Loka.

Lake Ti-ratana (tee-RAH-tuh-nah): Large freshwater lake that lies west of Avici.

Laylah (LAY-lah): Younger sister of Invictus.

Long breath: Fifteen seconds. Also called slow breath.

Mahaggata Mountains (MAH-hah-GAH-tah): Largest mountain range on Triken. Shaped like a capital Y.

Mala (MAH-lah): Former snow giant who was ruined by Invictus and turned into the sorcerer's most dangerous servant. Formerly called Yama-Deva.

Majjhe Ghamme (Mah-JEE GAH-mee): Means midsummer in the ancient tongue.

Mogols (MAH-guhls): Warrior race that dwells in Mahaggata Mountains. Longtime worshippers of the dragon Bhayatupa and the demon Vedana. Ancient enemies of Nissaya.

Mount Asubha (ah-SOO-buh): Dreaded mountain in the cold north that housed the prison of Invictus.

Nirodha (nee-ROW-dah): Icy wastelands that lie north of the Mahaggata Mountains.

Nissaya (nee-SIGH-yah): Impenetrable fortress on the east end of the Gap of Gati. Home of the Nissayan knights.

Noble ones: Monks and nuns who inhabit Dibbu-Loka. Also called deathless people.

Obhasa (oh-BHAH-sah): Torg's magical staff, carved from the ivory of a desert elephant found dead. Means *container of light* in the ancient tongue.

Ogha River: (OH-guh): Largest river on Triken. Begins in the northern range of Mahaggata and ends in Lake Keo.

Okkanti Mountains (oh-KAHN-tee): Small range with tall, jagged peaks located northeast of Kilesa.

Pabbajja (pah-BAH-jah): Homeless people who live in the plains surrounding Java. Little is known of their habits.

Pace: Approximately 30 inches, though among Tugars a pace is considered 36 inches.

Peta (PAY-tuh): Ghost girl of Arupa-Loka. In life, she was blind.

Piti-Loka (PEE-tee-LOH-kuh): Original name of Dibbu-Loka. Built by King Lobha ten thousand years ago as his burial shrine. Means *Rapture World* in the ancient tongue.

Podhana (POH-dah-nuh): Asēkha warrior.

Rathburt (RATH-burt): Only other living Death-Knower. Known as a gardener, not a warrior.

Rati (RAH-tee): Asēkha warrior.

Sammaasamaadhi (sam-mah-sah-MAH-dee): Supreme concentration of mind. Temporary suicide.

Sampati (sahm-PAH-tee): Giant condors crossbred with dragons by Invictus. Used to transport people and supplies to the prison on Mount Asubha.

Senasana (SEN-uh-SAHN-ah): Thriving market city that lies north of Dibbu-Loka.

Short breath: Three seconds. Also called quick breath.

Silver Sword: Ancient sword forged by a long-forgotten master from the otherworldly metals found among the shattered remains of a meteorite.

Simōōn (suh-MOON): Magical dust storm that protects Anna from outsiders.

Sister Tathagata (tuh-THUH-guh-tuh): High nun of Dibbu-Loka. More than three thousand years old. Also known as *Perfect One*.

Sivathika (SEE-vah-TEE-kuh): Ancient Tugar ritual. Dying warrior breathes what remains of his or her *Life Energy* into a survivor's lungs, where it is absorbed into the blood.

Slag: Stone-Eater defeated by Torg in ancient battle. Father of Gulah.

Snow giants: Magnificent beings reaching heights of 10 cubits or more that dwell in the Okkanti Mountains.

Sōbhana (SOH-bah-nah): Female Asēkha warrior.

Span: Distance from the end of the thumb to the end of the little finger of a hand spread to full width. Approximately nine inches, though among Tugars a span is considered 12 inches.

Stone: Equal to fourteen pounds.

Stone-Eater: Magical being that gains power by devouring lava rocks.

Svakara (svuh-KUH-ruh): One of the large tribes of the Mahaggata Mountains.

Tanhiiyati (tawn-hee-YAH-tee): Insatiable craving for eternal existence suffered by some long-lived beings.

Tējo (TAY-joh): Great Desert. Home of the Tugars.

Tent City: Largest city in Tējo. Home to the Tugars. Also known as Anna.

The Torgon (TOR-gahn): Torg's ceremonial name. Also Lord Torgon.

Torg: Thousand-year-old Death-Knower wizard. King of the Tugars. Means *Blessed Warrior* in the ancient tongue.

Triken (TRY-ken): Name of the world. Also name of the land east and west of the Mahaggata Mountains.

Tugars (TOO-gars): Desert warriors of Tējo. Called *Kantaara Yodhas* in the ancient tongue.

Uccheda (oo-CHAY-duh): Tower of Invictus in Avici. Means *annihilation* in the ancient tongue.

Ugga (OO-gah): Human-bear crossbreed who was a partner of Bard and Jord, trappers who lived in the forest near the foothills of Mount Asubha.

Uttara (oo-TUH-ruh): Specially made sword wielded by Tugar warriors and Asēkhas. Single-edged, slightly curved.

Vasi master (VUH-see): Martial arts master who trains Tugar novices to become warriors.

Vedana (VAY-duh-nuh): 100,000-year-old demon. Grandmother of Invictus and Laylah. Mother of King Lobha.

Vinipata (VEE-nee-PUH-tuh): Central shrine of Senasana.

Warlish witch (WOR-lish): Female witch who can change her appearance between extreme beauty and hideousness.

Wild men: Short, hairy men who thrive in the foothills of Kolankold. Their women do not fight as warriors and are rarely seen. Longtime enemies of Nissaya.

Worm monster: Nameless beast with more than a thousand tentacles that lives beneath Asubha. Largest living creature on Triken.

Yakkkkha (YAH-kuh): Magic word from the Realm of the Undead that brings corpses and skeletons temporarily back to life.

Yama-Deva (YAH-muh-DAY-vuh): Ruined snow giant that became Mala.

Yama-Utu (YAH-muh-OO-too): Snow giant. Brother of Yama-Deva. Husband of Yama-Bhari.

Coming Soon by Jim Melvin

Chained By Fear

The Death Wizard Chronicles
Book Two

Prologue

From his hiding place among the trees, the teenage boy had spied on the little girl for months. Though darkness was not his friend, he had endured it to be near her. How daring she was to leave her house all by herself in the middle of the night, seemingly undeterred by the specter of ghosts and goblins. How foolish of her, too. She would learn one day that monsters did exist, and that some of them were far deadlier than any her imagination might conjure. She would learn that it was better to stay locked in her room than wander the wilds after dark. She would learn because he would teach her.

Though she was little more than four years old, she already was beautiful. He admired her golden hair, which so matched his own. And though her gray-blue eyes were in stark contrast to his deep-brown ones, he permitted her this fallibility. No one was perfect. Well, almost no one.

When they were king and queen, she would birth many of his children. The first would be a son whom he would mold in his own image. After that, he didn't care so much about the rest. But the more products of his seed who walked the world, the better.

Yes, the little girl would become his bride—whether she liked it or not. He was a god, after all. And who in their right mind could refuse the hand of a god?

Not even the god's sister could do that.

Brother

1

Laylah first met her brother when she was five years old. He found her at the rope swing that hung from an ancient sycamore tree on the outskirts of the village known as Avici. With so many children flocking to the swing, Laylah sometimes had to wait forever for a turn. But she knew the best time to go. While her parents slumbered she snuck out her window and scampered through the darkness. The swing hung there—lifeless but inviting—and she had it all to herself. When morning came, she returned home to sleep.

On one especially beautiful night when the moon was full and the sky clear, Laylah sat on the swing and basked in the reflected light. Phosphorescent streaks emanated from her body as she swept back and forth. When she held up her arm she could see that her skin glowed magically. She didn't know why, but she didn't really care, either. To her, it was normal.

But the boy who came to her that fateful night was by no means normal. He wore calico robes embroidered with little golden suns, and when he lifted his hood to expose his face, Laylah saw something in his expression that felt familiar. He smiled at her, exposing perfectly white teeth and disturbingly clear brown eyes. His hair was an even deeper yellow than hers, hanging long and silky about his shoulders. He sat cross-legged in the grass near her feet and rested the palms of his hands on his knees.

"Are you afraid?" he said, whispering huskily.

"No," she said, telling the truth.

He smiled again. "Do you know me?"

"I don't think so."

The smile lessened. "I'm a stranger to you, but you're not a stranger to me. Do you understand?"

"A lot of the old people know my name, but I don't know theirs. Is that what you mean?"

He chuckled, but with a slight hint of irritation. "Not exactly. But it's obvious you're a very smart girl. And so pretty. I like you. Do you like me?"

"How old are you?" she said.

"I'm fifteen. And you're five?"

"You *do* know me," she said. "But I don't remember seeing you. Are you new here?"

"Yes . . . in some ways. I was born here, but I grew up someplace else."

"Have you come back here to live?"

"No . . . just to visit. With you."

"Why?"

"Because I like you. Do you like me?"

"I guess so."

"Well, that's a good start. I hope you'll like me more when you get to know me. But I have to ask you an important question. Can you keep a secret?"

"Yes!" Laylah loved keeping secrets. It made her feel like an old person.

"Good. Well, the secret is . . . *me*. I don't want you to tell anyone, not even your parents, that you talked to me tonight. If you tell them, do you know what will happen?"

"You'll be mad at me?"

"No . . . no. I won't be mad at you, but your parents will. They'll stop you from going out at night. They'll barricade your door and window. You won't have the swing all to yourself anymore and you won't be able to enjoy the moonlight without anyone around to bother you."

Tears welled in Laylah's eyes. Being imprisoned in her room at night would be the worst punishment she could imagine.

"But if you keep *our* secret," the boy continued, "you'll be free to come and go whenever you like. Tomorrow night, the moon will be round again. I'll come to visit. If you're not here, I'll know you broke *our* secret."

"I won't . . . I promise."

"Thank you, Laylah." He smiled so wide she could see his thick red tongue. "And I won't tell anyone, either. See you tomorrow night?"

"Yes," she said.

She went home before dawn and slept until almost noon. Her parents, Gunther and Stēorra, constantly told her how amazed they were that she slept so much. They put her to bed every night after dark, but she rarely got up on her own before lunch. Yet she was healthy and happy, so they didn't bother her about it too much, enabling her to continue to get away with her nightly wanderings.

He met Laylah at the tree again that night, lavishing her with praise for keeping their secret. He talked to her for a long time and asked many questions: What was her favorite food? He was an excellent cook. Did she have any pets? He had lots of them. Was she satisfied with her clothes? He could buy her some really nice gowns and shoes. Would she like that?

"Yes . . . YES!"

The third night, he leaned over and kissed her on the cheek.

"Do you love me, Laylah? Because I love you."

The kiss made her feel uncomfortable, and she didn't answer.

He became annoyed. "I won't be around for a while." And he walked away in a huff.

For several weeks afterward he didn't meet her at the swing. Laylah became used to being alone again. She once tried to tell her mother about the boy, but her tongue dried up and the words wouldn't come. She hated the feeling of helplessness.

When the moon rose full the following month he appeared again, strutting out of the darkness with a grin on his face. He gave her a light hug and another kiss on the cheek. Whatever anger he had displayed when she had last seen him was gone. He told her how much he had missed her and how much he loved her. Did she love him? She still didn't answer.

Four days a month around each full moon, he visited her at the swing. He taught her things, such as how to talk to him without speaking; or how to scorch patches of grass with fire from the tips of her fingers. He told her magical words. *Ratana*, repeated three times, turned pebbles into gems. *Khandeti* caused pottery to crack. *Avihethana* healed cuts and bruises. This delighted Laylah.

"Do you love me?" he asked.

"I *like* you, a lot."

"I *love* you, a lot."

One time, he taught her the word *Namuci*, which he told her had been conjured in a time eons past by the ancient demon known as Vedana. When a demon—or a human with demon blood—spoke the word, it gave life to invisible spirits called *efrits*, thousands of which dwelled in the Realm of the Undead. In that eternal darkness they were harmless. But when summoned to the Realm of Life, they became voracious meat eaters, gorging themselves on the internal organs of any living being unlucky enough to be near. The speaker of the word—because of his or her demon blood—was safe from harm.

If *Namuci* was whispered, one *efrit* responded and one person died. But if a being of great power screamed it at high volume, thousands of *efrits* emerged, and any human or animal within several hundred paces perished.

When Laylah said it, a sparrow tumbled from the sky and lay dead at her feet. She screamed and cried. He called her a "little baby" and stormed away.

For several months he did not appear. Laylah began to think she would never see him again. In some ways she was relieved. More than once she again tried to tell her parents or some other old person about her mysterious visitor. But the words would not come. She tried so hard, her eyes filled with tears. When they asked her what was wrong, she couldn't speak. Her tongue felt meaty and swollen.

By the time she was six years old, she had learned to spell quite a few words, but when she attempted to write something down about the brown-eyed boy, the quill smeared the ink. She even tried to draw his picture, but the same thing happened. It made her sick to her stomach.

Out of nowhere he appeared again, smiling as if he had never been gone. She told him she still was mad at him for making her kill the bird. He said he was sorry and wouldn't do it again. Instead he taught her good words like *Loha-Hema*, which turned copper to gold; and *Tumbi-Tum*, which caused vegetables to grow from seed to full ripeness in just a few days. He showed her how to conjure small spheres of flame that floated in the air, and the two of them tossed them back and forth like toy balls. When an adult villager, perhaps trying to walk off a bout of insomnia, wandered by the swing in the middle of the night, the boy blew smoke from his mouth and said *Niddaayahi*. The man collapsed on the grass, his insomnia cured.

Laylah worried about the old person. He was one of her father's many friends and often had been nice to her. The boy assured her he would take the man back to his house, and he picked up the old person and carried him away as if he weighed less than a feather. Laylah never saw the man again, but the boy came back the next night in a better mood than usual.

When she turned nine years old, the boy handed her an envelope, sealed with an insignia of a golden sun, and told her to wait until he was gone before reading the letter. He also told her to burn it with her special white finger-fire as soon as she was finished. When he disappeared from sight, she tore it open.

The letter was written in gold ink on a single sheet of silky white paper.

> *My dearest Laylah:*
>
> *You are so smart and pretty. When we are not together, I feel sad. I miss you all the time. I love you very much.*
>
> *Do you love me?*
>
> *We have known each other for four years, but you have never asked my name. Why is that? Aren't you curious about me? Don't you care?*
>
> *Remember our secret. Never tell anyone about me. Our parents will be angry at you if they discover we are friends.*
>
> *Your brother, Invictus*
>
> *P.S. Here's my present—another secret word. This one is very precious. The next time you are in bed or taking a bath, say 'Raaga' several times—but only if you are alone. It will make you feel good, but Mother and Father wouldn't like it.*

Our parents? Your brother? Mother and father? Laylah read the letter over and over. She decided not to burn it. Instead she would show it to her parents the next morning. But the moment that thought entered her mind, the paper burst into yellow flame. She cried again.

"You are *not* my brother," she said to him the next night. "I don't have a brother. My mom and dad would have told me."

He stomped around the swing, staring at her with fury in his eyes.

"You dare to call me a liar?" His body, now almost twenty years old and fully grown, glowed like a miniature sun. "Listen to me carefully, little one. I allow you to live because you're my sister, but even *you* need to be careful. Your powers are just a fraction of mine. Compared to me, you're merely a *reflection.*"

Laylah was terrified, and she burst into tears and ran all the way home. She didn't return to the swing for months. Instead she trembled in her bed until morning, when sleep finally took her, temporarily releasing her from misery. During that terrible stretch of time she never saw Invictus, the boy who claimed to be her brother.

Just a month shy of her tenth birthday, she relaxed in a warm bath while her parents made dinner in the kitchen. The magical word Invictus had written in his letter still teased her curiosity. Until this moment, she had managed to resist its supernatural lure. But the compulsion finally overcame her.

"*Raaga*," she whispered, guiltily.

Laylah felt a strange but enchanting sensation between her legs. She touched herself with her hand and the pleasure intensified.

"*Raaga*," she said again. "*Raaga. Raaga!*"

Afterward she lay panting in the bath, her face slathered with sweat. Her mother assumed she had come down with a fever, and she tucked Laylah into bed with a cold cloth on her forehead.

The next morning, Laylah said the word again. And then the following afternoon and evening. She said it every day, several times a day, several times a night. The sensation grew greater each time. But it took a severe toll on her prepubescent body. She lost her appetite and an excessive amount of weight. Dark circles formed under her eyes and her cheeks collapsed.

Her parents were convinced she was deathly ill. Shamans studied her but could find nothing wrong. She tried to tell them about the boy and his terrible powers. But no intelligible words came forth.

One shaman, who was filthy and stank, told Laylah's parents that he needed to be alone with the child to properly diagnose her condition. Out of desperation, they agreed. When they closed the door the shaman leaned over Laylah and told her that evil spirits possessed her. If she kissed him, the spirits would flee from her mouth into his, where he would devour them.

Laylah saw through his guise. Without thinking, she whispered, "*Namuci!*"

The shaman fell to the floor, spit out a glob of blood, and died. Her parents rushed back into the room and found her in hysterics. The shaman's death shocked the village, but no one thought to blame her.

For whatever reason the horror of what she had done strengthened Laylah's resolve, and she was able to resist saying the *nasty* word. In a few weeks her health was restored—and with it, her good humor. Her parents seemed so pleased.

It all fell apart for her the morning after her tenth birthday, when Invictus crept through her window and entered her room. She tried to cry out but could not manage more than a few weak grunts. Still wearing his golden robes, he lay next to her on her bed, pressed his chest against her back and then placed his hand on her stomach. She hated being so close to him, but somehow his presence froze her to the bed. A short time later, her parents entered the room and found them together.

"What are you *doing*?" her father said. "Get away from my child!"

He attempted to pull the young man off Laylah, but Invictus was far too strong, swinging his arm and knocking the older man against the far wall. Her mother lifted a small wooden table and smashed it against Invictus' shoulder, but it did not seem to hurt him at all.

He stood and faced her. "Mother, don't you recognize me?" Invictus said.

"I recognize you, but I wish I didn't," she said. "Why have you returned to torment us?"

"I love you, mother. Do you love me?" And then he spit a sizzling ball of sputum at her brown eyes.

Laylah's mother howled and pressed her hands to her face, staggering backward. When she removed her hands, most of the flesh on her skull was gone, though strands of long yellow hair still clung to the exposed bone.

Her father regained his senses, staggered to his feet, and pounced on Invictus, all the while yelling, "Laylah . . . *run!*"

"Father," Invictus said. "I love you. Do you love me?"

Invictus pressed his lips against her father's and blew hot breath down his throat. Her father collapsed and went into a wild spasm. Smoke exploded from his ears, nose, and mouth—and his tongue swelled absurdly. When he blew apart, flaming patches of tissue splattered across the room. This terrified Laylah and shook her out of whatever spell Invictus had put on her to keep her still. She sat up and screamed.

Though her mother was maimed and blinded, she continued to grope for Invictus. But she was no match for him. He grasped her disfigured face and kissed her too, and she met the same fate as her husband.

Afterward Invictus raised his arms and bellowed. Golden flames erupted from every pore. As if struck from within by dragon fire, the house exploded. Sizzling shards flew several hundred paces, casting Laylah into the yard like a piece of broken furniture. When the conflagration cleared, she saw Invictus standing naked amid the smoking debris, his robes incinerated but his body unharmed. Her parents were gone.

Laylah managed to stand. Amazingly she wasn't injured, but her clothes had been incinerated and she was now naked. The commotion drew hundreds of villagers, who rushed toward her. But when they saw Invictus they also ran. Only one man hesitated, as if daring to issue a challenge. For him, it was a death sentence. Invictus blasted a bolt of golden flame, ripping off the man's head.

Laylah could stand it no more. But at least she now had full use of her body. She ran . . . fast and far.

"Laylah! Come back. I love you." Her brother's voice shook the valley. "Laylah, do you lovvvvvveeeeeee me?"

She reached the Ogha River. The roar of its swirling waters drowned out her sobs. She felt her brother approaching from behind. She would rather die than have him touch her again.

Laylah cast herself into the Ogha. She could swim well, but she was used to the still water of lakes and ponds, not the nasty swells of the mightiest river in the world. The tumult swept her along, helpless as a leaf. Despite the dangers, she felt peaceful. Death by drowning was a small price to pay to escape such a monster.

But Laylah's life would not end on this day. Something grasped her thin arm. She glided along the surface of the river on her back and was dragged onto the steep bank on the far side.

She could still hear Invictus' desperate cries.

"Laylah, come back. I love you. Do you love me?"

Powerful arms lifted her and pressed her against wet skin that smelled like a wild animal. She screamed, struggling to free herself. Then a large hand clamped over her mouth, her nose, and everything went dark.

About the Author

Jim Melvin was born in New York but spent most of his life in Florida. He now lives in the magical foothills of the Appalachians, where he wrote *The Death Wizard Chronicles*. Jim has one other published novel to his credit titled *Dream House: A Ghost Story*. He currently is working on Book 1 of a young adult fantasy series. Jim graduated from the University of South Florida in Tampa in 1978 and went on to become an award-winning journalist. He occasionally plays golf, but has never won any awards for that.